**Rave reviews for Diana Rowland's
White Trash Zombie novels:**

"Angel continues to be a truly memorable character as she displays ample guts and determination when defending those she cares about.... With two stellar urban fantasy series running concurrently, Rowland expertly showcases the full range of her considerable talents. Awesome job!"

—*RT Book Reviews* (top pick)

"So far, this has been an incredibly fun series, and a breath of fresh air in an increasingly crowded field. While there's no denying that the basic premise is fascinating and entertaining, the real draw here is Angel's personal journey of growth and self-discovery.... Angel's a heroine worth cheering for."   —Tor.com

"If you haven't discovered this series, you're in for a treat. Angel is one of my favorite heroines in urban fantasy right now, and I can't wait to see what she's up to next!"

—My Bookish Ways

"This spiraling roller coaster is as full of heart as blood (and brains and guts), exploring themes of love, sacrifice, guilt, and vengeance amid splattery action. This orgy of super science, roadhouse rumbles, and slapstick supernaturalism should satisfy readers searching for blood-soaked fun."

—*Publishers Weekly*

"Rowland's delightful novel jumps genre lines with a little something for everyone—mystery, horror, humor, and even a smattering of romance. Not to be missed—all that's required is a high tolerance for gray matter. For true zombiephiles, of course, that's a no brainer."   —*Library Journal*

"Every bit as fun and trashy as the brilliant cover. The story is gory and gorgeous with plenty of humor and a great new protagonist to root for."   —All Things Urban Fantasy

Also by Diana Rowland:

SECRETS OF THE DEMON

SINS OF THE DEMON

TOUCH OF THE DEMON

FURY OF THE DEMON

VENGEANCE OF THE DEMON

LEGACY OF THE DEMON*

_____

MY LIFE AS A WHITE TRASH ZOMBIE

EVEN WHITE TRASH ZOMBIES
GET THE BLUES

WHITE TRASH ZOMBIE APOCALYPSE

HOW THE WHITE TRASH ZOMBIE
GOT HER GROOVE BACK

WHITE TRASH ZOMBIE GONE WILD

*Coming in 2016 from DAW

WHITE TRASH ZOMBIE GONE WILD

DIANA ROWLAND

DAW BOOKS, INC.
DONALD A. WOLLHEIM, FOUNDER
375 Hudson Street, New York, NY 10014

ELIZABETH R. WOLLHEIM
SHEILA E. GILBERT
PUBLISHERS
www.dawbooks.com

First Printing, October 2015

1 2 3 4 5 6 7 8 9

For Anna

ACKNOWLEDGMENTS

For their help and assistance—whether educational, informational, emotional, or physical—I owe the following people (and countless others) enormous thanks: Scott Knight, Jodi Levine, Matt Saver, Gerard Bultman, Sherry Rowland, Kat Johnson, Myke Cole, Mary Robinette Kowal, Peter Brett, Wes Chu, Roman White, Justin Landon, Jen Volant, Debbie Roma, Charlie Watson, Dan Dos Santos, Carrie Vaughn, Daniel Abraham, Kat Abraham, Ty Franck, Howard Tayler, Sandra Tayler, Betsy Wollheim, Marylou Capes-Platt, Joshua Starr, everyone at DAW, Domino's, Walter Jon Williams, Jack Hoffstadt, Anna Hoffstadt, Matt Bialer, Lindsay Ribar, and social media.

Chapter 1

Blood and fat greased the thick needle as I fought to work it through the slab of flesh. I'd closed up hundreds of bodies after autopsies, and could usually sew up the Y-incision in nothing flat. But of course the day I had *plans* for lunch, the corpse had a beer gut the size of a keg.

"Omentum," I said through gritted teeth, pulling the string through. "That's what all the lard in this dude's gut is called."

Derrel Cusimano looked up from his clipboard, wide mouth curving into a smile. "Look at you with all your college biology smarts."

"Yeah, well, Mr. Granger's omentum has too much *momentum*," I grumbled, earning me a laugh. A linebacker for LSU turned death investigator, Derrel had been my partner for most of my time with the Coroner's Office. We weren't permanent partners anymore, thanks to my ever-changing work schedule, but we still made one hell of a pair—short, skinny, white girl with bleached blonde hair, and a hugely muscled, bald, black guy who was easily the most compassionate person I'd ever met.

The faint scent of Mr. Granger's brain teased me from

the bag of organs between his knees. A rush of saliva filled my mouth, and my hands trembled. The smell of baking bread was as appetizing as dog shit compared to the delicious aroma of a fresh human brain. And hoo boy, I needed that brain. Now. "I thought you were leaving for lunch ten minutes ago."

"Leaving for the *day*," Derrel corrected as he scribbled notes. "Checking my last report now. I'm off 'til Tuesday."

The needle slipped against the slick flesh, drove into my gloved middle finger and ripped through the side. I clamped down on a yelp of pain and yanked it free, then shot a look at Derrel. To my undying relief, he was focused on his report and hadn't noticed a thing. Needle sticks were bad news, and no way did I want to deal with the paperwork and tests and other crap.

Especially since I had nothing to worry about. Not with my zombie parasite on internal cleanup duty. But the injury twisted my brain-hunger a notch tighter. Shit. I couldn't forage for that particular sustenance until Derrel left. At the rate he was going, he'd still be here tomorrow.

The blood from my finger and the body mingled as I continued to wrestle with needle and string. "You're almost done though, right?"

Derrel gave me a knowing look over the clipboard. "You trying to get rid of me?"

I batted my eyelashes. "Would I do that?" My stomach made an obnoxious gurgle.

Derrel chuckled. "Sounds like someone skipped breakfast. I can finish sewing him up if you want to head out for lunch."

"No!" I cleared my throat, annoyed at how nervous I sounded. "I mean, no. I'm on call tonight, so I'm taking a long lunch then cutting out of here early. Don't let me hold you up from your days off." I struggled to get the damn needle through for the next stitch. "I have this under control."

Derrel hung the clipboard on its hook and tugged on gloves. "I can see that."

Cripes. He was never going to leave. The scent of his warm, live brain wafted over me as he stepped close. Didn't he know I was starving? I focused on the needle.

Derrel held the dead guy's impressive belly together so I could stitch. "You going tonight?"

I didn't have to ask what he meant. For the past month, zombies and movies had dominated conversations all over St. Edwards Parish, even crowding out the juicy scandal involving the Chief of Police and a box of ferrets back on Valentine's Day. The movie *High School Zombie Apocalypse!!* had been filmed here in Tucker Point, and its nationwide release was this very weekend. A few hundred locals had made it into the movie in bit parts or as extras, and I couldn't think of a single person who didn't have plans to go see it, if only to watch the scene where the mayor—played by the actual mayor of Tucker Point—ended up covered in blood and zombie splatter.

And tonight Tucker Point was home to a big red carpet premiere, complete with celebrities and all sorts of other cool stuff.

"Yep, I'm going with Marcus." Three more stitches and I'd be done. Then I could get away from Derrel and his brain before I—

"You two back together?"

In my head, I let out a primal scream of frustration at his refusal to leave. Outwardly, I faked a casual shrug. "Nah, but we're still friends. It's nice having someone to talk to. We're both going through a lot of changes right now, with me starting college and him taking over his Uncle Pietro's business." I didn't mention that *business* also involved Marcus becoming the public head of our zombie Tribe.

"Uh huh," Derrel said with a dubious twist of his mouth. "As long as it stays 'nice' and he doesn't try and run your life again because he thinks he knows what's best for you."

I smiled as I made the last stitch. "You have the best brain ever."

Derrel let out a booming laugh. "Angel Crawford, I think that's the weirdest thing anyone has ever said to me."

Crap. So much for *think before you speak*. My stomach gave an almighty gurgle loud enough to wake the dead. I clamped a forearm over my belly. "Oh, jeez."

He clapped me on the back then steadied me as I staggered. "Let's get Mr. Granger into the cooler so you can go feed yourself."

Sigh. The guy was a seriously nice pain in my ass. He was thinking burgers. I was thinking brains. Didn't help one bit that all the effort to get the body bagged, on the gurney, and rolled into the cooler fired Derrel up like a brain-scented plug-in air freshener.

I breathed easier once we were out of the close confines of the cooler. "I can handle it from here," I told him. "Go have fun." I disposed of my gloves and protective gear, then hurried to wash my hands before Derrel could spy the blood on my finger. My parasite had done its job and stopped the bleeding, but I needed brains now for it to finish the healing.

Derrel tossed his gloves into the medical waste can. "I'll be hiding out at home." With that he smushed me against his massive chest in a hug—and immersed me in brain scent.

A low growl escaped before I could clamp down on it. *Oh god, Derrel, please leave before I eat you!*

"Call me if you need anything," he said, releasing me.

"Will do," I choked out and covered my dismay by pretending to push my nose back into place. He chuckled then grabbed his jacket and departed, leaving me alone in the morgue.

My hunger thrashed like a bobcat in a trap, yowling at me to chase Derrel down before my meal could escape. I tightened my hands into fists and breathed through clenched teeth until the monster within me settled. Now that Derrel was *finally* gone, I'd give it what it wanted.

I held my breath and listened for any hint of another living soul in the morgue.

The drip of the sink in the cutting room. The low hum of the cooler behind me. But no voices or footsteps. Not even the tiniest fart. I relaxed and exhaled, slipped back inside the cooler and tugged the heavy door closed. The cold air lifted goosebumps along my arms, and an underlying stench tickled the back of my throat—blood and rot and antiseptic. The morgue cooler had shelf space for ten bodies, but at the moment the only resident was the one on the gurney Derrel and I had rolled in here a few minutes ago.

Blood pounded in my ears, and a chill swept through me that had nothing to do with temperature. Even though I'd raided corpses more times than I could count, the fear-of-discovery adrenaline rush still hit me every single time.

"Get it done and get out, Angel," I muttered as I gave the zipper a tug. It slithered open to once again reveal Noah Granger, dull eyes half-closed and lips parted. White male, fifty-nine years old, dead of a heart attack—confirmed by the clot that Dr. Leblanc had found in his left anterior descending coronary artery.

Sucked for Noah, but good for me. The faulty heart rested in the clear plastic bag between his knees along with his kidneys, liver, lungs—and the brain I was after.

My mouth watered as I unknotted the bag. I snatched a chunk of frontal lobe and shoved it into my mouth. It slid down my throat with the consistency of a raw oyster but tasted a thousand times better. A warm tingle like life itself rippled through me. The tear in my finger closed, healing without a trace, and I breathed a sigh of deep pleasure. A second brain chunk settled the hunger enough that I wouldn't try to eat the next person I ran into.

It used to freak me out that human brains tasted so damn good, but I got over that in no time. The guilt was harder to shrug off, but the unpleasant truth was that I needed to eat human brains to stay alive and in one piece. Moping about it was nothing more than a waste of time and energy. At least I wasn't killing people for brains.

Not unless they tried to kill me first.

I scooped the rest of the brain pieces into a plastic freezer baggie then retied the organ bag and tucked it back between Mr. Granger's knees. Hunger urged me to scarf down another chunk, but my tattered self-control told the hunger to sit its ass down and wait until I was in a safer place. That settled, I sealed the baggie nice and tight then wiped a dribble of bloody yuck off its side.

The *clunk* of the cooler door handle sent my heart spasming like an electrified frog. I whirled to face the doorway, jerked the baggie behind me and shoved it into the back of my pants even as the Chief Investigator—my supervisor—stepped in.

"Allen!" I forced out a laugh and put on my best I'm-so-innocent face. "You, uh, scared the crap out of me."

He regarded me for an endless second then frowned at the body. Holy shit, was I ever glad I'd already closed the organ bag.

Allen flicked his eyes back to me. "What are you doing, Angel?"

"I was double-checking that all the property had been logged." I tried for an easy smile but it felt more like a freaked-out grimace. I'd rehearsed clever lies for this sort of thing a hundred times, and here I'd managed to blurt out the worst one to use on Allen. Ever since an incident last year involving missing property, Allen checked and logged each case personally. Shitfuckgoddamn.

Mouth tightening, Allen stepped to the gurney. I shifted away to give him space, and the baggie slipped down the back of my pants to the bottom of my scrawny butt. I froze as I envisioned the baggie sliding down my pant leg to flop onto the floor. That would be epic.

Allen pulled the zipper open all the way to Mr. Granger's feet. With his attention off me, I arched my lower back to stick my butt out, trapping the baggie between my pants and the crack of my ass, then edged back against a steel cadaver shelf until the baggie squished, pinned in place. Except now I was equally trapped, since I couldn't move without risking the baggie going *plop*. I also couldn't lean back and chill, since all I needed to make the day perfect would be for the bag to bust open and spill brain splooge down my legs. I doubted Allen would believe I was having the Worst Period Ever.

"Did you find anything amiss?" Allen asked.

My pulse stumbled. "With the, uh, property?"

"That's what we're talking about, isn't it?"

"Yeah," I said. "I mean, no, I didn't find anything. Looks like everything got inventoried." God almighty, I hoped nothing had been left on the body. I'd been so focused on the brains, Mr. Granger could've been wearing the Hope Diamond as a nose ring, and I wouldn't have noticed.

Allen's eyes lingered on the organ bag, and my gut did a somersault. If he noticed the missing brains, I'd be fired and charged with . . . hell, I didn't know what I'd be charged with, but I had no doubt that stealing organs was illegal. And I *knew* that Chief Asshole Allen Prejean would demand full prosecution. The pathologist, Dr. Leblanc, had my back for most on-the-job issues, but I couldn't see him stepping in to save me on this one. What was the punishment for corpse desecration anyway?

Damn it, why hadn't I made absolutely sure everyone was gone from the whole back of the building before doing something so risky? Hey, maybe for my next trick I could munch on a brain in the break room and hope no one noticed. Moron.

Allen zipped the body bag without checking the organs. My heart finally descended from my throat.

"I need to see you in my office after lunch," he said, words crashing over me like a wave of ice water.

"Is something wrong?" I squeaked out.

"We'll talk about it then." He shoved the cooler door open and exited.

I stayed where I was, breathing shallowly and certain that if I moved I'd fall over. *No way.* No way could he have any clue what I was really up to. No way could this be the worst case scenario. No. Way. None of my coworkers knew I was a zombie, and that was mighty fine with me. Allen probably wanted to see me for some stupid work thing. Yeah. That's all it was. That's all it could possibly be. Not a thing to worry about. I pulled the baggie out of the crack of my ass, slipped it into the thigh pocket of my cargo pants then staggered out.

The air of the hallway felt smothering after the thirty-four degrees of the cooler. A glance at the clock told me the entire incident had only burned five minutes of my lunch break, which meant I had an hour and twenty-five minutes to get my shit together. Plenty of time, but best done the hell away from the morgue.

I jerked in shock as my phone vibrated in my pocket, and I fumbled it out only to drop it to the tile floor. Cursing, I snatched it up then breathed a sigh of relief that it wasn't damaged. I'd earned a sweet bonus on my zombie R&D lab paycheck for helping rescue Marcus and Pietro Ivanov—who was now Pierce Gentry—from the Saberton lab in New York. After paying tuition, I had enough left to buy myself a fancy new smartphone *and* a MegaCase that would protect my phone from all sorts of awful things, including the perils of being owned by one Angel Crawford.

My mood eased as I saw I had a text from Marcus. He'd saved my life in more ways than one when he turned me into a zombie. We'd then dated on-and-off again for about a year but finally broke up for good a few months ago after he—once again—made plans about our life together without consulting me. Big plans that involved me quitting my job and moving to New Orleans. Despite all that, I was glad we'd remained friends. He was a good guy and would always be dear to me, no matter what else happened.

I thumbed in my passcode and read the text.

Have to back out on the movie tonight. Leaving with

Pierce, Brian, and Kyle on business. Back Wednesday. Sorry. Miss you.

I sighed. This was the third cancellation in a month.

What kind of business? I typed. *Anything interesting?*

A moment later. *On the way to the airport. Can't talk now.*

Great, now I was anxious *and* pissy.

Stepping outside the Coroner's Office building was like passing into an alternate universe. Harsh fluorescent lighting and questionable odors gave way to brilliant sun and the cool air of early spring. Not that I was in the mood to enjoy the weather. I hurried to my car then drove a half dozen blocks before I pulled into an empty parking lot. The instant I came to a complete stop I had the baggie open and half the cerebellum stuffed into my mouth. Blood and cranial fluid dribbled down my chin, and my eyes rolled back in pure bliss. The texture and taste of that particular section of the brain was too good for words. Once I swallowed that mouthful down, I noshed on the left parietal lobe then reluctantly tucked the rest back into my lunch box.

A year and a half ago, I woke up in the ER after a supposed overdose and without a scratch on me, yet with the vivid memory of being horribly injured in a car crash. I soon discovered that an anonymous benefactor—Marcus—had arranged a job for me as a morgue tech with the Coroner's Office. I'd been harvesting brains out of body bags to feed my zombie needs ever since, but this was the first time I'd come so close to being caught.

But Allen didn't *catch me*, I reminded myself as I wiped brain gook off my face and checked my teeth in the mirror. He wouldn't have let me leave on my lunch break if he had. So what if he wanted to see me in his office? Everything was okay. Most likely, he was going to pull an asswipe move and change my shifts and days off for the billionth time. No biggie.

Then why was my heart still thumping like a rabbit in a sack?

The lunch box remained open. My last vial of V12 modifier rested beside the baggie of brains. Unlike regular drugs,

V12 was a kick butt pharmaceutical specifically formulated to work *with* the zombie parasite rather than be neutralized by it. I knew too damn much about regular drugs—especially the not-so-good kind. I'd been a pill-popping loser until I was turned into a zombie. All of a sudden those drugs had stopped working on me and, just like that, my addictions disappeared.

The V12 mod was different, of course. I'd discovered its benefits a few months back, after all the godawful shit I went through during the rescue mission in New York. V12 was the one thing that kept me from turning into a complete basket case and, as a mega-super bonus, it countered a good portion of my dyslexia. I was currently struggling through Biology 101 and Basic English Composition, and I needed all the help I could get.

I peered at the milliliter of colorless liquid left in the vial. One cc. One full dose, which I needed to save to help me study tonight, especially since midterms were in a couple of weeks.

But I was supposed to meet with Allen after my lunch break, and I didn't need to be looking guilty and freaked out for that. Calm. Chill. Like ice. That's how I needed to be.

I opened the glove box and dug out a 3cc syringe—a special one with a coating on the needle that kept my parasite from trying to heal the cells around it.

I grabbed the vial then paused. Last dose, but I could obtain more soon enough. My shift at the morgue today ended at two, and my second job at the zombie R&D lab had a flexible schedule. I could squeeze in a few hours at the lab today and load up on enough V12 to get me through another two weeks. I'd do only a half-dose right now, enough to take the edge off my nerves. The rest would be a reserve in case I didn't make it to the lab today. Yeah, that worked.

Satisfied, I drew half of the remaining mod into the syringe, pinched my side and jabbed the short needle under my skin. With a sigh of anticipation, I pressed the plunger then pulled the syringe free.

Fifteen seconds.

I dropped it into a plastic bottle to join three other used syringes and returned the vial with its half-dose to my lunch box.

Ten seconds.

Later I'd dispose of the used syringes deep in the medical waste bin at the morgue, but for now I chucked them back into the glove box.

Five seconds.

I closed my lunch box and leaned back.

Three . . . two . . . one.

Delicious warmth spread through me like a smile. The sun shone brighter. My lips tingled. Diamonds glittered on the dash and sparkles tickled my nose. Laughing, I put the car in gear and left the parking lot.

All was right in my world. Time for a sandwich.

Chapter 2

The half-dose of V12 was enough to keep me from obsessing about the meeting with Allen. Knowing him, it was some teensy issue that gave him an excuse to give me grief. That seemed to be a favorite hobby of his. I sure wished he'd take up whittling or cake decorating instead.

Traffic was hellacious, and even the chill-out effects of the mod weren't enough to keep me from snarling as my lunch break ticked away. I only needed to go two miles, but at this rate I was never going to make it to Alma's Café. Ever. I'd starve to death behind the wheel of my car. Rigor mortis would forever preserve my hand with my middle finger extended, aimed at idiot drivers everywhere.

Screw this. In a desperate move of navigational brilliance and law-breaking, I whipped through a gas station and onto a quieter back street. Distance-wise it was longer, but at least I'd be able to go faster than three miles an hour.

As I passed Scott Funeral Home, a black Escalade SUV in the parking lot caught my eye. Brian Archer, head of our zombie Tribe security drove one, but of course lots of other people probably did, too. Well, maybe not *lots* since they weren't exactly cheap. And how many people also had the same black roof rack rails and front and rear molded splash guards and 22" five-spoke silver and black machined wheels?

Hey, I dated a car guy for four years. I noticed that kind of stuff.

But the kicker was the bright blue Ford F-150 pickup next to it. Marcus's truck, I was damned near positive. The Tribe owned a bunch of funeral homes—part of the supply network for brains—but Scott Funeral Home wasn't one of them. So why would Brian and Marcus be here when they were supposedly on their way to the airport?

I cruised on past. It was none of my business. Really.

Not my business, but curiosity wasn't a crime. Maybe those weren't their vehicles after all? I made the block and got another look.

Nope, that was most definitely Marcus's truck, right down to the small ding on the rear bumper. It was possible he'd lent it to someone while he was out of town, but that didn't explain Brian's Escalade. What the hell, I had time to spare. I pulled into a parking space where I had a good view of the two vehicles and the front door, but not so close that my surveillance was obvious.

I barely had time to come to a full stop before Marcus exited the funeral home and plopped onto the bench beside the door. He was a seriously good-looking guy, tall and fit with dark hair and eyes, and strong Russian features. As I watched, he dropped his head back against the wall and slumped, clearly tired in more ways than just physically. I winced. Looked like his sudden "promotion" wasn't all puppies and ice cream. Had to be especially tough considering he'd been deliberately excluded from the Tribe's inner circle right up until they actually needed him.

Damn. Now my curiosity felt more like stalking. I climbed out of my car and started his way. The funeral home door opened again, and security specialist Rachel Delancey prowled out like an elegant, athletic cat, dark-skinned and with braids to die for. I stopped, still on the far side of the truck from them, and watched as Marcus smiled up at her.

Rachel took his hand and gave it what I knew damn well was a squeeze. "Call me later if anything turns up."

"You know I will," Marcus said like a promise. Grr. I knew I had no good reason to get my hackles up over Marcus getting involved with another woman. Except that this was *Rachel,* who hated me for no good reason.

Rachel turned away from him and headed toward his truck—and me. I scrambled to get my game face on and managed to pull off *cool and natural* by the time she rounded the front.

Surprise flashed in her eyes for only an instant before she gave me a tight smile. "Angel. What are you doing here?"

I smiled right back. "Seeing what y'all are up to."

"Tribe business," she said with a haughty lift of her chin.

"What a coincidence! I'm Tribe, too."

She glanced toward Marcus then leveled a cool gaze at me. "For now."

I rolled my eyes. "Really? You're gonna talk Marcus into kicking me out? Your shit ain't that hot."

Rachel's lips pressed thin before she shouldered past me and climbed into Marcus's truck. As my shock settled, she looked down on me with a triumphant smirk then cranked the engine and backed out.

Bitch. Did she *know* I'd never driven his truck?

Marcus stared at me in shock as the departure of the truck left me exposed, then scrambled up from the bench. I closed the distance and gave him a sour look. "On your way to the airport, huh?"

"In a manner of speaking," he said a bit stiffly. "I was going to text you."

I snorted. "Is that why the big neon sign over your head is flashing 'guilty'?"

He frowned. Guiltily. "Nothing to feel guilty about." He gestured toward the Escalade. "We're leaving soon."

"Gimme a break, Marcus." I rolled my eyes. "You bailed on the texting when I asked for details on the business trip."

A scowl tugged at his mouth. "It's Tribe business."

As in, none of mine? I could take a big sucky hint. "You could've just said it was confidential Tribe business instead of *lying*," I said, grimly pleased when he flinched. "But hey, whatever. I obviously don't deserve to know shit. It's not like I proved myself in New York or saved your ass and Pierce's, too."

His face could've been carved from stone. "It's not my call."

"Your *call?*" Acid dripped from my voice. "You mean Pierce won't let you make the call." Marcus's uncle, Tribe leader Pietro Ivanov, had died in a fiery private plane crash on the way back from New York a few months ago. Except, he hadn't, and only a handful of people knew the truth. In order to escape Saberton Corporation's zombie dungeon lab, Pietro had been forced to make a bold move. He'd eaten the brain of enemy security guard Pierce Gentry and used the DNA blueprint to change from Pietro-shaped to Pierce-shaped. Only mature zombies had that freaky ability.

Unfortunately, once he became Pierce, he couldn't return to Pietro-shaped. After we returned from New York minus Pietro Ivanov, Pierce Gentry had joined the Tribe with the cover story—supported by Brian and Dr. Nikas— that he'd been a long-term mole in Saberton. However, Pierce couldn't exactly waltz into Pietro's vacated shoes as if nothing had happened. In order to keep everything running, he had to work from behind the throne.

And it was Marcus who now wore the crown.

I poked the zombie king in the chest. "Don't you dare let Pierce treat you like a figurehead! You gave up your badge and law school to take over for him. You deserve better than his bullsh—"

The funeral home door banged open, and Pierce himself stalked out, black eyebrows drawn together in a fierce glower. "Bullshit is right. I don't have time for it."

"A big ol' hello to you, too," I said with a healthy dollop of sarcasm.

Ignoring me, Pierce pulled Marcus a short distance away while I folded my arms over my chest and scowled. The two put their heads together, speaking too low for me to get the slightest whiff. Pierce was tall like Marcus and looked hella formidable in no-nonsense charcoal-grey polo shirt and black pants. On his belt he had a big-ass knife that I'd seen him use with scary-deadly ease. I still had trouble thinking of him as the same person as the older, stocky Pietro Ivanov. But there was no mistaking the Pietro confidence and attitude. And, occasional assholeishness.

Brian exited the funeral home, face set in unreadable mode. He took in the Pierce and Marcus conversation then gave me a faint smile, angled his head in the opposite direction in a clear "come with?" gesture. Suppressing a sigh, I nodded and moved down the sidewalk with him. Brian was guarding Pierce's privacy, but at least he was being nice about it.

Brian stopped after about twenty feet. "Don't mind Pierce," he said. "The FBI has him worked up."

I sucked in a breath. "The FBI? What's going on?"

"An agent visited three of his funeral homes in other states in the past two days."

"Did they show up here?"

"About an hour ago. Mrs. Scott says the agent asked a few simple questions about how they handle bodies. Showed her a photo of a man and asked if she'd seen him come through. That's it. The other funeral homes reported the same."

I chewed my lower lip as I considered that. "If the FBI is also poking around non-Tribe funeral homes, then isn't it less likely they're tracking zombie-related stuff?"

"At this point, we're baffled, but we can't take any chances," Brian said. "There've been some uncomfortable inquiries into Mr. Ivanov's *death* as well." His gaze drifted to Pierce. "We're checking all leads."

"Is that why y'all are here instead of on your way to the airport?"

Brian gave me a sharp look. I gave him a bland one in

response. I knew he'd realize who spilled the beans, but no need to throw Marcus under the bus. Even if he was a Lying LiarMcLyingPants. Besides, if I didn't let on how much I knew, maybe I could wheedle a few more details out of Brian.

But my wheedling hopes shattered when the door opened yet again, and a lanky black man. Tribe weapons specialist—and my trainer—Kyle Griffin. Pierce and Marcus broke off their conversation and moved his way.

"Her description of the photo is useless," Kyle told them. "I did find out that at least one agent will be in town over the weekend."

"Goddamn shitty timing," Pierce said through clenched teeth. He blew out an angry breath. "Let's roll."

Brian gave me an apologetic look and fished car keys from his pocket. "Take care, Angel," he said and headed to the Escalade with Kyle in his wake.

Marcus stepped close and gave me a quick kiss on the cheek. "Sorry, Angel." He pressed a movie premiere ticket into my hand. His. "I'll tell you what I can when I get back."

"Yeah. Sure," I muttered as he moved past me toward the SUV. That was probably yet another lie-to-Angel-for-no-good-reason thing. Brian was head of security, and *he* hadn't been so tight-lipped. I was no doubt being a petty bitch, but it sucked that once again Marcus hadn't trusted me enough to believe I'd act like a grownup. This day was already lousy enough with Allen's surprise visit to the morgue cooler, thank you very much. And what the hell would I do if Allen found out the truth? My gut tightened. If I got fired—

Pierce's gaze snapped to me. His nostrils flared as he stepped close and *sniiiiffffed*. "What are you afraid of, Angel?"

"Oh, for fuck's sake." Damn mature zombie super-senses. Still, it was probably smart to tell him. "I'm not *afraid*," I corrected primly. "I'm a little worried about a stupid thing at work, that's all." I gave him a quick and dirty rundown of my encounter with Allen and the impending meeting. "I don't think anything will come of it," I added. "He'd have fired me already if he knew the deal, but it still makes me nervous."

Pierce shot Marcus a dark look. "See?"

Marcus pressed his lips together, jaw tight as if holding back a comment.

"What's going on?" I asked.

"Far too much scrutiny," Pierce said. He took my shoulders in a firm grip. "Call Dr. Nikas ASAP if you have trouble at the morgue with Allen Prejean. Ari will get hold of me. Got it?"

"Sure. Okay." I had the uncomfortable sensation Pierce could see right through me. "What about the FBI agent here in town? Anything to worry about?"

"Rachel will be keeping tabs on the funeral homes. Naomi is undercover at the Zombie Fest, watching for anything noteworthy." He huffed out a breath of frustration. "Not that we know what we're looking for."

I perked up. "I'm going to the Zombie Fest tomorrow. I can be another set of eyes and ears there as well as around town."

Pierce regarded me for a long moment, giving me time to prep my I've-proven-myself-over-and-over speech. But he squeezed my shoulders and let out a weary sigh. "That would be great, Angel. We certainly need the help."

He meant it, I realized, and a tendril of worry crept through me. He shouldn't need my help. Not with Tribe security on the ball. But this was a job I could do. I had no trouble—

Without warning, Pierce leaned in close and sniffed again. I twitched in surprise then grabbed his head and licked his damn cheek.

He jerked back and stared at me.

"See how creepy it is on the receiving end?" I snapped. "Maybe a little warning next time? Or, I dunno, privacy?"

Eyes on me, he wiped a hand over his cheek then brought it to his nose. *Sniffed.* He gave me a frown I couldn't read then strode to the Escalade without a word.

Weirdest day *ever*.

Chapter 3

Normal food-hunger jabbed at me as I climbed back into my car, informing me that I needed to get my ass to Alma's Café before I starved to death. Brain-hunger chimed in as well, and I dug another chunk out of my lunch box to shut that one up for the moment. One of the few drawbacks of V12 was the way it tripled my brain hunger, but I figured that was a small price to pay for the benefits it offered. Besides, I only needed to use it until I finished the semester.

It also didn't suck that I felt more relieved than upset about the encounter with Pierce and Marcus. Though it irked me to be left out of the loop about the confidential business, I was more than happy for the others to deal with the big crap. New York had been a trial by fire of *enormous* crap, and I still felt singed by everything that happened. I'd killed people. A lot of them. And my nightmares didn't care that there'd been no choice, didn't care that those people would have done far worse to me and my friends.

So yeah, I'd done my time in the trenches. Being eyes and ears—and not much else—was fine with me.

The hideous traffic had eased, and I made it downtown with a minimum of stress. But once there, I slowed and gaped at the sight of an enormous putrid green banner strung over Main Street. Lurid red letters screamed "5th Annual Deep South Zombie Fest" with "-er" at the end, printed to look as if it had been spray painted on.

Fest-er. Because zombies rot and . . . fester. Heh.

The Deep South Zombie Fest was held in a different place each year, but it was Mayor Turnbuckle who deserved props for bringing it to town. He'd worked political magic and southern charm to convince Infamous Vision Studios— the makers of *High School Zombie Apocalypse!!*—that a return to Tucker Point as sponsors of the Zombie Fest would be great promo for the movie's opening weekend. With the studio's money and prestige as incentive, the organizers of the Fest had been more than happy to bring it here.

For a small town whose interests usually ran toward hunting season, NASCAR, and *Cochon de Lait*, Tucker Point seized onto the zombie mania with fevered passion. Not only did all the hoopla pump tourist money into the community, it also gave the locals yet another reason to let loose and have a good time. Not that they needed one. Hell, this was Louisiana. We partied when the weather changed.

I turned down a side street and into the lot behind Cathy's Candle Creations. Parking there meant I had to walk an extra block, but considering the earlier traffic I doubted there'd be any open spaces closer to the café.

The giant banner over Main Street turned out to be merely the tip of the festering iceberg. It looked as if the zombie fairy had paid a visit and waved her magic wand to transform downtown Tucker Point into an undead circus. Moans and groans and hungry growls issued through a town PA system usually reserved for holiday music. All the local businesses had jumped onto the rotting bandwagon in an effort to cash in on the weekend of zombie craziness. Roaming vendors peddled makeup kits and latex gore. Sidewalk sale zombie stuff was everywhere. Posters, bumper stickers, T-shirts, you name it. A local youth group was even selling tickets to the Zombie Petting Zoo.

I didn't want to know.

To add to the total weirdness, Mardi Gras was coming up in four days, on the heels of the Fest weekend, which made for a strange hodgepodge of decorations. Carnival and corpses. Putrid colors of zombie rot mingled with the glitter of gaudy purple, green, and gold. And no one seemed to mind one little bit.

Least of all me. I absolutely loved it. The last lingering worries about Allen or Marcus or the FBI slipped away as I took it all in and headed down the street toward Alma's Café.

Moe's Hardware had been in business for over a hundred years and was as much a museum as a store—filled with all sorts of tools made obsolete by technology. Not many people had a need for a two-man saw anymore. Gimme a good chainsaw, any day. But I also knew that if we ever had ourselves a real apocalypse, Moe's would be my first stop to load up on useful shit that didn't need gas or electricity.

The current Mr. Moe was the son of the original owner. He was ninety if he was a day, but that hadn't stopped him from joining in the fun. With a denture-baring grin, he shambled up and down the sidewalk in front of his store, fake blood smeared on his face.

I evaded a leering zombie hug—which, knowing Mr. Moe, would include a zombie ass-grab—but stopped in awe when I reached the next shop, Le Bon Décor. Displayed in the window were a pair of exquisite carnival masks. *Zombie* carnival masks with sculpted rot and realistic paint. The grinning one had teeth exposed in maggoty flesh, and the mouth of the frowning face dripped blood from rotting lips. Bedraggled feathers and tarnished sequins completed the cool risen-from-the-grave effect.

A deep yearning lust for wearable art filled me.

I wanted those masks.

I *needed* those masks.

Squaring my shoulders, I stepped into the shop and brazenly asked the salesgirl the price.

She told me with a smile. I thanked her with a smile, and stepped right back out. Okay, maybe I didn't really *need* zombie carnival masks. Moving on.

A guy wearing cheesy zombie makeup and sandwich boards shuffled along the sidewalk in front of Alma's Café. The front placard advertised "Zombie-licious Étouffée" and the back, "Fried Brain Po-Boys"—all made from calf, pig, and lamb brains. I shuddered. As yummy as I found a human brain, the idea of eating any other sort left me queasy. Only the human kind had the components my zombie parasite needed to do its thing. I'd stick to Alma's turkey club sandwich, thank you very much.

Alma's brain supplier was no doubt Wyatt's Butcher Shop across the street. My clue was the "Get Your Braaains Here!" painted in shocking pink on his window along with "Great addition to your zombie costume!" in smaller lettering beneath.

Before I could think too hard about fake-zombies wandering around toting animal brains—and what that would smell like after a few hours—my gaze fell on the red 1968 Dodge Charger parked in front of the butcher shop. The only person around here who owned a car like that was my *other* ex-boyfriend, Randy.

Maybe he'd come into town for sausage or steaks? He sometimes had friends over for beer, pot, and barbecue on Friday evenings. I shaded my eyes and scanned the butcher's shop. No sign of him through the window, so I shifted my looksee to the business next door: The Bear's Den Gun Shop and Indoor Range. A huge Zombie Fest poster filled one corner of the window, but beyond the poster, I saw Randy lounging against a counter inside. I'd known him since I was fifteen, and he'd never shown any interest in camping, hunting, or owning a gun. But his buddy Judd worked there, and they were most likely cooking up plans for the weekend. Judd wasn't my favorite person ever since he asked me out during one of my many breakups with Randy and got all kinds of pissy when I turned him down.

But, hell, lots of people weren't my favorites. For the most part, I put up with them anyway. Life was too short to hold more than a handful of grudges.

Randy and I had dated for about four years, breaking up and getting back together a couple dozen times. We finally broke up for good not long after I became a zombie but, when I got back from New York, we started hanging out again some. Randy knew me better than anyone else—except for the fact that I was a zombie—which meant I could relax and be myself and not worry about coming off as trashy or ignorant. And though I never *ever* wanted to date Randy again, it turned out we worked pretty nicely as friends.

And, as a friend, I was totally allowed to be a nosy bitch. Might as well go with my strengths.

I left Alma's brainy menu behind and jaywalked through the slow-moving traffic. A chime sounded as I pushed the Bear's Den door open, barely audible over the hubbub in the store. It was more crowded than I'd expected, and I took a couple of seconds to get my bearings. I wasn't exactly a gun shop kind of chick, especially since I became a convicted felon right about the time I was old enough to buy a gun. Fortunately, I wasn't a felon anymore. About a year ago, someone—most likely Pietro Ivanov—had pulled a few dozen strings to get me pardoned by the governor.

My adventures in New York had included shooting myself in the ass, an event that was sure to end up on the blooper reel of the life of one Angel Crawford. However, the upside of my little mishap was that Mr. Deadly Operative himself, Kyle Griffin, took me under his wing and taught me how to shoot a variety of firearms safely and precisely. I suspected his generosity was more a desire to reduce the chance that I might accidentally shoot him, but I didn't mind. Though my concealed carry application was still in process, Louisiana law allowed me to have a gun in my car, where I currently had a Tribe-loaned Kel-Tec PF9 in the glove box. As crazy as my life was, it made sense to keep a little heat close at hand.

Even though The Bear's Den took up a good chunk of the block, I hadn't realized how *big* the place was. To my left, half a dozen black-shirted salespeople prowled behind a glass-enclosed display case that ran the length of the shop. Handguns and knives and other deadly stuff filled the case, and the wall behind it was one long rack of rifles and shotguns. To my right, a mounted deer head with enormous antlers loomed over a broad archway that led to the hunting, camping, and archery supplies. Everywhere else, shelves and racks held all sorts of accessories, equipment, and clothing. Posters hung from the ceiling with warnings such as: "ALWAYS TREAT A GUN AS IF IT'S LOADED" and "FINGER OFF THE TRIGGER UNTIL YOU'RE READY TO FIRE." But my favorite was "ASSHOLES AND IDIOTS WILL BE MAULED BY THE BEAR" complete with a picture of a scary, burly man—the owner of the shop himself, Bear. He stood behind the counter, wide shoulders hunched, hands huge but nimble as he demonstrated to a customer how to break down a handgun. His T-shirt read "Don't just survive. *Thrive!*"—a testimony to his standing as the local expert on survival and disaster preparedness.

A murmured "Excuse me" to my rear jarred me out of my gaping. I stepped aside to let a Hispanic man in black tactical pants and a form-fitting grey shirt go by, then shamelessly ogled him as he continued past me and down the counter toward Bear. *That* was the kind of male body those compression shirts were made for. V-shaped torso, trim waist, and biceps that popped from the sleeves in a way that said "I have these muscles as a result of being fit and strong in a lot of different ways" as opposed to "I have these muscles because I do bicep curls while I stare adoringly at myself in the gym mirror." Sparkly fireflies danced between us. I took a step toward him. Holy crap, that ass was like two firm apples that—

Jesus, Angel, get a grip on yourself! The V12 was still kicking in hard. The sparkly fireflies side effect wasn't so bad, but the suppression of impulse control—a remnant of the original combat version of the mod—could be downright inconvenient. Useful in high danger situations to tweak reaction time, but not so helpful while lusting after a stranger. But I could handle it. I always got it under control before anything embarrassing happened.

I reined in my inner sexual harassment of Tactical Pants Man and looked around for Randy. The entire section by the front window was nothing but Deep South Zombie Fest paraphernalia—posters, T-shirts, caps, coffee mugs, key chains, and a buttload more novelty items. Randy stood by a pyramid of dark blue duffel bags emblazoned with the Bear's Den logo and *Zombie Hunter Survival Kit* in searing red letters. Long and lanky, Randy didn't have movie star good looks or a Tactical Pants Man body, but he had a nice face and a sweet, lazy smile. A bright blue Zombie Fest cap covered light brown hair nearly the same color as his eyes. He had a duffel slung over one shoulder and was talking to Coy Bates—a slim black man with tidy shoulder-length dreads. Randy and Coy had been friends since sixth grade, and Coy was one of a very small number of Randy's friends who I actually liked. He always seemed to have a smile for everyone, and though he smoked pot with Randy most weekends, he stayed focused on his growing taxidermy business.

I skirted a display of paintball supplies, edged past a gaggle of men who were enthusing over a catalog of reloading equipment, then sidled up to Coy and Randy and gave them matching light arm punches. "Hey, guys. Coy, is that deer head above the arch your work?"

Randy gave me a grin, and Coy's face lit up with pride. "It sure is," Coy said in a gentle drawl. "Bear's son bagged it last fall. I got a lot of new business after Bear trusted me with it."

"It's gorgeous. You did a great job." I smiled up at it.

Sparkles glittered over the antlers. It turned its head toward me, eyes glowing like hot coals, and winked.

I sucked in a breath. "Holy shit!"

"Angel?"

I flinched at Randy's voice and yanked my gaze to him. He looked perfectly normal, to my relief. "I mean, uh, holy shit, those are big antlers," I said with only the tiniest hitch in my voice, despite the thumping of my pulse. I'd never had a hallucination like *that* before. Could the V12 have caused it? The sparkles sure added weight to that suspicion. I shot a wary glance at the arch. The deer stared straight ahead with glassy brown eyes. Maybe it wasn't a hallucination. Maybe I'd just imagined it. Hallucinated having a hallucination. Right.

Randy eyed me, but Coy beamed. "It's a ten point that scores in the one-sixties!"

I managed to give Coy a winning smile. "I have no idea what that means, but I assume it's good." I glanced at the perfectly normal deer head one more time. Okay, so now I knew seeing weird shit other than sparkles was a possibility. It wouldn't catch me off guard if it happened again. Worst case scenario, I'd have to decrease my dose a bit to stabilize. No biggie. I could handle it.

Randy gave my arm a soft punch. "I was gonna give you a call later. Didn't expect to run into you."

"I was heading to lunch and saw your car outside. What-cha doing here?"

Randy swung a puzzled look around the store. "Dunno what you mean. I'm shopping."

I snorted. "You hate shopping unless it involves car parts."

Coy gave a low laugh. "She's got you there, dude. You don't even like doing beer runs."

Randy chuckled. "Yeah, well, I wanna get ready for the weekend." He patted the duffel he carried—one of the zombie hunter survival kits.

"You're going to the Zombie Fest?" I asked in disbelief.

"Sure," he said with a shrug. "Everyone's going."

I peered at the tag that dangled from the duffel's strap. "A hundred and fifty bucks? Are you crazy?"

"It's got a lot of great stuff!" He flipped the tag around to show me what the kit included. "It's good for any kind of disaster, not just a zombie invasion."

My shock at the price eased as I read the list of contents. Three days' worth of emergency rations and water purification packets for two, a LifeStraw personal water filter, fire-starter, multi-tool, paracord, rain ponchos, light sticks, first aid kit, compass, fishing hooks and line, knife, insect spray, sunscreen, whistle, and a survival blanket. And, to justify the zombie hunter survival kit marketing, a baseball bat and a machete. "Okay, that looks pretty cool," I grudgingly admitted.

"I'm getting one, too," Coy said. "It includes an equipment vest Bear had specially made for the zombie hunts at the Fest."

The hunts? That explained the pile of gear heaped on the floor between the two. A big pile. This was more than an impulse purchase of a survival kit. I pressed my lips together to hold back the laugh. "You two are dressing up like zombie hunters for the Fest?"

Randy held up three fingers. "Me and Coy *and* Judd." He gestured toward the long counter where a black-shirted employee—Judd Siler—was giving an animated demonstration of proper grip and sighting to a rapt audience of teen boys. Judd wasn't a bad-looking guy—decent teeth, tall and wiry, sandy hair in a military buzz-cut—but his arrogance tended to wear thin on me pretty quickly.

"You *three*," I said. "Gee, sounds great."

Randy grinned, unfazed by my lack of enthusiasm. "We got us a team together for tonight's hunt," he said. "We're also signed up for two hunts tomorrow. You wanna join us? We got space for a fourth. It's gonna be a blast, and we're closing down Pillar's Bar after we kill all the zombies tonight."

I couldn't hold back a laugh. "Randy, I've seen you shoot. You couldn't hit a broken-down bus with a target painted on its side."

"We'll see what you say when I got a kickass zombie body count." He flashed me a Randy smile. "Come with us. You know we always have fun."

Despite the personal squick factor of "zombie body count," a tiny part of me couldn't help but be intrigued. Randy's usual idea of fun was hanging out at a car show or smoking pot around his fire pit. He liked zombie movies, but I never thought he'd get into it on this level. Then again, the entire damn town was getting into it. How could I say no to that kind of enthusiasm? It was all about having a good time.

"Can't do tonight since I already have plans, plus I'm on call with the morgue," I said. "But tomorrow might work. I'll buzz you in the morning and let you know." No way was I dressing up as a hunter, though. That hit a little too close to home. "What happens if a zombie bites you? Do all your hunting buddies take you out?"

"I ain't gonna let no stinkin' zombie anywhere near me." Randy lifted a hand and pretended to shoot me. "Kapow! Right between the eyes!"

My stomach jerked into a knot as I forced a laugh and batted his hand away. "Or, in your case, twenty feet to the left." Would he shoot *me* right between the eyes if he knew I was a real zombie?

Coy gave me a wink. "Why do you think we wanted Judd on our team? He's a crack shot."

"I ain't *that* bad," Randy said. "But you won't know the truth if you don't join us, Angel. This paintball stuff is a blast and don't have much more kick than a BB gun." His eyes lit up. "Bear's letting people try the paintball guns in the alley out back." Before I could respond, he slung an arm around my waist and propelled me toward the counter. I cast a desperate look back at Coy, but he gave me a helpless shrug.

"Hey, Judd," Randy called out. "Angel wants to try out the paintball rifles."

I didn't give a crap about trying out rifles—paintball or real—but after one look at the excitement on Randy's face,

I didn't have the heart to shut him down. Oh well, at least I had plenty of time left in my lunch break.

Judd gave a sharp nod. "Gotcha covered, bro." He retrieved a paintball rifle from a shelf behind him, ducked through a gap in the counter then beckoned imperiously. "Come on, Angel," he said as he headed for the back door. "I'll show you how to hit the target, and if you manage to not shoot yourself or me, I just might teach you how to use a real gun someday."

I planted my feet and glared big pointy daggers at Judd's back, but Randy nudged me forward. "C'mon. He's trying to get a rise out of you."

"I'll give him a damn rise," I muttered but kept moving, only because I intended to show Judd how full of shit he was. It so happened that I had a fair amount of experience with paintball, thanks to the zombie Tribe. Not long after Hurricane Katrina, Pietro Ivanov had purchased two thousand acres of woods and wetlands. Though he maintained the property as a wildlife refuge, it was also the perfect secluded spot to conduct paramilitary-style training. Every other weekend since New York, I joined the Tribe security people and played paintball tactical scenarios.

Except that zombie paintball was a wee bit more hardcore than regular paintball. I suppressed a grin at the gruesome memory of the time Rachel I-Hate-Angel Delancey needed help removing a tree branch I'd driven clean through her torso. I probably shouldn't have enjoyed skewering her as much as I did, but I *really* didn't like her. Besides, it was her own darn fault. She'd missed her chance to nail me with a headshot—after peppering the rest of me with paintball rounds—so it was only fair that I retaliate realistically. It wasn't as if a little impalement would've killed her or anything.

I didn't particularly like Judd, either, but I'd be satisfied with making him eat his words.

Tactical Pants Man gave me a long look as I walked by him. He had incredible green eyes and a nice, rugged face that matched the rest of him. I had no idea why he was checking me out, especially since my Coroner's Office shirt didn't do much to show off my assets. Not that I had a whole lot of "assets" beneath the shirt. Still, I gave him a flirty smile, though as soon as I passed him I subtly checked to make sure my fly was zipped.

Yep, zipped. Good. I wouldn't have to slink off and die of humiliation.

Judd led us out the back door and into a broad alley with the rear entrance to Wyatt's Butcher shop to the left and a cinderblock-walled dead end fifty feet to the right. A large target spray painted onto it was heavily marked with hundreds of splotches of fluorescent color.

Judd leaned the rifle against the wall. "Thanks, Angel." He grinned at my baffled look and pulled a flat case from a pocket. "Bear doesn't like us taking a bunch of smoke breaks, and I was getting the shakes."

"Wow, so glad I could donate my break time to help you kill yourself." I pointedly glanced at my watch, but he ignored me and removed a cigarette from the case.

"I roll my own these days," he announced and held the cig up proudly to show off the little American flags printed on the paper. "Saves money, even with special-ordered paper like this. You should give it a try, Angel."

"I don't smoke anymore," I snapped. Not entirely true since I still occasionally enjoyed a smoke—despite the fact it burned up brains as the parasite cleared out the toxic shit. It wasn't a habit, though. And I sure as hell didn't get the shakes if I couldn't have a cig. Before I became a zombie I was as much of a nicotine addict as Judd was now, but I wasn't going to waste my time explaining the finer points to him. "Are we gonna shoot this thing or not?"

Judd produced a bright yellow lighter and casually lit the cigarette. "Don't get your panties in a wad." He took a long drag and left the cigarette between his lips as he scooped up the rifle. "Watch and learn, little girl." In a smooth motion, he lifted the rifle, sighted, and pulled the trigger three times.

Puht puht puht

Three new splotches appeared, right on top of each other in the center of the bull's-eye. Judd was an arrogant turd, but I couldn't deny he had serious skills.

Judd grinned around the cigarette and lowered the rifle. "Now, Angel, you gotta tell me if it's your time of the month, 'cause I got a policy of never giving a woman a weapon when she's crazier than usual."

I fixed my mouth into a sweet smile. "Now, Judd, I can't be all that crazy. I was sane enough to never fuck you."

Randy and Coy hooted in appreciation of my comeback. Judd's face tightened for an instant, but then he forced a laugh. "Okay, that was a good one." He thrust the rifle at me. "Now let's see if you can even hit that wall."

Still smiling, I took the rifle from him, handling it a bit awkwardly on purpose. The asswipe had flipped the safety on. If I'd been a total newbie, I'd've looked like an idiot while I tried to make it work.

Judd flicked ash off the end of his stupid red, white, and blue cigarette. "I'll give you a lesson if you want." He laughed and pointed to his crotch. "Won't cost much."

"Gee, lemme think about that," I said and walked to the center of the alley. With Kyle Griffin's instructions ringing in my head, I hugged the butt of the rifle to my shoulder, nudged the safety off, and sighted.

Puht puht puht

Three pink splotches appeared within a foot of the center. Not as perfect as Judd's, but it was close enough.

Coy let out a whoop while Randy busted out laughing. "Hell yeah, Angel!"

Judd dropped the cigarette and ground it into the concrete. "You got lucky. Even a blind squirrel finds a nut—"

Puht

Judd squawked in pain as fluorescent pink bloomed an inch above his belt. "Jesus fuck! You bitch! You shot me!"

I stood with my hands clenched on the rifle, sparkles

crowding the edge of my vision as Randy and Coy stared at Judd.

My pulse stuttered. *Oh, shit. I* shot *him. What the hell, Angel?* I'd lost control again. Because of the V12? But that didn't make sense. It was only half a dose. I'd been using the stuff for months and never lost it this much. Then again, I'd also never had a hallucination other than sparkles and fireflies.

Crap. It didn't help that normal ordinary pissed-offedness at Judd the Jerk had kicked in as well. At least I hadn't aimed for his pecker. Or maybe I had and missed. It happened so fast, I had zero memory of any of it.

Forcing a smile, I blew imaginary smoke from the end of the barrel then handed the rifle to Coy. "Thanks for the demo, Judd, but I don't think I need you to teach me how to shoot." With that I left the three men in the alley and slammed the door behind me. Good effect for them, not so much for Bear. He glared at me over the scope of an assault rifle he was showing Tactical Pants Man. I cringed and mouthed "sorry" then made it through the Bear's Den and out onto the sidewalk without getting shot in the back by either Judd or Bear. A small victory, but I'd take it.

Chapter 4

Between stalking Marcus, chatting with Randy, and school-
ing Judd, I managed to burn enough of my break that I had
to settle for a pre-made sandwich to-go from Alma's. Even
so, I had only four minutes to spare by the time I made it
back to the Coroner's Office. I sat in my car and gobbled
down my turkey club, chased it with a couple of brain
chunks from the lunchbox, and hit the morgue door with
three seconds left.

Unfortunately, I now had no valid reason to put off
meeting Allen any longer. Not without risking landing in
more hot water. On the other hand, three staff meetings
ago, Allen had gone on a tirade about departmental emails
going unread. I smiled. Yep, I'd be the solid employee who
followed every Allen-directive to the letter. Every one. Especially the one about checking my email.

I trekked up the hallway to the tiny office that the
morgue techs shared. The morgue took up the back of the
Coroner's Office building, with records storage and supply
rooms serving as a buffer between it and everything else. As
the Chief Investigator, Allen was senior staff with an office
at the front of the building. Not only did that mean I didn't

have to see him as often, but at the moment the distance allowed me to eke out a few more minutes before our meeting. Hell, I'd scrub the morgue floor if it would buy me more Allen-free time.

I stepped into the tech office then stopped at the sight of my coworker, Nick Galatas, leaning over my desk. I cleared my throat, amused when he jumped like a startled cat.

"Jesus, Angel!" He straightened to his full five and a half feet and gave me a mild glare. He was a nice-looking guy, with dark brown hair and green eyes, though it was only in the last six months or so that he smiled more than he sneered—at least with me.

"You'd better not be giving me more paperwork to do," I said with a teasing smile.

"Nope." He snatched a gaudy flier from the desk and jerked it behind his back like a kid hiding candy.

I moved toward him and tried to peer around him. "What's that?"

"Nothing." He shifted away, scowling when I refused to give up so easily.

"You came in here to put nothing on my desk?" I snatched for the flier, but he was a hair too fast for me. "C'mon, Nick. Let me see."

"It's stupid."

I folded my arms over my chest and leveled my fiercest look at him. "Cough it up."

His shoulders drooped as he accepted defeat and handed the flier over. "It's for the Zombie Fest." Color crept up his face. "I have an extra VIP pass. And . . . I thought you could use it tomorrow. You know. With me."

Awwwww. There was nothing in the world cuter than Nick the Prick squirming like a teenager. "Sounds fun," I said, then winced. "But I'm supposed to join up with one of the hunter teams."

"The hunters *suck*," he snapped, mouth turning down as if he'd swallowed sour milk.

"Couldn't agree with you more," I said, though I doubted

my reasons were the same as his, whatever they were. "Look, my plans aren't firm, but no way in hell will I dress up like a hunter. Promise to go zombie, and we've got a date."

His eyes widened in a priceless look of denial. "It's not a date!" he sputtered. "I just didn't want the ticket to go to waste."

"I'm messing with you, dude," I said, grinning at his reaction. "I'm totally cool with no strings."

The whisper of panic faded from his eyes. "Good. Sure. Okay. As long as we understand each other." He squared his shoulders and lifted his chin. "We can meet here tomorrow at one-thirty."

He was all Nickitude and business now, but I knew that was a mask he put on when he felt out of his depth. "Only if you dress up for real," I said. "No half-ass dollar store outfit. I need to *believe* you're undead."

He gave a prim sniff. "That's a done deal. You need help with a costume?"

I smiled for reasons he'd never know. Let me go without brains for a while, and I'd show him a costume that would send him screaming for his mommy. Rotten flesh, a dangling eyeball, maybe even a bone-grating broken arm that flopped with every move. Of course, he'd have reason to run if I got hungry enough to be in that state, since prying his brain from his skull would be at the top of my to-do list. "I could use help with the makeup."

He relaxed into a smile, genuine and open. "I have a kit. I'll fix you up when you get here tomorrow."

I dropped the flier onto the desk, fidgeted. "Allen wants to see me. I, uh, better get going."

"Yeah, me too. I need to write up the report on the hospice death from this morning."

Neither one of us moved. An awkward silence threatened.

I scrambled for something neutral to say. "Have you heard back about your med school application yet?"

To my surprise, Nick stiffened. "No. Nothing yet," he said, curt and sharp, then turned his back on me and stalked out of the office without another word.

Baffled, I stared at the empty doorway. What the hell? I hadn't even been trying to rattle his cage. For as long as I'd been working with Nick, he'd bragged nonstop about being pre-med. It seemed only natural to ask how everything was going. Grimacing, I tugged a hand through my hair. Crap. What if he'd been rejected and was too embarrassed to admit it? It'd be like him to get all defensive if he had to eat crow. He could be a dick, but most times it was all bluster and no bite.

Aggravated at the both of us, I kicked the wastebasket then had to scramble and pick up the crumpled paper that spilled across the floor. If not for Nick's relentless and patient tutoring, I never would have passed the GED and would currently be up shit creek in Biology 101. Nick was a solid friend, and it bugged me that I might have said something thoughtless. At least I'd be seeing him tomorrow. I'd try and find out then what bug crawled up his butt.

I dutifully checked my email then had no choice but to amble to the office marked Chief Investigator. Allen was on the phone when I poked my head in. I mouthed and gestured *I can come back later* along with what was no doubt a desperately hopeful look, but he shook his head and waved me in. Crap. My last hope of escape, gone.

He finished an irate conversation about a missing shipment of formalin and replaced the phone in its cradle with force. "Idiots." He yanked an invoice out of a folder and made some angry notes on it. "Close the door and sit down."

My stomach dropped. The only other time he'd told me to close the door was after I accidentally dumped a gurney and body bag into a rain-swollen ditch. The street had been dark and slick, and I never saw the pothole that grabbed the gurney wheel. All I could think was that I'd be written up or fired for losing the body, so I jumped right on into the ditch to grab it since I figured at the worst I'd get my pants wet.

Except it was a pretty deep ditch to begin with, and not only had I failed to take flash flood rainwater into account, but I'd also neglected to consider that there'd be a fierce little current. Could've been bad news if I was human but, after the first few seconds of panic, I stopped worrying about drowning, got hold of the body bag and dragged it out of the water.

Allen called me in the next day but, instead of giving me a damn pat on the back for saving the body and the gurney, he delivered a twenty minute ass-reaming lecture on safety and awareness and unnecessary risks and other stupid crap. Even told me I'd be fired if I pulled a "stunt" like that again. Asshole.

I clung to that slim thread of righteous anger like an emotional lifeline, sank into the chair in front of his desk and tried not to squirm. "So, what's up?" I tried for a casual tone, as if being in trouble was the furthest thing from my mind.

Allen pulled a Zombie Fest flier out of his drawer and dropped it on the desk in front of me. "You going?"

I couldn't have been more surprised if he'd asked me if my dad was an alien. This rated a closed door meeting? "Er, yeah, tomorrow with—" I caught myself before naming Nick. Allen might count it as a date and, if dating a co-worker was against the rules, he'd milk it for ammunition to give me grief. "—with a friend."

He leaned forward, eyes fixed on me. "As zombie or hunter?"

I fought back a twitch. "Why?"

"Curious."

The curiosity of a cat about to snatch a mouse. "Zombie."

Allen's expression remained inscrutable. "Why zombie?"

"Thought it might be fun to imagine what it'd be like. To be one. A zombie." I pushed my mouth into a grin and stuck my arms out in front. "*Braaains*."

Dude didn't crack a smile. He was seriously beginning to creep me out.

"How about you?" I asked. "Are you going?"

Allen pursed his lips. "Too real for me." He paused. "Thought it might be for you as well."

Too real? What was *that* supposed to mean? I knew for a fact Allen wasn't a zombie. I'd salivated over his very human brain many times before. And it was beyond impossible that a stick-up-the-ass like Allen would believe in zombies. "Everyone's going." I shrugged in the way a completely unconcerned person would shrug. "It's all just for fun."

A glower tugged his eyebrows down. "People get crazy."

"Paintball and beer have that effect," I said with a weak laugh and tried not to fidget in nervous discomfort. I couldn't handle much more of this Allen closed-door strangeness. "Is *this* what you wanted to talk to me about?"

He replaced the flier in the drawer, leaned back and laced his fingers together over his stomach. "There've been some irregularities with the organ bags."

My lips felt weird, as though all the blood had drained from my face. Allen regarded me as steadily as if I was under the dissecting scope in the morgue. I waited for him to elaborate. And waited.

"What kind of irregularities?" I finally blurted.

"It's gone on long enough, and I don't want any trouble for the department." His left index finger tapped a slow cadence. "You have anything you want to tell me?"

"Tell you?" My mind froze so hard icicles could've hung off my ears. *But if he knew about the missing brains, I'd be in the back of a cop car at this very moment, not having a cozy office chat.* That realization thawed my brain enough to squeeze out a reasonable response instead of a confession. "I've, uh, caught a few with leaks. I went ahead and double-bagged them." I bit down on the urge to add more cover-my-ass lies. My ex-boyfriend and retired-cop, Marcus, used to tell me how a lot of criminals tripped themselves up by complicating their lies with details. Good thing was, I *had* found a couple of leaky organ bags. Bad thing was . . . organ bags.

Allen's glower didn't budge. "As I said, I don't want trouble for the department. I intend to ensure—" His phone rang. He glanced at the caller ID then muttered a curse. "I have to take this." He snatched up the handset. "Allen Prejean."

A brief reprieve. I scrambled to get my thoughts in order. None of this made any sense. He hadn't called me in to talk about leaky bags. That was minor stuff and wouldn't rate a closed-door meeting. Something else was up.

Not that it mattered. For whatever reason, Allen was paying attention to the organ bags, which meant he would eventually notice that brains were missing. Shit. What was I going to do? I *liked* this job, but if it dried up as a source of brains, I'd have no choice but to look for alternatives.

"Yes, sir." Allen's face tightened but his voice remained calm. "I'll get the report to her this afternoon." A pause. "No, sir. No. Let me explain. Hang on a moment." He covered the mouthpiece with his hand. "Angel, we'll have to finish this on Monday. Be careful out there this weekend."

I forced a sickly smile and fled, out of the building and straight to my car. I fumbled the lunch box open and grabbed the vial of V12. The few remaining drops caught the light. It was enough to clear my head, help me stop freaking out. Brains were awesome but they couldn't deliver this kind of chill—like the difference between a great hamburger and a Xanax.

I scrambled for a syringe and drew up the half-dose. Under the skin and . . .

Fireflies twinkled around my head. I relaxed back into the seat, felt the panic recede and my thoughts clarify. Allen didn't know I'd stolen brains, but he was on alert about the organ bags. This was fixable. I hadn't been caught yet, and from here on out I needed to make sure there was no chance of that happening. But *how*?

The V12 hummed through my system as I looked for a solution. I couldn't afford to lie low and stop harvesting. Maybe I could take half brains? Cut the rest into chunks to make it harder to see any was missing. Except, I only had a week's worth of surplus brains left, thanks to the V12 and the increased hunger side effect. I'd starve on half brains. Normally the Tribe would help me out, except no way could I say, "Hey, Dr. Nikas, I need extra brains because I kinda borrowed some of the V12 mod."

But I couldn't risk Allen finding out that brains were missing. At this very moment, Mr. Noah Granger was tucked away in the morgue cooler along with a brain-free organ bag. He wasn't getting carted off until Monday, which gave Allen way too much time to check things out.

A laugh bubbled up from the very center of my being. Fireflies wheeled around my head in a merry dance. Duh. I didn't have to stop harvesting brains. All I needed was something to put in place of the brains I took—an imposter brain that would pass an Allen inspection. The only reason I'd never thought of this solution before was because, up until this week, there hadn't been a big ol' sign in the window of Wyatt's Butcher Shop.

Get Your Braaains Here!

I smiled. Tomorrow morning, I'd do me a little brain shopping.

Chapter 5

The rest of my shift whizzed by without a hitch, and I happily clocked out at two p.m. on the nose. I hit the road and cranked up the radio, then proceeded to sing at the top of my lungs with the kind of teen-pop music I'd never in a million years admit I actually listened to. But hey, that shit was catchy.

Twenty minutes later, I pulled into the gravel parking lot of a faded blue cinderblock building—the front for Dr. Nikas's super cool zombie research lab. Research *for* zombies, not *on* zombies. The only other vehicle in the lot was a dull bronze '79 Chrysler Newport that belonged to Raul, one of the full-time lab security zombies.

The camera by the front door was a decoy, with a cracked cover and dangling wires to make it appear totally useless. Even though I knew that the real—and well-hidden—cameras had picked me up the minute I turned off the highway, I still gave the door a pert salute as I approached. A second later security buzzed me through and into the drab, threadbare waiting room with its decade-old magazines. A faint odor of mildew hung in the air, adding to the impression that the room and the rest of the building held nothing of interest. I continued through and down a hall with the same dull color scheme, punched my code into the keypad beside the door at the end then proceeded into the "kill zone" corridor that led to the main complex. Its kill-zone-ness had been beefed up in the last few months, after a team of Saberton operatives made entry during an ultimately fruitless attempt to steal hibernating zombie heads. I waved at the mirrored window on the wall and pressed my thumb against a sensor plate, then entered as the thick security door slid open.

No more boring beiges and stuffy odors. Recessed lighting revealed a blue and gold hallway that continued to my left and right. Cool air carried a fresh scent that didn't come from any cleaning product. Across the hall and behind bulletproof glass doors was the central hub of the lab complex. The doors slid aside with an effortless *whiss* as I approached and whispered shut as soon as I passed through. A far cry from the creaky sliding doors at the local BigShopMart.

The central hub looked like a kickass science fiction movie set, with nifty computers and shiny equipment, but the open floor plan and high-domed ceiling made it feel comfortable and homey. And no wonder. Dr. Ariston Nikas and his two assistants made their homes here. Though the hub was unoccupied at the moment, instruments and computer screens flashed with work in progress, including a screen that showed a series of status updates along with progress charts and projected growth rates for Kang—the zombie who got his head chopped off by a serial killer and was now being regrown.

One of my jobs at the lab was tending to him, but he could wait. My bones were starting to itch. It wouldn't take long to complete my most important task for today—replenishing my V12 supply.

I headed down the corridor that led to the medical wing. Through the open door of the second treatment room I spied my zombie baby, Philip Reinhardt, sitting on the exam table. Not a real baby, of course. I'd turned him into a zombie about a year ago—forced to do so by Dr. Kristi Charish

during one of her unethical experiments. I'd never zombified anyone before then, but my zombie instinct kicked in
before Philip could die of Saberton-inflicted gunshot
wounds. I turned into a nightmare monster, mauled and bit
until the parasite spores took root to save him. If I'd failed,
Philip would have died, just like a second volunteer *had*
died when I couldn't turn him. But Charish didn't care. To
hell with human or zombie rights. All she wanted was documentation and data to impress Saberton Corporation and
establish herself as the queen of zombie research.

After I zombified Philip, she'd used him as a guinea pig
for her untested fake brain formula and royally screwed up
his parasite. He'd suffered physical consequences ever since
but, thankfully, Dr. Nikas's treatments kept him relatively
pain-free and functional. It was like having a debilitating
disease successfully managed by meds. Currently, the V12
mod kept him physically stable—and me chilled and dyslexia free.

Except Philip didn't have to use a needle. Dr. Nikas had
recently implanted one of his special zombie mod ports into
Philip's chest—a clever bit of biotechnology that fused
along a rib and allowed a syringe to screw straight onto a
reservoir. The mod port worked in cooperation with the
parasite to dose out combat, sense enhancement, or any
other zombie pharmaceuticals. I planned to write a long
letter to Santa this year explaining why I totally deserved a
shiny mod port of my very own.

The empty vial beside Philip told me he'd just received a
treatment. I'd last seen him a week ago, and he'd been his
typical buff and handsome self. But his hands trembled now
as he buttoned his shirt. His blue eyes were sunken, and his
skin an ugly grey. A full-blown case of pre-rot.

"You okay, ZeeBee?" I stepped into the room and
frowned at him. "I thought Dr. Nikas's treatment was doing
the trick for you."

Philip gave me a smile. I winced as the corner of his
mouth fissured.

"It was until a few days ago," he said, voice rasping. "He doesn't know why it stopped working."

I shifted, unsettled by the idea that Philip's pre-rot might be caused by V12. But then again, he took ten times what I did, *and* he had a screwy parasite. Plus, I was super careful. There certainly wasn't enough risk to make me stop using the V12. I was sure. "That sucks," I said with a wince. "Does Dr. Nikas have a plan?"

"He's going to reformulate."

Reformulate. My gut clenched. Dr. Nikas had cooked up the original version of the "super-mod" in a kitchen in New York as a combat enhancement. I'd used it during the high-stakes rescue of Marcus and Kyle in New York, which was when I discovered that, not only did the super-mod heighten senses and reaction times, it also delivered a serene calm and increased focus. After several attempts, Dr. Nikas had refined the overkill supercharge of the mod into a useful pharmaceutical for Philip's treatment—Version 12. I'd experimented with it until I found just the right dose for everyday use as well as for an occasional pick-me-up. It was by sheer accident that I discovered it countered much of my dyslexia. I'd have to hope and pray that Version 13 would have the effects I needed.

"Will Dr. Nikas still use the super-mod as the base for your new treatment?" I asked oh-so-casually.

"I don't think so." Philip gestured toward his very zombie-looking face. "Fresh approach because of this."

Crap. The super-mod base *worked*. That was what I needed, not a new concoction. When Dr. Nikas reformulated, I'd be cut off. No supply. What the hell was I going to do when I ran out? The chances that a completely new recipe would work the same were slim. I couldn't live without—

"Angel?"

Philip's worried voice cut through my flailing thoughts. I caught myself hyperventilating and took a slow, focused breath. "Sorry. I, uh, hate that you're going through this again." That much was true. I glanced beyond him to the glass-doored fridge and the tray inside that held three full vials. "Are you still using the old V12?"

"This was the last time. Dr. Nikas increased the dose, and it stopped the deterioration." He stood and re-tucked his shirt. "It didn't reverse it, but at least now I don't feel as bad as I look. He'll have the new formula ready to test in a couple of days, and I'll be back to working security in no time."

"Glad to hear it." I smiled, genuinely relieved for him, if not for my own predicament. I moved to the counter by the fridge and straightened containers of supplies. "I saw Marcus, Pierce, Brian, and Kyle earlier today. The FBI is sniffing around funeral homes."

"There's shit stirred everywhere," Philip said with a shake of his head. "Those four left here about twenty minutes ago." He moved to a mirror on the wall and peered at the fissure by his mouth.

My eyes narrowed. "Three hours ago they were supposedly off to the airport."

His eyes met mine in the mirror. "Plans had to be shuffled. Pierce showed up here in a *mood*, then he got a call from Rachel. Kristi Charish surfaced in Portland this afternoon. That's where they're heading first now instead of the out-of-state funeral homes and other business."

I let out a low whistle. After I managed to escape Charish's lab, the Tribe had captured her and put her to work with Dr. Nikas. Then, a few months back, Nicole Saber—CEO of Saberton Corporation—ordered a major strike on the Tribe, during which they grabbed Charish, along with Pietro, Marcus, and two other zombies. We'd rescued Pietro and Marcus from the New York lab, but Charish and the other two zombies had been sent to the Saberton dedicated zombie research lab in Dallas. The Tribe conducted a raid there and successfully freed a number of zombie captives but failed to recapture Charish. As far as I knew, today's appearance in Portland was the first time she'd been seen in months. No wonder Pierce had dropped everything to head to Oregon.

"If they do track her down, are they gonna . . ." I swiped my finger across my throat.

Philip grimaced, either at my question or his reflection. "I think they'd prefer to capture her. But our security resources are stretched thin at the moment, between Saberton, FBI scares, and the exodus project. Whatever our head honchos decide, they need to do it fast—and without making any waves—so they can move on to the next fire that needs dousing."

My mind scrambled back a few seconds. "Wait. Exodus project? Exodus of what?"

He turned back to me, expression serious. "The Tribe. It's vital that we have a plan in place in the event the Saberton or FBI shit hits the fan and it looks like we're close to being exposed. The logistics of how and where to go to ground is the honchos' big project."

I gulped. "Temporarily, right? Until the threat blows over?"

"If and when we go, we vanish for good."

"No." I shook my head, mouth dry. "It won't come down to that." *But it might.* I couldn't deny the possibility.

Philip exhaled. "Pierce says he goes through an exodus once or twice every hundred years, on average. Sometimes more often."

"Whenever regular people find out about his Tribe's zombie-ness," I said in dismay. Mob mentality was ugly stuff. "But it's in Saberton's best interests to keep the zombies secret. Their hands are dirty. Plus, once word got out, every bio-tech or pharmaceutical company in the world would be racing to study the parasite in the hopes of making billions on cures of diseases and old age." I licked dry lips. "Saberton wants that monopoly. And they'd likely get scooped on the whole super zombie soldier idea as well." The ultimate point of Saberton's secret and inhumane zombie research was to make a buttload of money from the parasite in any way possible. It helped my peace of mind to know that, if push came to shove, I had a passel of naked sex pics of Saberton CEO Nicole Saber that she knew I'd cheerfully upload to every website in the world if she screwed with us. But she wasn't the only head on the Saberton monster, just the biggest one—at the moment.

"As it stands now, Saberton has no reason to out us," Philip said with a nod of agreement. "But they're only one worry." He sighed. "The thing is, non-zombie friends and family members are notorious for stirring shit. That's why Pierce advocates keeping the number of humans who know the real story to a minimum. That number has been growing recently."

The truth of his words slid home like a knife to the gut. Families fell out over all sorts of things, even after years of harmony. What better way to get back at the sister who slept with your husband than to expose her as a brain-eating monster? And, whether malicious or not, it would only take one wrong thing said to the wrong person to bring about a totally different kind of zombie apocalypse.

In the last six months, I myself had told two people about zombies—my dad and Pietro's ex-fiancé, Congresswoman Jane Pennington. I trusted my dad with all my heart, and I'd trusted Jane as long as Pietro was alive. Unfortunately, I hadn't seen her since Pietro's faked death. I had no idea if Pierce had broken the news to her that he was her lost love in a hot new body. Jane was an amazing woman and deserved to know the truth, but a shocking revelation like that could be a deal breaker and put her on shakier ground.

Now I understood why Pierce had shot Marcus a *look* earlier today when I told them how Allen nearly caught me stealing brains. One step closer to discovery—and to exodus.

"Well, it's good they're making a plan. Like Bear and his survivalists stocking up on ammo and food and stuff in case aliens invade," I said with fake cheeriness. "Disaster preparedness and all that. Like a fire drill."

Sympathy swam in Philip's eyes. "All I know is that a few weeks ago the exodus plans shot to top priority. Makes me think we're on the verge, even if not yet there."

My chest ached. "Pierce will keep all this under control. He always does. He's just being cautious." I waved my hand as if to disperse the unpleasant thoughts. "We'll keep doing what we've been doing."

"Angel, I've never seen Pierce overwhelmed. Ever. But after he got the report that Charish had turned up in Portland, he was like a shell of himself. Too much on his plate."

I remembered his weary sigh at the funeral home—and that was *before* he'd been forced to add "hunt Kristi Charish" to his to-do list. Pierce looked young and vibrant, but it was easy to forget that he was *old*. Hundreds of years, at the very least. I used to think it would kick ass to be immortal, but now I wondered how horribly exhausting it must be, especially with his sense of responsibility for his people. "He'll pull it together."

Philip put on a reassuring smile. "Sure thing. No worries." He said it as if he was humoring a kid, but I didn't get mad. No matter how much I tried to deny it, the reality was that the Tribe *did* teeter close to being outed. Even if Nicole wanted to keep a lid on the zombie stuff, we still had to consider the Saberton guards and techs who witnessed or participated in atrocities against captive zombies. Mutilation. Amputations without anesthetic. Vivisection. What if one of those pieces of shit decided to sell secrets to another interested company? Or interested government? Or, what if one of them grew a conscience and decided to publicize the plight of the zombies? Then again, Nicole was smart enough to have anticipated all of those possibilities. Knowing that bitch, she had something nasty up her designer sleeve to keep her underlings in check.

But it would only take one credible person blabbing to destroy our way of life.

Philip swayed and grabbed at the exam table for support. "Sorry. I have to go rest and let this treatment do its job."

"No prob." I gave him a quick hug. "Take care of yourself." Moving carefully, he left the treatment room. I waited until he was far down the hall then yanked the fridge open and pulled out the three vials of precious V12. The last three in existence. A tremble went through me as I stared at them, and I quickly closed my hand, suddenly terrified of dropping the vials and losing this last bit of the mod. I carefully tucked the full vials into the right side pocket of my cargo pants then stowed a new empty vial, a bottle of saline, and a syringe in the left.

I clenched my hands to control their shaking. Too much was happening at once. Exodus project? Permanent relocation? I didn't want to leave St. Edwards Parish and my job and school. Hell, I'd finally settled into this whole responsible adult thing, and now I was supposed to start over?

And what about my dad? If family members were considered problematic, would the Tribe leave non-zombies behind? No way would I leave him. But if the situation was so bad the Tribe had to skedaddle, then my dad would be at risk simply for being my dad.

My pulse raced, and my chest tightened to where I could barely suck in a breath.

I can't handle this right now. Running out of V12 forever. Giving up everything I have here. Leaving.

A dose. I needed one, more than ever. Needed to take the edge off, enough to let me function and get through all this crap.

I scurried to the bathroom down the hall and locked the door, put the toilet lid down and sat. I had my skimming routine down. Suck ten percent out of each full-strength vial and squirt it into an empty vial. Replace the missing mod with saline. Easy. V12 looked like water, so no one ever noticed the dilution.

Syringe in hand, I hesitated as sick guilt rose. Was Philip's current state of pre-rot the result of the diluted mod?

No. I'd been skimming for almost four months, and only a little from each vial. He would've shown symptoms before now. A wave of relief washed through me. That made sense. Besides, no matter what caused it, Dr. Nikas would fix Philip up with a new formula and he'd be fine again.

But what about me? I wouldn't make it through school and all the other crap without V12. I lined the three vials up on the edge of the sink and stared at them glumly. Now that Philip wasn't using it anymore, this was the last of the formula—ever.

So, why do I still need to skim and dilute?

Why indeed. It didn't matter how much I diluted the vials this time. Ten percent? How 'bout a hundred? Replace *all* of it with saline. The vials were going to get tossed out anyway, and it'd be a crying shame to let all that pretty V12 go to waste. All I needed was two more empty vials from the drawer by the fridge.

But, first things first.

I sucked a dose into the syringe and injected it under my skin. Worry slipped away like a greased pig on ice, and I let out a pleased sigh. There was no need to get all worked up about a zombie exodus. Anyone who started blabbing about brain-eating zombies would get locked up in the psych ward. Only crazy people believed in real zombies. A laugh bubbled out. *Yup, we're all crazy here!*

Okay, *now* I was ready to take care of the rest of my business. I shoved the vials back into my pocket and dashed back to the treatment room accompanied by a whirl of happy snowflake sparkles. It sucked that the formula would change, but in about two minutes I'd have more V12 in my possession than ever before. Philip used a full vial at a time, but I only needed one cc to do the trick. If I rationed it out carefully, I'd be set for two months at the very least. That would give me plenty of time to test other formulas until I found one that worked as well.

Delighted with the genius of my plan, I fished two empty vials from the drawer and did a happy dance as I dropped them into my pocket.

"Angel."

My heart nearly exploded as I spun to face Dr. Nikas. The vials clinked in my pocket with the movement. "Uh, hey, Dr. Nikas. How's things?"

Soft brown eyes regarded me from his ancient, unwrinkled face. "I wasn't expecting you today."

I put on my best innocent expression and casually sidestepped to stand in front of the fridge. "I figured I'd come in and change Kang's tank today instead of tomorrow. That way I can go to the Zombie Fest. You know, because Pierce needs me to keep a lookout for anything weird." The premeditated lie stuck like sawdust in my throat. Dr. Nikas was the kindest person I'd ever met. I shifted to open the fridge, quickly pulled out the bottle of nutrient sludge I needed for Kang's tank and waggled it. Fireflies crawled over my skin like a mass of ants wearing high heels.

"I shouldn't have taken—" The confession fought to spill out, but I clamped down on it. Hard. My suppressed impulse control from the V12, trying to bite me in the ass. Sweat dribbled down my sides. "I, uh, shouldn't have taken advantage of your flexibility without calling first."

His nostrils flared, and my paranoia imagined his ancient zombie senses picking up my fear, smelling the vials in my pocket, and knowing exactly what I was up to. But to my relief he simply nodded then gestured at the fridge. "We should decrease the temperature to two degrees to accommodate a batch of new samples. It is set on four now, yes?"

"I can take care that." I fumbled with the number pad of the thermostat. Being sneaky around Allen and my coworkers about stealing brains didn't bother me since that was a life-or-death issue, and therefore I'd never worried about the lowered impulse control leading me to confess. But lying to Dr. Nikas's face about the V12 was a whole different matter.

"When was the last time you saw Philip?"

"About ten minutes ago. He said you're making a new formula for him." I punched in the new temperature with a shaking hand. "Two degrees Celsius. Done."

"He's had a difficult week."

"He sure looked bad. Poor guy." I pretended to make

another adjustment on the refrigerator. "Do you need blood from me for the new treatment?"

"No. That won't be necessary. I know what the problem is now and will address it."

"That's terrific. Lemme know if there's anything I can do to help."

"I will. You have a good afternoon."

"You too, Dr. Nikas." I listened to him walk out of the room then slumped, relieved to have dodged another bullet. Had I missed the memo about it being Almost-Get-Caught-By-Your-Boss Day? This close shave stuff was going to wear me out.

Maybe I needed to abandon the whole drug heist plan? A millisecond later I squashed that idea. This was the last of the V12. Forever. It would be pure insanity to let this opportunity pass by.

Dr. Nikas's voice drifted in from the central lab as he spoke to one of his techs. I hurried to the bathroom and made the switch. Three new vials full of V12. Three original vials full of saline. I shuttled the saline-filled vials back to the refrigerator and arranged them on the shelf in perfect alignment. No one would be the wiser.

So why did I feel like shit? I'd skimmed lots of times before. Or maybe it had nothing to do with a guilty conscience. The side effects of V12 were unpredictable. Every now and then a yucky everything's-my-fault feeling came on the heels of I-can-handle-anything. I could deal with a measly side effect. Bottom line, I wasn't hurting anyone. What was there to feel crummy about?

I closed the fridge. In fact, I was a goddamn conservationist. I'd saved all of that perfectly good V12 from being wasted.

Chapter 6

Humming under my breath, I damn near skipped down the corridor to the Head Room. In an hour, maybe less, I'd be done with work and safely out with the vials. An odd cinnamon scent wafted over me as I made my way with a spring in my step, but I didn't see a source and put it out of my mind as I reached my destination.

The Head Room was, hands down, the creepy-coolest place in the lab. Within, four stainless steel vats the size of big crockpots held zombie heads, grim remains of Ed Quinn's zombie hunting rampage. A lifelong friend of Marcus, Ed was another victim of Dr. Charish's manipulation. She'd molded him into a murdering zombie hunter by playing on his belief that a zombie had killed his parents, all so he'd collect the zombie heads she wanted for research. And, of course, she'd let him take the full rap once the cops identified him as a serial killer. Cold-blooded bitch.

The good news was that the Tribe managed to recover the heads, and five currently survived in stasis—a form of parasite hibernation. The bad news was that the nutrient stuff they floated in wasn't quite right yet, which was why only one of them had started regrowing. Dr. Nikas had said that if he could determine the missing factor, he'd also be a step closer to creating fake brains, and zombies wouldn't have to rely on human brains anymore.

Despite the not-quite-right nutrient, one head had made significant progress. Over the past six months, a fetus-like body had budded from his severed neck and developed rapidly. John Kang, the first zombie I met after I was turned. In the short time I'd known him, we had several rocky interactions, including one where I tried to warn him that the serial killer was targeting zombies. He hadn't listened and ended up decapitated. Still, I learned a lot about being a zombie from him, and I liked the idea that he might not be permanently dead.

He'd grown out of the crockpot and now lay suspended in slug snot within a glass coffin-like tank. It wasn't actually slug snot. Or any kind of snot. Dr. Nikas called it Nutrient Medium 42, but it looked and felt like a bucket of slug slime mixed into a barrel of cloudy mucus with a cup of blood thrown in to give it a gross pink tinge. Barf.

Changing Kang's gloop was one of my regular duties, but as I entered I noted snot already blop-blopping into the floor drain from a hose attached to the spigot of his tank. No complaints from me. That meant I'd be out of here that much faster.

I put on a plastic apron, then hosed water into the tank, thinning the snot to help it drain quicker. Soon Kang lay exposed, naked, grey-skinned, and as still as a corpse. I skimmed a gaze over him. He'd grown. Last week he'd been a good half a foot shorter and a lot more wrinkled. Now his body looked full-size, no longer too small for his head.

The lab had tablets to track data, and an app especially for Kang. I dutifully took and entered all forty-four measurements—everything from overall length to circumference of his chest to size of his boy parts. I smiled as I noted that he'd made significant growth on all counts.

The door clicked, and Jacques Leroux entered, pushing a cart loaded down with a giant crockpot, a bucket, and a

case of gauze bandage rolls. He was one of Dr. Nikas's
live-in lab assistants—slender and with skin so pale it was
as if he hadn't set foot outside for a century. He had the
most amazingly expressive hazel eyes, though they always
held a faintly haunted look as if he'd just woken up from a
nightmare.

The cinnamon scent came with him and seemed to orig-
inate from the crockpot.

"Length?" he asked.

I didn't take his brusque manner personally. He wasn't
much of a talker. I checked the tablet entry. "Up sixteen
point five one centimeters."

Jacques set the tray on the counter then snatched the
tablet from me. "Length, one seventy-three point four."

Weird. He wasn't usually *this* abrupt. "Isn't that full
growth?"

Jacques ignored me and muttered under his breath as he
scanned the measurements. After about half a minute of
waiting for a reply, I gave up and started to unseal a fresh
barrel of slug slime for Kang's tank.

"No nutrient medium," Jacques snapped. "We're wrapping him." With that, he shoved the tablet back into my
hands and departed.

MegaWeird. I peered into the crockpot and saw that it
held melted paraffin with plenty of cinnamon. The bucket
contained brains pureed with . . . something. I leaned close
and sniffed. Honey? I groaned under my breath. I had no
idea what all this was for, but anything that involved wrapping Kang was sure to take longer than refilling the tank.
Guess I wasn't getting out of here anytime soon.

Jacques returned with a gurney and pushed it close to
the side of the tank.

"Why are we wrapping him?" I asked as I helped lift
Kang onto the gurney.

Jacques busied himself with opening the case of gauze,
then shifted to stir the paraffin. "Pierce wants Kang awake
sooner rather than later," he said at last, stress winding

through his normally calm and even voice. "And now that Kang has reached full growth, Pierce will be relentless."

Ever since Kang's head had been brought to the lab for regrowth, Pierce had pressured Dr. Nikas about how much memory Kang would retain, if and when he woke up. I couldn't imagine what he wanted from a small-time local zombie like Kang, and Pierce flat out refused to share. "What changed?" I asked.

"Pierce is impatient."

Only about this. In everything else, as far as I could tell, Pietro/Pierce had always displayed careful patience. "Do you know what he wants from Kang?"

He set the bucket of pureed brains on the edge of the gurney. "Rub this on him. Every bit of exposed skin."

I stuck my hands into the puree then dropped a glob on Kang's chest. "What exactly are we doing?"

Jacques went still for a moment, then I jerked in surprise as he hefted the case of gauze and hurled it to crash against the wall, sending bandage rolls flying out like popcorn. I stared, flabbergasted, while Jacques stood among the scattered bandages, his chest heaving and color high in his cheeks.

I'd never even heard Jacques raise his voice before now. "Is something wrong? I can call Dr. Nikas. I mean, if you—"

"No!" he said then, more quietly, "No." He squatted and began to gather bandage rolls and toss them back in the box. "Mobility."

"What?"

"That's the other reason we're going to wrap Kang. The tank is unwieldy."

"Where's he going?" Yet as the words left my mouth, the ugly picture came together. Scowling, I smeared the brain puree over Kang's chest. "Pierce's top priority is prepping for the exodus of the Tribe. Kang's some sort of asset to him, and he wants to kickstart Kang's recovery *and* make sure he survives the move."

Jacques gave a sharp nod. He stood and dropped the

case of gauze onto the cart, then began to unwrap bandage rolls, jaw tight.

"You don't *want* to be mobile, do you," I said. "You've been through this exodus thing before."

He released a long breath. "Twice."

Jacques had never revealed even this much personal information to me before. "It's bad?" I asked.

He lapsed into silence. I took the hint and returned to goop-smearing while I did my own quiet pondering. Jacques's reaction to a possible exodus didn't put me at ease.

Once I had Kang slathered in brain puree, Jacques tossed me a bandage roll, then unwound one of his own and dipped it into the melted paraffin and cinnamon. I followed suit, and together we worked meticulously to mummy-wrap Kang.

I finished Kang's right arm and pressed the end of the gauze to seal it. "Fake brains would help. Stop the need to run, I mean." Non-zombies would have a lot less reason to condemn us as monsters if we didn't rely on eating their relatives.

Jacques met my eyes. "Pseudobrains are our greatest hope of salvation."

"Dr. Nikas is close to developing them." It was a statement and a question.

Jacques smoothed out a lump of paraffin. "It's Pierce's belief that Kang knows what we're missing, or part of it, at least."

"So that's what he wants so bad," I murmured then frowned up at Jacques. "Hang on. Is that why Kang's the only one who's regrown his body? Because he has the missing whatever it is?"

"That's Dr. Nikas's theory."

I started to run my goopy fingers through my hair and caught myself in the nick of time. "Holy crap. Did Kang *know* he had this super thingy that'll save us all?"

Jacques spread his own goopy hands. "That, I don't know."

More questions crowded in, but I realized Jacques likely wouldn't know the answers. Plus, if I kept pestering him, we'd never finish wrapping Kang. Better for now to see if I could come up with answers on my own, like I had with my theory of why Kang regrew.

"I don't want to do this exodus bullshit either," I said as I helped sit Kang up to wrap his torso. "We'll have to do everything we can to avoid being exposed until Kang's awake and Dr. Nikas creates the fake brains."

"And pray that Dr. Nikas succeeds before Pierce decides the risk is too high for us to remain." He exhaled, shoulders drooping. "The noose tightens."

He sounded miserable, as if he was watching hope unravel. Anger stirred in my gut on his behalf. To hell with the tightening noose. None of us wanted exodus. Even though I wasn't working with the head honchos, there was plenty I could do to pull my weight and do whatever needed to be done. We'd get out of this mess. Somehow.

We finished Kang's torso and laid him flat again, then I began on his lower legs while Jacques wrapped his head. Brain hunger nipped at me as a tingle began in my fingers, but the simple rhythm of dip-and-wrap helped me ignore it. We worked in silence, and at long last Kang was a fully wrapped, bona fide, zombie mummy thing.

Jacques stepped back and peeled paraffin from his hands. "Thank you," he said with sincerity as he headed for the door. "I'll get the final data and meet you in the hub."

I gave him a smile as I cleaned up. "It's not over yet. We'll hold it together until Dr. Nikas concocts the fake brains to save us from the mobs."

"To save us from ourselves." His eyes were liquid sorrow as they met mine. "I slew and ate those I held most dear. We *are* monsters."

By the time Jacques gave me the readings from Kang's assessment, I'd managed to shake most of the sick fear his statement had created. Ate those he held dear? No wonder he looked haunted. Monsters. He'd nailed it. There was no sugar-coating the truth.

On a less horrific but more annoying note, the tingle in my fingers had crawled up my arms. My typing speed wasn't epic to begin with, and it took me twice as long as usual to enter the information in the computer. It was way past time to get my butt out to the car and top off with brains. I glanced at my watch. Only two hours since my last dose of V12. It usually lasted closer to six, but I'd no doubt burned through it faster with all the stress. I'd give myself a little bump as soon as I made it to the car. After all, I wasn't going to run out of my special mod any time soon.

Humming to myself in happy anticipation, I grabbed my bag and headed for the sliding doors.

"Angel."

I stopped and gave a bright smile across the hub to Dr. Nikas. "Did I forget something?"

He didn't return the smile. "Could I see you in my office, please?" He gestured toward his door.

My expression felt as brittle as a frozen spider web. I followed him into his office, heart thudding unevenly. We had a tight-knit work crew at the lab: Reg, Jacques, Dr. Nikas, and me. Not much was said behind closed doors. The urge rose to stick my hand in my pocket and close my fist over the vials, and it took every speck of my self-control to resist it.

I blinked into brilliant sunshine streaming from a screen that covered the entire far wall of the office. Gulls wheeled over white sand and a turquoise sea, their cries mingling with the rustle of surf. A breeze carried the scent of salt and subtle flowers. An ambiance immersion system. Dr. Nikas tapped in a code on the system console and plunged us into silent darkness. Another tap, and the wall displayed a rainforest, the light subdued and filtered by the leafy canopy. Birdsong. The babble of a stream. Calm. Peaceful.

He stood with his back to me, as still as a column of granite, his gaze on the sanctuary of the forest. He didn't go out much, and I suspected the ambiance systems in his office and living quarters helped keep him connected. And sane. Centuries ago, a brutal zombie-hating mob—tipped off by his wife after she discovered what he was—broke him in ways I didn't even want to consider. He coped by withdrawing. But he'd never really recovered.

The seconds dragged by. I fidgeted and tried not to worry. Not easy with the borrowed V12 vials in my pocket. But this meeting wasn't about that. He needed a little break, that was all. Dr. Nikas's statue impersonation had nothing to do with me. Not one thing.

He finally heaved a deep sigh and dropped into the chair behind his desk. "Close the door, Angel."

My pulse lurched. *Déjà vu Allen.* I pushed it closed. The latch clicked like the slamming of a cell door.

Dr. Nikas's mouth was drawn down, and his ancient eyes held a deep sadness. "Have a seat."

The vials felt like lumps of lead in my pocket as I sank into the chair. "Am I getting fired?" I tried for a joking laugh, but it came out as a strained croak.

He laced his fingers together on the desk before him. "I know about Philip's doses."

Blood drained from my head, and my vision swam for a second. *Yes, let me faint. Let me pass out and escape this nightmare.* My breath shuddered in my chest, but I remained stubbornly conscious. "Wh-what do you mean?" *Still a chance to talk my way out. There's always a way out. Just have to find it.*

"You've been removing a portion of the dose and diluting the remainder with saline to cover it." His words slashed at my defenses, all the sharper for the gentle tone. "It's been going on for some time, hasn't it."

My hands shook. I clenched them in the fabric of my pants and stared at the whiteboard on the wall. I couldn't look him in the eye. Physically impossible. I scrambled to think of a convincing lie. Excuse. Explanation. Anything.

Nothing came up. This was Dr. Nikas. I couldn't bear the thought of him knowing what a stinking lowlife I really was, but I also couldn't bring myself to lie to him again. Tears stung my eyes, and I gave a jerky nod.

The single soft breath of his sigh practically shouted his disappointment. "And using it. Why, Angel?" His voice remained calm and even and *nice*, which made the whole thing that much worse.

Sweat stung my palms. Coherent thought felt like a distant memory. My throat clogged with fear and self-loathing but I forced the useless words out. "It h-helps me."

A hint of a frown touched his brow. "Helps you? In what way?"

Faint hope flickered. "To read." I swallowed, throat dry as a stone. "It, uh, helps with the dyslexia."

Dr. Nikas leaned forward, gaze boring into me. "How does it affect the dyslexia?"

I gave a helpless shrug. "I dunno. One day I noticed that things made sense when I was using it. Like, I could read a paragraph one time and understand it, and it didn't take me forever like it usually does." I wiped my hands on my pants. "It's not a cure, but I can keep up with my classes when I use it. When I don't, I can't."

He sat back and regarded me. "You started using it *before* you noticed it helped the dyslexia."

Shit. I'd walked myself into that. The hope sputtered out, and I dropped my gaze to the floor. "I'm freaking out with the whole college thing," I said in a shaky voice. "I'm in over my head, and the mod helps me handle the stress. Lets me chill enough to keep at it and not quit."

"And you like the way it makes you feel," he said in the same tone he would've used to say *And you like the way chocolate tastes.*

Except we weren't talking about chocolate. "Guess I'm kicked out, huh." Better for me to get it out in the open, no matter how much it hurt. I didn't want to hear him tell me to get out and never come back. I'd lose it for sure.

He didn't answer, which was answer enough. Instead he stared off over my head, eyes narrowed and mouth pursed in his familiar deep-thought mode. "Why dyslexia?" he murmured then went to the whiteboard and wiped a section of equations clean with the sleeve of his lab coat. The red marker squeaked against the board as he began to fill the cleared space with his unique shorthand.

I pulled the vials out of my pocket. I could leave them on his desk and go while he was in his own world. No point in sticking around any longer. It wasn't as if he was going to suddenly turn to me and say, "Oh, yes, of course you can still work here even though you totally lied to me and stole from me and betrayed my trust." No, I'd come clean and get out. Leave now so I wouldn't have to see him looking at me with disappointment, knowing what kind of loser I really was. I placed the vials on the edge of the desk—a gorgeous antique buffed to a shine so deep it reflected the vials like a dark mirror. My hand shook as I withdrew it. This was the right thing to do.

Dr. Nikas continued to scrawl on the board, muttering to himself in Greek.

I stood and backed to the door.

The vials shimmered. Sparkles danced over them. Alluring. Mocking.

My last hope of calm in a stupidly unfair universe.

The V12 is all I have left. Damn it. I'm not hurting anyone.

Pulse racing, I snatched up the vials and fled the office. I didn't slow down until I reached my car and then only to fumble my keys into the ignition before I peeled out.

When I reached the little highway I dragged the wheel over and coasted to a stop on the shoulder. My chest was so tight I felt as if I was about to implode. Away from Dr. Nikas, away from the lab and the Tribe and the world I'd come to love, I let it out. My chest heaved, and my gut felt like it was turning inside out with sobs.

My phone beeped with a text message. Dr. Nikas. *Come back.*

Coherent thought returned in a panicked rush. Only one reason why he'd want me to come back. I twisted to scan the highway behind me. Even though the head honchos were out of town, there was always the chance that Dr. Nikas might send Tribe security after me. I couldn't deal with that. Not until I *had* to. Tears blurred my vision as I pulled back onto the highway, but I drove another ten minutes before I turned onto a side road and parked. I grabbed a syringe and a vial and drew up a dose, then paused before sliding the needle under my skin.

"And you like the way it makes you feel."

Dr. Nikas's words took on a vicious edge as I mentally replayed them. I scowled, unsettled. He was off base there. Sure, it felt good, but I wasn't an addict. I was *nothing* like the old Angel. And I could prove it. Jaw set, I squirted the dose back into the vial and continued on my way.

A mile later I stopped and clawed for the syringe.

"I'm not an addict," I muttered. The mass of ants dug their marching feet into my skin. I slid the needle between their bodies and pushed the plunger.

A haggard blonde woman looked back at me from the rearview mirror. Sparkling tears slid down her face.

I dashed them away.

"I'm *not.*"

Chapter 7

The Kreeger River boat launch was my go-to sit and think spot, and I drove there in a numb, sparkly fog. No way could I be around anyone I knew. Couldn't handle it, couldn't risk that I'd see in their eyes, "We knew you were a loser. We were right all along. Who were you trying to kid?"

After I parked, I climbed out and sat on the hood. The boat launch didn't always hold the best memories. I'd been attacked there by Philip and Saberton goons—back when Philip was undercover. It could be downright creepy at night, but the only darkness at the moment was my mood.

A low sun sparkled across the water, silhouetting a young couple kayaking side by side. A man with a battered pickup loaded a boat onto a trailer and drove off, streaming water across the gravel. Two preteen boys stood on the dock, trying in vain to skip rocks across the water. After a few minutes they climbed onto bicycles and raced off, leaving me alone in the lot.

Grief swelled, and I let it fill me and spill over. I'd loved working at the lab. Loved it. And it was my fault and no one else's that I'd lost my place there. I'd been so cocky, full of excuses. Not an addict? Yeah, sure. *Who are you trying to kid?* And what about the Tribe? Was that gone as well? I didn't want to think about how Marcus would react when he found out. So much for us remaining friends.

I stared out at the river until the agony faded to merely a horrible ache. Boats motored by, and three warning hoots from farther up the river signaled an opening bridge. A sweet scent rode the breeze to me, a contrast to the less pleasant smells of boat exhaust and dead fish. I glanced around for the source and spied a determined stand of bushes at the very back of the lot, exploding in tiny white flowers.

On impulse, I walked over and snapped off a sprig of blooms. A bee, legs heavy with pollen, alighted on one of the blossoms, and I watched as it burrowed into the flower to do its pollinating thing. It didn't care whether or not the flowers were still attached to the bush. When it finally buzzed off in search of more gold treasure, I returned to my car, deep in thought.

My time with the Tribe didn't have to be over. So what if I didn't work at the lab anymore. I stuck the sprig in my cup holder, mustered a smile as the sweet odor filled the air. I was like that little worker bee, digging out useful info. I'd been damn useful to the Tribe over the past year, and if I continued then they'd pretty much have to keep me around, right?

Feeling a little better, I started my car and headed home. If Dr. Nikas decided to send security to pick me up, so be it. Until then, it felt good to have a plan, or at least a sense of direction. Enough shitty stuff. Tonight was movie night. Pierce needed eyes and ears around town, and I was going to have a nice time if it killed me.

My grand plans for a nice time free of shitty stuff hummed along up until the moment I walked into my house. There on the living room couch sat my dad, obviously waiting for me, with a Very Serious Expression on his face.

I stopped dead, door still open. "What's wrong?"

He lifted his chin. "I got something I need to say, Angel."

Not Angelkins. Angel. That was never a good sign. I shut the door. "Did someone die?" I asked then narrowed my gaze at him. Dark circles rimmed bloodshot eyes. He looked tired, sad. Fear squeezed my heart. "Are you sick?"

He shook his head. "I ain't sick, and no one died that I know of." He exhaled, and he seemed to deflate as the breath left him. "I didn't sleep real good last night 'cause my mind kept racing and worrying."

"Jesus, Dad, what the hell's going on?" I plunked down on the other end of the couch and toed my shoes off. "You're scaring the crap out of me."

"I'm scaring *you*?" He snorted and got to his feet. A dark scowl pulled at his mouth. "You been acting odd and moody, and I wanna know what's eating you up."

No. Not twice in one day. I barely survived the last goddamn *intervention*. No way was I going through this again.

"I'm really fucking busy," I snapped. "That's what's eating me up. I have school and work to deal with, and I'm trying to avoid flunking out my first semester."

"Nah, it's more than that," he said, eyes hard on me. "I ain't as dumb as I look. I seen you like this before. I dunno how you're doing it, but you're using again!"

"No! That's bullshit!" I shouted. "Drugs don't work on me anymore, remember? How 'bout you get off my goddamn back?"

"Don't lie to me, Angel! I swear to god, I'll—"

I didn't remember getting up from the couch, didn't remember advancing on my dad. But next thing I knew he was backed against the door, with my left hand clenched tight in his shirt and my right cocked back in a fist.

My breath spasmed in my chest. Memory swept through me of another confrontation almost three years ago, back when we still lived in the old, crappy house with the roaches and leaky roof and duct-taped windows. My dad had found a bottle of Vicodin in my sock drawer and, even though I'd been drinking and smoking pot since I was seventeen, he decided it was time to do more than just yell at me. This time he was going to lay down the law and set me straight. But I was out with Randy when my dad found the pills, and I didn't come home for another four hours. That gave Dad plenty of time to work up a good head of steam, along with ample opportunity to plow through a six-pack of beer and half a bottle of Old Crow. The instant I walked in he started yelling at me about how I was a piece of shit and worthless and all that crap. We screamed at each other for a minute or so, then I must've said the wrong thing because he backed me up against the door and smacked me so hard I couldn't see out of my left eye for three days.

It was the first time he'd ever truly scared me.

And now . . .

Dad's eyes were wide and full of fear. Nausea rose in my throat, and I stumbled back with a gasp. "I'm sorry. Oh god, Dad. I'm sorry."

For a spindly guy pushing fifty he was quick. He back-pedaled into the kitchen, grabbed a cast-iron skillet off the stove and brandished it in front of him with both hands. "Stay the hell where you are," he said, voice shaking.

"Dad." The word choked out. He knew what the monster in me was capable of doing. What monsters like me had done to loved ones in the past. This was different, but how was he supposed to know that? "Dad, I—I'm sorry."

He lowered the skillet but didn't set it down. The fear in his eyes shifted to wariness.

"Look, I had the crappiest day ever, and—" I shoved my hands through my hair. "Shit. That's no excuse. I screwed up."

The skillet clanged onto the counter, and he had me wrapped in a hug before I could blink. "Yeah, Angelkins, but I shouldn't've accused you like that." His arms had a wiry, gentle strength as he held me against him. He'd filled out a bit since he stopped drinking and was definitely healthier. I could have pulled free if I'd wanted to, but I didn't.

"I got no proof or nuthin," he went on, voice thick, "and I just been worried 'cause you ain't been acting like my

Angel. Maybe it's your medical condition. I dunno what's going on, but whatever it is I want you to know I love you and I'll help you any way I can."

Guilt dragged claws through me as I leaned into him. "Thanks," I croaked out and tried to blink away tears. "I'm sorry. I don't know what got into me." A lie. I knew what made me react without thinking, and it scared me senseless.

"It's gonna be okay, baby." A tremble went through him as he held me, then he pulled away and offered me a teary smile. "Hang on. I know you gotta get ready for the movie, but I got two things that might put a smile back on that pretty face."

I dragged a hand under my nose as he yanked open the coat closet door. He reached all the way to the back then straightened with a pair of rain boots in his hand. Pink rain boots. The brightest eye-searing pink I'd ever seen in my life. On top of that, they were bedazzled and painted with silver glitter in swirls so distracting I almost didn't see the fake fur trim around the top. At least I assumed it was fake. If not, somewhere there was a purple cheetah missing part of its hide. "I—"

"Before you say anything," Dad began, "you need to know I got these on a crazy whim thinking you'd like 'em, and then realized they might be a little much. But that ain't the part that's gonna make you smile."

"Oh?" I said faintly. A *little* much? There was fake fur on the rain boots.

Fake fur. On rain boots.

"See, I bought 'em from Tammy's booth at the Farmer's Market this morning." He chuckled as my eyes narrowed. The loud and flamboyant Tammy Elwood was a bartender down at Kaster's, and my dad had been dating her since a bit before I left for New York. To say that me and her had never clicked was like saying that the carpets on the Titanic got a little damp. "Then, I overheard her gossipy ass telling Maylene from the diner that you was all creepy weird for working with dead folk. Broke up with her then and there."

"But Dad, y'all were getting along so—"

"It's been coming for a while now, what with her whining about how I ain't asked her to move in with me and dropping hints like how great it'd be to honeymoon in Cabo." He cracked a grin at my shudder. "This morning was the last straw on this camel's back. 'Sides, I'm the only one who gets to say how creepy weird you are."

"Damn straight." I smiled and kissed his cheek.

"Anyway, I figure maybe next time it rains you can have fun stomping these ugly-ass things through the mud."

Laughing, I took the boots from him. "That's so perfect."

Dad let out a whistle. "Damn, those fuckers are butt-ugly."

"They're so ugly, they're awesome."

"Just like me," he said. "Go on. Get yourself ready for the movie. You don't wanna keep Mr. Highfalutin waiting."

"Marcus bailed. I snagged his ticket, so go get your ass changed."

His face lit up as if I'd told him he'd won the lottery. "No shit?"

"No shit. Get moving. All the cool movie premiere stuff starts in less than an hour."

"Dibs on the bathroom!" he cried out and scrambled that way. I could have beat him there, but I let him have the victory. Maybe this day wouldn't end up as awful as it had started.

Chapter 8

The population of St. Edwards Parish included a variety of ethnic groups, income levels, religions, political views, and sexual orientations, but one thing everyone agreed on was that the Royale Cinema in Tucker Point was hands down the best movie theater in the entire parish. Best popcorn, nicest seats, cleanest bathrooms, and biggest screens, it was damn near the only place I'd go see a movie anymore now that I could afford the extra fifty-cents it cost compared with the Multiplex Six. The last time I'd been to the Royale was when that movie came out about a chick who had kinky sex with a hot billionaire and then they teamed up to save the world from giant robots, then had more kinky sex. I didn't watch it—preferring a shoot-em-up car chase action movie instead—but I swear to god every woman in the parish apart from me was at the theater to see it. Twice.

Tonight the theater was closed to all but the two hundred and fifty premiere ticketholders, which made my job of keeping an eye out for suspicious stuff easier. I had no idea what I was looking for, but I'd know it when I saw it. I hoped.

Two searchlights swept the sky, and Mr. and Mrs. Paul

and Julie Wood from the *Tucker Point Sentinel News* snapped pictures as the local version of paparazzi. Gigantic posters for *High School Zombie Apocalypse!!* draped the building on either side of the entrance, and red carpet covered a chunk of the parking lot. To add to the fun, zombies moaned and reached for people from behind the velvet ropes, turning the walk into an absurd and awesome gauntlet. Dad glared at the zombies until we reached the end, but pulled a smile as a pert blonde with impressive breasts handed us each a numbered fake finger bone.

"Hang on to that," the woman chirped. "There'll be a drawing before the movie starts for all sorts of nifty prizes!"

"So, what makes a prize nifty?" I murmured to my dad as we moved on.

"Nifty means it's something you'll toss in the garbage in a few months 'cause it takes up space and ain't worth shit." He gave me a knowing nod. "You'll see."

I laughed and hooked my arm through his. People milled and conversed. A lot of local big wigs were here, no doubt taking advantage of the chance to network and call in favors and make promises. Champagne flowed, but Dad took a soda. I gave his arm a squinch, proud of him for staying off the booze.

A wall display proclaimed *Coming Soon! Zombies Are Among Us!! The documentary THEY don't want you to see.* Then, in smaller lettering: *Ten minutes that will change everything you thought you knew.* Beneath the words, a smiling woman in scrubs stood beside a patient's bed. I had to hand it to the studio. They were milking this silliness for all it was worth. When we moved on, the new angle showed the woman rotted and horrific. I took a step back. Normal. Forward. Zombie-riffic. Okay, that was cool.

Stationed around and through the crowd were at least a dozen men and women in bright blue shirts with SECURITY stenciled across the back. Justine Chu, one of the stars of the movie, signed autographs at a table near the theater door. Asian-American and damn pretty, she had sharp eyes and a quick smile, and appeared to enjoy interacting with the fans.

I spied a familiar figure stepping onto the red carpet—a good-looking man with honey-blond hair and a strong bearing. Andrew Saber, a high-ranking muckety-muck at Saberton Corporation and the son of CEO Nicole Saber. The company was one of the financial backers of the movie, which explained his presence here.

But he was also a zombie. *My* zombie baby, in fact. Andrew had been on the brink of death after getting shot during the Saberton raid in New York, and I'd offered him a chance to survive. I often wondered if he regretted his decision. He was a covert zombie in a company that did fucked up things to zombies. Dying might've been easier.

We weren't exactly enemies, but we weren't allies either. His eyes met mine, and the tension crackled between us. I had a thing or two I wanted to say to him. But not here. Not where it could put my dad in the spotlight.

My phone buzzed in my pocket. A chill snuck through me when I checked the display.

We need to talk. From Dr. Nikas.

I shoved the phone back into my pocket. Shoved the ache and worry from my mind.

"Everyone's dressed up as sumthin," my dad remarked, lifting his chin toward a gaggle of people who were helping run the event. "The workers and movie people. Every one of 'em's in a costume." He grinned, clearly delighted. "It's a hoot."

"A hoot," I echoed. "Who the heck says 'hoot'? Besides, that lady in the pink suit isn't in costume."

"I say 'hoot,' and yeah, she is." He gave me a smug smile. "She's dressed up like the school principal."

I rolled my eyes. "C'mon, Dad. How on earth could you know what the school principal looks like?"

Amusement danced across his face. "I been watchin' the trailers and behind the scenes stuff online for months now. They even got Twitter and Instagram for the movie. Couple weeks back they posted a Vine of the principal whacking a zombie."

I stared at him in astonishment. "I don't believe this. My redneck dad has more internet savvy than I do."

He cackled in triumph.

Smiling, I watched the production company people with new eyes. The majority were zombified, with varying degrees of rot, but even though I obviously wasn't as much of an expert on the movie as my dad, I'd seen the trailers enough times to pick out half a dozen characters. They all seemed to be having fun, too, which was cool. That or they were faking it *really* well.

Except for one zombified dark-haired guy with seriously cool shoes—high tops with zombie pinup girls painted along the sides. He paced and fidgeted and kept glancing over his shoulder as if the bogeyman might pounce on him at any second. How could anyone be in a bad mood with shoes like that? He edged up to one of the security people, leaned close and spoke low. The security guy gave a crisp nod, then Zombie Shoe Guy moved on to another security person and did the same thing. And again, with every blue-shirt out front.

Ooooh boy, that had my zombie-sense tingling. What had him spooked? Whether it was real-zombie related or not, I wanted to know.

"Hey, Dad," I said, "I need to go take care of something real quick. Will you be okay without me for a sec?"

"I'm a big boy, Angelkins," he grumbled. "I can handle myself just fine. Next you'll be wanting to tie a balloon to my ass so you can find me if I get lost."

Laughing, I handed him my numbered finger bone. "Fine. I'll only be a couple of minutes, but if I win a nifty prize you can collect it for me."

"Better be real damn nifty," he said with a snort, but he tucked the bone into his shirt pocket.

I kept an eye on Zombie Shoe Guy as I slipped through the crowd, and after a moment I realized he was heading for Justine Chu's table. Being short and skinny didn't have a lot of advantages, but getting through a crowd fast sure was one of them. By the time he made it to Justine, I'd already staked out a spot a few feet from her table where I pretended to gawk at a display that was nothing more than a picture of a judge with the title *Zombies Are Among Us!!* splashed above it.

Justine glanced over at my guy as he slipped behind her table, then leaned in as he bent down and spoke close to her ear. Even with my brain-enhanced hearing, it was tough to hear much over the buzz of the crowd, but adding in a bit of amateur lip-reading helped me get a few snatches.

". . . tell your security . . . on their toes . . . watch yourself . . ."

She drew back and gave him a skeptical look.

He nodded fiercely. " . . . feds wanted . . . believe me . . ." He made a sharp gesture at the display in front of me then froze as he caught me looking at him.

Shit. I knew enough not to jerk my gaze away. Instead I let it wander off. With any luck he'd believe I was casually taking in the sights.

Nope. He started toward me, suspicion in his bearing. Behind him a relieved Justine returned her attention to the line in front of her table.

"I love your shoes!" I blurted.

He stopped, eyes narrowed. "Excuse me?"

I let out a nervous giggle. "Your shoes. They're so awesome, and I know I was staring, but I was trying to figure out who you are in the movie."

The wariness hovered on his features for another second, then he relaxed, apparently deciding I wasn't a terrorist. Or a fed. Could his muttered "feds" be referring to the FBI agent in town? But what on earth could the FBI want that might connect to the *Zombies Are Among Us!!* film?

"I'm not *in* the movie," he said in a deep warm voice that put a wobble in my knees. "I'm a producer. And a friend custom-painted the shoes for me." His smile sent a coil of lust into my belly. "You're local?"

"All my life." I gave him a dazzling smile of my own.

"I love the south," he said, adding a rich chuckle. His gaze roamed over me, hot and searching. "The food. The women."

He dragged me close for a scorching kiss, and I didn't fight it. Heat seared my bones as his tongue invaded my mouth. My hands gripped his shirt, and his grabbed my ass. I shuddered, wanting all of—

"Miss? Are you okay?" He peered at me in concern from a good two feet away. Sparkles flickered over his face, danced in the cleft of his chin.

No. Oh god. He'd never kissed me. I'd hallucinated the entire thing. What the hell had I *done*? Did everyone see me making out with no one?

Color flooded my face as I groped for an excuse, an apology. Before I could get a word out he slipped an arm around my shoulders and steered me to a quiet spot behind a display.

"It's all right," he said. "I have a cousin who has petit mal seizures."

Oh, thank god. "Y-yeah. A seizure," I managed, gulping. "Did I, um, do anything?"

"Stared off into space for a few seconds," he said, blue eyes gentle and reassuring. "No one besides me noticed a thing. Are you steady now?"

"I'm good." I forced a smile. No, I wasn't good. I was anything but good. I was a fucked up mess. *That's it. No more V12. None.* "I, um, better go find my dad. Thanks for watching out for me."

"Anytime." He gave my hand a friendly squeeze then tilted his head. "Have we met before? You look familiar."

"I don't think so." No way would I forget a face like his.

"Hmm. Strange. Déjà vu." He shook his head. "Anyway, I hope to see you around." With a parting smile, he strode off through the crowd.

I took a minute to recover from the close call. I needed to notify Dr. Nikas about the bit of conversation I overheard and the security alerts—

No. I couldn't call Dr. Nikas. I was on his shit list.

Tears stung the back of my eyes. Being on Dr. Nikas's shit list was shittier than being on Santa's shit list. It was like being on *Mr. Rogers'* shit list. You had to fuck up like a champ to get there. No way could I talk to him. Not yet. Besides, it wasn't as if I knew there was trouble brewing. No point in calling until I had more info on Mr. Hot Zombie Shoes Guy and his paranoia. I'd keep an eye on the situation myself and see what was up at the Zombie Fest tomorrow. By then I'd be off the V12 and it would be easier to face Dr. Nikas. Tell him how sorry I was.

Squaring my shoulders, I set off to find my dad. It didn't take long, considering he was toting a life-sized cardboard cutout of Justine Chu.

"Hey, Angelkins!" A grin split his face. "Look what I won. Now *this* is nifty!"

High School Zombie Apocalypse!! rocked. I was the last person in the world to be a fan of zombie movies, but this one was funny and clever with a great plot, lots of action, and a few truly touching moments. Plus, even though the actors were pretty much unknown when they were cast, they were fantastic. Justine Chu played the plucky nerdy girl who saves the day and rescues the jocks and cheerleaders who were mean to her before. I particularly enjoyed the part when the hunky captain of the football team came up to her at the end, said he was stupid to have never realized how cool she was and asked her to be his date to the prom, at which point she laughed in his face and walked off.

The one negative was my stress during the big climactic scene when the heroes had to retreat to the football field and fend off the rampaging zombie students. During the filming of the movie, Saberton Corporation had used the extras as unwitting test subjects and turned them into temporary pseudo-zombies. Mistakes were made, hijinks ensued, and the zombie-rampage scene ended up being a little too real. I'd kinda crashed the filming of that scene, but to my relief I was nowhere to be seen in the movie, and none of the "real" rampage was either.

After it was over, my dad carefully stowed the cardboard Justine in the back seat of my car.

I cranked the engine. "I can't believe I didn't win anything," I said with a pout.

"You did."

I glared at him. "You're holding out on me? Well, where is it?"

He dug in his pocket, pulled out two little stuffed brains, each about the size of an apricot and connected by a string. "Better than fuzzy dice," he said as he looped the string over my rearview mirror.

"Fuzzy brains." Smiling, I flicked one to set them swinging. "They're perfect."

I sat on the edge of my bed, opened my lunch box, and unloaded an uneaten brain burrito and two vials of V12 into the mini-fridge. The third vial went on my nightstand.

A buzzing itch began deep in my muscles as I changed into a sleep shirt. I scrubbed at my arms, my face. Something had changed in the past couple of days. Worse side effects. Hallucinations. Less impulse control. An increase in my already near-insatiable brain hunger.

My fingernails dug into my palms. But I needed to be sharp to follow up on Zombie Shoes Guy tomorrow.

I drew up a dose, set the syringe aside.

I gotta quit.

My dad deserved better than this. *I* deserved better. It wasn't worth risking my job or the Tribe or my life. Come hell or high water, I was going to do the right thing, get off this crap, for me and my dad. I'd figure the rest out. School. Stress.

A roll of duct tape sat on the floor by my dresser. I grabbed it, took the partly used vial, added it to the other two, and wrapped several layers around all three vials. That would help me remember to keep my hands off. I tucked the bundle in the fridge then downed a bottle of brain smoothie. The itch eased a little.

Only a little. The filled syringe still gleamed on my night-stand.

I gotta quit.

The liquid bliss of the dose wound through me, made all the bad go away. Self-loathing, worry, doubt, fear—gone. Pride swept in as I disposed of the empty syringe. I was already making progress. For the first time in forever, I hadn't drawn up a dose to be ready and waiting on the nightstand in the morning.

I turned off the lamp, relaxed back on the bed. Fireflies blinked in the darkness. Hungry lips found mine. Hands caressed. I shuddered and moaned in pleasure.

I was gonna quit. Cold turkey. No problem.

Tomorrow.

Chapter 9

The shrilling of my phone jerked me out of a dream of being chased by zombies in Mardi Gras masks as they groaned *Throoww meee sooommethinggg misssterrr.* Letting out my own zombie groan, I pushed aside the weird images, groped for my phone and blearily read the text message from the dispatcher. I still wasn't used to the rudeness of people dying in the wee hours of the morning, but I'd been doing the on-call thing long enough that I knew to immediately flick on the nightstand light and get my sleepy ass moving. Now was *not* the time to risk falling asleep again. After screwing things up with the lab, I needed the morgue job more than ever.

Rain drummed on the roof, a hypnotic beat that made me want to dive back under the covers. Razor blades of brain-hunger sliced my belly, and my bones itched. I reached for the syringe of V12 on the nightstand.

Nothing.

I felt around then switched on the lamp. *Gone.* No syringe. Pulse racing, I scrambled out of bed, searched the floor—

Jesus, Angel. I forced myself to breathe. Cold turkey. Right.

I fumbled open the lock on the mini-fridge then stared at the three vials duct-taped together. Reaching for them, I froze at the sight of the mottled grey skin on my arm. *No.* I touched my face and let out a whimper as skin sloughed.

Trembling, I grabbed a bottle of brain slush and chugged it down. The mottling faded, but the grey persisted. I only had one bottle left, so I snatched a brain burrito, peeled the foil back, and scarfed it. I scrambled up and peered in the mirror. My skin had pinked back up—for the most part— but still had a greyish cast. It wasn't *bad,* but it shouldn't be grey at all. Not after eating a double helping of brains *and* chugging a bottle before bed.

Cold turkey. No more V12. Ever.

Resolved, I hurried to dress, then shoved my feet into the obnoxious Tammy boots. Trashing them in the mud would make the day better. A packet of Tribe-issued brains—labeled as ProteinGel—went into a pocket as a quick-fix if I needed brains fast and easy. Raincoat and lunch box in hand, I crept down the hall so as to not wake up my dad. His door was a few inches ajar, and I peeked in. He slept in a sprawl, face down on the bed and with one leg sticking out from beneath the blanket. His breath whistled softly, and I drank in the sound for several seconds. Spring allergies always kicked his ass, though it wasn't as bad since he'd stopped drinking. Used to kick mine as well until I was turned.

The rain was coming down in buckets as I dashed to the van, but it slowed to a drizzle not long after I left my house. I murmured a relieved thank you to Mother Nature. Picking up bodies in pouring rain *sucked.* Plus, the address the dispatcher gave me was *Highway 180 between Rat Tail Road and Catfish Drive*, which meant this was an outdoor pickup. Good thing was that finding it would be a snap. That bit of highway wasn't far from Randy's place, which meant I'd driven it about a billion times and knew every cross street by heart.

By the time I passed Rat Tail Road, the rain had stopped.

The rising sun merrily burned through the retreating clouds in bright and cheery slashes of color as if to say, "Isn't spring *awesome*?" Unfortunately, I had a feeling the glorious display would be wasted on a bunch of people this morning. Either there was one hell of a cop party going on, or this was a murder scene. Stretched along the side of the highway were five marked police cars, four unmarked detective units, three SUVs, and two TV trucks. *And a partridge in a pear tree.* A flash of yellow from beyond the line of cars drew my gaze to where several knots of people worked behind crime scene tape on the opposite side of the highway. Yup, it was a murder.

I pulled in behind a TV truck at the end of the long line of vehicles. A reporter I vaguely recognized leaned against the bumper as he struggled to wipe off mud caked halfway to his knees with a handful of tattered napkins.

Wincing in sympathy, I snagged one of the towels I kept in the van for emergencies and jogged up to him. "I think this will work better."

He accepted the towel with a grateful TV-worthy white smile. "Thank you from the very bottom of my heart." He got to work on the mud then glanced at my footwear and chuckled. "If I thought there was any chance your boots would fit me, I'd pay top dollar."

I cocked a gaudy boot out. "Women's size six and a half?"

"Darn. Men's size twelve, extra wide." He grimaced at the now mud-covered towel. "Do you have a plastic bag to put this in?"

"It's cool," I said. "Just toss it by the van when you're done. I'm betting I'll need it once I finish up."

"I'm sure you will. It's a bog out there." He glanced toward the crime scene tape. "Both the sheriff and the captain of investigations are on scene, which tells me this is a big deal. They're being awfully tight-lipped, though." He slanted a look at me. "Know anything?"

"Clueless as a newborn babe," I replied with a sweet

smile. "Not that I'd tell you if I did." That would be a sure way to get fired.

He laughed. "Understood. I owe you one anyway."

Hey, I needed all the favors I could get. With my good deed done for the day, I snagged a body bag from the van then tromped down the road. A "big deal" could be darn near anything in St. Edwards Parish. It was rare to have more than a handful of murders in a year, and most of them were of the alcohol-plus-redneck-plus-dumb-fight variety. The majority of the deaths I dealt with were from natural causes or accidents, but year before last had seen an unusual uptick in the murder rate, thanks to Ed Quinn's zombie hunting spree.

After what felt like a half-mile hike, I made it to the scene. Yellow tape started at the edge of the highway and marked off a half-acre square of low grass and scattered brush. Within the perimeter, rubber-booted crime scene techs and uniformed officers prowled in organized search patterns. At the center of the taped-off area, orange privacy screens shielded the body from curious eyes—and cameras—while knots of detectives and other officials conferred nearby.

Nick stood slightly apart from the others as he made notes on a pad. I signed the crime scene log, ducked under the tape and made my way through the mud toward him. He turned as I approached then glanced down. A faint smile danced across his mouth. "Wow. Those are obnoxious."

"Sure are!" Even a thick layer of mud did little to hide the tacky glitz. "Makes it easy to find me, though." I lifted my chin toward the orange screens. "What's the deal? Why all the attention?"

His smile vanished. "The sheriff thinks the serial killer may be back."

My breath seized, but an instant later common sense swept in. No. There was absolutely no way he was back. First off, the killer—Ed Quinn—had been horrified to learn

Dr. Charish had manipulated him into killing zombies, which meant he damn well wasn't going to start up again. Second, and more importantly, he was tucked away in Costa Rica with a new identity, thanks to Pierce—back when he was Pietro.

"Why does he think that?" I asked.

"Well, our guy is a lot shorter than he used to be."

"Shiiiiiiit." I knew what he meant. A head shorter. If this was a copycat murder, was the victim a zombie? Though that was pretty unlikely since pretty much no one but zombies knew the nature of Ed's victims. "Is the head here?"

"They're still searching the area. Got a dog out." Nick waved a hand toward a far corner of the yellow tape where a German Shepherd sat patiently in one of the few non-muddy spots. A tall, dark-haired man with his back to me held the lead as he spoke with Detective Mike Abadie. Abadie was a solid detective and an asshole—at least to me. We'd settled into a mutual dislike of each other and traded insults and jabs whenever the opportunity arose. The dog handler talking to him had broad shoulders and a narrow waist. My gaze drifted further down to—

Holy shit. I knew that ass. Tactical Pants Man. He worked with a cadaver dog? My lustful thoughts poofed into smoke. My habit was to keep my distance from cadaver dogs and their handlers. Even if the guy had no clue that zombies were real, it would get his attention if his dog indicated that I smelled like a corpse.

"I don't recognize the dog guy," I said. "Is he new around here?"

"Nah, he's not a local," Nick said absently as he jotted notes. "The sheriff knows him, asked if he could come help out. Word is the guy has a ton of search-and-rescue experience, and his dog is top notch." He looked up as a burly detective with a scruffy mustache approached us. Ben Roth, who I liked as much as I *didn't* like Abadie.

"Sorry to make y'all wait," Ben said. "Crime scene is still tagging and bagging crap by the body. Lucky for us, one of those things was his wallet. No cash, but credit cards and driver's license were in it."

"Name on the DL?" Nick asked.

Ben consulted a pocket notebook. "Grayson Seeger, white male, thirty-four years old, from Venice Beach, California. 'Course, we don't have a face to verify that's actually our victim."

"It's a start," Nick said. "We'll try and verify with fingerprints."

"Was he robbed?" I asked Ben while Nick jotted down the info.

"Looks like it. The pockets were turned out, but no way to know if that was the reason for the attack."

I cocked my head. "Tell me the truth, Ben. Do *you* think Ed is killing people again?"

Ben gave a rueful smile. "Nope. I don't think the sheriff does either, but it's easier for him to get resources if he says it's a possibility." He shrugged. "Ed's gone to ground, and he's not stupid enough to come back and start that crap again. My theory is that it's some asshole from the Zombie Fest pulling a copycat."

"The Zombie Fest? Why?"

Ben snorted. "We found one of those stupid Bear's Den zombie hunter survival kit duffels."

Nick jerked his head up, blinked, then curled his lip in derision. "Way to leave evidence."

The presence of the zombie hunter kit pretty much ruled out that a real zombie hunter had killed a real zombie. Way too cheesy. But maybe a clueless copycat got lucky and bagged a real zombie? Or was this an ordinary everyday decapitation? I sure as hell preferred the last option. "Maybe the duffel belonged to your victim?"

"It's possible," Ben said, "but my gut instinct doesn't agree with that." He patted his belly for emphasis. "We found a car a mile or so up the road. Tags came back as a rental, and the company confirmed it was rented to the vic. Looks like Mr. Seeger ran out of gas."

"Cell phone reception is lousy out here," I commented. "He couldn't call for roadside assistance. He was probably hiking to the XpressMart."

Ben nodded, grim. "That's how it looks, and is why I don't think the duffel belonged to the victim. It was found a hundred feet in the wrong direction if he was going to the XpressMart. Plus, the kits come with a bat and machete, and both are missing."

I shuddered. "How many of those things did Bear sell?"

Ben blew out his breath. "A shitload. I just got off the phone with him. Between the website and the store, he's sold a hundred and seventeen so far. He's putting a list together of everyone who paid by credit card, but thirty-four were cash purchases."

I boggled. "A hundred and seventeen? Are you serious?"

"Hell, fifty-five of those were through the website," Ben said. "Several as far away as Oregon."

Nick cleared his throat. "He'll sell out of them before it's over," he said, eyes on his notes. "There are a lot of survivalist types who hang on his every word. If Bear suggested that artificial poultry would be useful in the event of a governmental collapse, there'd be a sudden run on rubber chickens."

"I don't doubt it," Ben said, mouth twisting, then looked around. "Unfortunately, the rain wiped out any footprints or tire tracks, so the duffel is the best lead I have. The lab's going to try and get prints off the survival crap that was in there, but the mesh bag it comes packed in didn't look like it'd been opened. As soon as I clear from here I'm gonna head into town and get the list of buyers and a copy of the surveillance video to try and track down people who paid cash."

"Can you get fingerprints off the wallet?" I asked.

"It's one of those canvas deals. Crime scene bagged it, but I doubt they'll get a useful print. The FBI has a way to lift prints off fabric, so I'll submit the wallet and duffel to them and see what we get back." Ben sighed. "It'll take weeks to hear anything, though."

"Maybe you'll be lucky and the dude will have DNA under his fingernails."

"That would make my day." He glanced toward the privacy screens and got a nod from a tech. "Okay, y'all are up."

Nick and I followed Ben around the screens. I thought I heard someone snicker at my gaudy rain boots, but screw 'em. My feet were obnoxious, but they were also dry and mud-free.

The victim was, indeed, missing a head. A messy, hacked stump of neck topped what looked like an otherwise healthy body. He wore a disturbingly familiar flannel shirt, unbuttoned to reveal a white t-shirt with several long rips in it, smeared in mud and blood. My gaze traveled down similarly ripped and stained jeans, to the hand-painted Zombie Pinup Girl high-tops on his feet.

"Oh my god!" I blurted in shock. "I know this guy!"

Ben wheeled toward me so fast he almost fell over. "How?"

"I don't *know* him, but I talked to him last night at the movie premiere. He was with the production company." I waved a hand at his shoes. "He had those on. I told him they were cool." A sharp pang went through me, and I couldn't speak for a few seconds. "He was really nice," I finally managed. Damn it. I took a long breath and got the ache settled to where it wouldn't interfere. "He was in these clothes, dressed up like a zombie. The rips were in his shirt, and I bet some of that blood is paint." I yanked gloves on and crouched, lifted one of his hands and peered at it. "See, there's a bit of makeup here."

Ben waved a tech over to take pictures of the makeup. "Angel, I could kiss you."

I smiled. "I don't want to make your boyfriend mad."

"He'd understand, once I explained the reason," Ben said. "Can you describe the vic's hair and face?"

"Dark brown hair, almost black. Blue eyes." And he wasn't a zombie. I'd been close enough to know. At least I'd confirmed that real zombies weren't being targeted again.

"He had a cleft in his chin, like a friggin' comic book super-hero."

Ben nodded. "That description matches the DL pic."

"Still need to verify with the prints," Nick muttered as he shone a penlight onto the neck stump. "He might've swapped clothes with someone else after Angel saw him. Not likely, but can't assume he didn't."

"I'll take his prints as soon as I get him to the morgue," I reassured Nick, but my own thoughts weren't as comforting. Grayson Seeger had been nice, but he'd also been fidgety and nervous. Concerned about security. It was possible that whoever he was freaked about had caught up with him. I drew breath to tell Ben about Seeger's paranoia then released it. Shit. That info might help Ben's investigation, but what if the "fed" thing Seeger was worried about tied into the FBI agent who was checking out funeral homes? And what if the funeral home thing tied into the Tribe and brains and real zombies? Ben was a damn good detective because he was a tenacious son of a bitch who never gave up on a case and pursued every possible lead to its very end. If there was even the slightest teeny tiny thread of a link between Seeger's murder and real zombies, Ben would dig it out. And the last thing we needed was the cops poking into our business. I felt as if I was betraying Ben by keeping the Seeger paranoia thing to myself, but I simply couldn't risk the Tribe. Best to keep my mouth shut until I knew more.

But, damn, it would have been a whole lot easier to find out what Seeger was up to if he hadn't gone and gotten himself murdered. As soon as I had what was left of him tucked away in the morgue cooler, I needed to call the Tribe. I'd keep *them* in the loop, even if they didn't do the same for me. 'Cause *I* was considerate.

As soon as Nick finished his examination, I paper-bagged the dead guy's hands to preserve potential evidence, then rolled him over to let crime scene take pics of his back and the ground beneath him.

A tiny wink of sunlight on chrome caught my eye. "Ben, there's something in the mud here."

Ben squinted at where I pointed then signaled to the tech who deftly uncovered what turned out to be a battered yellow disposable lighter.

The tech bagged it. "No telling how long it's been here, but I'll see if I can bring up any prints."

A yellow lighter.

Judd. Lighting his stupid hand-rolled cigarette in the alley behind the Bear's Den.

Which had nothing to do with a brutal murder. Crazy how the mind stuck random details together. Millions of those lighters were sold every year. I probably had a couple in a kitchen drawer at home.

Randy. With a zombie hunter duffel slung over his shoulder.

Along with a hundred and sixteen other buyers. Sure, one of those might've been Judd. But that still didn't mean anything. Judd was with Randy and Coy last night. No way in hell would those two do something like this.

"Angel?" Nick said. "You going to bag the guy or what?"

I realized with chagrin that everyone was waiting for me. "Oh. Sorry." I got the guy into the body bag and zipped it up, then Ben and Nick were nice and helped me carry it up to the highway. Leaving them to babysit the corpse, I returned to the van to bring it closer, stomping my way there in a futile effort to get the mud off the boots. Not that I gave a crap about the condition of the boots, but I didn't want to spend the rest of the day cleaning out the van.

Both TV trucks had left, creating a big gap between the van and the next vehicle as if I'd parked far away on purpose. The news guy had left the towel by the front right wheel along with a neatly printed note, weighted down with a piece of gravel.

Thanks again for the towel! Call me if you ever want to cash in that favor, or even just to grab a coffee together. — Brennan Masters

I smiled in amusement. He'd included his phone number and email address as well. My cynical side told me he was simply hoping to get an inside contact and maybe pump me for info, but I allowed myself a bit of preening. There was no law that said a polished and spiffy TV guy in his late thirties couldn't be interested in a bedraggled twenty-two-year-old morgue tech—

Okay, yeah, he wanted the inside scoop.

Still, I stuffed the note into my pocket and grabbed the towel. The piece of gravel dropped off and bounced into the grass, and my blood went cold as it landed beside a piece of red, white, and blue paper.

A hand-rolled cigarette butt with little American flags printed on it.

Chapter 10

Heart pounding, I stared at the cigarette butt as if the thing was a water moccasin about to bite me. *Another coincidence. That's all.* Judd drove this highway damn near as much as I did. This stretch probably had a few hundred of his stupid butts. Didn't matter that this made three coincidences. The number didn't make them any less coincidental. Circumstantial evidence. That's what it was called. What I needed to do was call Ben over, let him make his own determination as to whether a cigarette butt a quarter mile away from the body was the least bit important.

Randy was with Judd and Coy last night. The thought ricocheted within my skull. But Randy wasn't a murderer. None of them were. Couldn't be. Coy had a good reputation that didn't need to get screwed up by dumb suspicions. And Randy didn't need to be hassled by the cops.

I snatched up the cigarette butt before sanity could return. It wasn't tampering with evidence if it wasn't actually evidence. Right? My hands shook as I unrolled the paper to dump the tobacco out, and I cursed under my breath as a greasy smudge of dark green smeared across my fingers. Bug shit, with my luck. I crumpled the paper and shoved it into my pocket, then scrubbed my hand on my pants to get the green crap off.

I got my ass into the van and drove to Nick and Ben, loaded the body up while anxiety and brain hunger stewed in my gut. Nick gave me a funny look, likely wondering why I was acting like a guilty spaz, but he backed off quick after I mumbled something about female trouble.

Once I was on my way, I grabbed a brain smoothie out of my lunchbox and chugged it down. Though the grumbling hunger settled, my tension and worry stuck tight. Randy lived just a few miles away. It would only take a couple of minutes to swing by and see what he was up to, ease my mind, and confirm that my imagination was running wild.

Shit. No, that wouldn't work. The Coroner's Office vehicles had GPS trackers on them. While van drivers on call were allowed to run personal errands in the van, protocol was no stops or detours between picking up a body and reaching the morgue except for absolute emergencies. I didn't need to give Allen any more ammunition to use against me. Not to mention, Randy might get a little suspicious if I showed up in the van with a body in the back.

I pulled the cigarette paper from my pocket. Too late to put the thing back where I'd found it, especially since now my fingerprints were all over those dumb American flags. But I didn't want to be caught with it, either.

Another two miles down the road, I rolled my window down, checked for witnesses, then flicked the crumpled paper into a water-filled ditch.

At the morgue, I transferred Mr. Seeger from the gurney onto a rolling table then unzipped his body bag. Even though Nick and I had performed a cursory search of the body on the scene, I still needed to do a full property inventory.

Hunger grabbed my belly in a sneak attack and squeezed a sharp gasp from me. Hissing, I grabbed the edge of the table as an itch began in my bones. Invisible ants walked up my arms. A mini-dose, a tiny hit was all I needed to —

No! C'mon, Angel, don't be a fucking wimp.

Jaw clenched, I sucked air through my teeth and focused on a spot on the wall. The clock behind me ticked out seconds, and I used the sound, imagined myself shoving the need a little farther back into its hole with each *tick*.

The hunger eased. The itch faded to mild buzz. The desire to climb out of my body went away.

Straightening, I wiped my mouth and let out a strangled laugh. I'd won. I'd fought that bitch down. It was all good. I could do this "no more V12" thing. A tendril of fear slid through a crack, and I slapped it down hard. No. Everything was going to be just fine. Beating this shit was all about willpower, and I had plenty of that. Time to get my head back in the game.

I went to the bathroom and washed my face and hands, then pulled on fresh gloves and began a meticulous search of Mr. Seeger. No jewelry, watch, keys, or phone. Jeans pockets were empty except for a damp Kleenex, and the front pocket of the flannel shirt held lint and nothing more. Shoes and socks contained feet and nothing else. I even tugged his jeans down to check his underwear and found only the expected boy parts and shaved pubic hair. Interesting, but not at all what I was looking for.

Sighing, I pulled his clothing back into place. Later, I'd remove them for good, after I photographed him on the table and before the autopsy. It was silly, but I hated leaving the bodies naked in the bag before autopsy. Why not let them have a few more hours with that tiny shred of dignity?

Something crinkled beneath my hand as I adjusted the flannel shirt. A quick investigation revealed an inner pocket that held a folded piece of paper. My pulse quickened as I slid the paper out. *Bingo*.

It was a list of filenames, on battered Infamous Vision Studios letterhead, with several handwritten notes scribbled on it. The word "zombie" leaped out at me from several places, but that didn't surprise me considering Grayson Seeger was a producer for a *zombie* movie and was in town for a *zombie* fest.

The list header read *Contents of USB Flash Drive from D.R.* and was followed by more than a dozen filenames such as **zombie_feeding* and ***zombie_turn_1*. One file named **zombie_frenzy* had a hand-drawn arrow pointing to it with *Zombie Frenzy!* written beside it. I snorted. Gee, that was a tough code to crack.

Most of the filenames were marked with asterisks or double asterisks which matched up with a handwritten note at the side:

* approved by DR for ZAAU

** use for deal with SASA

Seeger sure liked his acronyms. DR was most likely someone's initials. The others could be studio names or—

ZAAU. Zombies Are Among Us? That was the short film title on the "coming soon" display I'd seen at the movie premiere. Could be the asterisk meant the file was used in the *"documentary THEY don't want you to see."* But I had no clue at all what SASA could stand for. Sharks Are Sexy Also? Secret Aardvark Social Action?

My focus sharpened on a double-asterisk filename. ***Zombie_heal_2*. I frowned. Heal? The zombies in *High School Zombie Apocalypse!!* were typical mindless rotters. When they got blown to bits or chopped up they stayed that way—no healing involved at any point. An uneasy chill walked down my spine even though plenty of reasonable explanations came to mind. Maybe the zombies would get to be badass and heal up in the sequel, *College Zombie Apocalypse!!* Or, more likely, the filename had zilch to do with zombies healing. It probably stood for "zombie_ healthy" and was a video of zombies who weren't all rotted yet.

Whatever the reason, it hit too close to home, especially since I was already on high alert for anything zombie-like and suspicious. I didn't care if the paper might be evidence. Hell, I didn't care if it could lead to the cure for the common cold. It damn sure wasn't staying here for anyone else to find and speculate about.

Mr. Seeger went into the cooler, and the paper went into my bra.

As soon as I left the morgue, I headed straight to Randy's place. Casual visit, nothing more. Dropping in to say Hi, that sort of thing. After all, I knew there was no way Randy could've been involved in the murder. Knew it. He could be a Grade-A Prime Loser, but murder? Nuh uh. I was *sure*.

Almost sure. Only a teensy bit of doubt lingered, but it was like a grain of sand in my eye. I'd swing by and see how he was doing, what he was up to. Laundering bloody clothes. Burying a machete. Innocent shit like that.

Randy lived at the very end of a long-as-hell rural road, on several acres of land that held a rusty corrugated metal garage and a halfway decent trailer. The garage was where he made his living as a mechanic and—when he needed some extra cash—it served as the occasional chop-shop. After I parked, I made my way around puddles to the trailer steps where I could hear a TV blaring the morning news from within. Worry twisted in my chest. Randy *never* watched the news.

I knocked, hard enough to be heard over the TV. The sound went off, and a few seconds later Randy yanked the door open, looking surprised, relieved, and disappointed to see me. He was fully dressed, with a half-smoked cigarette in one hand. His eyes flicked to the van and then farther down the driveway. Checking to see if I'd brought anyone with me?

"Dude!" I put on my excited-and-horrified act. "Did you see the news about the serial killer?"

"Uh." He glanced at his TV then gave me a nod. "Yeah, I was listening to it."

He made no move to invite me in, but that was a minor

obstacle for a pushy bitch. "The body was found not far from here," I said and slid past him before he could stop me. "Figured I'd make sure you were okay."

Randy made a face as if I'd just pissed in his Cheerios but went ahead and closed the door. He picked up a plastic cup and knocked ash into it. "I'm good. Crazy shit, huh?"

"Totally crazy!" I flopped onto the sofa and made myself at home. "Did you hit Pillar's Bar after the Fest?"

He shrugged. "For maybe an hour."

Was he acting guilty? Hungover? Hell, I couldn't tell a damn thing. "Oh man, you might've knocked back a beer with the sicko who chopped off that guy's head and never known it!"

Randy gave me a sharp look. "The cops think the guy was at Pillar's before he—?"

"Before he murdered the guy?" I spread my hands. "I don't think they've made any *public* statements about it." I wasn't lying. It was Randy's fault if he took that to mean there were *private* statements floating around.

He sucked on the cigarette and sat on the arm of the sofa. "The news said the cops didn't have any leads."

I scoffed. "You believe that? The dumbass left plenty of evidence at the scene. It won't take long."

Surprise flashed across Randy's face, as if he suddenly remembered what I did for a living. "You were *there*?"

"Sure. I was on call. Picked up the body. Dude, that shit was gruesome. Y'know, it ain't like the movies where it's one clean slice." I warmed to my topic as Randy paled. "Nah, it must've taken a dozen hacks with a dull ass machete to get this poor dude's head off." Hunger shimmered through me. The brain would've been nice and warm and fresh and—

Saliva flooded my mouth, and I quickly swallowed before I started drooling. The smell of Randy's brain filled the room, overpowering the scent of bacon grease and cigarettes.

"Jesus, Angel. I don't need the gory details." Randy

crushed out the cigarette then shook a fresh one from a pack and lit it. In the next instant he jerked to his feet, eyes wide in rising horror. "Is that body out in the van?"

Randy's reactions would've been awfully funny if the stakes weren't so high. "Nah, I already took it to the morgue. What was left of him, at least." I plastered on a grin. "Why'd you leave Pillar's so early? I thought you and the guys were gonna stay 'til closing."

His expression turned sour. "Judd thought we were about to get ambushed during the zombie hunt, spun around and accidentally whacked me in the head with the butt of his paintball rifle." He pulled his cap off to show me a small butterfly bandage atop a decent-sized goose egg. "I left Pillar's 'cause I couldn't deal with the shitty band pounding my skull."

Frowning, I peered at the lump. That wasn't faked. And such a fine brain under it. I quickly stepped back. "You feeling okay? You don't want to mess with head injuries."

"Hell, I got knocked a lot worse that time Chester Albertson dumped me off the back of his four-wheeler." His shoulders twitched in a shrug. "The EMT at the Fest checked me out and told me I just needed to take it easy."

Well, that was good. Hard to be up for cold-blooded murder with a splitting headache. If it was true. What if Seeger had walloped Randy in self-defense? I might have to track down the EMT and verify.

Randy's phone shrilled on the end table, startling us both. He grabbed it and stared at the caller ID as if the phone was poisonous, then glanced at me, hesitating.

"You get that. I need to use the can." I popped up off the sofa and headed down the hallway, then snuck a quick peek into the open lid of the washer. Bone dry and empty. No late night laundering, at least not here. I stepped into the bathroom and closed the door, then eased it open a crack and listened.

"Okay okay, now hang on," Randy said, low and urgent. I heard a scuff of shoes on carpet as he moved farther away.

"Yeah, gotta show up for the zombie shit today and tonight, both hunts, as we planned." Stress gave his words a sharp edge that made them easier to hear. "We're already registered." Another pause. "I know, but we'll have to deal with it tomorrow."

Deal with it? That could be anything from hiding evidence to scrounging lunch. I did a quick search of the bathroom and laundry hamper for any sign of blood—or murder weapons. Randy's zombie hunter equipment vest lay in a crumpled heap at the top of the hamper. My heart skipped a beat as I spied scattered dark spots of dried blood.

He got conked on the head, I reminded myself. The blood was probably from that. Plus, I was no blood spatter expert, but I knew there'd be a lot more than a three or four drops if he'd been anywhere near a head being chopped off.

Hunger spiked again, this time joined by the bone itch as the need for a dose clamored. The scent of Randy's brain filled my nose, and a growl built in my chest. *No, not now!* Aghast, I fished the emergency brain packet from my pocket and slurped it down, then stared at the peeling wallpaper and focused my willpower to shove the beast away again. It grudgingly settled back, but I had a sinking feeling this was a temporary truce.

"Yeah. That works," I heard Randy say. "See you at the gun shop in an hour."

I closed the door, flushed the toilet and ran water over my hands, then opted to dry them on my pants instead of the grungy towel. "Hold your shit together," I snarled at my reflection. I'd never find out the truth about the murder if I ate my ex.

Back out in the living room, Randy was peering out the blinds.

"Everything cool?" I asked.

He let them flick closed and gave me a crooked smile. "Uh huh, just gotta get my shit together and head to the Zombie Fest."

"I'm on call 'til noon," I said, "but I'm supposed to go over there this afternoon. Maybe I'll run into you."

A frown tugged at his mouth. "Yeah, since I'm the one what invited you."

Crap. Forgot about that. "Oh, um, a guy I work with has two VIP passes. I figured it'd be dumb to turn down free shit."

Randy took a drag off his cigarette, shrugged. "Good for you."

Not even a weensy bit of disappointment. "Where will y'all be this afternoon? Maybe I'll stop by."

"Hard to say. We're gonna be hunting . . . and stuff."

"Gotcha," I said. "I need to run, so I'll let you get ready."

He nodded, flicked off ash. "See you around."

I gave him a quick hug then left the trailer, skirting puddles as I returned to the van. Though he hadn't given anything away, he hadn't acted normal either. Randy was a pro at being a piece of shit, but I'd never known him to be cold-blooded. If he'd been involved in a murder, he'd be a helluva lot more freaked out.

Okay, great. I was *almost* certain Randy hadn't killed anyone. But my Angel-sense told me there was a big stinking pile of shit not far off.

The beast awoke the instant the van door closed. Fire raced through my marrow, and blades of ice sliced at my gut. Whimpering, I fumbled the lunch box open to grab my brain burrito, then stared at the three duct-taped vials that should have been at home in my fridge. But of course they'd be here. Even though I didn't remember packing them, the beast had taken care of it for me. I couldn't possibly leave home without V12 because what if something happened and I *needed* it?

Oh thank god. I snatched the vials and held them in a shaking fist.

No. Fuck no. Cold turkey, goddammit.

Sweat beaded my lip as I willed my fingers to open. A

gasp of relief and despair sagged out of me as the vials dropped back into the lunchbox. Another battle won? No. Bullshit. That was like saying the beach won every time the surf retreated. That wasn't victory. The waves would keep coming, keep scraping away at the sand.

A harsh sob clogged my throat. I peeled out of the driveway, palms slick against the wheel. As soon as I was out of sight of Randy's place, I pulled onto the shoulder.

Cold turkey was kicking my ass. I got myself into this state all on my lonesome, but now I needed a boost to claw my way out. Time for me to put my big girl panties on and ask for help before I ruined what was left of my life. I'd have to face Dr. Nikas eventually. Might as well be now.

I called the lab, and a baritone voice with a lilt of French accent answered. "Angel."

"Jacques. Hi." Shit, could my mouth get any drier? "Um, I need to talk to Dr. Nikas."

"He's working with Philip."

Guilt shuddered through me. I scrubbed a hand over my face. "Did Philip get worse?"

"You sound like shit." His words slapped out. "When was your last dose of V12?"

Oh god. Jacques knew. Shame and humiliation rolled through me in waves of hot and cold. Of course Dr. Nikas would've told him. "I . . . last night."

"Are you out?"

My blood cells turned into spinning razor blades as they flowed through my veins. I sucked air between clenched teeth and clung to the outrage. "You think I took *three whole vials* since yesterday?"

"I don't know what you may or may not have done. Right now, anything is possible." His voice remained icy cool and professional. "Are you out of V12?"

"I don't need the third degree," I snapped. "I just need to talk to Dr. Nikas." Damn judgmental ass. Who the hell did he think he was? Sure, I'd borrowed a few doses, but that didn't mean I couldn't be trusted at all. And no way was I going to tell him how much V12 I had left. What if he sent security to take it away from me? "When will he be done with Philip?"

Jacques huffed out a breath. "Take a dose if you have one. I'll let him know you—"

I ended the call and hurled the phone. It bounced off the dash and skittered to a stop on the passenger side floorboard. My chest heaved, and I screamed in fury. Useless, backstabbing asshole. Take a dose? I was trying to get off the crap! Calling had been a mistake. Jacques probably resented that I'd ever been allowed to work at the lab. Trashy loser Angel, horning in on his turf. He wanted me to take a dose to make sure I never got my job at the lab back.

The phone beeped with a text. I snatched it off the floor: *Where are you? Take a dose.*

My bones burned. I slammed my fist into the seat over and over then typed in a reply, barely able to keep my hand steady enough: *Headed south on Fuck You Street.*

My gut twisted as if it was about to burst out of my belly like an alien. I needed brains. I needed a goddamn dose. How was I supposed to drive after he got me all worked up like this? What if I got a call to pick up a body? Asshole. He knew what he was doing. He knew I only had one option.

I fumbled the lunch box open. Grabbed the vials and prepped a dose right through the goddamn duct tape. Jabbed the needle under my skin.

"This one's *your* fucking fault, Jacques." My breath hitched as I pressed the plunger. "This one's on you."

Chapter 11

The V12 had me nicely chilled out by the time I got home, yet resentment stewed despite the effects of the mod. If Jacques hadn't screwed with me, I wouldn't have needed to chill in the first place. Asshole.

I headed inside and changed into clean jeans and T-shirt, then stuffed my impromptu zombie costume items for the Fest into a plastic grocery bag. He *had* screwed with me, hadn't he? Doubt butted up against the resentment. I struggled to replay the incident, but my memory of it was fuzzy. And downing an entire bottle of brain-enhanced chocolate milk did nothing to clear it up.

My phone beeped. *Jacques again?* Annoyance flared as I snatched it from the dresser. "Why can't you leave me the f—"

Not Jacques. The text was from Nick.

It was an early morning. Still good for meeting up at 1:30?

My ugly mood melted away, and I smiled. *You wimping out and need a nap?*

Hell no. I was worried about your dainty self.

I grinned as I thumbed in my reply. *My delicate butt will be there on schedule.* I glanced at the clock to be sure. Yep,

I'd have enough time to buy calf brains from the butcher then get to the morgue and stick them in Mr. Noah Granger's organ bag before Nick got there.

Good deal. See you then.

Feeling more settled, I put my phone aside then sat on the floor of my bedroom and glowered at the contents of my fridge. One bottle of brain smoothie and two brain burritos. Before I'd started using V12, that would have been enough to last a week. Now, at my current mod-stimulated hunger levels, it was barely enough to get me through the day.

In addition to the dismal contents of my fridge, I had a small for-absolute-emergency-only stash here at the house, a baggie of chips, and less than a week's worth in the freezer in my storage unit. At the rate I was going, I'd need a buttload of "patients" to come through the morgue. Maybe a derailment of a train carrying a bunch of prisoners destined for death row?

Sighing, I chugged the last smoothie then closed the door and clambered to my feet. Surely the crazy hunger would die down as soon as I quit the V12 for good. The craving faded as I drained the bottle, but I threw the last two burritos into my lunch box and tucked the brain chips into my pocket, to be on the safe side.

I shoved down the worry. It would all work out. Somehow.

Humming with V12-fueled confidence, I grabbed the grocery bag with my costume pieces and headed off to Tucker Point. It sucked big milky turds that I'd been forced to take the V12 after swearing off the stuff. Now I'd have to start over from scratch on the cold turkey withdrawal crap. But at least this dose would help me get through the day. It was silly to try and stop cold with everything that was going on: Randy and trouble at the lab and the murder and snooping and being on call and school. I *needed* that dose.

Traffic slowed as I neared downtown Tucker Point, and the dozen brightly colored parade floats in the BigShopMart parking lot reminded me that the Krewe of Swampfoot parade was due to start in an hour. I drummed my fingers on the steering wheel as I ducked down side streets and through neighborhoods. The police wouldn't start blocking streets off until the parade was ready to pass by, but I *needed* to get to the butcher shop. I pumped a fist in triumph as I scored a parking place a mere three blocks away, though I knew I couldn't take too long with my shopping. The last thing I needed was to get trapped by the parade until it was done—which would be a couple of hours at best. In and out. That was the plan.

Main Street bustled with a strange mix of parade goers and Zombie Festers, and it wasn't easy to tell which was which. Plastic beads and fake rot. Only in Louisiana.

I walked past Le Bon Décor and the zombie carnival masks, then stopped, went back, and peered at the sign beside them. *40% off.*

Ooooooo. That put them in the "not stupidly expensive" territory. Nick had bought VIP tickets for the Zombie Fest, so it was only right for me to give a little back in return. And, it would be fun to surprise Nick and use the masks for part of the day. Besides, I wanted them. Grinning in delight, I marched into the shop, plopped my debit card down, and became the proud owner of unique zombie Mardi Gras mask awesomeness.

With my treasures boxed and bagged in a fancy-schmancy artsy bag, I continued on my way. A pair of jugglers were entertaining a crowd in front of the Bear's Den and Wyatt's Butcher Shop, so I ducked around the corner and into the alley to hit the back entrance. Judging by the number of new paintball splodges on the practice wall at the end of the alley, Bear was no doubt making a killing from sales for the festival.

I set the bells on the back door jangling as I entered the butcher shop.

"Be with you in a minute," Mr. Wyatt called out from the processing room.

"Take your time," I called back as I strolled to the front display cases. A sign on the wall advertised game processing—everything from whitetail to alligator. Every hunter I knew brought their kills here.

Mr. Wyatt emerged through swinging doors, wiping his hands on a blood-covered white apron. Stocky, with hair the color of dark steel, the first impression was that he wasn't someone to be messed with. Yet he always had a ready smile, like the one he sent me now.

"G'morning, Miss Angel. What can I do for you today?"

"Hey, Mr. Wyatt. I need calf brains."

He shook his head solemnly. "Fresh out. Cletus Crowe picked up the last of them this morning. Got some nice pig brains, though."

I hid a wince. "Can I see what they look like? I mean, how big they are?"

He moved behind the right display case and tapped the glass. "That's them in the front. This for special effects?"

"Nah, for eating." I peered at the brains nestled in crushed ice. Damn. They were a quarter the size of a human brain, if that. "Any idea when you'll get more calf brains in?"

"I can order them special, but Wednesday would be the soonest."

My plan could still work, though I'd need more than I'd thought. "I'll take four of the pig brains for now."

The front door bells clanged, and Mr. Wyatt looked up. "Mornin', Miss Savannah," he said with a broad smile. "Be right with you."

Savannah. I glanced at the woman who'd entered. Shit. Savannah Prejean. Allen's wife. And, outside on the sidewalk, the boss-man himself watched jugglers with the rest of the crowd.

"Take all the time you need, Wyatt." She smiled at me. The kind of polite smile you give to strangers. "Angel, it's nice to see you."

Damn, so much for hoping she wouldn't remember me. I'd only met her twice before—at the Coroner's Office

Christmas party and a crawfish boil at Derrel's place last spring. I managed a nice smile in return. "Good to see you too, Mrs. Prejean."

Wyatt prodded a brain with his gloved finger. "Miss Angel, you want me to special order for next week?"

"Uh." I stole a glance at Allen. I needed to order three calf brains, but having his wife listen in while I schemed made me more than a little antsy. "Lemme get back to you. I'll cook these up for my dad, and we'll see how that turns out."

"Good enough. Call me by ten Monday." He flopped the pig brains onto butcher paper, wrapped them.

Savannah lifted her chin toward the display case. "Allen tried to talk me into taking a bite of his sandwich at the diner." She gave a prim shudder. "I can't get past the thought of them being *brains*."

I shoved a ten across the counter. "I had the same problem the first time I had brains, but they grew on me."

Wyatt passed me a bag with the brains and my change.

The jugglers had moved on, but Allen remained on the sidewalk in front of the shop. No way was I going to carry contraband pig brains past him. Sure, I was being paranoid, but he—

My gaze froze on a man across the street, phone to his ear as he looked straight at the butcher shop.

Philip.

My heart thundered. A thousand scenarios flashed through my head for why he was here, each more heinous than the last. But one stood out: Jacques had sent him here to pick me up. Made perfect sense that he'd use Philip. The Tribe didn't have a lot of manpower to spare right now, and he was the one who'd suffered most from my bullshit.

I had no idea how long he'd been out there, but I wasn't going to wait around. While Savannah waffled over ribeye vs. T-bones, I hustled out the back door.

The door jangled shut behind me. I hurried toward the street then skidded to a stop as a black SUV pulled across the mouth of the alley. *That's a Tribe vehicle*, I thought wildly, followed by, *I'm trapped*. No way forward and no way back with the paintball dead end behind me. If I cut through the Bear's Den, I'd come out on Main Street where Philip was waiting.

My one shot was to dart past the SUV. Surely the driver wouldn't be desperate enough to tackle little old me in front of a bunch of pedestrians.

No way to tank up on brains for zombie-speed, so I sprinted as fast as possible for regular Angel. The driver's door flew open as I squeezed past the SUV. Jacques clambered out. "Angel! Stop!"

Heart pounding, I dodged down the sidewalk away from Main Street and Philip. I needed to be a damn grownup, stop and give myself up, but my inner third-grader insisted that if I just kept going maybe they'd give up and leave me alone.

Footfalls behind me told my inner third-grader she was a moron, but I scooted through a cluster of parade-goers and kept going.

"Angel!"

Different voice. Not Jacques. *Dr. Nikas.*

I stumbled to a halt, spun in horrified shock to see Dr. Nikas climb out of the back of the SUV and take several steps toward me. Jacques had also stopped and was looking back at the reclusive doctor. I could practically hear the thoughts clamoring through his head. *Dr. Nikas is out of the vehicle in a crowd!*

"What are you *doing* here?" I blurted.

People whooped on Main Street. Dr. Nikas flinched, then paled as pedestrians crowded past the SUV. "Come to the car, Angel," he said, voice strained. "Please."

Shit. Dr. Nikas had a horrific phobia of crowds, and for damn good reason. No way could I put him through more pain because of my idiocy. Shoulders slumped in defeat, I headed his way, reaching him as Philip rounded the corner of the Bear's Den. I couldn't bring myself to meet Philip's eyes. I didn't have the energy—or the courage—to handle the condemnation and anger that I knew they held.

Dr. Nikas fled back to the SUV. Worry and fear and embarrassment battled it out in the hard knot in my chest as I climbed in after him. Fuck it. I had no choice but to be a grownup and take my licks now.

Philip closed the door behind us, but remained outside with Jacques, to my very small relief.

"I'm sorry," I croaked, and clenched my hands together to try and control the shaking. "I'm so sorry. Oh god, why did you come here?"

Dr. Nikas took a long drink from a thermos, and a bit of color returned to his face. "You left the lab, then wouldn't answer texts, and hung up on Jacques. I need to talk to you."

My throat tightened. "What's there to talk about?"

His calm eyes rested on me. "We have yet to sort out the issue."

"What's to sort out?" I said, miserable. "I'm an awful person who stole drugs."

"Yes, you did," he said then sighed. "And it is partially my fault. I hope you can forgive me, Angel."

"Huh?" I stared at him. "How the hell is it your fault?"

"I'm the one who authorized you to use the combat mod in New York," he said. "I knew of your addictive nature yet didn't take care of you when we returned."

It was several seconds before I could speak. "You had more important problems. I'm the one who made the decision to steal from Philip's doses." My eyes filled with tears as I glanced at the broad back of my zombie baby where he stood near the front of the vehicle. "That's why he's messed up again, isn't it? I hurt him."

Dr. Nikas's expression of regret told me I was right. "I didn't catch it sooner because it took months for the cumulative dose decrease to show an effect." He touched the back of my hand lightly. "Now that I know, I've made corrections and the reversal is well underway."

"But I hurt him and made him suffer," I said. No way could I ever look Philip in the face again.

"It's you I'm concerned about now," Dr. Nikas said.

The lump in my throat thickened. "Don't worry," I said. "I won't come back to the lab. I understand."

"No, you don't understand," he replied with a shake of his head. "I *need* you to come back."

Baffled, I struggled to make sense of his words. "Come back? Why?" Punishment or imprisonment seemed unlikely at this point. Dr. Nikas wasn't the type to be all sneaky like that.

He gave me a gentle smile. "You're part of my team. You, Jacques, and Reg. I don't want to lose you."

Tears spilled down my cheeks. "Even after everything I did?"

He covered my hand with his. "It isn't what you did, but what you *didn't* do that I'd like to change."

I blinked. "What didn't I do?"

His eyes met mine. "You didn't trust me. I would very much like it if you would."

Damn. I bit my lip. "I was using the V12 for a few weeks before I realized it was helping the dyslexia." I sniffled and wiped at my eyes. "By that time I didn't know what the heck I could say, y'know? 'I've been skimming drugs, but hey, they have a cool side effect.'"

His gentle understanding didn't waver one bit. "I'm sorry I didn't catch it sooner."

If he'd yelled at me and been angry it would have been easier to handle than his quiet patience. *It ends now,* I thought fiercely. *The bullshit ends now*. I'd rather pull my own guts out than see his compassion turn to disappointment.

"I tried to quit, but it hurt so bad," I managed to croak out. "I called this morning to get help, but Jacques told me to take another damn dose."

"Because stopping will *kill* you. Your parasite is addicted too."

I stared, dumbfounded. "I *have* to stop! I've started having hallucinations, and my judgment is crap, and I'm eating enough brains to feed five zombies. I'm gonna fuck up everything if I don't—"

"Angel," Dr. Nikas said sharply. "I know. I'll develop a non-addictive formula and wean you off the V12. It'll take time and experimentation to get it right, but as long as you're committed, we'll get there."

I blew my breath out. "Does everyone know?"

When he shook his head, a thousand pounds of pressure lifted from my shoulders. "No one knows but Pierce, Jacques, and me," he said. "Not even Reg, Brian, or Philip. And it will stay that way as long as you work with me honestly."

"I will." Gulping, I nodded. "I swear."

"It's vital, Angel. For your sake. Pierce smelled it on you yesterday and alerted me." Dr. Nikas paused. "He wanted you to have *in-house* rehab."

In-house. Locked down in the lab medical wing until I was clean. It was a few seconds before I could speak around the panic that clutched at me. "You talked him out of it?"

He squeezed my hand, and I realized he was willing to trust me to the ends of the earth. I had no idea how I'd managed to earn that sort of faith—especially after this dumbass stunt—but it tripled my resolve to never let him or myself down again.

"In-house would be easiest and safest for others," Dr. Nikas said. "But our world—the zombie world—is at a crisis point. Matters are heating up, and exposure is a very real possibility. Easy and safe are luxuries. Pierce needs you in the field as an operative. I need you." He took a deep breath. "It would also likely cause more problems than it would solve for you to take an extended leave from your job, even if a suitable explanation was offered." His eyes met mine, serious and unwavering. "But I'll lock you down myself in a heartbeat if you stray off course."

Resolve shoved fear aside. "I'll do whatever it takes." No

more screwups, not when so much was at stake. Hearing of the exposure crisis straight from Dr. Nikas made it a thousand times more real.

"Your addiction has an upside," he said, smile returning. "The dyslexia puzzle gave me new insight into parasite interaction with pharmaceuticals. I'm a half-step closer to pseudobrains."

"That's awesome!" I gave a strained laugh. "But I think it's better if I don't make 'exercising really poor judgment' a permanent research technique."

Dr. Nikas chuckled. "Many great discoveries have been made quite by accident," he said, but then his amusement faded. "The downside is that you have an addictive personality and need counseling. It's not optional."

I gave a quick nod. "I'll do it."

"I'd like you to speak with Jacques," he continued. "If you prefer an outside practitioner, I'll arrange it."

Jacques? He was the last person I'd have expected Dr. Nikas to suggest. "He told me he killed people he held dear."

"I created him during the last days of the Franco-Prussian war," Dr. Nikas said, expression sad and grave. "Less than six months later, he lost control and ate his wife and son." He exhaled. "The parasite wouldn't allow suicide, though his pre-zombie addiction to laudanum drew him to the opium dens of Paris to try. He succeeded only in damaging his parasite and, between subsequent behavior and rotting in public, triggered an exodus. He has much insight to offer. As do I."

If I ate my dad or Derrel or Nick, I'd want to kill myself too. My gaze went to where Jacques leaned against the hood of the Escalade, his thin shoulders drawn in. Though I couldn't see his face, I knew his eyes would have their characteristic haunted look.

"I'll talk to him." I said. "Thanks."

"Good. You can do so next week when I have your new formula ready. For now, take half-doses of V12 twice daily." He leveled a stern gaze at me. "Do it by the clock, not by perceived need. And do not take less in a misguided attempt to wean more quickly."

Gulping, I nodded. In return he retrieved a pill bottle from his jacket pocket and pressed it into my hand. "Take one capsule along with each dose. It will help withdrawal symptoms until I can reformulate for you. And if you feel yourself faltering, call me. Yes?"

"I will," I promised. It was almost too good to be true, except that this was Dr. Nikas, and this was exactly how Dr. Nikas handled shit. I summoned up a crooked smile. "Speaking of field operative crap, today has been one hundred percent psycho." I filled him in on the events of the last twenty-four hours: my suspicions about the decapitated Seeger, the list of zombie-related file names from Seeger's pocket, the possible involvement of Randy, Judd, and Coy, as well as my plan to check out more at the Zombie Fest.

He nodded as I wound down. "I'll pass the information on to Pierce. Call me next time, yes?"

The mild admonishment in his voice stung worse than any chewing out I'd ever received. I'd been an idiot to avoid him. "I've learned my lesson."

"Good. Brian is available by text today for urgent matters, and Naomi is on surveillance at the Zombie Fest if you need physical backup."

Absurd relief flooded me as if he'd handed me two lifelines. Though not a zombie, Naomi was a fierce advocate for our kind and worked as an operative for the Tribe. Brian was my usual go to resource but, with him off doing secret stuff with the other honchos, Dr. Nikas was the next in line. Even if I didn't *need* Brian or Naomi, it felt good to have them as options.

Dr. Nikas retrieved a handful of brain packets from the console and handed them to me. "That should help bolster your diminishing supply. Be careful out there."

I shoved the packets into the bag that held the pig brains, opened the car door then turned back and threw my arms around him in a hug. He stiffened, and for an instant I thought I'd made a horrible mistake by intruding on his personal space, but before I could pull away his arms came around me and he returned the hug. It only lasted a couple of seconds, but it was full of warmth and comfort and support. It was the best goddamn hug in the history of hugs.

He released me, eyes glistening, and I suddenly wondered how long it had been since he'd been hugged.

"Take care, Angel," he said, voice soft.

"You too, Dr. Nikas," I whispered, then climbed out of the car and closed the door.

Philip turned to me as I exited. "You cool, ZeeEm?"

"I am now." I paused. "I need to get something off my chest." He frowned, but I forged on before I could chicken out. "It's my fault you've been feeling like shit. I was skimming your doses for my own use, but I swear I didn't know it would affect you like that, and I'm really really sorry." The words tumbled out in a jangled rush, leaving me breathless and anxious at the end.

"Ah." He flicked a glance toward the back of the SUV then to me, face as unreadable as granite. "Dr. Nikas is helping you?"

My eyes welled up again. Did he hate me? If so, I deserved it. Nothing I could do about it except not fuck up again. "Yeah. He is."

"Good deal. I'd better get him on back to the lab." He slid into the driver's seat. "I'll, um, catch you later." He looked as if he was poised to say more, but closed the door instead.

"He'll be all right," Jacques said. "You'll be all right."

"What about you?"

His eyes told me everything I needed to know. My throat tightened as he climbed into the backseat of the Escalade. A smile flickered on his face. "It's not too late for you. Call me."

The door closed, and the SUV pulled away. People—

non-zombies—laughed and chatted and strolled toward Main Street for the parade. They had no idea they'd just passed four monsters living right alongside them.

And I would do my damnedest to make sure they never did.

My phone rang as I put the brain packets in the console of my car. I didn't recognize the number, but I answered with a professional *hello* since it might be work-related.

"Angel, it's Andrew Saber." He spoke in an urgent whisper over muffled crowd noise and distant music.

I instinctively tensed. "Is something wrong?" Andrew had never called me before.

"No. I don't know. My sister isn't answering."

"Is that all?" I relaxed again. After I saved his life by turning him into a zombie, he and the Tribe had forged a loose deal. We supplied him with brains and "new zombie" counseling, and in return he promised to give us the heads up if Saberton hatched any new nasty plans to use zombies in research. His twin sister, Naomi—formerly Julia Saber—was his usual Tribe contact. She'd fled Saberton after she witnessed their zombie atrocities and killed one of their researchers. Today she was busy at the Zombie Fest. If she wanted to contact him, she would. "So you stooped to calling me?"

"Grayson Seeger was murdered," he said, still in the hoarse whisper. "What do you know about it?"

"Not much. Why?" If he knew anything regarding Seeger, I wanted to hear it without showing my cards. We had a truce, but we didn't have an open exchange of information.

"It has nothing to do with you," he replied, to my annoyance. "I'll keep trying to reach Nao—" A sharp sound like gunfire erupted in the background, followed by cheers.

"Where the hell are you?"

"Zombie Fest," he said as soon as the noise died down.

"Seeger got his head cut off," I offered, throwing him a bone to keep him talking.

"Was he a . . . ?"

"Zombie? Nah. But it's possible somebody thought he was."

"How? Why?" Andrew said, quiet tone ratcheting up in stress. "He called me yesterday out of the blue. Said he had important information for me and wanted to meet today. But if someone thought he was a zombie and—"

A hollow knock sounded on his end. "Mr. Saber? Is everything all right in there?"

"I'll be out in a minute," he said in a normal voice then whispered to me, "I have to go."

I burst out laughing. "If you gotta *go*, you gotta go. You're hiding from your goons in a goddamn porta-potty?"

"Shut up, Angel! It's not funny."

"Yeah, it is. I'll find you later at the Fest."

He made a noise of either relief or dread before he disconnected. A touch of guilt shimmered through me. He could be a dick, but I probably shouldn't have screwed with him. It had to suck living a secret zombie life right beside people who'd kill him or worse if they found out. But, then again, the same applied to all zombies.

Pedestrians hurried toward Main Street as I eased through traffic. Even with all the sucky stuff, the day was turning out to be pretty okay. I had a mental image of the mighty Andrew Saber hunkered down in a porta-potty, making an illicit call while his security people hovered outside. I had leads to follow on Mr. Seeger. I had a clear-the-air understanding with Dr. Nikas. I had pig brains and cool masks. On top of it all, I made it out of downtown before the cops barricaded the streets.

I headed for the morgue to meet Nick, heart lighter than it had been in ages.

Chapter 12

I swiped my ID card and slipped into the morgue. Even when people had the misfortune to die during non-business hours, the on-call investigator and morgue tech rarely stuck around longer than the few minutes it took to stuff the decedent into the cooler and log basic info in the computer. And autopsies were performed on the weekend only when the need was critical. As a result, the morgue tended to be quiet as a tomb on the weekends. And, fortunately, today was no different.

I dropped my plastic grocery bag with my zombie costume clothes on the desk along with the butcher-paper wrapped pig brains, then checked the other offices and the cutting room to make sure no one was around. There was no valid reason for me to be poking through a body bag on my day off, so I needed to be one hundred percent *sure* I wouldn't get caught.

Not another living soul in the entire building. And a quick check of the computer reassured me that dispatch hadn't sent anyone out on a call, which meant I wouldn't be rudely interrupted by a body coming in.

Satisfied, I ducked into the cooler with the packet of pig

brains, but left the heavy door open. If anyone came into the morgue, I'd hear the outer door. Besides, I wouldn't be more than a minute or two. Good thing, since the trip into town had taken longer than planned.

The cooler held just two bodies: Mr. Omentum-has-momentum Granger—whose organ bag I'd already raided, and Mr. Grayson-headless-Seeger. I yanked the zipper of Omentum's body bag open, but froze as I reached for the organ bag. The knot in the bag. Was that mine? It looked too tight. Then again, I'd been munching brains when I tied it. It was *possible* my zombie strength had kicked in. I worried my lower lip, uneasy. What if Allen had checked the bag after I went to lunch, found the brains missing, and retied it?

If he had, I was already up shit creek and a few pig brains wouldn't make any difference one way or the other. But if he hadn't, the little oinkers could save my scrawny zombie ass.

I worked the knot open, then tore the pig brains in half and dropped them into the bag. Organ stew with extra brains. Convincing enough. And, as far as I knew, once the body left the morgue, no one opened the organ bags. Score one for Angel.

Feeling pretty damn good about the whole thing, I grabbed my bag of festival clothes and headed into the bathroom. My fake zombie costume consisted of a pair of hole-y jeans and a ripped white tank top with old barbecue stains and fresh fake blood.

The door from the parking lot clanged as I finished slipping into the tank top. "Angel?" Nick called out.

"Be right out!" I checked my reflection and adjusted the tank top. Crap. Was my bra showing? And why the hell was I nervous? It wasn't as if this was a date. Nick and I spent loads of time together outside work, especially with all the tutoring. I stuffed my good clothes into the plastic bag, and headed out. "Okay, I'm almost ready for—"

Zombie Nick shambled toward me, arms outstretched. "Braaaiiins." He wore a suit and tie frayed and aged to appear as if it had been moldering in a crypt for half a century. Grey makeup covered his hands, neck, and face.

I let out a delighted laugh. "Dude, that's awesome!" A hole in his shirt revealed a fake wound that wriggled with mealworms sealed behind a near-invisible mesh. "And seriously gross," I added with a grin.

"Braaaiiins." Slack jawed, he reached for me.

Laughing, I ducked under his arms and thwacked him with the grocery bag. "I'm a zombie too! Save it for the hunters. Besides, zombies don't eat zombie brains. Ewww!"

Nick grinned and ceased his shambling. "All right, Miss Zombie-Expert. I need a bit of help with this." He held up a realistic dangling latex eyeball.

"Niiiice," I said with a nod of approval. It would look great hanging out the eyehole of one of the zombie Mardi Gras masks I bought, if he wanted to wear one. "But you have to do my makeup first."

"What? You don't want me slathering goop on you when I'm half blind?" He closed his eyes and groped toward my face.

I laughed and batted his hand away. "I want to look like a zombie, not a clown. And I don't want you poking makeup brushes in my eyes!"

"Chicken." He grinned. "I'll grab my kit."

I plunked down in the chair, still smiling. Nick returned, carrying a small plastic tackle box. He sat in the other chair and set the box on my thighs. "Let's see what we can do to ugly you up."

I let out a tragic sigh. "You've got your work cut out for you."

He flipped open the lid of the box, and I blinked in surprise at the contents. Makeup and brushes and sponges galore, and all of it appearing well-used. He fished a black stick out of the bottom. "Start simple. Sunken eyes."

"How do you have so much makeup?" I grinned. "Do you do drag on the side?"

His lips twitched. "I'm not *that* good. I used to do theater. Did tons of plays with Tucker Point Little Theater up until I was seventeen."

"That's so cool!" I breathed. That was the most Nick had ever told me about his background in all the time I'd worked with him. Other than his rub-it-in-your-face crowing about being pre-med and going to med school, he didn't mention his personal life much. "A friend and her mom took me there to see *Wizard of Oz* for my tenth birthday. It was amazing."

Nick grinned. "You liked it, huh?" He rubbed the stick under my eyes then used his thumb to expertly smudge the color.

"Sure did. The way they did the smoke for the wizard. And the costumes!" I smiled, shrugged. "It was probably crap for real, but back then it felt like magic. I'd never seen anything like it. Real people singing and dancing and performing a *story*."

"It wasn't crap." He exchanged the black stick for a small pot of white goop. "That show won the Louisiana Community Theater award for best children's production."

"You remember that?" My phone beeped with a text message. A quick glance told me it wasn't anyone in my contacts, which meant it could wait.

A smile played around his mouth as he dabbed goop along my cheekbones. "I sure do."

My slow brain finally put two and two together. "Wait. Were you *in* it?"

"Yep." He closed the pot then wrung his hands and screwed his face into a mask of worry.

"The cowardly lion!? That was you?" I stared at him in awe. "I loved the lion!"

Nick beamed as he brushed powder on my nose. "Really?"

"Yeah. You were great." I sighed in happy memory. "Such a scaredy cat, then you found your courage."

Nick's smile slipped a little. Had I said something wrong? But he seemed to be proud of the role. "How'd you get the tail to swish like that?" I asked. "It had a mind of its own."

He perked up again. "A munchkin's dad rigged it up with fishing line and—" His phone rang. He glanced at the ID and couldn't hide a grimace. "Sorry, Angel. I have to take this."

He hurried out, far enough to be out of human earshot. Of course, I wasn't exactly human. I pulled a baggie out of my pocket and munched a few dehydrated brain chips. And then a few more. The stupid V12 in my system meant I needed more brains than usual to activate my zombie senses. But hey, I wasn't *spying*. I was hungry.

Nick's voice carried to me. *I can't believe you want to do this today.*

Pause.

No. That's not what I mean. I just don't—

Pause.

No. I told you, everything's fine. Monday's better for me. I'm on my way to the—

The stress in his voice ratcheted up.

Okay. Okay. Sorry.

Pause.

No! Not your house. How about a restaurant instead. Crawfish Joe's. It'll be good. And if we go at five, we'll beat the festival crowds.

That sure was a hard sales pitch for the restaurant instead of whoever's house. Public rather than private?

Yes. I'll be there.

Pause.

I said I will, so I will. I have to go.

The phone beeped as he ended the call.

Fuck. Fuck!

I barely got the brain chips back into my pocket before he swept in, his face set in his arrogant Nick the Prick sneer.

"Change of plans." He slammed the makeup box closed and snatched it off my lap. "Something came up. You go. Your name's on the pass, so it's useless to anyone else." For all his bluster, his voice shook.

I grabbed at his arm. "Nick, what happened? Is there anything I can do to help?"

He wrenched away from me. "Yeah. Mind your own god-damn business." He threw a laminated Zombie Fest pass on the desk then stomped out.

Holy shit. Damn good thing I'd eavesdropped, otherwise I'd be chasing him down to tell him exactly how to shove his makeup kit up his ass. Sideways. Instead, I was worried. It sure didn't sound like he wanted to meet with the jerkwad caller. Plus, if they were supposed to meet at five, we'd still have several hours to go to the festival. But he was upset enough to bow out altogether. Was he in some kind of trouble?

I needed more info, and I knew one possible way to get it. Crawfish Joe's Cajun Cabin made a great catfish po-boy, and a girl had to eat. Who knows, maybe I'd feed myself there around five p.m.

First, though, I had business at the Zombie Fest. Why had Grayson Seeger wanted to meet with Andrew? Did it tie in to why Seeger had been so worked up? And did the Three Dumbass Stooges have anything to do with Seeger's murder? With luck, a little quality Angel-spying would put those questions to rest for good.

I had a VIP pass, and I wasn't afraid to use it.

Chapter 13

Though Tucker Point was the primary hotbed of Zombie Fest hoopla, the site of the Fifth Annual Deep South Zombie Fest was about fifteen minutes east of the city on sixty acres of former farmland owned by Ms. Charlotte Glaspy. Her father had bought it almost twenty years ago with the intention of building an outlet mall, but had been nice enough to choke to death on a strawberry before cutting down a single tree. Ms. Charlotte, his only heir, apparently decided that an inheritance of several million dollars was plenty and saw no need to add to it by messing up a really nice chunk of land. With plenty of open pasture and wooded areas, the Glaspy property soon became a popular spot for a variety of outdoor concerts and festivals.

And, to my shame, I'd never once been out there despite living in the area my entire life. Fortunately, a multitude of signs between the highway and the festival grounds made it easy to figure out where to go. Dozens of people in zombie makeup and reflective vests directed cars down back roads, toward broad fields, and into neat rows. Once parked, I joined the line to get in and grinned up at the awesome entrance gate—a barrier ten feet high and fifty feet long that resembled a pile of hundreds of rotting zombies. Animatronic heads moved, and arms reached out toward the arriving crowd. At the very top, actors in zombie getup crawled and moaned and made grabs at people. A ragged tunnel cut right through the middle of the pile and led to the Fest itself.

When I managed to drag my ooo-ahh gaze from the gate, I did a double-take at a woman in line who looked as if her face was falling off. She wasn't the only one with a kickass makeup job. A teen girl had gore dripping down her throat and wiggly intestines poking out of her stomach. A man with salt-and-pepper hair gestured with a skeletal hand that still had bits of flesh clinging to it. It took me several confused seconds to realize he was an amputee wearing the bone-and-gore hand in place of a prosthetic.

Fortunately, I was hungry enough to verify that all these people in amazing makeup really *were* humans with nice juicy human brains. If not for that handy little superpower, I'd have been hard pressed to tell they weren't rotting. It was too bad Nick hadn't been able to finish my makeup before getting that phone call. And what the hell was that about anyway? I intended to damn well figure out what happened.

At the gate, a round-faced man in a black DSZF T-shirt smiled as he took people's tickets but, when I handed over my VIP pass, his face positively lit up.

"Welcome to the Zombie Fest-er, Miss Crawford!" He pulled a blue and green lanyard out of a box, looped it through the hole in the top of the pass then slipped it over my head with a flourish. "This pass gets you into the VIP Graveyard!" He gestured with excitement toward an enormous white tent off to the right beyond the gate. "VIP members *only!* Plenty of free food and drink as well as trained experts who'll help with makeup and costumes. *Plus*, you get to have your picture taken with Justine Chu." He quivered in glee. "Oh, and don't forget the sneak preview of the 'documentary'"—he even made air quotes—

"*Zombies Are Among Us!!* You can see the trailer in the Graveyard today at two and four, and there'll be a special screening of the whole thing tomorrow."

With that, my VIP pass and I made our way through the gate. It looked as if half of Tucker Point was already inside with the other half waiting to get in, and twice as many out-of-towners. Less than a third or so were in costume or makeup, but everyone seemed to be in the spirit of things.

To my left stood dozens of booths selling merchandise or food, with a large Bear's Den booth dominating the pack. Several delightfully cheesy carnival rides occupied the center of the main Fest area, and a large and deliberately crude sign pointed beyond the rides to "Hunting Grounds." And that barely scratched the surface of the spectacle. It was as if the Fest and studio people had started with one of those great big church fairs with all the rides and crafts and game booths, added a dash of Louisiana Crawfish festival with beer trucks and every kind of amazing food, then piled on zombies, paintball, and Hollywood. It was insane and utterly awesome.

I checked at an information booth for the times of the afternoon hunts and learned that prep didn't start for another hour and a half. Good. That meant I had time to track down Andrew Saber before I went searching for Randy, Judd, and Coy. And I knew right where to start.

Like a fancy white circus tent with six peaks, the VIP Graveyard sprawled over enough real estate to house a jumbo jet. Framing the entrance were two humongous statues locked in mortal combat: one a fierce huntress with a machete and the other a rotting high school football player.

I half-expected to be turned away despite my VIP pass, since I hardly looked like a Very Important anything. But the security guard simply flashed a UV light at my pass then waved me in. I walked between the statues and stepped from bright afternoon into an incredible moonlit graveyard. Clever lighting transformed the top of the tent into starry blackness, and a full "moon" high in the center cast pale light over everything. Props, plants, and landscaping combined to create a realistic and creepy graveyard about the size of a tennis court and ringed by a wrought iron fence. People milled beyond it, crowding around exhibits and clustering in social groups. I followed a gravel path through the graveyard and a creaky gate, and then into the main affair of food and fun.

A scan of the other VIPs showed me that this was the Rich People tent, no doubt about it. Perfect teeth and smooth skin, trim bodies honed beneath a surgeon's knife or a hot-yet-stern trainer's eyes, jeans that cost what I made in a week, elegant manicures on both genders, and not a split end or bad dye job in sight. Even the people in costume were in niiiiiice costumes, hunters and zombies alike. I also noted way too many men making idiots of themselves over actress and zombie-hunting heroine Justine Chu, which proved once again that money couldn't cure stupid. Then again, she was plenty gorgeous—almond-shaped eyes, high cheekbones and full lips, and an athletic figure that still had enviable curves. Fortunately for her, two crew members kept the line moving and discreetly intervened whenever it looked as if a fan was getting a bit too adoring.

I spied Andrew near a giveaway table stocked with zombie farmer dolls riding Saberton farm equipment. To my amusement, he was damn near as popular as Justine even though he wasn't *quite* as pretty. I spared a moment to watch him deftly handle a variety of wannabe business partners as well as several women who were wannabe Mrs. Andrew Sabers, each angling to become the heiress-by-marriage of the Saber fortune.

Oh, if they only knew they were fawning over a real zombie.

I helped myself to a sparkling juice and several way-yummy crawfish canapés, and watched Andrew in my peripheral vision as he talked to people and smiled the kind of smile you put on when you don't feel like smiling. Standing a dozen feet to his left was a woman in a crisp pantsuit and a serious expression. Thea Braddock, the Saberton head of security from New York. During our raid, Pierce had spared her life because he considered her a decent person and believed she'd been unaware of the atrocities inflicted upon zombies in the Saberton subbasement.

Her gaze skimmed over me and stopped. She recognized me from the New York showdown. I gave her a polite nod. Her eyes narrowed, but she offered a micronod in return which clearly said *I'm watching you, and if you pull any stunts I'll flatten you.* Off to Andrew's right stood another Saberton bodyguard, Tom Snyder, dressed in a tailored dark suit. As far as I knew, he hadn't been involved in the zombie lab shit. Good thing. If he was one of the fuckers who'd helped torture and abuse zombies, I'd be starting a whole different kind of zombie hunt at this shindig. In any case, neither of them knew their boss was a zombie.

The gaggle of hopefuls around Andrew finally moved on, and his smile dropped away as if it weighed a hundred pounds. He reached behind a sign on the table, retrieved a blender bottle and gave it a shake. He took a long drink—of brain shake, I figured—then closed his eyes and pinched the bridge of his nose as if he had a headache. My stomach growled, and I gave it a pat. *Hush now, Mama will give you a brain packet as soon as I have a little privacy.*

I sidled to within a couple of feet of him, well aware that Thea Braddock had her eye on me. "Ohhh, Mr. Saber!" I purred in a mockery of the women who'd been fawning over him. He startled and snapped his eyes open. "You're so handsome," I gushed and fluttered my eyelashes as he glared. "And RICH!"

Braddock moved toward us but stopped when Andrew waved her off. She eased back but continued to give me the stinkeye.

"You're a laugh a minute, Angel," Andrew sneered, putting on a scowly face which was as much a show for onlookers as it was directed at me. It wouldn't do for the Saberton security peeps to see two supposed enemies acting cozy. He continued more quietly, "Did you get my message?"

Crap. That must have been the text that came in when I was talking to Nick. "Things were hectic after you called. What's up?"

"I found out that my mother is flying to Portland today."

Double Triple Crap. I nibbled at my canapé. "Kristi Charish is in Portland." And, as of yesterday, so were Pierce, Marcus, Brian, and Kyle.

"From what I've heard, Charish has notes and documentation from the Dallas lab."

"So?" I frowned. Surely a lab like that had copies of documentation all over the place. "Were all the backups destroyed? And why doesn't she just FedEx them to Nicole?"

"I'm not in the loop, but it's clear there's more going on. When Charish esca—" He stopped and cleared his throat. "When she disappeared the week before your people raided the Dallas lab, she took files with her. This is the first we've heard of her since then."

Escaped? That was damn interesting. Sounded like Saberton had been holding her as a captive researcher in their Dallas zombie lab. I'd last seen Kristi Charish right before New York, when she was working with Dr. Nikas—as *our* captive researcher. Saberton was responsible for her escape from the Tribe, and I would have bet anything that she'd pounce on the chance to work with Saberton—and their resources. Orrrrrr maybe she *had* pounced on the chance and then, once she discovered that she wasn't going to be top dog at the Dallas lab, got pissy and had to be locked down. That sounded like the Kristi Charish I knew and loathed. "Are you telling me Saberton had no idea where she went after she fled Dallas?"

"That's right. I notified Naomi yesterday when Charish contacted my mother. That's all I know." He took another long pull from the bottle and gave a barely perceptible shudder. I doubted it was because of the taste of the brains in his "protein drink." Way more likely that he was having a tough time adjusting to the scent of so many fresh live brains around him. I remembered how crazy hungry I'd been as a new zombie. Poor dude was going through the same shit. I could sympathize since my own brain hunger clamored as if I hadn't eaten in days and days. If it wasn't for the pesky fact that Ms. Braddock would have me face down on the grass with a knee on my back in the blink of an eye, I'd probably try to snag the bottle out of his hand and chug it down.

I lowered my voice more. "Top off more than you think you need when you have to go out in public."

His hand tightened on the bottle, and his eyes flashed in frustrated outrage at his situation. Yet he took another long slug. "What the hell am I supposed to do if my mother brings Charish to New York?" he muttered.

I crammed the rest of the canapé into my mouth, chewed and swallowed before speaking. "You get up in the morning, take a shit, eat breakfast, work out, shower, or whatever the hell you usually do, then go to work and do the same crap you've always done. Charish has worked around zombies, but she's only human. She can't smell brains and doesn't have any superpowers that'll tell her you're *different.*"

Andrew didn't look convinced. "No one has suspected so far." He took another drink from the bottle as if drawing reassurance. "If I get outed, I'll end up as a test subject. My mother is heartless."

"No one's outing anyone," I said with absolute certainty. Too much at stake. For me as well. If Andrew got outed, it would push the Tribe closer to exodus. "No one will suspect." I shut up and plastered on a bland smile as Braddock approached.

She touched Andrew's arm. "Mr. Saber? You're on in ten minutes, and the promoter would like to go over a few things with you beforehand."

Andrew nodded. "Thank you, Ms. Braddock."

Braddock gave me another pointed once-over then returned to her former position.

I finished my juice and tossed my cup into a trash barrel. My bladder politely informed me that I was going to need to do something soon about all the juice I drank, which in turn reminded me of Andrew's porta-potty call. "How do you know Grayson Seeger?"

"Only in passing from Saberton's association with the movie."

I gave Andrew a stiff smile. "You mean Saberton's abuse of extras for unethical zombie experiments?"

He glared at me. "I mean Saberton's position as a financial backer to one of his productions."

"Whatever." I rolled my eyes. "Why did he want a meeting?"

Andrew's face bunched in a perplexed frown. "I don't know. He said it was an important deal that I didn't want to miss. I agreed to meet him for lunch. But . . ."

"He got whacked before he could give you the deal of a lifetime." My frown echoed his. More clues and bits of info, but still nothing resembling a full picture. Yet. "Whatcha doing in ten minutes?"

He scowled, and this time it wasn't for show. "Promo for the *Zombies Are Among Us!!* documentary. Part of the deal with the production company. Stupid shit."

I snorted. "Well, try and act like you're having fun, 'kay? After all, you're *Andrew Saber!*" I fluttered my lashes again.

Andrew drained the last dregs from the bottle, then casually flipped me off. "To keep up appearances," he said with a tight smile. "You understand."

"Ditto," I said brightly and returned the gesture, then sauntered off as if I didn't have a care in the world. But as soon as I was well away from him, I texted Brian.

Queen Bitch is flying to that place you went yesterday. Her puppy says there's funny business. If the FBI was monitoring my texts I didn't want to make it easy for them.

Nicole. Portland. Got it. Tell the rest to the doc.

I rolled my eyes. Jerk. See if I ever tried to be cautious again. *And you're an asshole.*

10-4. No argument there.

Smiling, I sauntered around the tent until I found a quiet corner where I was sure no one could overhear me, then called Dr. Nikas and filled him in. He asked a few questions, clarified a few points, thanked me and hung up.

Cool. Phase one of my Fest mission complete. Now for phase two: get more free food.

Chapter 14

The crawfish things were gone, but in their place were cream cheese and salmon rolls. I scarfed several down, not only because they were seriously delish, but also because I hoped real food would help keep the other hunger at bay, at least for a little while.

My next stop was the makeup table where I got a shockingly realistic protruding skull fragment attached to my forehead by a woman who kept up a cheerful stream of chatter about the various movies she'd worked on. Damn, Nick would've loved this shit. And he must have paid a rotting arm and leg for the VIP passes. It *sucked* that he couldn't be here.

By the time my forehead was nicely uglified, the line to get a picture taken with Justine Chu had dwindled to nothing. Probably because she was finishing up for the day, I realized as I noticed her security guard helping the two crew members carry plastic crates full of promotional materials out the back of the tent.

My watch said I still had five minutes before the picture-taking ended, and so I trotted my scrawny ass over. I missed being first by a matter of seconds, beaten out by a tall blond guy in his mid-twenties in red skinny trousers and a dark blue polo shirt. He was tanned and fairly good-looking, and I might have been attracted to him except for his smirk that told me he was used to getting his way. Plus, it was clear he'd already paid several visits to the open bar.

Justine Chu was only a few inches taller than me, which I hadn't expected. I'd always figured that being crazy tall was a requirement to be a movie star. She gave the blond guy a bright smile as he stepped up, but I didn't miss the quick flash of dislike.

"Back again!" he announced with a self-satisfied grin. "I know you missed me. I thought of another pose to do with you. You'll *love* this one."

Her smile turned brittle. "Sounds great, Sergei," she said, making zero effort to sound convincing.

Sergei? I bit back a snigger. He didn't look like a Sergei to me. Bradford or Ambrose maybe—something more Ivy-League-preppy-I'm-so-entitled.

I waited at the front of the line, marked by a square of red carpet to the right of the photographer. The photo area consisted of three backdrops showing different scenes from the movie. Justine moved to stand in front of the one for the science classroom, but stiffened when Sergei slung an arm around her waist and leered at the camera. Okay, it was official: I never ever wanted to be a movie star. Not if I had to put up with that kind of shit. My opinion of Justine's acting skills climbed higher as she maintained the smile despite having been through this crap a few hundred times today.

But Justine sucked in a shocked breath when Sergei shifted his hand to cup the side of her boob. I whirled in search of help, but the poor camera girl stood frozen in horror, and everyone else in the tent seemed to be distracted by a door prize drawing. What the hell was taking Justine's security so long?

To her credit, Justine didn't stay shocked. "Get *off* me!" Eyes blazing in fury, she dug an elbow into Sergei's ribs to push him off, but he shifted his hand to grab even more tit.

"C'mon, one more pic!" He laughed and wrestled her closer. "Let's make it a good one!"

Screw this. "Oh my god!" I shrieked. "It's Val Kilmer!" I didn't have zombie speed at the moment, but I had fuck-this-asshole speed. I bounded forward, and before he had a chance to register the skinny form hurtling toward him, I leaped, and threw my arms around his neck in a death-grip.

"What the—" His words cut off with a croak as I tightened my bicep against his windpipe. He staggered a step then—as I'd hoped—let go of Justine to deal with the crazy chick latched on like a face-hugger. The instant Justine backed off, I released my super-affectionate hold and dropped to the ground, then stepped between Justine and the sleazeball.

"The hell?" I said in outrage I didn't have to fake. "You're not Val Kilmer! How dare you pretend to be him!"

Sergei coughed. "Wait, what?"

I planted my hands on my hips. "You're not Val Kilmer, asshole, which means it's my turn with Justine."

His face darkened. "Get out of my way, you crazy bitch. I—"

"*No,*" Justine said with seething force. "You're finished. Move along before I have you arrested."

I clapped my hands like a manic pixie. "Run along now, you big faker!"

"Bullshit." He leveled a haughty sneer over my head at Justine. "My father invested heavily in this movie. I'll make sure you never work—"

He stopped as a throbbing growl built in my throat. Teeth bared, I met his eyes steadily, watched his ego war with the overworked survival instinct that told him not to tangle with the scary trashy chick.

"Screw this," he muttered and managed a pathetic glare before slinking off.

"Oh god," Justine said, voice quavering. I whirled, dismayed at the sight of tears rolling down her cheeks. "Val Kilmer," she gasped. "Oh Jesus, Val Kilmer."

Those were tears of *laughter*. I grinned, relieved. "It was the first thing that popped into my head. Sorry. I didn't see any security, and you didn't look real happy."

She flicked the tears away without smudging her makeup then gave me a brilliant smile. "You're right, I wasn't happy at all. Since no one was in line, I asked my security guard if he'd help Mandy and Chad carry the crates to the van. I'm sure that's what Sergei was waiting for. I was about to do something violent and no doubt bad for my career when you stepped in."

"He's a douche-nozzle," I said. "Who's his daddy? I'll go beat him up next."

Justine sighed. "His father passed away a few months ago—Pietro Ivanov, who seemed like a nice man when I met him last year. But his son is nothing like—"

I snapped my hand up. "Hang on. That asstard told you *Pietro* was his dad?"

Her eyes slitted at the edge in my voice. "That's what he told me the first time he came through the line." Her mouth tightened. "And I believed him. I'm an idiot."

"Nah, he's just an ass who figured he could get away with it since Pietro isn't around to say otherwise."

She arched an eyebrow. "You knew Pietro?"

Still do, I thought, hiding a smile. "I used to date his nephew," I said with a shrug.

Her security guard jogged up, consternation on his face. Justine filled him in on what happened, managing to make the part where I jumped on "Sergei" sound way more heroic than it actually was. The guard summoned the deputies, the camera girl showed them the boob-grab pics, and Justine and I watched in delight as the asshole—a.k.a. Boswell Carlton—was arrested and carted off. *Ha! I knew he wasn't a Sergei!*

"Oh, crap." Justine grimaced. "You never got your picture. I have to go introduce the *Zombies Are Among Us!!* trailer, then I have a gig right after. Are you going to be around tomorrow?"

"Probably not," I said, "but I don't need the pic anymore. Jumping the guy was a lot more fun."

She chuckled. "Well, stop by tomorrow if you decide to come. And skip the line!" With that she hurried off toward a harried studio-type who didn't seem pleased that so much time had been wasted with Boswell's shenanigans.

I snagged a bottle of sparkling guava juice then found a spot not far from the stage where short little me could see. Andrew and Justine stepped onto the stage to a wave of mild applause, both smiling as if they were having the absolute best time EVER. Andrew gave a mercifully short and sweet speech about how excited he was for the movie release and how much it benefited the area, blah blah. He turned the microphone over to Justine who enthused about how terrific all the locals were and how she was the luckiest actress ever to have such a great role. Yeah, this lady was one hell of an actress to say all that with a straight face. Of course, everyone applauded.

Justine lifted a hand. The "moon" that lit the tent dimmed. "And now," she intoned, deep and dramatic, "a few scenes to whet your appetite for Infamous Vision Studio's latest short film release, premiering tomorrow at two p.m. here in the Fifth Annual Deep South Zombie Fest VIP Graveyard. It's the documentary *they* don't want you to see. You've been warned: *Zombies Are Among Us!!*"

Applause swelled again as Justine leaped nimbly off the stage. The moon went black, leaving only the stars above. Ominous music swelled, and the clapping died away.

The trailer began with a dark screen and narration in a James-Earl-Jones-deep voice.

"The Shocking Truth of monsters living *Right Next Door*."

I rolled my eyes at the "B-movie meets documentary" style, but I had to give props to the studio. The production quality was even better than *High School Zombie Apocalypse!!*, which did a lot to reduce the cheese-factor.

Subtitles flashed up, echoed by the narrator.

The Hidden Zombie. Faux-news footage showed a smiling woman working as a barista.

The Truth. A night scene with the same woman crouched beside a mangled corpse, gore on her face and hands, and a savage look in her eyes.

Several more scenes of people in ordinary jobs with quick scene cuts to show them killing and eating customers or patients or neighbors. I snorted. Please. I'd never once killed and eaten a customer or neighbor. And the bodies at the morgue could hardly be counted as patients.

"You've seen what zombies are like in movies." The narrator's voice resonated through the tent.

Another subtitle flashed. *Zombie Frenzy!*

The football field melée scene from *High School Zombie Apocalypse!!* filled the screen, except this clip was from a different camera angle than the ones used in the movie. It showed plenty of general movie zombie madness, but there I was at the back of the crowd, leaping on Philip and biting his neck to calm him down. I gulped, mouth dry. At least it didn't show either of our faces.

"Are you prepared for the reality?" the narrator asked, dark and serious. "The truth will *shock you*."

Dramatic music punctuated each word as it filled the screen—

ZOMBIES
ARE
AMONG
US

—followed by a rapid-fire series of gory images, too fast to register individually.

Short credits rolled, accompanied by eerie snarls. I spotted my murder victim's name, Grayson Seeger, listed as a producer. The final line told viewers to visit zombiesare amongus.com for more information.

Well, shit.

I managed to clap along with everyone else, forced a grin

onto my face as the moonlight returned. People jabbered in excited voices about the film as they milled toward the food, and the tent suddenly seemed way too hot and crowded. It shouldn't have surprised me that the studio used footage from that melée on the football field, but never in a million years did I expect them to make a "mockumentary" about it. Those fake documentaries were great and funny and all that, except for the pesky fact that there were always a few people who either didn't get that the shit was fake or wanted to believe it and started looking for mermaids and monster sharks. Despite the presumed absurdity of the subject matter, this little film did a damn good job of portraying the issue as legit and serious. The last thing any of us needed was for a moron viewer to get worked up and believe that zombies were real and needed to be hunted down. Especially with the angle of zombies living like ordinary people.

I made my escape through the graveyard and stepped out into the daylight. The abrupt shift helped drive away the creepiness of the video. Why the hell was I letting it get to me? It was just a silly piece of studio promotion. Besides, one of the reasons I'd come to the Fest was to get a read on the Three Dumbass Amigos about the murder. I needed to stop fiddlefucking around and get moving on that.

But my mind kept going back to the *Zombie Frenzy!* subtitle that had accompanied the melée scene. I'd seen it before, handwritten on the paper I found in Seeger's pocket, with an arrow to the filename *zombie_frenzy*. I ducked into a porta-potty and took care of my insistent bladder, then pulled the paper from my bra. *Zombie_frenzy* had one asterisk, which meant "approved by DR for ZAAU," according to the notation. As I'd suspected, ZAAU was short for *Zombies Are Among Us!!* I scanned the other files marked with single asterisks: *zombie_heal_1, zombie_amputation, zombie_feeding_3, zombie_speed.* My uneasiness increased. Would there be healing and speed segments in the documentary too?

No question—I was definitely coming back tomorrow afternoon to see all of *Zombies Are Among Us!!* Maybe I'd get that picture taken with Justine after all.

Clear skies and brilliant sunlight lorded over a Fest in full, raucous swing. Merchants hawked everything from munchies to zombie puppets, and kids squealed in fearful delight on the carnival rides. On the big stage, a zydeco band played to a lively crowd, with at least a dozen couples twirling in a high-energy Cajun two-step. And through it all wound the mouth-watering aromas of crab boil and jambalaya, café au lait and beignets.

My Deep South brethren were doing what they did best: enjoying the hell out of a party.

A packet of "ProteinGel" quieted my brain hunger and sharpened my senses a bit. Smiling, I wove through the rotting rabble toward the Hunting Grounds. Laughter and applause broke out from the crowd gathered in a hay bale amphitheater, and an announcer's voice cut through the clamor. "You can't fool the Marquise de Saber, folks! She'll root out zombies every time."

The Marquise de what? A sharp bark issued from the direction of the stage. Curious, I wormed my way through clusters of people until I had a decent view. On the stage stood a man dressed in a military-style zombie hunting outfit with a sheathed machete slung across his back. A German Shepherd sat beside him. I narrowed my eyes. That was Tactical Pants Man and his goddamn cadaver dog.

"For the last demonstration, it's your turn to see if you can trick her," the announcer continued from the edge of the stage. "Dante will take her offstage so she can't peek."

Dante? At least he looked like a Dante. Man and dog disappeared through the back stage curtain. Yep, definitely Tactical Pants Man. I'd know that ass anywhere.

The announcer gestured with one hand. "Everyone who received a box at the beginning, come on up!"

A dozen people made their way to the stage, ranging in

age from preteen to a couple in their eighties. Each carried
a wooden box about the size of a loaf of Bunny Bread and
sealed with a padlock. While the announcer lined up the
participants, the words *Dante Rosario and the Marquise de
Saber* filled the screen above the stage, followed by *Paws of
Service. Paws of Pride.* Stirring music swelled as the video
showed Rosario and the dog picking through smoking rub-
ble, working next to cops as they combed through woods,
and locating a missing child. It closed with a shot of the pair
standing proud as a list scrolled by of the places where
they'd volunteered, with a giant Saberton Corporation logo
at the very end. Even I had to admit it looked seriously
cool. Damn it.

The announcer swept his arm toward the participants.
"One of those boxes, and *only* one, contains a zombie hand.
It's up to the Marquise to find that hand. If she fails, every-
one in this audience wins a pair of tickets to *High School
Zombie Apocalypse!!*" He paused and smiled for the ap-
plause. "Of course, if she succeeds in finding it, you all lose!"
He grinned at the chorus of boos. "But not to worry. No
matter the outcome, each of our contestants here on the
stage will win a free item of their choice from the Tasty
Brains booth *and* a ticket for tomorrow's raffle!"

The crowd cheered again, and Rosario returned to the
stage with the dog trotting along happily beside him. I
edged behind the woman next to me. Cadaver dogs made
me more than a little nervous, even when they were just
doing their job.

"All's fair in a zombie war," the announcer told the people lined up across the stage. "Feel free to try and distract
the Marquise. Dance or holler or stand on your head, but
no touching her." His gaze swept the audience. "All y'all can
help, too. Remember, *everybody* wins if she gets it wrong!"

The participants and audience started enough whooping,
hollering, and gyrating to rival the antics of Saints fans
when their team played the Falcons. Rosario and the Marquise de Saber paced in front of the participants. She didn't

so much as twitch an ear in reaction to anyone, but I had a feeling Rosario hadn't given her the command to seek yet. He knew what he was doing. Playing it up big for the crowd. Building the suspense. At the perfect moment, he tapped his thigh in what I suspected was the signal for the dog to do her thing. She made one pass down the line, sniffing. Then she came back, halted in front of a teenage boy and dropped to her belly, ears perked and eyes riveted on the box in his hands.

Rosario called the dog off, and an assistant unlocked all of the boxes. One by one, the contestants opened their empty boxes, leaving the boy until last. He opened his box to reveal a fake zombie hand, to an uproar of applause and cheers. The announcer lifted it and waggled it at the crowd. I had little doubt that there was a bit of dead human hidden in that hand for the Marquise to scent. Not all that shocking considering that cadaver dogs were trained with donated cadaver tissue.

"There you have it, folks. Give a big round of applause to Dante and the Marquise de Saber. Catch their demos twice every day of the Zombie Fest. Bring your friends!"

Rosario waved at the crowd. The dog lifted her paw, too, eliciting a round of laughter and applause and waving back. The Marquise's ears perked as the breeze shifted, and she looked my way. Shit. I was a little on the rotten side due to the V12. Not enough for people to notice, but plenty of stench for a cadaver dog. I stepped back, but not before Rosario met my eyes. It was only for an instant, until I let the crowd swallow me, but cold settled in my belly. A Saberton-sponsored guy with a cadaver dog. Even though it was obvious the pair did a lot of demos, and Tucker Point might simply be one stop on the tour, I didn't trust anything that connected Saberton and zombies. I'd keep my Angel-sense sharp around this guy.

"Your donation to support training of service dogs is greatly appreciated," the announcer continued. "Cash, check, or card! And remember, Saberton Corporation will match your donation two to one. You heard that right! For every dollar you give, the dogs get three!"

Because Saberton is so kind and fucking charitable.

But enough of that shit. Time to put it behind me and get on with finding the guys.

After following the signs to the Hunting Grounds—and hitching a ride on a passing four-wheeler—I found the Three Dumbass Amigos in their zombie hunter outfits near a pair of stately oak trees. They had their heads together, engaged in discussion intense enough that they didn't notice me walk up.

"HI, GUYS!" I said, nice and loud, tickled when all three startled and made various *Jesus fuck, Angel!* type of exclamations.

Randy recovered first and gave me a sour look. "Thought you weren't coming out with us." He flicked my VIP badge on its lanyard. "Where's your boyfriend?"

Was that jealousy? I flicked his earlobe in return. "Oh, you mean my *girlfriend* Justine Chu? She's getting her picture taken with the other VIPs."

Randy stared at me for a second then snorted and gave my shoulder a light shove. "Almost had me going there."

Judd took a swig from a bottle of ginger ale, scowled. "Randy, c'mon. We gotta get our shit together." He gave me a tight smile lacking any hint of friendliness. "Sorry, sweetcakes. We have work to do."

"That's cool!" I chirped. "I don't have anything else going on. Happy to tag along and help out."

Coy gulped, eyes wide. "Nah, it's for hunters only. You said you didn't want to hunt, and uh, you even came as a zombie." He gestured frantically at my makeup and clothing.

"Oh! No, I'm really a hunter," I said. "See, I dressed up as a zombie to make the other zombies less suspicious. It's like wearing camouflage." No way was I giving in that easily. "Okay, it's settled then. Let's roll!"

Judd's face reddened. "Hang on, we don't have you registered, which means you can't go on the hunt with us." He shot a Do Something glare in Randy's direction. "Right?"

Randy jammed a hand through his hair. "You two go get set up," he told Judd and Coy. "I'll take care of this." After a brief hesitation, the men moved off. Randy turned to me. "Look, Angel, forget the hunt. I didn't register you."

I acted hurt. "What the hell, man? Are you really bent out of shape because a coworker gave me a VIP pass?"

"You're the one who told me you weren't gonna come out with me this afternoon," he shot back. "Don't blame me."

"I was still dealing with my shitty morning when I said that. A five a.m. call to pick up a dude with his head chopped off tends to throw me off my rhythm."

"I'm supposed to know you changed your mind? That's bullshit, Angel."

If this was a real argument, he'd have a point. "Okay, well, I changed it." I softened my voice. "Can't you put my name down for the team?"

He glanced at the retreating Judd and Coy. "They won't let me," he said. "The, uh, registration people."

Right. I knew who he meant. "Could you at least try?" I jiggled my VIP badge. "I betcha this will get me in."

Randy looked down at the badge as if it was a horrible truth—which it likely was. His shoulders slumped. "Sure. Let's go see what that thing can do."

Giving a great impression of a man heading to his execution, he walked with me to the registration table. Once there, I was delighted to learn that Randy had in fact included me when he'd turned in the team members, which meant I was already signed up. All I had to do was fill out a couple of forms and sign the release and waiver of liability. *Take that and shove it up your ass, Judd.*

As soon as I finished the paperwork, we headed to the prep area. Randy appeared calm and laid back, but I'd known him for too long not to notice the little signs of stress. The way he rubbed his left thumb and finger together. His lack of friendly banter. The creases on his forehead.

Not that I had any room to talk since I was just as stressed. I wanted desperately for my suspicions to be wrong, but it wasn't easy with how squirrelly all three were acting. It also didn't help that I kept getting annoying stabs of brain hunger despite the recent "ProteinGel" brain packet. To my relief, Randy wasn't paying close attention to me, and I managed to sneak a few brain chips into my mouth and gulp them down. That settled the hunger again—for now.

"So, how's this zombie hunt thing work?" I asked Randy as we neared the prep area.

He blinked as if he'd been deep in thought. "We gear up and load weapons, then around fifteen minutes before our hunt the coordinators come around and check the shit for safety. Once that's done, we climb in the truck," he lifted his chin toward a big black pickup with a giant zombie decal plastered along the side, "and they take us to the beginning of the course. When it starts, we have thirty minutes to get through the course without getting painted by any zombies, and at the end you're scored for how many hits you get on them."

"Painted?" I asked, frowning. "The zombies have paint-ball guns, too?"

Randy shook his head. "Nah, see, the only zombies on the course are the ones the Fest hires, and they have gloves that leave paint on you. Plus they have all sorts of people out there watching for cheaters. You lose points any time a zombie grabs you, and if you get grabbed three times you're dead, though your points still count for your team. If you get disqualified for safety violations, none of your points count."

A six-foot-tall sign near the pickup had THE RULES emblazoned at the top. A quick scan showed plenty of sensible guidelines such as No open-toed shoes, No shooting point blank/within five feet, No touching or grabbing zombies, NO DRUGS OR ALCOHOL. A line at the bottom stated that Zombie Fest officials reserved the right to eject anyone at any time based on whatever criteria they wanted to use. Nice.

"I gotta know," I said to Randy. "Does Judd really think people believe he's drinking ginger ale?"

Randy's mouth twitched. "Dunno what you mean. Looks like ginger ale to me."

Judd and Coy stood by a sign with a big red "13" on it. Coy tugged on his equipment vest while Judd checked his paintball rifle. Judd's mouth tightened at the sight of me. He nudged Coy and murmured something. Coy glanced my way then suddenly became super concerned with the positioning of his gear.

I spied a foam machete lying on the ground a few feet away. "You bringing this, too?" I asked Randy as I scooped it up.

"Nah, that's not allowed in the hunt," he said. "There's a group of people who do a kind of role-play zombie attack thing after hours where they bash each other with hard foam stuff. One of 'em must've left it behind."

"That sounds like fun." I made a few chopping swings with the foam machete then let out a laugh. "Whack whack whack! Hack a zombie's head clean off."

Coy's throat worked. He turned away and busied himself adjusting the vest.

"Put that down before you do something stupid!" Judd snapped.

Gee, touchy much? I shifted to a two-handed grip. "C'mon, it's foam." I batted his arm. "How stupid can I get?"

Judd made an angry grab for the machete, but I jerked it out of his reach. His face reddened, and he balled his fist as if he was ready to take a swing at me, but Randy stepped between us.

"Hey, stop it! Both of you!"

"Jeez, lighten the hell up, Judd," I said.

Coy seized Judd's arm before he could respond and

dragged him away. "Dude, you're gonna fuck everything up," he murmured, and it was only because of my recent brain snack that I could hear him. He tugged Judd back another step and toward the pile of equipment. "Get your shit on so we can get this over with," he said at a more normal volume.

Randy let out a strained chuckle. "Yeah, I'm ready to be done with the prep shit and get to the good stuff."

Judd muttered a curse, stomped to the equipment, and started rooting through a bag. A sinking feeling threatened to tug my heart right into the ground. This was supposed to be a recreational activity. Coy and Judd were a bundle of nerves, and Randy was obviously trying to cover for their odd behavior.

Judd flipped open a small plastic case and began smearing on camo face paint. The sinking feeling abruptly tripled in strength. Green goop. Maybe it hadn't been bug shit on the cigarette butt.

"Y'know, I think maybe y'all will do better without me," I said and dropped the foam machete. "I need to take care of a few things anyway."

Randy couldn't hide his relief. "Yeah. Yeah, I under-stand." Not even a token effort to talk me into staying. He took my elbow to walk me out of the prep area, and I didn't resist. "Sorry, Angel," he said after we were a couple dozen yards away from the others. "It's . . ." He sighed. "Sorry."

Stress carved his face into sharp angles, as if he was car-rying the world on his shoulders. It seemed utterly wrong for him to look like that. This was Randy. Easy-going. Laid back. Barely ever worried about anything. "Randy," I said, voice soft, "is everything okay? You know you can tell me anything, right?" *Please, tell me*, I silently urged him. *Spill your guts so that we can fix this. I know something's wrong, dammit.*

Indecision flickered in his eyes, but then he shrugged it away. "What've I got to tell?" he said. "Oh, yeah. Ol' man Brody's truck needs a new tranny, and I'm here instead of working on it."

He'd have told me everything if it was only about him. But he wouldn't do that with others involved. *IF they're involved*, I reminded myself. I didn't know anything for certain yet. But, damn, the circumstantial evidence was piling up like crazy, and my zombie-senses were tingling.

"Okay. Just remember I'm here for you if you ever get in over your head." I exhaled. "I'll see you later."

He mumbled a goodbye then turned and walked back to the others, head bowed.

I stopped at the registration table on my way out, unsurprised to find that Randy's team was signed up for the night hunt as well. Didn't make sense to do so many hunts if they weren't actually having fun. But it *did* make sense if they were doing these stupid things as a cover, to act natural and throw off suspicion.

Fine with me. While they were busy hunting fake zombies, this zombie was going to hunt down a few clues.

Chapter 15

I had a few hours to kill before diving in to clue-hunting, since I wanted to be certain the boys would be occupied with the evening hunt while I snooped. That way I could count on at least a solid hour and a half to do my thing. Plus, it would be dark, which was always a bonus when doing a little lawbreaking.

I debated heading straight home to wash the makeup off, but my hunger pangs—both normal and brain-related—were kicking up a fuss. Besides, there were plenty of other people around town with zombie makeup on. I'd blend right in.

Not to mention, Nick was due to begin his mystery dinner meeting fairly soon. He could be secretive if he wanted. Dude was entitled to his privacy. Far from me to pry. Not my style. I *never* butted in where I wasn't wanted. Ever. Yup, I was mind-my-own-business girl. It was sheer coincidence that I happened to be on the road to Crawfish Joe's, and that I had a sudden craving for takeout.

Crawfish Joe's Cajun Cabin didn't look like much—a squat, wood frame building with a corrugated metal roof and colorful fish painted on the walls—but it had a reputation for the best seafood in three parishes. Legend had it that Joe's great granddad spent a week naked and alone in the swamp and came out with the secret recipe for the best seasoning ever.

Nick's car was in the parking lot—good thing, since I was so hungry I was going to get food here whether I could spy on him or not. Inside, half a dozen people waited for tables. Several gave me startled glances, which was when I realized I still had the skull fragment plastered to my forehead. Oops. The overworked hostess seemed relieved when I told her I wanted takeout, and waved me toward the bar. Several patrons occupied stools, and at the far end was a dude with green and white grease paint smeared on his face and wearing overalls spattered with fake blood. He glanced my way and gave me a thumbs up which I assumed was for my own far more professional and awesome makeup job. That or he could see my bra through the rip in my shirt.

A low wall and potted trees separated the bar from the restaurant. I grabbed a spot by the wall and peered through the branches to covertly scope out the customers. It didn't take me long to locate Nick. He sat angled away from me, enough that I could barely see the side of his face. But the mystery caller was . . . Bear?!

Yup, no question about it. The burly owner of The Bear's Den sat across from Nick. Bear had the remnants of a seafood platter in front of him and idly scooped fried shrimp through cocktail sauce. Nick's plate held a soft shell crab sandwich, though as far as I could tell he'd only taken a few bites.

The bartender handed me a menu. I ordered a Catfish po-boy and onion rings, then peered between the plants as soon as she left. Nick and Bear were too far away for me to hear their conversation, but it appeared pretty darn one-sided. Bear was doing most of the talking while Nick shrugged a few times and seemed to be focused on the sandwich he wasn't eating. Though I couldn't see much of his face, Nick's body language telegraphed *I'm not having fun, and I'm ready to go*.

Why had Nick agreed to what sure as hell seemed to be a not-very-friendly dinner? Job interview? Business deal? Maybe Bear was a second cousin, once removed, who Nick was forced to tolerate for the sake of family harmony? Whatever the reason, Nick looked miserable. Great, I was reduced to gawking through foliage at two people enduring a dinner together. Unexciting *and* uninformative.

Nick pushed his plate away then spoke. Bear went quiet and kept his eyes on Nick, but as the seconds ticked by his expression shifted from calm to shock to disbelief and, finally, to stony controlled anger.

The bartender brought my food out all nicely packed up, and I dragged my eyes from Nick and Bear long enough to hand over my debit card. When I resumed my spying, Bear was speaking through clenched teeth with an expression of Pissed to the Max. Not so unexciting anymore. I scooched my chair over a smidge to get a potted ficus between me and their table in case either of them glanced in my direction. Nick held his hands up, palms toward Bear, but whatever he said wasn't enough to placate Bear, who jabbed a finger toward the door in a clear *We're taking this outside* gesture.

What the ever-loving hell?

Shoulders slumped, Nick stood and headed for the door, his expression an awful mix of humiliation and anger and despair. I snatched up the menu and held it up to shield my face, but I had a feeling I could have been dancing naked on the bar and Nick would have been oblivious.

Bear tossed bills onto the table and stalked after Nick. The bartender was busy taking a drink order, my debit card in her hand. So much for following the men outside and maybe finding out what was going on. I clamped down on my impatience as the bartender dealt with a spill before she finally ran my card. She looked frazzled when she brought me the bill, so I added a decent tip then grabbed my food and left. It was only my amazing self-control that kept me from shoving an onion ring into my mouth before I was outside.

I dug in the bag for one as I walked across the parking lot then stopped in surprise at the sight of Nick's car, still parked in the same place and unoccupied. Weird. I'd expected both Nick and Bear to be long gone by the time I finished paying for my food. Or maybe he left with Bear to—

Muffled shouting issued from a big pickup on the far side of the lot. I stood between two cars, riveted in place by shock as I watched a red-faced Bear rant at Nick in the passenger seat. Snatches of the tirade drifted through the pleasant spring air.

"... *pea-brained decision* ..."

"... *how dare you* ..."

"... *plans don't include* ... *whiny bullshit* ..."

Nick sat with his shoulders hunched, not yelling back. Or even talking back, as far as I could tell. In all the time I'd worked with him, I'd never seen Nick cowed by anyone. He was usually confident to the point of arrogance.

At last Bear wound down and finished with a *Get the hell out.* White-faced, Nick almost fell out of the big truck as he complied, staggered a step, then pushed the door shut before stumbling off. Bear watched him go then slammed his hands against the steering wheel in either frustration or rage. In the next instant the truck engine revved, and Bear sped out of the lot.

Nick fumbled his keys from his pocket and dropped them. The thud of metal against asphalt shocked me out of my daze. I lurched forward.

"Nick?!"

His entire body tensed as if I'd punched him. Face flooding with color, he snatched the keys up and hurried to his car, acting as if he hadn't heard me. He yanked his door open and practically dove in, but I poured on the speed and wedged my body between car and door so he couldn't close it.

"Angel, I gotta go," he gasped.

"Nick." I groped for words, a way to tell him I understood, that I knew how it felt to be called worthless and stupid and worse.

Nick's hands shook and his breath wheezed as he groped in his messenger bag. Damn it. I also knew how shitty it was when an outsider saw—when the private pain became public shame.

I pulled his inhaler from his bag and pressed it into his hand. Waited for him to take a puff, then another. His breathing eased, but he continued to tremble and was as pale as death.

"Nick," I said. "How do you know Bear?"

His distress increased to agonizing levels, as if he'd break into a million pieces if touched. He shoved his keys into the ignition and started the car. "I gotta go," he repeated, still refusing to meet my eyes. He reached for the door, but I didn't budge.

"Please listen to me," I said, trying my best to project calm understanding. "I know a little about—"

"*YOU DON'T KNOW SHIT!*" Nick screamed, face blotchy and eyes wild. "Get out of the fucking way!"

Goddammit, Angel. I'd pushed too far. Shit. I should have known better. I used to get pretty goddamn defensive when people tried to reach out to me. Throat tight, I stepped back and closed the door for him then walked away. Behind me, tires squealed on the asphalt as Nick peeled out in an eerie echo of Bear's departure.

As soon as I was in my car, I pulled out my phone. "Okay, Bear," I muttered. "Who the hell are you to Nick?" I had a gigantic suspicion, but I needed to be sure.

The owner of The Bear's Den turned out to be Owen "Bear" Galatas. And a search on people associated with that name turned up Nicholas Galatas. Before tonight, I never would've guessed it in a million years.

Bear was Nick's dad.

Chapter 16

I sat in my car for several minutes, nerves jangling as I struggled to process the entire incident. It didn't help that it hit way too close to home. My mother had been mentally ill, and I'd been the easiest and closest target whenever she lashed out. She'd gone to prison for it and died there—committing suicide on my sixteenth birthday. But life hadn't turned perfect when she went to jail, not when my dad was an alcoholic who had no idea how to keep a screwed up kid in line. He eventually resorted to slaps when he reached the end of his rope, though by that time I was old enough to get away from him until he could sober up and cool down. But the emotional abuse and outright neglect were a lot harder to escape.

Dad was better now, god almighty so much better. My zombification had helped him damn near as much as it had helped me, and we'd broken the horrific cycle of Angel-fucks-up followed by Dad-doesn't-know-how-to-help which would inevitably lead to Dad-gets-pissed.

Bear didn't appear to be mentally ill like my mother was and, if he was any sort of addict, he hid it damn well. Not that either was a requirement or excuse to be abusive. Bear was scary and intimidating under ordinary circumstances. I couldn't imagine being on the receiving end of his anger.

Yet there was every chance that what I'd witnessed was an isolated incident. Parents and kids argued for all sorts of reasons. Even the most well-adjusted families had the occasional screaming match—which was one of the reasons why Pierce worried about family members of zombies being in the know. Nick never mentioned his family or personal life, but then again neither did most of my other coworkers, not in any sort of depth. How was I to know if there was a pattern of abuse—verbal or otherwise—from Bear? And, if I did know, what the hell could I do about it?

Thoughts stewing, I drove out to the park behind the municipal auditorium. Dusk turned the western sky purple and maroon as I sat on the hood of my car. And, while I consumed my monthly quota of fried food, I continued my internet search of Bear Galatas.

It was common knowledge around these parts that Bear was a survivalist who preached the virtue of preparedness. What I hadn't known was how serious he was about it. A frequent contributor to *Survive This!* magazine, he wrote articles on everything from how to escape handcuffs, zipties, and duct tape to the increase of martial law in the U.S to how to grow a survival garden. He even had a popular blog called "Bear Talk" where he discussed how to prepare for and survive various catastrophes, from house fires to hurricanes, terrorist attack to alien invasion.

I added this info to my own observations of the man. Big, tough guy, smart and confident enough to run a very successful business, a planner with strong opinions, and openly dismissive of anyone he deemed a slacker. Worked out hard, and a big believer in mind-and-body strength.

Shit. And then there was Nick—not at all big and tough and strong who no doubt embodied everything that Bear considered wimpy and worthless. But damn it, Nick was smart. Surely that was an important survival trait?

Worry for Nick gnawed at me, but I had zero idea what

to do to help him. Maybe I could talk to Derrel—without naming any names—and get his advice.

Nothing else I could do right now. Damn it.

Frustration simmered as I continued home, but by the time I arrived, I'd wrenched my thoughts back to murder-clue hunting. In the bathroom, I peeled the skull fragment off my forehead, then attacked the makeup and glue residue with makeup remover, baby wipes, and cold cream. It probably would have been quicker to claw my skin right off, eat brains, and grow my face back, but I figured mopping up the blood and flesh bits would burn more time than I saved.

It was full dark by the time I finished removing all of the makeup. I checked my watch, changed into dark jeans and a black t-shirt, killed another fifteen minutes with a skim-through of my Biology notes, then got my ass in gear.

Zombie Spy Powers, Activate!

Judd lived in Bob's Trailer Park, a rundown shithole with a dozen lots and a driveway that had more potholes than level ground. The owner, Bob, was a real prince who dealt meth on the side and by some miracle had yet to be busted for it. The residents were the kind of people who either didn't give a shit about the nasty conditions, or were desperate enough to tolerate them for the cheap rent. Judd wasn't desperate. He simply preferred to spend his money on the finer things in life. Guns. Pot. Prostitutes. Antibiotics. Judd had lived there the longest of any of the residents, and was one of the few with anything resembling a steady—and legal—job.

The good thing, for me at least, was that I seriously doubted any of Judd's neighbors would call the cops if they saw weird crap going on since everyone here had something to hide. The bad thing was that the neighbors would likely just shoot anyone they deemed suspicious.

In other words, I needed to be super-ultra-sneaky. I parked a street over, ate a packet of brains, jumped a ditch, and cut through a thin stretch of woods. At the edge of the trees I watched, listened, and scented. Neither of his neighbors on either side were home, and I thanked baby Jesus for that little advantage. Both the front and back doors of his trailer were locked with padlocks, but that didn't bother me. I'd been here a few times before, back when I was dating Randy. Though, at the time, I'd hated hanging out with Judd, I was glad now that I'd listened to his dumb ramblings about escape routes and secret trap doors in case of terrorist attacks. Because, god knows, if I was a terrorist, a piece of shit trailer park in bumfuck Louisiana would *totally* be my first target. Totally.

After tugging gloves on, I crept up to the back of Judd's trailer, crouched, and peered beneath it. Cobwebs and trash and way too many bugs made a nasty, creepy jungle, but at least it was relatively dry. Though I had a mini-flashlight in my pocket, I didn't dare use it outside where it could draw attention. Lucky for me, the recent top off of brains gave my vision a decent boost, and I spied a difference in the floor near the very back of his trailer.

Judd's idea of an escape hatch wasn't fancy—nothing more than a two foot square hole covered by a piece of plywood and an area rug. I had no trouble shoving them aside to shimmy into the trailer, then took a minute to brush spiders and other yuck off me. Ugh. I'd been through nastier places, but that didn't mean I had to like it.

No bed or dresser in this room. Old mail and miscellaneous trash littered a floor that had never known the sweet kiss of a vacuum. A gun safe hunkered in one corner, and a matte black crossbow that looked like the lovechild of an assault rifle and Satan's longbow hung on a rack beside it. A workbench covered in reloading equipment and fletching supplies took up the entire back wall, and on the opposite wall hung a huge image of Bear in camouflage gear and toting an axe, surrounded by posters of naked women with guns. Wow. Talk about hero worship. Ew.

I did a quick search of the room and found a vast collection of porn, but no murder weapons or bloody clothing. The gun safe seemed to mock me. That was the most logical place to stash evidence, and its big lock would keep out anyone who didn't have the combination or major explosives. I didn't have any explosives, but I did have experience. I'd been on a lot of crime scenes in the past year and a half, and I knew that a whole lot of people didn't trust their memory. In less than two minutes I found the scrap of masking tape on the underside of the workbench, and in another thirty seconds I pulled open the safe in triumph.

"Well, crap." So much for triumph. Guns of every possible variety were cram-packed into the safe, but no machete, no blood, and no car keys or anything else that might have come from the murder victim Seeger. Annoyed, I shut the safe door and locked it. There'd been no room to spare in the safe, so maybe he hid stuff elsewhere?

I proceeded through the trailer, searching as quickly and carefully as possible. The second bedroom held Judd's bed and dresser along with a three-foot high pile of dirty laundry that I forced myself to root through. I even got on the floor and peered under his bed, and found only a collection of cum-crusted socks and several pounds of weed.

The kitchen was surprisingly clean, and I realized I hadn't seen dirty dishes or food in any of the mess elsewhere in the trailer. That explained why I hadn't seen any roaches. Okay, so Judd was gross, but he still had standards. Nice to know. I dutifully checked the cabinets and found jack squat of interest, then moved on to the last room—a marginally tidy living room. But disappointment reigned as I turned up nothing but enormous dust bunnies under the couch, and desiccated Cheetos in the cushions.

Crap! My hopes of getting this done nice and quick vanished. Failure here meant I had to check out Coy's place, and it would take me at least fifteen minutes to get there. Still, it was that or give up the search, and I wasn't going to do that. Not if there was any chance Randy was involved or that a clue about the murder might surface.

Fuming in annoyance, I turned to leave but stopped as my gaze fell on a small table in the corner. It held an ancient computer that I didn't think Judd had ever used in all the time I'd known him—probably because he bought it cheap and second-hand, and only later discovered that whatever part it needed to connect to the internet was busted. He'd insisted he was going to fix it, but that was at least four years ago. Not surprising since Judd had less computer smarts than me, which wasn't saying a whole lot. I hadn't bothered to check the computer during my search since it didn't seem like a place to hide evidence of murder but, beneath the dust, a red light winked on the front of the computer tower.

A tingle started at the base of my spine, spread up as I moved to the table. Papers cluttered its surface along with a yellow legal pad and a bubble pack for two USB flash drives—with one drive missing. Penis-shaped flash drives, because this was Judd.

What was so important that Judd decided to crank up this dinosaur? I wiggled the mouse and was rewarded with a Windows ME screen. It took me several frustrating tries to find a list of his files, but as far as I could tell everything was several years old. There also wasn't a damn thing on the computer that looked to be worth saving onto a flash drive.

My eyes dropped to the legal pad, and the tingle increased. I grabbed up a pencil and rubbed the lead over the surface of the paper, like I'd seen in every detective TV show. Words appeared, light against dark, and I had to bite back a whoop of delight. Hot damn. The shit worked! Now I could see exactly . . .

zombie heal
zombie turn
zombie speed

"What the . . . ?" Comprehension seared through me as if I'd grabbed a live wire. These matched the filenames on

Grayson Seeger's printout. If Judd knew the filenames, he either had a second copy of the list, or—

I tugged a crumpled receipt from beneath the penis drive package. It was from the XpressMart with a time stamp of four-nineteen p.m. today. He wouldn't need to buy a flash drive if all he had was a printout of the list. The only thing that made sense was that Judd somehow had the actual files themselves.

I chewed my lower lip as the implications came together in ugly patterns. Judd must have gotten the files from another flash drive—and the most obvious suspect was one belonging to Seeger. Shit. Judd had bought the penis flash drives between the afternoon and evening hunts. In other words, he checked out the files on Seeger's drive and *then* decided he wanted a copy—so badly that he ran out and bought flash drives during the break between hunts. What the hell could've been that important?

Mouth set, I continued rubbing the pencil lead over the paper.

zombie feed
zombie frenzy

"Frenzy" was circled. Could be Judd saw the *Zombies Are Among Us!!* trailer this afternoon and thought that the zombie_frenzy video file—the one I suspected matched up with the film—was interesting because lots of locals were in the big melée scene.

zombie turn 2

The last was underlined four times with a heavy hand. I chewed my lower lip as I pondered those fierce underlines. The sneak preview today hadn't shown anything that matched up to that filename, but I figured the full mockumentary would. I'd find out for sure at the Fest tomorrow. I rubbed lead over the last few inches of the paper.

ANGEL

The pencil slipped from my fingers. *What the shit?* My pulse stuttered, and my mouth went bone dry. My name. Why did he have *my* name listed with the files?

Panic sent waves of cold running over my skin, and my thoughts jabbered like a room full of angry people. I stumbled back from the table and pressed both hands to my stomach. My name on a page of zombie crap. He knew. Judd knew. It was over. I needed a dose so I could chill and figure out what to do. I—

"Stop it!" I gasped, both frightened and furious at myself. "Stop being *stupid!*" This wasn't me, wasn't the Angel who'd remade herself. This stupid freakout was Old Angel, the one who couldn't handle shit and took the easy way out. I didn't *need* a dose. Not for this. Goddammit, I'd survived worse.

The panic gradually crumbled as I forced myself to breathe, steady and deep. The mad galloping of my heart slowed to an unsteady trot. Straightening, I moved back to the table. There, see? I could handle this. No need to freak out. Without the panic gibbering in my ear, I had no trouble thinking of any number of perfectly logical reasons for why my name was on the paper. Judd might have written it on the pad earlier, and it had nothing to do with the files at all. Or could be he wrote my name down because he spotted me in the *Zombie Frenzy!!* clip of the mockumentary. Hell, maybe he met some other chick named Angel and wanted to hook up with her.

Calmer now, I ripped the sheet from the pad, folded it, and shoved it into my pocket. Best case scenario was that I got my hands on those files to see for myself. Nothing else I could do now except make sure I didn't miss the full mockumentary tomorrow—and track Judd's worthless ass down as soon as possible to recover both Seeger's flash drive and the penis drive copy.

Unfortunately, the list of files still didn't *prove* Judd's involvement in the murder. Seeger could have dropped the drive after he left the movie premiere, and Judd then picked it up completely innocently. I knew in my gut that was bullshit, especially when added to the other evidence from the crime scene—the American flag cigarette with the smear of camo makeup, the yellow lighter, and the zombie hunter kit. Top it off with the squirrelly way the guys were acting, and I had a really bad feeling that Randy, Coy, and Judd were in neck deep. Damn it. But I needed to be sure.

Next stop on my breaking and entering spree: Coy's place.

Chapter 17

My phone vibrated seconds after I settled into my car. I slid it from my pocket and glanced at the screen.

V12

"Holy shit." I blinked at the message on my alarm. Unfamiliar pride swelled within my chest. I'd made it. Even though I'd really fucking wanted a hit, I'd made it until it was time for my dose. A smile pulled at my mouth as I got out the syringe and vial. I still craved the V12 like no one's business, but that wasn't the point. Not yet, at least. I hadn't caved, and that's what mattered.

Warmth spread through me as I injected the half-dose. Stress melted away and the world brightened. I was an addict, and I'd always be an addict, but I was facing it now. For the first time ever, I was facing it.

I took one of the capsules Dr. Nikas gave me to counter withdrawal side effects, downed a packet of brains, and got on my way, body tingling delightfully. And, when my tires hummed on the bridge over Bayou Zaire, the water laughed with me.

*　　*　　*

Coy's closest neighbor lived half a mile away from him, which meant I didn't have to be as sneaky. All I had to do was park behind his house so no one could see my car from the road. Oh, and avoid setting the place on fire. That might draw a bit of attention.

Breaking into Coy's house was even easier than Judd's since I knew he kept a spare key taped to the top of the hummingbird feeder. After I pulled on fresh gloves and let myself in, I checked the place out. It was about half the size of my house, which meant it was damn tiny. Main room, bedroom, bathroom, and kitchen—all spotless. A nice change of pace after Judd's trailer, and quick to search, too. With a sigh of relief, I finished my sweep and shoved the sofa back in place. Not a speck of blood or murder weapon to be found.

My next stop was the detached garage where Coy did his taxidermy. To my annoyance, it was locked tight, and no amount of searching under rocks and potted plants turned up a key. My lock pick experience was limited to the time I broke off a bobby pin in the outside door of an XpressMart bathroom. The clerk was being a major prick and wouldn't give me the key to the crapper, so I'd tried to pick the lock. When that failed spectacularly, I made tracks before the clerk discovered the ruined lock or the surprise I left him. Hey, I *really* needed to go.

Breaking Coy's lock—or taking a shit by his door— weren't my first choices. I circled the building and searched for a way in. Two small windows near a dryer vent in the back. A skylight on the roof. Nothing easy or open.

Crap. I was going to have to break in for real. But surely busting one little window wasn't *that* much worse than sneaking through a trapdoor or letting myself in with a key. If Coy was guilty, it had to be done. If he wasn't, I'd make it up to him. Later.

I found a rock the size of my fist, smashed the window then went still, listening. No alarm sounded. A dog barked twice in the distance. Doing my very best to not slice my hands to pieces, I unlocked the window and slid it open.

A variety of scents swirled around me as I clambered through the window and onto the washing machine. Epoxy and paint. Musk and blood. I scrambled down and panned the beam of my mini flashlight around. I'd never been in a taxidermy studio before, and I took a few seconds to gawk. It was obvious Coy was serious about his work. The space was orderly, with cabinets and shelves filling one wall, and printed labels organizing everything from glass eyes to glue. I grinned at a shelf of protective gloves, aprons, and filter masks. I had a shelf like that back at the morgue. A large chest freezer took up the wall by the door. Two broad wood tables filled the center of the garage, with a pole between them that held three unfinished deer heads. Several finished pieces perched on the far wall—squirrels, ducks, and even a wild boar head. Bare polyurethane animal forms hung from a rack along the ceiling.

"This is so cool," I breathed then got my ass in gear.

Like the house, the neatness of Coy's garage made it a snap to search for things that didn't belong. I combed through shelves, storage bins, cabinets, and every nook and cranny. No murder weapons. No blood. Nothing suspicious.

But my heart dropped to my toes at the sight of a black garbage bag inside the washer.

Be cool, I told myself as I tugged the bag out. Maybe it was Coy's dirty laundry. He could've been in a hurry and chucked the bag in the washer with plans to wash it later.

I untied the bag, gazed in dismay at the bloody shirt at the top. It was dirty all right. A brief inspection told me the bag held the same outfits Coy and Judd had worn on Friday. Shirts and pants were spattered with blood, and Coy's was smeared with ground-in mud as if he'd decided to roll around in the muck.

Son of a bitch. Coy was smart enough not to wash the clothes in this washer and leave blood evidence behind. But not smart enough to stay out of the situation in the first place. The guys had gone to the Zombie Fest today to avoid raising suspicion. Stick to the routine and all that. That's what Randy had said to Judd on the phone this morning. They probably intended to sink everything out in the swamp at the first opportunity.

I stomped down a brief and moronic urge to take the bag with me. With my luck I'd get stopped for a busted taillight or something equally stupid, and then I'd have to explain why I had a bag of bloody clothing in my car.

Doubt curdled in my stomach as I stuffed the bag back into the washer and closed the lid. What if I was wrong about Coy and Judd being murderers? Sure, the clues lined up, but what if I was too focused on the guys? For all I knew the blood was from an animal Coy had worked on. I didn't have a DNA test in my back pocket. I didn't want it to be them. Even though I barely tolerated Judd, I didn't want him to be a murderer.

Finish searching. Now wasn't the time to lose my nerve. If I found a murder weapon here, I'd know for sure whose blood it was. The chest freezer was the one place I hadn't checked, but when I swung the lid up, the unmistakable scent of human brains swirled out with the chilly air.

I couldn't breathe, couldn't think past the crashing wave of sadness and anger and frustration. Only one reason why I'd smell a brain in the freezer. An instant later my mouth began watering like that Pavlov dude's dog when he heard a bell.

Pissed and hungry, I shoved aside frozen, plastic-wrapped skins of three deer, a squirrel, and a raccoon. There at the bottom of the freezer rested a garbage bag that held a basketball-sized object.

Jaw tight, I lifted the bag out and set it on a table, prayed that I was wrong and this was all a giant mistake. I opened the bag and tried to ignore the scent of brains that told me the truth.

Though I'd handled hundreds of corpses before, a shudder went through me as I peeled frost-stiffened newspaper away from Grayson Seeger's face. His eyes were open, clouded and shocked. Frozen mud and blood caked his hair, and grey matter leaked from where his skull caved inward a couple of inches above his left ear. Baseball bat. One shot, and lights out, just like that. He'd been so animated and friendly last night at the movie. And now here he was . . .

"Fucking hell," I muttered, wiping at my eyes with my sleeve. "Goddamn it, you stupid fucks." No denying it now. Coy and Judd were responsible for a vicious, senseless murder. I liked Coy and hated to see him get in trouble, but I was pretty sure Grayson Seeger had liked having his head attached.

And now Randy was in deep shit, all because he wanted to help Coy out, but how far had he gone? I needed to call Detective Ben Roth. Except I sure as shit couldn't tell him that I'd destroyed evidence. I couldn't even tell him I'd suspected the guys were involved and decided to go search their residences on my own. Yeah, that would be a quick trip to handcuff-ville. No, I'd have to spin him one hell of a yarn and tell him I'd been thinking about the murder, point him in the right direction. Ben was sharp. He'd figure it out.

But Randy would burn. He wasn't a murderer. He was simply too loyal a friend to Coy. I wanted to give him a chance to do the right thing, to fess up. Maybe he could scrape off some of the shit and catch a break with the law.

There was only one hitch. If the guys came back after the hunt tonight and ditched all this evidence—which I had zero doubt they planned to do—they might just get away with murder. And Seeger deserved better than that.

Fine. I'd make sure they couldn't get rid of *all* the evidence. Easily taken care of with a smear of Seeger's blood on the bottom of the table leg. It wasn't immediately obvious, but a thorough search would turn it up.

DNA, bitches.

I started to rewrap the head then paused, salivating. *Screw it.* If my guess was right, the head would be in its new home in the swamp in the next couple of hours. Waste not, want not, and all that crap. I pried up a section of skull, dug out two good-sized handfuls of the brain slush beneath and gulped them down. *Sorry, Seeger, but if I'm gonna find justice for you, I need a boost.*

After I washed the brain slush off my gloved hands, I re-wrapped the head and shoved it beneath the frozen skins, then got the ever-loving hell out of there.

Chapter 18

After I left Coy's garage, I drove around aimlessly to do some serious thinking.

Randy was involved. I had zero doubt. But I *did* doubt that he'd been there when the murder happened. As squirrelly as he was acting, he'd be a thousand times worse if he'd been there when the dude got his head chopped off. Randy wasn't violent or mean—his lawbreaking tended toward smoking weed and the occasional chop of a stolen car. He'd fight when provoked, but it took a lot to provoke him.

But even if he didn't help kill the guy, he was helping those other two idiots. If he got caught, he'd be in shit nearly as deep as theirs. I needed to try and talk a bit of damn sense into him. I owed him that much.

No. That wasn't true. I didn't *owe* him anything. But he was my friend. And I couldn't stand idly by and watch him sink himself. That said, I wouldn't let him sink me either.

Resolved, I pulled out my phone and signed into the Tribe's encrypted email account. Every detail I knew and suspected about the murder, including tonight's discoveries, went into an email addressed to Brian and Dr. Nikas. I finished up by detailing my plan to reason with Randy and that, if I didn't email or call by morning, they should do whatever needed to be done with all this info.

With that bit of life insurance sent, I ate two packets of brains then retrieved the Kel-Tec PF9 from the glove box, placed the gun on the seat and headed to Randy's place.

The driveway was empty, but I figured I wouldn't have long to wait. The Fest crap had ended not too long ago, and I doubted that he'd be going out partying after. I chambered a round in my gun and clipped the holster into my waistband at the small of my back, then went and sat on his trailer steps. It was a nice clear night, the stars were out, and the mosquitos weren't interested in my zombie blood.

Less than ten minutes later, Randy pulled into the driveway in his Charger. I caught a look at his face as he registered my presence, and it was full of *what the fuck*. For an instant I thought he'd stop and back right on out, but he must have known I'd follow him. I was stubborn and bitchy like that.

He parked next to my car, climbed out and managed to give me a crooked smile. "Hey, Angel. Did I forget we were gonna do firepit or something?"

I stayed right where I was and didn't smile back. "We need to talk, Randy."

Dismay lit his eyes, but he shook his head. "It's been a long day, babe. I wanna get a shower and drop into bed."

"And it's gonna get longer if you don't give me ten minutes right now." I stood at the sight of headlights coming through the gate, narrowed my eyes. "Who's that?"

"It's just Coy," Randy said with a shrug as he headed toward me, but I didn't miss the tension in his shoulders.

My pulse gave a little flutter. At least it wasn't Judd. Tanked on brains, I could deal with these two if things went tits up. I hoped. "You two planning to up your zombie body count?"

Randy stopped in his tracks. "What the fuck is up with you, Angel?"

"The fuck is up with me?" I shot back. "What the fuck is up with you being involved in a murder?"

Shock flashed across his face before he gave a strained laugh. "You're a real kidder."

I kept my expression stony. My heart beat an intense staccato as Coy parked on the other side of my car. "Hey, Coy. You need to hear this too."

He gulped as if holding back the urge to spew. "What's going on?"

"Shut up, Coy," Randy snapped then glared at me. "Best you forget whatever notions you got in your head."

"That ain't gonna happen," I said with a lift of my chin. "And, in case y'all get any stupid ideas, everything I know is in the hands of people who will make you beg to die if anything happens to me." With confidence buoyed by the gun, brains, and Brian's efficiency, I nailed them with a glare. "What the *hell*, dudes? Y'all are better than this!"

Panic widened Coy's eyes. "What's she talking about, Randy?" Stress made his voice shrill. "Did you tell her?"

Randy rounded on Coy. "Would you shut up? I'll handle this!"

"No one had to tell me anything," I said, planting my hands on my hips. It helped my badass act that I was a touch higher than the guys thanks to being on the steps. "I worked the crime scene, remember?" I scowled. "First of all, you dumbasses left the damn zombie hunter survival kit duffel there. Second, Judd left his lighter and one of his stupid cigarettes behind." I wasn't about to say that I took the cigarette. They needed to stay worried. Coy was my weak link here, so I turned a pleading look on him. "What *happened?*"

"Aw shit." Coy grabbed his head with both hands as panic vibrated through him. His breath came in short pants, and his eyes darted around as if seeking escape from a trap. "I gotta get out of here."

"No!" I shouted. "Goddammit, Coy, you need to listen to me first."

Tight lipped, Randy stalked up to the side of the trailer. "Say what you gotta say, Angel." He crouched and pulled a six-foot length of heavy chain from beneath it. I hoped it was meant to weigh down a head and bloody clothing and not to shut me up.

"I'm saying that you idiots need to turn yourselves in." I scorched them both with a glare. "*Maybe* that way you'll be able to come out of this without spending the rest of your lives in prison."

"No. Oh god, no." Distress warped Coy's face as his nightmare took a turn for the worse. "W-we gotta stick to the plan." His throat bobbed as he gulped. "Stick to the plan."

Randy slung the chain toward Coy to land in a pile at his feet. "Throw that in the car," he ordered. Coy stooped and struggled to pick it up as a heap. Randy scowled back at me. "We got other options here that don't mean no one going to prison."

I stared at him. He was an idiot. "What other options? Run like hell? Give up everything? Leave behind your entire life and live in hiding forever?"

Randy narrowed his eyes. "You going to the cops?"

I threw up my hands in frustration. "I won't have to! They're going to come to you soon enough." Possibly a lie, but Randy and Coy didn't need to know that.

Randy shifted from foot to foot. "I didn't do anything, and we're getting rid of the other shit. Just chill."

Yeah, he was the polar opposite of chilled at the moment. I looked at him sadly. "If you didn't do anything, then why are you setting yourself up to be charged as a principal—or at the very least an accessory. You're better than this." I shifted my focus to Coy. "And, dude, you're no cold-blooded murderer. C'mon, there's a way out of this, but you both need to let go of this *fantasy* that the cops won't come knocking at your door. I mean, goddamn, Coy, there's evidence all over your place."

Coy dropped the chain with a jarring clatter. "Evidence? What? How do you know?"

"A little birdie told me," I snapped. "You want to charge me with trespassing? Sure, let's call the cops right now and tell them that I broke into your shop and found a *severed head*."

"Dammit, Angel!" he said, voice cracking. "Whaddya have to go poking around for? Oh god."

"Don't you get it? You *have* to go to the cops," I told Coy, trying hard to sound nice and calm. "If you don't, and they come to you first, then you're screwed. And you too, Randy."

"No," Coy said. "No, Randy wasn't there." He sagged to sit on a low pile of tires, while I did my best to hide the relieved shaking of my knees.

He wasn't there. Randy's not a murderer. "Tell me what happened," I said when I had control of my voice again.

"This guy flagged us down out on Highway 180," Coy said. "Judd pulled over. So we could help, y'know?"

"Yeah, 'cause Judd's a soft-hearted kind of dude," I said, voice dripping with sarcasm. "Go on."

"The guy went nuts, and, uh, dragged Judd out." Coy's words came out in a thin monotone. "He was trying to kill Judd. The bat was there with the kit in the back of the truck. I couldn't think what else I could do. Whack him. I, um, I whacked him right on the head. Didn't mean to kill him."

Wow. This was one disjointed story. "Who opened Judd's door?"

"The guy." Coy's gaze darted around like a horsefly on steroids. "Judd didn't do anything. The guy started it."

I regarded Coy with naked disbelief. "A random out-of-towner flagged you down and, for no reason, dragged Judd out of the truck and tried to kill him? Seriously?"

"That's what happened. I swear." Coy pulled a cigarette out of a pack, but his hands shook so badly he couldn't hold the lighter in place long enough to get it lit. After a few seconds he gave up and threw the lighter as hard as he could, then dropped the cigarette and jammed his heel onto it.

"Sure it is." I rolled my eyes. "How many times did you practice that story?"

Randy stepped between Coy and me. "Why're you fucking with him? He's been through enough."

"*He's* been through—? What about the *dead* dude?" I jabbed a finger at Randy. "You're not helping anyone by buying this line of bullshit."

Scowling, Randy turned and moved a few feet away then stopped, as if waiting to hear how this all played out.

I swung back to Coy. "And *you* need to come clean, but for god's sake, get your story straight first. The cops will rip that pathetic lie to pieces—after they stop laughing their asses off. Your story has holes big enough to drive a semi through."

Coy stared at me, aghast, then his entire body drooped in defeat. He slid a look toward Randy's back. "Judd said we had to tell it like that," he mumbled then stared at the ground between his feet.

Okay, *now* we were making progress. "I'm not surprised. Why don't you tell me what really happened."

"It was after Pillar's," Coy said, voice dull. "Out on 180."

I lowered myself to sit again and gave him a *go ahead* nod.

"Judd was driving. There was this zombie walking on the shoulder." He grimaced and rubbed his eyes. "I mean, the guy was wearing zombie makeup and all that stuff. He tried to flag us down for a ride. That much was true." His eyes went hollow. "We were drunk. And you know how Judd is when he's plastered."

Mean. And ready to pick a fight with anyone. "Yep, I know," I replied with as little expression as possible.

"We passed him, then Judd swung around and we went back. He pulled onto the shoulder." A shudder passed through Coy. "Said we were gonna hunt some zombie ass."

That sounded like Judd. And Coy, the follower, went along with it. "But y'all weren't planning on killing the guy, right?"

He jerked his head up in shock. "God, no!" But then he groaned. "It was just gonna be like a prank, y'know. Mess with the guy."

"A prank," I echoed.

"I was drunk." Shame and grief passed over his face.

"The zombie hunter kit was in the back seat." His throat worked. "I swear we were only gonna scare him."

A pretty clear picture was forming. "And the dude didn't want to be fucked with," I said. Car broken down, starting to rain, and then two drunk dumbass rednecks decide to screw with him instead of being decent human beings and giving him a ride.

"Some shit got said. It's hazy." Coy stared down at his hands. "It all happened so fast. He tried to back off, but Judd grabbed him. I got between them to break it up, and the guy shoved me. We ended up in a tussle on the ground."

"And *Judd* hit him with the bat," I murmured. I knew the sound a bat made when it hit a human skull. Last year I'd caved a man's head in with one then feasted on his brain. But that had been self-defense. Made all the difference in the world.

Coy looked as if he could still hear that sound, too. "Yeah." He gulped. "I had the machete but dropped it when we started fighting. Judd had the bat and—" He couldn't finish.

Randy spun and took a lurching step toward us. "Wait a goddam minute, Coy. You and Judd both told me *you* had the bat."

Coy pushed to his feet. "I know. But I didn't. I swear!"

"Coy." I snapped his name out. "You said you were rolling on the ground with him?" At his shaky nod I glanced at Randy. "Coy was wearing his blue plaid flannel shirt. It's in a garbage bag in his washing machine, covered in mud. And Judd's *isn't* all dirty. So unless they switched clothes, I know who was rolling around in the mud." I paused to let that sink in. "Hard to hit someone with a bat when you're wrestling with them."

Coy gave a frantic nod. "Yeah. That's right. You remember, Randy? That's the shirt I was wearing! And it was Judd who decided we needed to chop the head off to make it look like the serial killer did it." He gripped his head. "Judd said . . . he said you wouldn't help us if you knew he did it."

"Judd knew Randy would stick his neck out for *you*, not him," I said. "Y'all played him like a patsy."

"You *lied* to me." Randy took a step toward Coy then stopped short, dismay in his eyes. A whisper of dread tugged at my chest as he dropped his gaze to the phone in his hand. He'd been turned away the whole time he was listening to us.

"Randy?" I said. "What were you just doing?"

He shoved his phone into his pocket, like a five-year-old hiding a cookie behind his back after being caught red-handed.

I gave him a withering look as I came down off the steps. "'Cause if you texted Judd, he's going to be ready to throw both your asses under the bus." They were all a bunch of goddamn idiots, every single one of them. I glared at Coy. "What do y'all know about the guy you murdered?"

He flinched at the m-word. "Dunno anything. I didn't look at his wallet. All I wanted was to get the hell out of there."

"Did the guy say anything before y'all got in the scuffle?" I narrowed my eyes at Coy. "Think hard."

Coy raked a hand over his hair. "It's all fuzzy. Something about it not being too late. That the deal wasn't done, and he'd keep his mouth shut. That's when he tried to back off." He shook his head, eyes hollow. "None of it made sense."

A deal? It sounded as if Seeger thought Judd and Coy had been sent to make sure he kept his mouth shut about it. That part matched up with his paranoia at the movie premiere, but what kind of deal had he cooked up that could possibly warrant sending thugs after him? And who was it with? Saberton? Andrew said Seeger wanted to meet with him in reference to a deal, but Seeger had died before they had the chance to do so. The files marked with double asterisks had been for a deal with "SASA." Was that an acronym for a Saberton branch, or was there another player in the game? And did the mysterious deal have anything to do with the video files and real zombies?

"Did you take anything off him?" I demanded.

"Judd went through his pockets. Took a couple hundred dollars from his wallet and his keys 'cause there was cocaine in a pill holder on the ring. That's it."

And I bet the USB flash drive and its zombie files happened to be on that key ring.

"I'm done," I said. "This has been a messed-up day, so I'm going to leave you two upstanding citizens now with this piece of Angel advice: Both of you, do the smart thing and turn yourselves in before it's too late." I started toward my car then paused and met Randy's eyes. "Grayson Seeger is *dead*. Do the right thing. For everyone. You're better than this."

I opened the door and slid behind the wheel. Coy stumbled toward me, hand outstretched. "Angel, wait! What are you gonna do?"

"Not a damn thing. *If* you grow a goddamn pair by morning. I'm sure you can figure out the rest." I slammed the door and did my best to pepper them with gravel as I sped out. I didn't know yet exactly how I'd expose them. But, if they turned themselves in, I wouldn't have to worry about it.

Headlights washed over me as I pulled out of the driveway. I slammed on my brakes as a pickup swerved and screeched to a stop in a half-ass diagonal to block a good chunk of the road. Pulse thrumming, I jerked the gun from my waistband and held it in my lap.

Judd flung his door open and scrambled to stand in the beam of my headlights, red-faced and with his hands fisted by his sides. "Get out of the goddamn car!"

I shot him the finger. He took a step closer.

I bared my teeth and stomped on the gas. He yelled a curse as he dove out of the way, and I raced around his truck, wheels skimming the edge of the ditch. *Asshole.* I kept half an eye on my rear view mirror, waiting for the flash of headlights that signaled his pursuit. I finally slowed as I reached the highway with no sign of him chasing me, and I let my breathing slow as well. After a moment of hesitation, I returned the gun to the glove box. They had no reason to come after me. After all, I hadn't taken any of the evidence, and it was my word against theirs. At least that's how I figured they'd see it. Besides, they had no reason to doubt that I'd shared the murder info with someone else. And *that* could definitely fry their asses.

Before I could forget, I pulled over and sent an "all clear" to Brian and Dr. Nikas. By morning I'd know whether Randy, Coy, and Judd had decided to turn themselves in or hide all the evidence and hope for the best.

And if they chose the second option, I fully intended to be their *worst* nightmare.

Chapter 19

It was almost nine a.m. by the time I dragged my sorry ass out of bed after lousy nightmare-filled sleep. Bleary-eyed, I shuffled out to the kitchen. No sign of my dad, but the coffee in the pot was still warm enough to drink without being gross. Good enough for me. Why was coffee great hot or over ice, but disgusting at room temperature? "A mystery for the ages," I murmured as I poured a mugful and added milk. That essential task taken care of, I settled at my desk and fired up my computer. It wasn't much better than Judd's, but it got me online and did the email, word processing, and web-stuff that I needed for my classes.

The cobwebs in my brain melted away beneath the onslaught of caffeine, and it only took me a few minutes to scan the local news sites and discover a complete lack of stories about murder suspects turning themselves in. Surely the sheriff's office would have released a statement if they had a big break like that? Or maybe the guys had decided to wait until morning before going to the cops, start the day off right.

Yeah. Sure. I wanted to be optimistic and have faith that all three would make the best available choice. But the reality was that Judd and Coy were going to end up in jail, and very possibly Randy as well. Didn't matter that they had a better chance of getting *less* jail time by turning themselves in. Judd was more prone to skip town, in my opinion, though Coy would do whatever Randy decided. Problem was, Randy always went for the road that seemed easiest but never looked ahead to see the mountains.

Hell, I'd been just like that before I became a zombie. Still was, in a few ways, as galling as it was to admit. That's how I got myself into the mess with the V12. The zombie parasite was a magic cure for all sorts of physical ailments, but it couldn't fix Stupid. Or Denial.

Or Addiction.

I was an addict. I would always have that mountain in my path. But, goddammit, I intended to keep my eyes on it from here on out.

Randy's cell phone went straight to voicemail when I called, as did Coy's. There were any number of reasons for that. Their phones might be off because they'd been arrested. Frowning, I pushed up from the desk and refilled my mug, then brought up Judd's number. I didn't want to talk to him, but chances were good he was with the other two, and any information was better than none.

Nope, voicemail.

Or they might have ditched the phones and skipped town.

It was an unpleasant thought, but I had to accept it might be true. I returned to my room and took a dose and a pill, then a boiling hot shower to chase the rest of the cobwebs from my head. Clean and dry, I dressed in jeans, light sweater and boots. Though I intended to make it to the Zombie Fest once more, I couldn't get into the spirit of costuming again. Besides, I wanted to look normal today. Well, as normal as I could manage. I ate a brain burrito, then started in on a second one. Though my brain-hunger clamored for me to eat all of it, my stomach couldn't hold another bite. With a sigh, I re-wrapped the half burrito and tossed it into the fridge. At least I had packets in the car console for later.

Heading out, I stopped at the first XpressMart with a working payphone and called the information number for the jail. No sense using my own phone and potentially drawing attention. The deputy who answered was terse and not very polite, but he informed me that none of the three men had been booked in the last twenty-four hours.

Not a good sign.

I went to Randy's place next, and my heart lifted at the sight of Coy's battered Chevy Blazer next to Randy's Charger. Good. They were just ducking my calls. I could handle that.

But the trailer was silent, even after I banged on the door and shouted for them. Okay, so either Randy and Coy were staying quiet and hoping I'd go away, or . . .

Or they left the cars here because they're on the run.

Only a tiny twinge of guilt poked at me as I retrieved Randy's spare key from under an old tire and let myself in. It was cold inside, which gave me pause. Randy was surprisingly frugal about some things and always turned down the thermostat before he left. But this had the feel of a place that hadn't been heated all night. And Randy didn't skimp on his climate comforts when he was home.

A quick check of the kitchen revealed a cold coffeemaker and dirty dishes in the sink. "Damn it, Randy," I murmured then checked his bedroom. Not that it helped. I had no way to tell if he'd grabbed a few changes of clothes since most of his clothing lived in a pile in a corner.

I returned the key to its hiding place, then raced to Coy's house. Dread wound through me at the sight of the garage door standing wide open, and I felt nothing more than a resigned disappointment when I determined the head and bag of bloody clothes were gone — no doubt resting in their new home at the bottom of the swamp.

Sighing, I returned to my car. *Now* I could think the worst.

I sat in Coy's driveway for a solid five minutes while I ran through my options, and my disappointment shifted to *seriously pissed.* I'd put my own ass on the line to give those guys a chance—the only chance they were likely to get considering the horrific nature of the murder—and they'd shit on it. What the hell else could I have said to get through to them? I didn't want to throw them under the bus, but did they really think I was going to let this go and walk away? Grayson Seeger deserved better than that.

Frustrated, I grabbed my phone and found Detective Ben Roth's number, but hesitated before hitting the call button. How on earth was I supposed to convince him that the guys might be persons of interest? I had no evidence. Great, so I saw Judd use a yellow lighter. Big whoop. I'd cleverly destroyed his cigarette, so couldn't point to that. And "they were acting weird at the Fest" was hardly probable cause.

And, of course, I couldn't tell Ben I found the head and bloody clothes then waited all night before telling him. And then having to explain how I knew to look there in the first place. Here I was thinking I was so clever leaving the smear of blood in Coy's garage, but now I didn't have enough info to give Ben for him to get a warrant. But I had plenty to get myself into trouble.

"Shit!" I'd screwed up, waited too long. Judd and Coy might very well get away with murder, and I had no one to blame but myself. That wasn't okay. And there was always the chance that Judd was crazy enough to come after me, despite my insistence that I'd told other people what I knew.

So fix it.

I blew out my breath. That was all I could do. Fix it. I'd watch my back and find a way to point Ben in the right direction. Somehow. And, in the meantime, I could focus my worry on the rest of the shit on my plate.

Lucky me.

Chapter 20

My VIP pass got me past the lines and through the gate of the Zombie Fest in nothing flat. I went straight to the Hunting Grounds on the slim chance that the guys were continuing to play their "everything is normal" game, but a check of all the prep areas turned up nothing. And though all three were registered for the hunt that was due to start in ten minutes, they hadn't signed in yet.

The last whisper of hope vanished that Randy might get out of this unscathed. Grief swam through me, and I let it linger for a few seconds before I ruthlessly pushed it down. Nothing I could do at the moment about the potential well-deserved arrest of the Three Dumbasses, and I'd already gone way *way* above and beyond the call of friendship to help Randy. I'd have to let the problem simmer of how to involve the cops without getting myself in trouble. Right now it was time to focus on my other big headache: the *Zombies Are Among Us!!* fiasco.

I returned to the VIP tent, slipped inside the Graveyard and paused to let my eyes adjust to the dimmer light from the fake moon. The crowd inside was thicker today, most likely because of the hype for the mockumentary premiere.

After a quick detour to grab a snack, I wound my way through the crowd then staked out a spot with a decent view of the screen.

Andrew was near the stage, conducting a meet-and-greet thing with VIPs, while Thea Braddock and Tom Snyder did their bodyguard impressions from a discreet distance. Braddock spotted me in less than ten seconds and gave me a hard look before continuing her surveillance of the crowd. Yep, I heard her loud and clear: *I'm watching you, and I will take your ass down with zero prejudice if you step out of line.*

Y'know, I was beginning to really like her.

The crowd near Braddock shifted, and I tensed as Dante Rosario stepped through with a German Shepherd—the Marquise de Saber—on a lead. Rosario strolled casually, but to my horror the dog zeroed in on Andrew. *Shit.* All zombies carried at least a micro-whiff of decay, no matter how tanked up they were on brains. And that dog was trained to smell rot.

Heart pounding, I wormed past people toward the impending disaster. Rosario moved to Andrew and offered his hand as if they knew each other—which they probably did considering Rosario was the face of Saberton's so-called commitment to public service. Andrew smiled and took Rosario's hand while, at their feet, the Marquise dropped her belly to the ground like a furry sphinx, her eyes riveted on my zombie baby.

Double shit, though so far it didn't seem as if Rosario had noticed his dog's behavior. Time for me to create a distraction and keep it that way.

"Andrew!" I called out, all bright and cheery, pairing it with a big wave. Both men looked my way, along with everyone else in earshot. Andrew stared at me with a *What the hell are you doing?* expression.

Distraction level one achieved.

"Oh my god," I gushed as I closed the distance. "I'm so glad I caught you before the premiere!"

Braddock stepped forward, eyes hard with suspicion. In

the same instant the dog snapped her head toward me, growl rumbling as her nose worked. Awesome. Let the bitch indicate on me. The dog, not Braddock.

Eyes on me, Rosario crouched and stroked the dog's head. "Quiet, Marla."

Marla. I stopped dead as the name punched through me. New York. I'd taken the subway to try and find Brian and boarded a car with what I thought was a blind man and his seeing-eye dog.

The man's hair had been reddish-brown, just like Rosario's, and the dog had growled at me.

It's because you're a pretty girl, the man had said. *Marla gets jealous of pretty girls.*

He'd been wearing sunglasses on the subway, which was why I hadn't made the connection before now. It might have been sheer coincidence that we'd been on the same subway car, but there was no mistake. Same voice. Same dog. Same man. But he wasn't blind. And now I knew he was with Saberton.

Focus, Angel. Bright smile. "Hey, Andrew, can I talk to you? Like *right now*?"

Though taken off guard, Andrew kept his cool and turned to Rosario with a professional smile. "Would you excuse me a moment, please?" he said then moved away with me without waiting for a reply.

"That's a cadaver dog!" I growled as soon as we were out of earshot. "What were you thinking letting it get so close to you?"

Andrew scowled. "I *know* she's a cada—" Color drained from his face. "I wasn't a zombie the last time I saw him. Does that mean Rosario knows?"

"If he noticed his dog indicating on you and knows zombies are real, he does." I gritted my teeth as stress woke my hunger.

Sweat beaded Andrew's upper lip. "Oh god." He rubbed a trembling hand over his mouth. "Yes. He knows about zombies."

"Can't catch a break," I muttered. I needed a hit. Or brains. *No.* I needed to keep my goddamn head. I squared my shoulders. "Look, I saw Rosario on the subway in New York. The dog growled at me then, too, so he already knows I'm a zombie. That is, if he didn't already know about me from working with Saberton." I had tons more questions concerning Rosario and his job description, but they would have to wait. "It doesn't matter if Marla pegs me as a zombie again today."

Andrew's face lit with understanding. "So I'll make an exit, and you'll—"

"I'll do something brilliant to make Rosario think the dog indicated on me and not you so that you can maintain your I'm-still-human cover," I said. "Now *go*. You getting outed won't help any of us."

Without another word, he gestured sharply to his bodyguards and stalked away toward Justine Chu.

Rosario stood beside Marla, a damn nice smile on his face as he watched me. Asswipe. I rushed his way. "Andrew had business to take care of," I said. "He'll be—" I stumbled to a stop as Marla stood, growling at my whirlwind approach and smell. Good doggie, doing exactly what I wanted.

"Will she bite?" I asked, wide-eyed. Marla's growl deepened, no doubt fueled by my apparent unease. I crossed mental fingers that she wouldn't actually bite me since that would pretty much suck—especially with me in perpetual brain deficit.

Rosario rested his hand on the dog's head. "Shhh. Easy, Marla," he murmured. "She won't bite you, Angel."

He knows my name. Bastard. Had he used that dog to torment Saberton's captive zombies? Maybe the dog would tell me herself. I bit my lip oh-so-prettily. "Will she let me pet her?"

"I promise she won't bite you," he said. "It's okay, Marla."

His words were like dog Valium. Marla's ears dropped and her tail thumped. I extended my hand—with caution—

and scratched behind her ears. I didn't have to fake the residual nervousness, especially after her previous aggression. To my relief, she appeared to love the attention and gave no sign that she was used to ripping zombies apart.

"How'd you know my name?" I asked, glancing up in time to catch his slight start and the whisper of chagrin that ran across his face. Aha! He'd slipped up.

But he recovered smoothly and gestured toward my lanyard. "It's on your badge."

"Oh, right!" I giggled. "Duh." *Slick cover, dude.* I hadn't imagined his "I'm busted" look, though.

He stuck out his hand. "Dante Rosario."

After an instant of hesitation, I took it. He had a confident grip, sure of himself but not too cocky. "I'm Angel Crawford. Nice to meet you." *Not.* "Your dog sure is cool. I mean now that she's not acting as if she wants to eat me."

Rosario gave me a long and guarded look. "She's like that with some people," he said slowly, as if choosing each word with care. "But she's fine now that you've been introduced." He flicked a glance around the tent. Looking for Andrew?

I snuck a peek behind me, relieved to see Andrew safe on the far side of the tent and surrounded by studio people. "I thought her name was the Marquise de Saber."

Amusement lit his eyes. "That's her official name. It's a little too snooty for daily wear."

"You're right about that," I said, keeping everything nice and agreeable. "Are you sticking around for the screening?"

He shook his head. "I'm on my way out. We did two demos today, and Marla needs a break."

That was fine by me. "Aw, puppy naptime." I made a kissy face at the dog and gave her one more headscratch before lifting my eyes back to Rosario. "Well, I hope I run into you again soon," I lied. Unless it was with my car.

"I'd like that," he said and gave me a nice enough smile. "Come on, Marla."

Eyes narrowed, I watched the Saberton dude and his

zombie-sniffing cadaver dog depart. I'd be keeping close tabs on those two. If they were up to anything besides doing charity demos, I intended to find out.

The light dimmed, and I scooted back to the place I'd staked out earlier. A spotlight hit Justine Chu as she stepped onto the stage. Everyone applauded because it seemed like the right thing to do, but she held up a hand, expression grave, until the clapping died away.

"Ladies and Gentlemen," Justine said in a campy Deathly Serious mode. "The documentary that you are about to see contains images you may find disturbing." She paused, shook her head. "No. You *will* find them disturbing. Prepare yourselves. Because—zombies are among us!"

The lights went out, leaving the interior of the tent far darker than I would have expected considering the bright daylight outside. Excited and nervous laughter tittered through the crowd. After all, this was what they were paying for. They *wanted* to be scared and shocked and disturbed.

"Those of you with weak stomachs should turn away now," Justine warned.

Ominous music swelled to a nerve-jangling discordance. Images of bodies and panicked mobs flashed in chaotic patterns, gradually resolving to longer shots of the melée at the Tucker Point High football field during the filming of the movie.

"Zombies—a source of primal terror," a deep-voiced narrator intoned as soundless chaos reigned on the screen. "Implacable. Hungry. A threat to all we hold dear. The mythology is as old as time, from the slow and relentless to the fast and strong. From conscious creations to viral-infected monsters." More images of shamblers. Rotting arms reaching through broken doors. I slowly relaxed. Okay, this was nothing more than a bunch of cheesy shit to get people fired up over the movie.

"Yet, the nightmare," the voiceover continued, "the *truth*—is worse than we ever imagined."

More long shots of the high school melée scene, then the

image jerked as if the camera had been bumped. The video transitioned to a jerky handheld news camera style in the thick of the action. It swung to a broad-shouldered zombie just as he smashed a man's head against a cinderblock wall.

Every cell in my body went numb even as a gasp and delighted shudder swept through the crowd. Not a special effect. That was *Philip* killing a Saberton operative.

Philip dropped into a crouch as the body fell, tore the man's skull apart and began to shove chunks of brain into his mouth. His dead-grey face was plenty horrifying without a speck of movie makeup, and his entire body jerked every few seconds as though jolted by electricity. He screamed through a gory mouthful, spattering the pavement with blood and brain bits.

I watched in growing horror while the rest of the crowd laughed nervously and applauded the realistic "effects." *That was real,* I thought in shock. *Someone filmed the whole thing. It doesn't look like studio footage, but surely they realized it wasn't their special effects when they put the documentary together?*

"A new generation of zombies is here," the narrator continued. "They aren't slow and stupid." I held my breath, tense and sweating as a shambling zombie woman morphed into a smiling college professor. "They look like us, but don't be fooled. When they get hungry—" The scene changed to the campus at night, where the now-rotting professor stalked a lone football player. "—they must feed." The crowd sucked in a collective breath as the professor took the football player down and cracked his skull like a walnut against the sidewalk.

And, in the next scene, the professor—smiling and whole again—gave a lecture as if nothing had happened. I breathed in shallow sips. Didn't matter that these were actors. This whole scenario hit too damn close to the truth.

"They're fast and strong." A very realistic zombie ran down a sprinter, lifted him over his head then let out a terrifying scream.

"These zombies can't be stopped by the swing of a machete." The shot zoomed to a dark-skinned arm strapped to a wall. I jerked as one swift stroke of a machete hacked off the hand with too-real-for-prime-time brutality. Even as the horrific image registered, time-lapse video showed a new hand regrowing from the stump—starting out as a bud then growing to full size. Just like Kang's body had been regrown from his head.

That shit was *real*. Saberton lab footage. It had to be. Dark skin. Oh god. Was that Kyle Griffin's arm? When I'd found him in Saberton's New York lab, he'd been mutilated and tortured, with his entire lower jaw removed. My gorge rose, but I forced myself to stay put, focused on the words and images. I needed to know exactly how fucked up it was.

"They're smart. They're strong. They're fast. They can heal." The shocking scene shifted to a postal worker walking down a street. To a nurse in a hospital. A church choir. A dentist.

"They live among us. Right here. Right now."

Scenes bled together showing everyday people going zombie, feeding on neighbors and customers and patients and students and coworkers. Actors and special effects. Mostly. But too real. Too goddamn real.

"Don't get caught. ZOMBIES. ARE. AMONG. US!"

The screen went dark. The lights came back up, and wild applause broke out an instant later.

I didn't clap. Couldn't. Not even to pretend I was part of the crowd. Nausea threatened to bring the canapés right back up. The hideous documentary had segments that matched each of the single asterisk filenames on Seeger's list. But what about the double asterisk files? What else was out there? Were there videos of Marcus being broken over and over? And would anyone recognize the crazed zombie at the melée as Philip?

More importantly, would anyone wonder if it could be real?

I looked around wildly for Andrew then froze like a rabbit beneath an owl. A broad-shouldered man stood on the other side of the tent with his arms folded over his chest. Bear, with Nick beside him. I wasn't surprised to see Bear here since his shop was one of the main sponsors. But knowing that Nick had seen the real zombie footage—even if he didn't know it was real—left me feeling weirdly off-balance.

The tent slowly emptied, and at long last I spied Andrew sitting in a folding chair near the back of the stage. Shoulders hunched and face sheet-white, he looked every bit as appalled and freaked as I felt. It was a double whammy for him. Real zombie stuff on top of insider footage from his company.

Braddock stepped into my path when I was a dozen feet away from him. "Now isn't the time," she told me, gaze hard and voice firm. "I'm taking him out of here."

Damn it, why did she have to be such a good bodyguard? "I know," I said. "Everything's screwed up, and he needs to leave." I gave her my best sincere and pleading look. "But it's vitally important that I talk to him, for his own sake. I swear I won't cause a scene."

Her eyes narrowed in distrust, but uncertainty flickered in them as well. She glanced toward the screen as if remembering the horrors shown there. Months ago she'd caught a glimpse of the atrocities taking place in the Saberton basement. She couldn't help but wonder how much of the film was real.

Mouth tight, Braddock shifted her regard to Andrew. He clutched his phone in one hand, and his cool business attitude was in tatters. With Snyder's help, he waved off eager fanpoodles but gave Braddock a nod when he saw me.

She glared the mother of all glares at me then stepped aside with obvious reluctance. "No trouble."

I breathed a thanks and moved to Andrew. He gestured for Snyder to back off.

"How did that footage get out?" I demanded, voice low. "Do you know anything about this?"

"I have no idea how the studio got their hands on it," he said. "I swear."

"All right. Shit." I pulled my thoughts together. "What's Dante Rosario's deal? What does he do for Saberton besides the doggie demonstrations?"

"He's worked security for close to a decade," Andrew said, slowly regaining his composure. "He became Marla's handler five years ago and was assigned to the Dallas lab for the past six months, up until you people raided it. He's on extended leave now."

"Sonofabitch," I breathed. "If he worked the Dallas lab, he was deep into the zombie research crap." An ugly suspicion stirred in my gut about the video files, but I wasn't ready to share it with Andrew yet. After all, he was first and foremost a Saber of Saberton.

He gave me a grim nod. "I have an exit strategy in the event everything goes to shit," he murmured. "It's an absolute last resort, but—"

"That's damn good to hear," I said fervently. "Let's hope it doesn't come to that." I did my best to keep my tone calm and casual. "Any updates on Kristi Charish?"

"Nothing yet. I'm scheduled to talk to my mother in the morning."

"Good luck with that." I made a face. "Keep us posted, and I'll stay out of your way as much as possible."

He snorted. "Why start now?"

My thoughts whirled as I left him in the tender care of his bodyguards. Dante Rosario had worked at the Dallas lab while Kristi Charish was there. According to Andrew, she'd taken a buttload of documentation with her when she escaped from the lab. What if *she* was the source of the leak?

Contents of USB Flash Drive from D.R. I didn't know yet how it all fit together, but I had a crazy-strong suspicion that the mysterious "D.R." from the file list was none other than one Dante Rosario.

Chapter 21

Rain from a sneak-attack Louisiana shower splattered my windshield and sent less adventurous Fest goers scurrying to their cars. My stomach growled as I briefed Dr. Nikas, and I switched the phone to speaker and set it on the dash. "Can't security pick up Rosario?"

"He's high profile Saberton," Dr. Nikas said. "An acquisition would require finesse, even if we had sufficient personnel for the op."

"So he walks?" I scowled and ripped the top off a brain packet.

"Other projects have priority."

"But—"

"I know," he said. "It's frustrating. Potentially damning zombie videos have been made public, and you've uncovered fragments of intel that seem to fit together. But we don't *know* Rosario is in league with Kristi or whether he has a Saberton agenda. It's conjecture."

"Then we find out for sure. Put a tail on him. Naomi or Rachel or—"

"Naomi and Dan flew out an hour ago to back up Pierce in Portland. Saberton is there in force, which makes recapturing Kristi impossible. Pierce is now hoping to convince Kristi to come with us willingly, but his only contact with her so far has been by phone."

Ugh. I despised the idea of Kristi Charish working with us while being free to come and go as she pleased, but I also knew that the bitch had smarts and skills the Tribe needed.

"All of our available security people are deployed elsewhere or are working short-handed," Dr. Nikas continued. "Jacques and Reg are armed because lab security is at half-strength. We don't have the resources for a local non-emergency operation." Dr. Nikas went silent for several seconds. "Angel, you're the only available person who can deal with this."

Jacques and Reg were carrying *guns*? Aliens taking over city hall would be less shocking. I sank back in my seat. "Well, damn."

"I agree wholeheartedly."

By the time we disconnected, the rain had passed, and a fat rainbow floated over the Fest grounds. Maybe it was a sign that everything was going to be A-okay.

I sipped the packet of brains as I mulled over my options. The most inviting one was to go home, kick back, and watch a bit of mind-numbing reality TV. But I was the Tribe's only hope for gathering intel on Rosario. I was *it*, thanks to a perfect storm of a ton of crap happening at once. It wasn't enough that FBI agents were snooping around funeral homes. No, the universe had to throw in the Kristi Charish wrench, forcing the Tribe honchos to scramble and change their plans to check their out-of-state funeral homes, and instead head to Oregon. Add in Saberton's usual hijinks, Grayson Seeger's murder, and Rosario possibly leaking the video files, and we were running around with our hair on fire while the universe laughed its ass off.

Well, screw the universe. I could handle the Rosario shit. There was always the chance he was still at the Fest, despite his earlier claim that he was leaving. It would be easy enough to check at the gate and find out. If he *was* still here, then I'd wait and tail him when he left. If not, a few calls to hotels within twenty miles might give me—

My phone rang with an unknown number. I stabbed at the answer button. "Hello?"

"Angel."

Not Randy. Disappointment flashed through me, with anger on its heels. "Judd! Y'all are a bunch of fucking morons! Skip town? Seriously? That's the best plan y'all could come up with? Where are you?"

"Shit. Calm your tits! Yeah, we skipped." He spoke fast, stressed. "We all talked it over and figured we're gonna stay low 'til shit cools off."

Cools off? For a murder? He was acting like it was a lousy prank. I clamped down on the urge to scream at him. That wouldn't help. I needed him to believe I agreed and was on his side. "Shit." I blew out a breath, faked a sigh. "Okay, that might work. Where's Randy?"

"He and Coy are busy setting up where we're gonna be staying," Judd said. "He asked me to call because he needs you to get something he hid and bring it to me."

My Angel-sense prickled. "What kind of something?"

"Just a couple of things that need to be properly disposed of, if y'know what I mean."

Incriminating evidence. The machete and baseball bat. It had to be. "Where are they?"

Judd let out a strained laugh. "I'm telling you in code in case phones are tapped, okay?"

My god, he really was an idiot. "Sure, I'll do it."

"Good. That's good. They're in the place y'all fixed a wheelbarrow after the river dried up. You know where that is, right?"

Only one place Randy and I had ever fixed a wheelbarrow. But what the hell did "after the river dried up" mean? Did he mean the flood last year when the spillway collapsed? I started to ask then stopped as my Angel-sense did a tap-dance on the back of my neck. "Yeah, I know where it is," I said instead, "but why can't you just go get them yourself?"

" 'Cause we're fucking hiding out." Judd's voice shook. "I need you to go get the stuff, and then I'll meet you someplace safe. Out by Lock Three."

I mentally replayed the twenty seconds or so of conversation. It was a code, all right, but it sure sounded as if Judd didn't know what it meant. Which begged the question, why would Randy use a code that I understood but Judd didn't? Randy wouldn't dick around with a murder rap on the line. My pulse pounded unevenly as pieces of an ugly picture fell into place. After the murder, Coy and Judd went to Randy for help covering it up. Coy hid the head and clothes in his garage, Randy hid the weapons on his property, and Judd didn't have a damn thing incriminating at his place. Not to mention, Judd had done his best to throw Coy under the bus by saying Coy had the bat. Maybe deep down Randy hadn't trusted Judd enough to tell him where he stashed the weapons. But whatever the reason, it gave him an ace in the hole.

And he was playing that card right now.

"Let me talk to Randy."

"I told you, he ain't here!" Judd said, voice rising. "You stupid bitch. Stop fucking around and go get the goddamn things."

"You're a real sweet-talker, Judd," I said with a sneer. "But I ain't bringing you jack shit until I talk to Randy."

"Bring the fucking weapons to the lock in one hour," he screamed, *"or you can talk to the pieces of Randy that I cut his worthless ass into!"*

I kept my head, only because I'd suspected that was the deal. "Bring Randy and Coy with you, alive and well," I yelled right back, "or you can stuff the weapons up your ass!"

He went silent, and for an instant I thought he'd hung up. "Fine," he choked out. "I'll trade you those two fuckers for the weapons. One hour at Lock Three."

The line went dead. My hand trembled as it gripped the phone. Had I said the right thing? What if Randy and Coy were already dead? No, Randy was still alive. Judd wouldn't kill him until he got hold of the weapons. But Coy . . .

Sick dread swam through me. Judd had killed once already. The second time would be easier. Randy would protect Coy, though. That's what he always did. God, I hoped he could.

I scrambled to find Ben's number in my contacts and hit the call button. A split second later I hit disconnect. No. I couldn't tell Ben. Not yet. The cops wouldn't be on board with any kind of exchange for hostages. I'd learned that from Marcus. That wasn't how they worked. Never give the suspect what they want. Besides, there was no way in hell Judd would let Randy and Coy walk free—not when they could testify against him. Any fantasy I had of handing over the murder weapons and getting Randy and Coy back safe and sound was just that—a fantasy.

I pressed my fingers to my eyes as I struggled to line up my thoughts. Randy would have known that Judd would kill him as soon as he got the murder weapons. Hell, he'd know that Judd would want to take me out as well, since I knew what happened. So why give Judd what he wanted?

A laugh began in my belly as the answer came to me. Randy was a laid back, pothead, gearhead with little ambition, but beneath all that he was pretty clever. In fact, most people tended to underestimate his smarts. Randy had indeed told me where the weapons were. He didn't have a choice since he knew it was possible Judd would eventually find them.

But my smart, loser ex-boyfriend had also snuck in a clue about where he and Coy were being held.

Chapter 22

Randy said to tell you it's in the place y'all fixed a wheelbarrow after the river dried up.

Not too long after I turned seventeen I got a job at the Jolly Burger—one of the many minimum wage jobs I scored in my young life. Two weeks later a cute guy named Randy Winger came in and started chatting me up, and that night we had our first date—if drinking cheap wine and making out at the boat launch could be considered a date. I quit my Jolly Burger job five days later, already deep in the throes of young love and blissfully certain that in a year or so I'd be changing my name to the awesomely cool "Angel Winger."

Randy's dad was still living with him back then. Mr. Hank was gruff but kind and never had a problem with me spending the night when things were bad with my dad—though he first made absolutely sure I was above the age of consent. He wasn't stupid. He knew Randy and I were banging like jackhammers, and he wanted to be sure his son didn't get in legal trouble. Mr. Hank also sat me down a week or two after Randy and I started dating, and gave me a *very* detailed lecture about teen pregnancy, STDs, abortion, and contraception. Hearing all this from a grizzled man who watched NASCAR as if it was his religion was disturbing and uncomfortable and more than a little emotionally scarring. That said, it was also damned effective. After he finished, I practically ran to the nearest health department clinic and got on the Pill, which was almost certainly why I didn't end up as a teen pregnancy statistic.

While Mr. Hank had apparently accepted that two people with raging hormones were going to go at it as often as possible, he made it clear that he didn't want to hear it going on under his roof. As a result, Randy and I found a variety of places to screw, but our favorite was an old treehouse in a sprawling oak near the back of Randy's property. Draped in camo netting for extra concealment and hard to find unless you knew which game trail to follow, it was the perfect pot den and sex nook for a horny couple. But the most memorable fuck was the time Randy wanted to try a bunch of different positions from a sex book he'd swiped. Most were okay, but about a minute into the wheelbarrow position my arms started to hurt, and I told Randy that my wheelbarrow was broken. He thought it was the funniest thing ever and, after that, whenever he wanted to go to the treehouse to fuck, he'd ask me if my wheelbarrow needing fixing.

In other words, I knew without a doubt that the weapons were stashed in the treehouse. There was no way Judd would ever figure out that part of Randy's clue. But it was the second part of the clue that had me wondering.

I fretted as I sailed down the highway toward the east end of the parish. "After the river dried up" couldn't possibly mean the spillway collapse last year. Randy and I sure as shit hadn't fixed any wheelbarrows since then, though Judd had no way to know that. There was one possible location that came to mind—one that *did* make sense and would be a horribly good place to keep a couple of people prisoner.

When Randy was in high school, he had a buddy whose

family owned a fishing camp on the East Kreeger River, and several times a year he and his buddy would go out there to fish and swim and just hang out. Unfortunately, during Randy's senior year, the East Kreeger River decided to shift its course, as rivers do, and the fishing camp ended up stranded a mile from the new riverbank. The buddy and his family moved away not long after, and Randy took over the camp and made it a man-cave hideaway. Later he brought in other friends, including Judd and Coy, making them all swear to keep the location secret. And, of course, Randy had taken me there a time or two without the guys knowing. Hey, we needed another place to fuck.

Judd hadn't started going to the camp until years after the river shifted, and at the moment I was counting on him not twigging to the "river dried up" bit of the clue and realizing Randy had tipped me off. But what if Judd was there at the camp with the guys? He'd told me he would exchange Randy and Coy for the weapons, in which case he'd be there right now to collect them for the swap.

"Yeah, right," I said then added, "*Ha!*" for good measure. Judd was a lying piece of shit who had everything to lose if he let Randy and Coy go. Right now he was getting ready to meet, ahem, *ambush* me at Lock Three.

And, if Judd is at the fishing camp with the guys, I'll call the cops—anonymously—and let them rescue Randy and Coy, I promised myself.

I made a turn onto a gravel road marked by a bent and rusted sign that said Pickstick Mill Road. After half a mile through towering pines I veered onto a rutted dirt lane then slowed to a snail's pace. Fresh tire tracks stood out in the drying mud. At least I knew my hunch was right, but my worry ratcheted up a few more notches. Peering ahead, I eased around the last curve, ready to back the hell out of there if I saw another car.

I let out the breath I'd been holding. The clearing was barely large enough to hold three cars, but at the moment nothing but winter-brown grass occupied it. There was no other place to park that didn't mean a mile hike through the woods, and I couldn't see Judd putting in that much effort.

As soon as I parked, I grabbed a brain packet from the console and gulped the contents down. Though I couldn't get super-tanked because of the V12, the snack would bump my senses and reflexes up a tad, doubly helpful since I'd be going in armed with more than my sunny disposition. I popped the glove box open to snag my gun out.

No gun. Cursing, I leaned over and dug through crap, pulled papers out and dumped them onto the front seat. No gun! *Shit!* I was absolutely positive it had been in there before the Zombie Fest. I'd shoved a gas receipt in and bumped the metal of the barrel.

"Someone stole it," I murmured in disbelief as the gun refused to materialize. *Fuck!* It had to have been while I was parked at the Fest. Another ugly truth swept in, and I gritted my teeth. This wasn't random. No broken windows or any other sign of forced entry. Whoever took it was a pro, most likely some asshole hitting cars in the Fest parking lot. Then again, it was also possible my car had been specifically targeted, though it seemed a lot of risk just to take away my gun.

Fine. I didn't need a gun to kick ass. I had plenty of weapons at my disposal: My cutting wit, my hot temper, and my never-say-die attitude. Oh, and the tire iron from the trunk of my car.

Beyond the small clearing, pines crowded together with water oaks and swamp hickory, thick enough to hide anything past a hundred feet. I'd only ever been out here four or five times, and the last had been around three years ago. But a towering magnolia marked the direction as effectively as a neon sign, and closer inspection revealed scuffs and crushed grass along the old game path we'd used.

Spurred by urgency, I broke into a jog and threaded through the trees. Even if Judd wasn't with the guys now, he might return at any moment to check on them.

Or kill them.

Eventually, the trees thinned to reveal a small building that looked completely out of place in the middle of the woods, like the witch's house in Hansel and Gretel, but with less candy. About half the size of a single-wide trailer, with a corrugated tin roof and wood siding stained green in patches by moss, it rested on low pilings at the edge of a shallow valley where the river used to run. In place of the water a forest of young trees now stood, dominated by fast-growing tallows and peppered throughout with the small white flowers of blackberry vines.

Clamping down on the urge to shout Randy's name, I crept onto the sagging excuse for a porch and peered cautiously through a Plexiglas window. My knees wobbled in relief at the sight of Randy sitting slouched against the far wall, while Coy—nicely alive—lay curled up on the floor a few feet away. Each was secured to a thick 8" x 8" support pillar by chains padlocked around their necks. Two gallon jugs of water sat nearby along with another plastic jug that held about three inches of what looked like piss. And, best of all, no sign of Judd.

The door was unlocked, and I yanked it open. Randy jerked in shock, fury blazing in his eyes until he registered that I wasn't Judd. Anger stirred in my belly at the sight of a dark bruise that spread across his jaw.

"Angel." He let out a shaky laugh. "Coy, wake up! She did it!"

Coy sat up with a groan, blinked at me blearily with one eye. My rage climbed higher as I realized the other was swollen shut. Dried blood flaked off his cheek, and his smile revealed a broken front tooth.

"You did it," Randy said with a lopsided grin. "I knew you'd figure it out."

A warm flush of pride went through me. "It was a good clue," I said then crouched to inspect the chain and padlock at his neck. Not heavy duty, but no way could I break either one, even at top zombie strength.

"I guess I kinda knew in my gut that Judd was up to

something," Randy said, "which is why I hid the weapons in a place he didn't know about. I was crossing fingers big time that you'd get what I meant about the river. I counted on him thinking I was talking 'bout the spillway." He winced. "Wish I coulda figured out a way to tell you to bring bolt cutters."

I snorted. "That would've been nice, but I think I have something in my car that'll work. Are either of y'all hurt more than just banged up?"

"Coy caught it worse," Randy said with a worried glance at his friend.

"I'm alive, and you look like an angel, Angel," Coy said with an uneven smile. "That's all that matters."

Randy scowled. "Judd went ballistic. I had a feeling he'd be against going to the cops, but I never expected him to go this far." He jangled the chain.

"Judd was out of his damn head," Coy put in, brow furrowing. He had a weirdly charming lisp and whistle to his words now, thanks to the broken tooth. "He was gonna kill us."

"Asshole missed his chance," I said. "I'm getting you out of here."

Randy caught my wrist. "He was raving about real zombies," he said. "Had this notion you was one. Said he had proof."

"Yeah, he's crazy." I forced a laugh and pulled out of his grasp. "Be right back."

I ran to my car then leaned my hands against the trunk and tried to rein in the panic that squeezed my chest. Judd *knew*. It hadn't been a coincidence that he wrote my name on the notepad. Something in those files convinced him. I needed to get Seeger's damn flash drive—and the copy Judd made—before he caused real trouble, then figure out what the hell made him think I was a real zombie.

I took a deep breath and let it out slowly. Even if I got the drives, the original files would still be out there. Nothing I could do about that yet, but I could sure as hell deal with Judd.

And how much did Randy believe? Before New York, I told him I had a medical condition that was only manageable with an illegal drug. If he could get past the weird factor, he was sharp enough to figure out that "medical condition" equaled "zombie," and "illegal drug" equaled "brains." I'd have to play this one by ear and hope he was too stressed to think straight.

Slightly calmer, I rooted through my trunk until I found a found a can of compressed air that I'd bought to clean my keyboard at home and then kept forgetting to bring inside. Randy and Coy looked at me like I was insane when I turned the can upside down and sprayed freezing air on the chains, but their distrust shifted to outright awe when I smashed the tire iron on the frozen links and shattered them. Fuck yeah, science!

They each still had a section padlocked around their necks, but I didn't give a shit about that right now. "It's a fashion statement," I told them, tone sharp, then hurried them up the trail, chains jangling. When we got to my car I ordered them to hunker down in the back, then I got us the ever-living hell out of there.

"Can we sit up yet?" Coy ventured once I was on the highway.

"No," I snapped. "Randy, are the machete and bat wrapped up in anything?"

"Yeah, a couple of black garbage bags," he said. "But you won't have any trouble finding them. They're right in the middle of the treehouse floor."

"I'm not going to get them." I pulled off the highway, came to a stop on the shoulder, then leveled a fierce look at the two men. "*Now* you can sit up."

Chains clinked as they shifted upright. "What's going on?" Randy asked, looking around in puzzlement. "Why'd you stop? Why aren't you gonna get the weapons?"

"I stopped because there's a gas station about a quarter mile up the road," I said. "You two are going to walk your asses in there and call the fucking cops." Distress flickered in their eyes, but I glared them down. "You're going to tell them everything that happened without once mentioning my fucking name. You're going to tell them where the weapons are and that Judd kidnapped you when you were about to turn yourselves in, and you're going to tell them you escaped from the fishing camp because you found a can of compressed air under a cabinet and got all sorts of clever." I paused, put every ounce of pissed-off-and-fed-the-fuck-up I had into my tone and expression. "And if you don't walk to that gas station and call the cops and spill your guts—except for the parts that pertain to me—I *will* make you fucking wish you were still chained up in that goddamn place. Am I making myself absolutely clear?"

It was empty bluster on my part, but they must have understood that I needed to vent all the worry and fear for them that I'd kept pent up until now. They sighed in unison. "Yeah," Coy said. "Should've listened to you last night."

"No shit. Now get the hell out and have a nice walk."

They slid out of the car, then Randy poked his head back in. "Thanks, Angel. You saved our asses."

"Yeah, I did. Don't you dare fuck up again."

He gave me a sweet and lazy smile, closed the door then started limping with Coy toward the gas station. I watched them for about a minute then pulled back onto the highway and zoomed past.

Thirty minutes until Judd was expecting me to meet him. I had no desire to disappoint the prick.

Chapter 23

"Lock Three" was local slang for the area at the end of Hickory Horn Road by the Kreeger River's third river-control lock. It was also a damn good place for a clandestine meeting, which raised my estimation of Judd's smarts ever so slightly. Not only was Lock Three in the middle of nowhere with the nearest house at least two miles away, but this particular chunk of "nowhere" was at the ass end of the parish, where cell phone service and police presence were equally spotty.

I stopped where the road ended at a broad field by the river. Several unnamed dirt roads radiated off the field, along with over a dozen four-wheeler trails, creating more escape routes than you could shake a stick at.

The sun wasn't due to set for another hour, but it was low enough to cast long shadows of pines across the field like dark claws. This was a prime spot for teen hormones to rampage, and I was confident that more than a few parish residents had been conceived in this very field. Fortunately, it was still several hours shy of prime nookie time.

It's not too late to call the Sheriff's Office, my conscience whispered. With Randy and Coy most likely in custody by now, every cop in the parish would be on the lookout for Judd. All I had to do was find another pay phone and make an anonymous call.

My hands tightened on the steering wheel. No, there wasn't enough time for the Sheriff's Office to mobilize and discreetly set up a trap. Not to mention, I needed the stupid flash drives. A whole lot of zombie lives could be affected by those files, and if Judd had the drives with him—which I sure hoped—the last thing I wanted was a bunch of redneck cops watching the videos. Especially since at least one of those videos convinced Judd I was a zombie. Besides, if all went according to plan, I'd be wrapping up Judd's worthless butt like a Christmas present for Ben Roth and the Sheriff's Office. I'd waited too long to tell Ben what I suspected, and this was the best way to fix all that. *And* avoid getting myself busted for interfering with an investigation.

Judd was nowhere in sight, though my gut told me he was watching from the treeline. I was a few minutes late, thanks to a couple of vital errands. The first was a detour to Marcus's house—which I still had a key to—where I borrowed his ballistic vest. It was at least ten sizes too big for me and easily the most uncomfortable thing I'd ever worn, but I needed every possible advantage I could scrape up. I'd also hoped to borrow a gun from Marcus, but he'd acquired a fancy new gun safe and wasn't dumb enough to leave the combination written down anywhere. Damn it. I wasn't thrilled about meeting Judd without firepower, but I had no other way to score a gun quickly. Then again, my parasite was already one hell of a weapon.

My second errand was to BigShopMart where I shelled out fifty bucks for Judd-conning supplies and a butcher knife that could fit up my jacket sleeve. Back in the car, and wearing gloves to avoid leaving fingerprints, I bundled the newly acquired gardening machete and cheapo baseball bat into a couple of black garbage bags then wrapped them up tight with duct tape. Best case scenario was that he'd never touch the bundle. But, if he did, it had to feel like the right stuff.

Ideally, a third errand would have been to my storage unit to stock up on brains from the last of my freezer reserves. I only had three packets with me, but the side trip would have cost too much time. Forty minutes late would make Judd think I'd gone to the cops. But he'd wait it out for at least five. He wanted the murder weapons.

He also wanted me dead—hence the borrowed vest. At least, if I was him I'd want me dead. Loose ends, and all that. Judd would hopefully be operating on the assumption that Randy and Coy were still chained up in that cabin—two more loose ends to snip as soon as he took care of me. I was counting on the fact that he'd want to be sure I had the weapons and wouldn't simply sniper me in the head from a few hundred yards away. After all, he wasn't stupid. If he killed me and I'd left the weapons elsewhere, he'd be up shit creek.

All I needed was to get close enough for my zombie skills to matter. Knock his ass down a few times, get the damn flash drives from him, wrap him up in duct tape, then—anonymously—let the cops know where to find him.

Right. Easy. So why was my heart pounding a mile a minute?

I scarfed down two packets of brains. Time to get this show on the road.

As soon as the all-is-well brainy tingle set in, I drove to the middle of the field and stopped, doing my best to not look at all anxious as I scanned for any sign of Judd. The field was big enough that it was next to impossible to sneak up on anyone waiting near the center. Yet another reason why this was a good spot for a meeting of this sort.

About half a minute later, a dull blue car cruised slowly from one of the dirt roads. It wasn't Judd's pickup, but I knew it was him. He stopped about fifty feet from me, climbed out and stood behind his open door. I took up a similar pose behind my own car door and silently prayed that it and the dim light would hide that I had the bulky vest on under my jacket.

"You have the stuff?" he hollered, scowl visible even from this distance.

"Sure do," I replied. "But I don't see Randy or Coy in your car."

"They're not far from here," he said. "As soon as I have the package in my hands, I'll tell you where to find them."

Lying sack of shit. "Guess I don't have a choice."

Judd grinned, cocky. "That's right."

What an ass. But I was fine with letting him think he had the upper hand. For now. I opened the back door, slipped the butcher knife up my sleeve and scooped the garbage bag bundle off the seat.

"Bring it over here," he ordered.

I clutched the bundle to my chest and walked toward him. I knew he had a gun—probably in a back-of-the-pants holster. He made no move to meet me halfway, but that didn't matter. All I needed was to get within twenty feet of him before he reached for his gun. From that distance I'd be able to pour on the zombie speed and take him down before he could react. Forty feet, thirty. He watched me, tense. I kept my face expressionless.

He stepped from behind his car door when I reached the halfway point.

Shit. Still too far away! I tossed the bundle of decoy weapons aside, pulled the knife from my sleeve and charged him. But instead of reaching for his gun, Judd lifted the bad-ass tactical crossbow he'd been holding out of sight behind the car door.

The vest won't stop a crossbow bolt! Adrenaline punched through me at the horrid realization, but it didn't come with the surge of zombie super-speed I really fucking needed. Goddamn V12. Panic robbed me of breath as I ran full out at slug-ass human speed. Judd should have been gasping on his back with my knee in his chest and the knife at his throat, but instead he raised the crossbow and sighted in a smooth and practiced motion.

Oh god. Not a headshot. Please.

The bolt punched me hard in the chest, followed by searing agony. The knife flew from my grasp, and I stumbled and fell hard to my hands and knees, then stared at the purple and gold fletching two inches from my jacket. *It went through me,* I thought in near-hysterical annoyance. Through the front panel of the vest, through my chest, and would have continued on out the back if it hadn't smacked into the rear panel of the vest. Way easier for my parasite to deal with the injury without a bolt in the way, but how was I to know Judd would bring his friggin' *crossbow?*

Blood bubbled into my mouth as I fought to get up. The pain dimmed slightly as my parasite trudged into action, and I willed it into higher gear. *Any* gear. If I didn't get my shit together quick, Judd would be able to take me out with a head shot. My parasite would really have its work cut out for it then.

"Figured you'd pussy out and wear a vest," Judd said with a nasty sneer. He retrieved the bundle of decoy weapons then tossed it and the crossbow into his car. Numb shock turned my limbs to lead when he pulled a gun and started toward me again.

He's going to finish me off now. One in the head won't kill me dead-dead, but only if someone shoves brains into me. No one's here to do that. What if I end up at the morgue? Will my dad know what to do when he finds out? But Judd knows I'm a zombie. He'll chop off my head and chuck it into the swamp.

No.

Fuck this prick. I lurched to my feet. Zombie speed or not, I wasn't going down without a fight.

Judd's eyes narrowed as he lifted the gun and fired. The bullet smacked into the vest like a giant fist, sending me sprawling and knocking what little breath I had from my lungs. The crossbow bolt grated against ribs, and fresh pain seared through me as even as I reeled in confusion. Judd *knew* I was wearing a vest, *knew* I was a zombie, so why shoot me in the chest instead of between the eyes? Not that I was complaining but, what the hell?

I sucked shallow breaths through gritted teeth and managed to roll to one side. Hunger clawed my belly as my parasite struggled to deal with the damage. Judd holstered his gun then yanked a set of handcuffs from a pocket. My thoughts moved sluggishly, refusing to make the connection, and I stared stupidly at him as he seized my left arm.

"You're coming with me, you fucking monster-freak bitch," he snarled as he snapped one cuff around my wrist.

The cold touch of the steel jolted me from my daze as effectively as a bucket of ice water. *That's why he didn't shoot me in the head. He's capturing me.* For Saberton? Someone else?

Didn't matter. Wasn't going to happen.

As Judd reached for my other wrist, I jerked my cuffed hand back, yanking the handcuffs from his grasp. He let out a surprised cry that turned into a yelp of pain as I whipped the unlocked side of the cuffs across his leg like a mini-flail. My zombie superpowers were being lazy little shits at the moment, but I'd scraped my way up to two whole stripes on my white belt in *jiu jitsu*, and I had a black belt in redneck pissed-off-bitch dirty fighting.

"Shit! You fucking b-aaagh!" Judd went to his knees as my kick slammed into the back of his leg. Red-faced, he groped for the holster at the small of his back. My chest was a fiery ball of agony, but I knew if he shot me again it was all over. No way was I going to let this asshole take me down.

With a cry of primal rage, I shoved up past the pain, launched myself at him and slammed my elbow into his face as hard as I could. Cartilage crunched in beautiful melody, bringing a manic grin to my face. While Judd

roared in pain, I wrenched his gun from the holster and
flung it as far into the gloom as I could. I hated to throw a
weapon away, but I didn't want to give him a chance to
wrestle it from me.

"Bitch!" Blood fountained from Judd's nose, but apparently he was equally determined to not go down without a
fight. He smacked his head into mine hard enough for me
to see stars, then followed up with a heavy punch to my ribs.
White hot pain seared through my entire body, and I crumpled, whimpering. Yet the scent of his brain wrapped around
me, taunting the hunger, and my whimper turned into a
growl.

Judd let out an ugly laugh. "Think you're tough, huh? I
can't wait to break every fucking bone in your body. Twice."
He grabbed the dangling cuff and gave my arm a vicious
tug.

My parasite wasn't doing much to control the pain, but
when he yanked my arm it was as if my precious little brain-
starved zombie parasite dumped one last dose of "fuck this
asshole" into my system. I lunged, clamped my teeth onto
his forearm, and bit down as hard as I could.

Judd screamed and released the handcuff. I held on like
a tick and bit down through skin and the top layer of muscle. He screamed again, a high-pitched sound of panic and
revulsion, then jerked back, dragging me to my feet as I
clamped down harder and my mouth filled with blood.
Beating at me with his free fist, he thrashed, struggling to
shake me loose.

I let go and retreated a few steps. No point in losing my
teeth to this prick for something as trivial as an arm. Not
with his luscious brain waiting for me. My growl burbled
with blood as he staggered back. I shambled in pursuit, then
fell to my hands and knees, still reaching for him.

Face pale and eyes wide, Judd stared in horror at the
bleeding wound on his arm. He jerked his eyes to me as
sheer terror flooded his face, then he let out a strangled cry
and fled to his car. I gathered myself to dodge if he tried to

run me over, but instead he peeled out in a sharp turn and sped off toward the highway.

The sound of the engine died away, leaving the rasp of my breathing and the croak of frogs by the river. I spat blood into the dirt, wiped at my mouth with a shaking hand, then stumbled to my car while pain and hunger raged through me.

Chapter 24

Every breath sent lava through my veins. I dragged myself half onto the driver's seat and fumbled a brain packet from the console. My hands shook too much to tear it open, but my teeth got the job done. I sucked the packet dry then shuddered as my parasite went to work and dulled the white hot edge of the pain. Not enough, though. *More. Need more.* I searched the console and the glove box, scrabbled through pens and maps and receipts. Nothing. *I'm out.* Shit.

Not the end of the world, I told myself firmly, though panic scrabbled at the edges of my mind. No need to freak. The situation was ten tons of fucked up, but that meant I was justified in calling for backup. Brain delivery in thirty minutes or it's free. A manic giggle slipped out as I grabbed my phone off the dash and—

No Service

A sob escaped before I recovered the shreds of my composure. Okay. Fine. So I didn't have backup. That meant I had two choices: give up, or save myself. And fuck giving up. I'd take this step by step, and the first step was to get my ass out of here before Judd checked the stuff in the garbage bag bundle and realized it wasn't the murder weapons.

I shifted to sit upright, and pain flared like a red-hot coal in my chest. With a breathless scream, I jerked forward to take the pressure off the head of the crossbow bolt then hugged the steering wheel. Tears snaked down my cheeks as I shuddered. *Hey, moron, you can't lean back and chill when you have a triple-bladed bolt head sticking out of your back!*

Seconds ticked by, but at long last the red haze of agony lifted enough that I could work through a plan of action. I needed to be able to drive without leaning on the wheel, but the fucking bolt had a carbon shaft that I couldn't break with my ordinary wimpy Angel strength. And, with that barbed tip in place, no way could I pull it out from the front. Desperate, I twisted my arm up behind me only to discover that, because the vest was so damn huge, the bolt hadn't gone through the back panel. Couldn't pull it out with the vest in the way, but the good thing was that the front and back panels attached with Velcro. It took me half a minute of agony and cold sweat to remove my jacket and the back panel, but then, even though I managed to get my fingers on the bolt, I had zero leverage to pull it out.

Great. From bad to worse. *Nice going, Angel.* The front vest panel was still nailed to me, and several inches of carbon shaft currently protruded from my back—with the tip poised to snag the seat every time I shifted. *This is gonna suck.* Straightening, I clenched my hand around the purple and gold fletching, gritted my teeth, then tugged. Pain raced through my chest, and brain-hunger twisted my gut in a vicious dance, but I didn't stop until I felt the blades touch my back and six inches of bloody shaft stuck out the front.

My breath came in shallow gasps. I let my hand drop then clenched it into a fist. Home was a twenty-mile drive away, and here I was barely able to see straight through the pain and hunger. Maybe it would be better to head to my storage unit instead? I had more brains there, though that wasn't saying a whole lot. But the storage unit was farther away, and I already knew it was going to be touch-and-go to simply make it home.

A dose would help. V12. Hell, pain control was part of its design. My reminder alarm wouldn't go off for another two hours, but then again, Dr. Nikas had simply said "twice a day." A little early shouldn't matter, and this *was* an emergency.

With the ease of habit, I injected a dose then chased it with a capsule. Barely a hint of the feel-good whispered through me, and a scant handful of faint sparkles glimmered on the dash. The hunger only calmed a tiny bit, but the pain eased off to dull numbness as my parasite stumbled into action. Good enough. Now I could get the hell out of here.

Driving while sitting up perfectly straight was way more awkward than I expected, but leaning back was out of the question. I kept my hands clenched on the wheel and drove as safely and law abidingly as possible since, not only did I have zero plausible explanation as to why I had a crossbow bolt sticking out from below my right tit, but I had a feeling my reputation with the police might suffer if I *ate* whichever unlucky officer pulled me over.

I drove the three miles back up Hickory Horn Road then another two on the narrow, unlit country highway before I saw another vehicle. I hunched as the headlights approached, even though I knew the chances were nonexistent that anyone would catch sight of the crossbow bolt as we passed. Still, best to play it safe—

The church van zoomed by, and the scent of warm brains swirled in its wake. A brief whiff, but enough to stoke the hunger to full flame. It scorched nerve endings, fanned higher every time a car passed, while I stared straight ahead and counted the miles. Ten miles left. I'd managed to hold on so far, passed half a dozen cars without chasing anyone down to peel the vehicle open like a can of tuna. I could hold on a little while longer. Thank god the night was chilly enough that most people were driving with their windows up.

As if to mock my gratitude, a pickup rattled by with its

windows wide open. The heady bouquet of a redneck brain caressed me, wringing an ugly rasp of a growl from my throat. I bared my teeth at the piece of shit truck in my rearview mirror. A quick U-turn and I could chase down the driver, get the brains I needed.

Pull it together, Angel! So fucking hungry. And no point calling the lab at this point, either. They were on the other side of the parish. The closest refuge was home, and that's where I needed to go. Brains waited for me there, my emergency stash and—

I pulled onto the shoulder and fumbled for my phone, breathed a *thank you* for the two bars. "Dad!" I gasped out the instant the call connected. "My f-fij." Shit. My speech was going. "Fihj!" Combination. I needed to give him the combination to my mini-fridge, but the numbers jumped and jumbled in my head. Change of plan. "No, feesa. In feesha. Bag of fash . . . foshen bussa spouss."

"What? Brussel sprouts? In the freezer? Why the hell do we got brussel sprouts? I hate those things."

"Yesh. Thassa point. Put bahg . . . on pash."

"Put bag where? Angel, what the fuck's going on?"

"Porsh." Just a few more miles left to go, but only if I could get him to understand me. "Bahg on porsh." I focused everything I had on each word. "Lohck . . . door. Lohck me . . . awt."

A beat of silence. "Shit. Brussel sprouts on the porch, and lock the door 'til you're yourself again."

I'd have wept if I had any tears. "Yesh."

A rustling came through the line, then the closing of a door. "Okay, it's done. Now get your ass home."

A motorcycle whizzed past as I ended the call. *Brains.* Before I even realized I was moving, I opened my door and stuck one foot out, then froze as I fought the instinct that urged me to chase down my prey on foot. Shaking, I pulled my foot in, closed the door and locked it.

Maybe going home was a bad idea? But what choice did I have? My other options would take too long. If I didn't do

something about the hunger real damn soon, I was going to
go full monster.

No.

My fingers felt like clumsy lumps of cold dough as I drew
up a syringe of V12. I hesitated, breath wet and raspy. Two
doses less than fifteen minutes apart. I'd never taken so
much so quickly. *I don't have a choice. I'm not going to make
it without a second dose.* I stabbed the needle in, jammed
the plunger. Within seconds, the hunger settled, and my
breath eased. *Okay, I got this.*

For added insurance, I dug a Bayou Burger napkin out
of the console, tore it in half, twisted the pieces and stuck
them in my nostrils. A zombie won't eat what a zombie can't
smell, right?

I tensed as headlights approached and prayed I was right
about the nose plugs. The car whizzed past, and I relaxed as
the chase instinct didn't trigger. *Paper boogies for the win.*

Weird heat like an alcohol rush abruptly surged through
me. Pain faded, and the black night outside lightened to
eerie late twilight. Whirs and chirps of insects mixed with
the distant huff of an eighteen-wheeler's air brakes. A laugh
built in my throat. I knew what this was. Zombie superpowers, high on overdrive. *Aw, yeah. I can do anything.* I
gripped the steering wheel and gave it an experimental
torqueing tug. It creaked, and I had no doubt I could break
it if I wanted to. *Yeah, baby.* Grinning, I pulled back onto
the highway.

Five miles down the road, the overdrive kicked me out
of the airplane without a parachute. I swerved and barely
managed to stay out of the ditch as pain returned with
crushing force along with a bone-deep exhaustion.

Wonderful. Half a dozen minutes of kick all the ass, followed by the zombie hangover from hell.

My world narrowed to keeping it together enough to
make it home. Eyes on the road, obey the speed limit, ignore passing cars. Try and distract myself by naming all the

functions of organelles. Nucleus, chloroplast, ribosome, lysosome . . .

Home.

Home and Dad. Just a few more miles to go. Or light years. Felt like I'd been driving forever. Cars whizzed by, but I barely noticed them, thanks to the V12 and napkin-nose-plugs.

A couple dozen antique and classic cars filled the parking lot of Chicory Chick Coffee and Wings, along with twice that many people. Holding my breath, I punched through the thick cloud of brain scent. Didn't fool the hunger. It sensed the drifting molecules and burst out of its restraints, surging up like an alligator gar ambushing a tasty duck. I let out an anguished scream and hit the gas. Home. Feed at home.

Home. I parked and ripped the napkin from my nose. Stumbled out of the car and sniffed the air, took in the scent. *Brains*. Hunger vibrated through me and dug sharp nails into every cell. Brains, in the house. A twitch of movement in the window. *Prey*. Mine. I lurched toward the house, snarled as the prey moved away. Up the steps and onto the porch. Brains. Cold brains. But in the house was a fresh brain. Yes. *Want fresh*. A door, closed. I hammered my fists on it, clawed and yowled. I smelled the fear of my prey, but the door stayed closed. *Feed*. Needed to feed. I turned back to the cold brains, ripped at the bag. *Feed*.

The frost raked my mouth, froze my gullet as I chewed and swallowed. *Yes. Oh god, yes, that's it.*

The hunger settled down, content as a kitten full of milk. A shiver racked me as I sat on the porch and scraped out the last pieces of my emergency-only brain stash. Too close. That had been way too close.

"You better, baby?" Dad shouted through the door. Blood streaked the wood, as if rotting fingers had clawed at it.

"Yeah," I called back. My voice still held a raspy edge, but my hands looked whole enough. "I'll finish off the burrito in my fridge, and I'll be good as new." Well, except for my pointy body modification.

Dad opened the door with the chain on and met my eyes through the gap. "Y'look grey as a concrete slab."

I sighed. "The bad part's over. I promise."

Apparently he believed me. He closed the door and took off the chain, then pulled it open long enough to drag me inside. His eyes widened at the sight of the crossbow bolt. "Jesus fucking Christ, Angel." He gulped. "Sit. Goddamn. You need to sit. I'll get the burrito. Holy fuck."

"It's not as bad as it looks," I said with a weak smile, but I went ahead and sat gingerly on the couch.

He gave me an exasperated glare. "Well that don't mean shit, 'cause it looks godawful fucked up."

"I'll be okay as soon as I eat," I reassured him then rattled off the combination.

"Got it. Be right back."

I watched him fondly as he trotted down the hall. I had one more emergency bag of brains labeled as brussel sprouts in the freezer, but those *had* to stay untouched, now more than ever. Use only in event of monster-mode. I didn't want to think what would have happened tonight if my dad's brain had been the only one available.

My vision swam and I struggled to focus.

"Angel!"

I was sitting on linoleum, staring at the . . . dishwasher? Kitchen. On the floor in the kitchen, right shoulder leaning against the fridge. But how? My left hand throbbed, and I saw that three nails were ripped off. I blinked stupidly at my hand then registered the frigid air flowing over me. Above me, the freezer door stood wide open.

I gulped. No. The freezer door was on the other side of the room. I scrambled to my feet, clutched the counter as I swayed. The freezer door hinges hung, twisted, and broken.

"Angel?"

Dad stood a foot from the linoleum, eyes wide as he took

in the damage. In one hand he clutched a foil-wrapped half of a burrito.

"Oh god." I swallowed, aghast. "I'm so sorry. I don't know what happened."

"I do. But you better eat while I talk." He tossed me the burrito which, by some miracle, I managed to catch. He waited until I started eating before he continued. "I'd just got into your fridge when you started caterwaulin' like a bear with a hornet up its ass. I grabbed your food and ran back out in time to see you trying t'get into the freezer." He gestured helpfully. "But you was yanking on the wrong side from the handle. Next thing I know, you done ripped it clean off."

My gaze went to the bag marked "brussel sprouts" resting in the center of the freezer. Still full, to my relief. I'd been going for the brains in there, I was absolutely certain. A blackout. I'd had a few of those before, at the peak of my drug use. But not like this. It didn't make sense.

Or did it? Huge loss of impulse control. Crazy strength. Aftereffect of the double-dose overdrive from the V12? That had to be the culprit.

"I'll pay for a new one, Dad. I'm so sorry."

"Never you mind," he said. "I mean, yeah, we gonna need a new one, but first let's get you taken care of." He shepherded me back to the couch and got me settled again. "Wait right here, and don't tear up any more appliances."

"You're going to give me grief about this forever, aren't you?"

"'Til the day I die," he shot back with a wink. He returned to the kitchen and a few seconds later came back with a hacksaw. "I seen on the news that Randy and Coy got themselves into some trouble," he said conversationally as he pulled up a footstool.

"No shit?"

"No shit." He squinted at the bolt, frowned.

"Cut the head off," I suggested. "Then you can pull it out from the front."

He blew out a breath, nodded and set the blade against the bolt at my back. "Yep, Coy turned himself in for the murder. Him and Judd done it." His face darkened as he sawed. "Though we all know it was mostly Judd. Seems Randy talked Coy into going to the cops, but Judd didn't want no part of that, so he kidnapped 'em both. Chained those two boys up in the Pichon's old fishing camp." Dad paused. "Turns out they found a can of compressed air in a drawer. They froze the chains to break 'em and escaped."

"Wow. Pretty darn clever of them."

His mouth twisted. "Uh, huh. Real clever. And real lucky. Judd woulda killed those two, no question." The head of the bolt thumped to the floor. Dad set the hacksaw aside then moved in front of me and took hold of the fletching. "There's a big ol' manhunt going on for Judd now." He pulled the bolt free in one swift move, wringing a gasp from me. After a few seconds to catch my breath, I gave him a weak thumbs up.

Dad tossed the front panel of the battered vest aside, then handed me the rest of my burrito. As I ate, I tugged my shirt aside and peered at the wound in my chest. It was closing, but it sure was taking its sweet time.

My dad cleared his throat. "Do I need to worry about seein' you on the news?"

"I think it's going to be okay." I leaned in and kissed him on the cheek. "Thanks, Dad."

His eyes were misty as he smiled. "Anytime, Angelkins." He helped me up then gave me a gentle hug that damn near had me bawling.

"I need to take care of one thing," I said then moved to the kitchen, hoisted the freezer door and stuck it back into place. "Break out the duct tape. I don't want to lose all this food."

"A redneck toolkit," he said with a snort. "Duct tape and WD-40." He grabbed a roll from a drawer and taped the door in place, then stepped back and regarded our handiwork. "Well, at least it ain't a driveway paved in crushed beer cans."

I laughed. "We're hicks with standards."

"Damn straight." He carefully looped an arm around my shoulders. "How 'bout I draw you a hot bath?"

"With bubbles?" I asked with a cheeky grin.

"The only way you're gettin' bubbles is if I put dish soap in there."

"I'll take it."

Chapter 25

Jangly music cut through my sleep, pushy and obnoxious. I groped for my phone to shut off the V12 dose alarm then let out a long groan as the light streamed through the blinds and stabbed my eyes. My entire body was one gigantic ache, and my head pounded like the worst hangover ever. *Thank god today's Lundi Gras and a holiday.*

This was the first headache I'd had since becoming a zombie, and I struggled to pull my thoughts together. I hadn't meant to sleep so late, not with Judd on the loose with the flash drives. And I still needed to track down Dante Rosario. Judd's call had interrupted that plan. Now half the morning was shot.

Squinting against the light, I dragged myself up and blearily pulled on clothing. My wound was healed over—one less thing to worry about—but I didn't have the slightest idea where to start searching for Judd. He would have heard by now that Randy and Coy had gone to the cops, and was smart enough to stay away from his trailer and his usual haunts. Hell, he could already be halfway to Canada. On the plus side, with Randy and Coy spilling their guts to the cops, and Judd's picture splashed all over the news, he had no reason to come after me.

I frowned as I buttoned my jeans. But he knew I was a zombie. He'd been trying to capture me, not kill me. So why had he run away? I backtracked through memory fogged by brain hunger. *Handcuffs. A struggle and threats. Judd's scream of horror. His blood in my mouth as—*

"I bit him," I murmured. A laugh started in my belly and worked its way out until I collapsed on the bed, tears streaming. Judd ran away like a little bitch because he thought he was going to turn into a zombie.

I wiped my eyes and grinned. *He should be so lucky.*

My amusement dribbled away when I stepped out of my front door. My car was parked—for lack of a better word— cockeyed and with one wheel in the flowerbed. A garden gnome lay smashed to bits except for one eye that stared accusingly up at me, and tire tracks revealed that I'd missed crashing into the porch by inches.

My head pounded as I scooped up the gnome pieces and chucked them into the trash bin. I had approximately zero memory of my arrival home, which I didn't like one bit. But, hey, at least I hadn't taken out the mailbox.

The V12 vial and capsules were right where I'd left them, in my lunchbox, but I didn't draw up a dose. Instead, I called Dr. Nikas and proceeded to give him a semi-coherent account of the clusterfuck with Judd, the flash drives, and the whole fight at the lock, then told him about the awful hunger and my reasons for taking a double dose, and finally finished with everything I could remember about the V12 overdrive superpowers and how it affected the hunger and pain.

Dr. Nikas listened without interrupting until I trailed off. "I am truly relieved you made it through the ordeal," he said. "Though I'm surprised by the headache. Philip only suffers them after a high dose, but then again his parasite is damaged in a way that yours is not."

"I've taken as much as three doses in a day without any problems." I lifted the vial and swirled the liquid. "Maybe the headache this time is because the doses were so close together?"

"It's possible. I don't—"

"Wait." I stared at the vial, then scrabbled for the other two. "I . . . I think I took more than two doses. At least four are missing. How could I have taken *four* doses? I took one at the lock, and I stopped one time. Two doses. I remember—"

"Angel!" he said, calm but firm. "What size syringe did you use?"

"The size I always . . ." Memory of the chaotic stop on the side of the highway shifted into focus. "Oh god. I wasn't thinking straight and drew up a full syringe. That's a triple dose! And I'd already had a regular dose." Shit. No wonder I felt hungover.

Dr. Nikas let out a long breath, and I imagined him rubbing his temples. "Any other side effects? More hallucinations? Changes in the dyslexia?"

I shifted to peer at myself in the rearview mirror. "I'm grey, almost to pre-rot," I told him, fighting to remain clinical and not burst into tears. "No hallucinations, and I haven't been reading much so I don't know about the dyslexia. No sparkles since the big dose either, and that's a first." I rubbed my eyes. "How bad did I screw up?"

"I don't know." Not the words I wanted to hear from Dr. Nikas. "You're the only normal zombie to have used V12." He muttered to himself in Greek for a bit before continuing. "The V12 has a cumulative effect. Take no doses today. But continue to take the capsules. Return to the twice-daily half-dose regimen tomorrow. And don't let yourself go hungry. Do you have brains?"

"I'm heading to my storage unit as soon as I hang up. I have enough for a few days."

"Good. If you truly get into a bind, there's a Tribe emergency stash at the swamp training ground. A case of eight ounce packets." He gave me instructions on how to find it then added, "If you take any, let me know so they can be replaced."

"I will. Thanks for everything."

"It's my true pleasure, Angel." He paused. "In, ah, other news, you should know that Kristi Charish is in full swing negotiations with both Saberton and the Tribe." While I listened in growing outrage, he explained how Kristi was trying to use herself as a hot commodity bargaining chip. It wasn't a stupidly bad ploy, since both organizations *needed* her damn research expertise, even if she was a heartless psychopath. But it meant that everyone involved was now scrambling to gain advantage and protect themselves. Saberton had sent goons to Portland, and the Tribe had everyone available deployed in a variety of locations.

I thanked Dr. Nikas for the update and hung up. Time for me to get my ass in gear, stock up on brains, and do my part locally. I'd start by checking out Dante Rosario at the Zombie Fest. Lucky for me, between the Fest and zombie Mardi Gras, I could get away with the grey skin as makeup. Pleased with that solution, I fished black eyeliner from my purse and smudged it under my eyes. Even better.

I'd made it only halfway to the storage unit when my phone vibrated, and I groaned at the sight of *Allen Prejean* on the caller ID. I'd forgotten all about the organ bag issue. Obviously, he hadn't.

"Hey, Allen," I said, all casual and pleasant-like. "What's up?"

"I need you to come in." Firm. Not even a hint of a smile in his voice.

"Oh, man. I sort of have plans with my dad. Y'know, 'cause it's a holiday?"

"This is important. I need to see you. Now."

That was his asshole I'm-the-boss voice. Technically, since I wasn't on call, I could play the holiday card and not go in. But I knew that if I did, he'd make my work life hell when I came back. I sighed. "Sure. I'll change my plans. See

you in an hour? There's a parade today, and traffic's going
to be a bitch."

"Get here as soon as you can. I'll be in the morgue."

I gave my phone the finger after he disconnected. What
a prick. At least I was already up and out, and still had
enough time to swing by the storage unit freezer and load
up my cooler with the last of my brain stash.

Because no way did I want to deal with Allen Prejean on
an empty stomach.

A sawhorse stood in the middle of the morgue parking lot
entrance, bearing a sign that threatened death, doom, de-
struction, and a hefty towing bill for all unauthorized vehicles in the lot. A must for parade days, when hundreds of
cars fought for space within easy walking distance of the
parade route. Apparently the sign had the desired effect.
The only cars in the lot were Allen's and a dark green Chevy
Impala parked beneath the overhang at the morgue entrance. I skirted the sawhorse and backed into a space in the
second row, then slugged the rest of a brain smoothie. Allen
was guaranteed to stress me out, and I really didn't want to
add "ate my boss" to my list of lifetime accomplishments.

I shoved the cooler onto the passenger side floorboard
to get it out of direct sun, locked my car and headed for the
entrance. I slowed as I neared the Impala, noting government plates and dark-tinted windows in the back. Did the
driver have anything to do with why Allen called me in?
Curiosity and caution prickled, and I made sure my path to
the entrance included a casual stroll alongside the vehicle
and around its front. A well-used leather file case sat on the
passenger side floorboard, and a stack of papers rested on
the seat. But it was the FBI parking pass on the center console that sent my gut plunging.

What if Allen called them about the missing brains? I'd be
walking right into an ambush. But that didn't make sense.
Law enforcement wouldn't sit around and wait for me to

come in if they had something on me. And they certainly wouldn't park in front of the door if they were lying in wait. *Jesus, Angel, stop being a paranoid twit!* Most likely the visit had to do with Ben's request for the FBI to process evidence from the murder. Or, possibly, whatever investigation had the feds poking around funeral homes. Neither of those involved me. Not directly anyway.

Inside, the intake area was quiet and empty, but my almost-tanked zombie hearing picked up voices from the direction of the cooler. I eased down the hall then stopped when I was close enough to make out the words.

"Are you looking for something in particular?" Allen.

"Is this all you have?" A woman's voice rasped as if air had to fight its way through her vocal cords.

The cooler only held two bodies at the moment, and one belonged to the murder victim, Grayson Seeger. There was only so much I could learn by eavesdropping. I needed eyes on this, too. I pulled the cooler door open. Beside Allen was a tall black woman with close-cropped graying hair. A keloid scar ran from the angle of her jaw down across the front of her throat.

I faked a slight startle. "Oh, sorry. I didn't mean to interrupt."

"Come on in, Angel," Allen said then gestured toward the woman. "This is Special Agent Sorsha Aberdeen." He glanced my way and his eyes widened. An expression of alarm and dread filled his face, as if I had purple boogies hanging out my nose, but a second later he recovered and cleared his throat. "Uh, this is Angel Crawford, morgue assistant." His eyes darkened with unease as they flicked over me. "She, uh . . . I called her away from the Zombie Fest. She really gets into dressing up for it."

Huh? I didn't know what Allen's game was, but—

Oh. The grey and makeup. Yeah, not exactly the most professional appearance, but at least he was giving the agent a reason for it—or what he thought was the reason. I faked a bright smile. "Anything for you, boss." Just in case, I very casually wiped a hand beneath my nose. Good. No boogies of any color.

Agent Aberdeen looked me over with sharp eyes. "Angel Crawford," she said as if trying out the name. "It would be a tremendous help if you could assist me while Mr. Prejean attends to the report I requested."

"Sure!" I said before Allen could protest. Who knew what juicy info this woman might drop.

Allen glared, though I couldn't tell if was at the dismissal or my enthusiasm. Probably both. "I'm happy to stay in case you have a question Angel can't answer," he said. "Dr. Leblanc performed the autopsy yesterday morning, and compiling the report won't take long."

"I'm in a bit of a rush," Aberdeen said with a whisper of steel behind her polite smile. "I'd greatly appreciate it if you could take care of the report now."

Allen's jaw tightened, but it was clear he knew he'd lost the battle. "Not a problem." He departed, but not before throwing me a firm look of *Mess this up, and I'll make your life hell.*

"You're here about Mr. Seeger?" I asked after the cooler door swung shut. A clear plastic bag containing Seeger's property rested on top of his body bag alongside a clipboard that held the property list and chain of custody.

"How long have you worked here?" Her eyes lingered on my face in an unsettling way.

"Year and a half." I smiled. "I know all the procedures, if that's what you're worried about."

"No. Not at all." She scanned through the property list then tapped the signature at the bottom. "You brought him in. Is this everything he had on his person?"

"Yup." *Except for a certain list of video files.* "The sheriff's office has items from the scene and his car."

"I've been through all of what they have," she said. "Are you certain there was nothing else on him when you brought him in?"

"Other than clothes, yeah." I gestured toward a paper bag in the corner. "But I went through 'em pretty good." I didn't have to be a brain surgeon to know she was looking for something specific. The flash drive? "You guys sure are quick. Detective Roth said he was going to call y'all this morning about processing evidence."

"I have nothing to do with that," she said, mouth pursing. "I was in contact with the victim on Friday."

Holy crap. Seeger had mentioned the feds to Justine. Another possible reason why he was so nervous at the premiere. "Oh, man. Not a personal friend, I hope."

Aberdeen's gaze skimmed over the body bag. "No. It was the first time I'd met him."

"He was a producer for the zombie movie, right?"

She signed the property sheet and the chain of custody and passed the clipboard to me. "I asked him for an early screening of the *Zombies Are Among Us!!* documentary," she said in a tone so conversational every single one of my warning signals lit up. "Have you seen it?"

I faked a laugh. "Yeah, out at the Fest. It was pretty silly. And the way it was trying to get people paranoid and all was really dumb." I paused. "No offense. I mean, if you're into that sort of thing."

"Gruesome and inflammatory. I agree. I'm keeping an eye on the public response." Her expression darkened. "There is enough hatred in this world without unfounded enmity turned on innocent people." The forced rasp of her voice emphasized the sentiment. It was clear this issue was personal to her. Did it tie in to how she got her throat cut?

"Good thing the mockumentary is attached to a B-movie and not a blockbuster," I said wryly.

Her piercing gaze lifted to my face. "The video was uploaded yesterday and has already had over a million views." While I stood speechless in shock, Aberdeen smoothly extended a business card. "In case you remember anything else about the victim," she said. "Or, if any thoughts come to you about the video." She exited the cooler without waiting for an answer. I stuffed the business card into my pocket and followed her out.

Allen was waiting for us in the intake area, holding a blue folder that he passed to Agent Aberdeen. "Everything I can give you without a warrant is in there. It's not much. Sorry. Preliminary tox screen showed cocaine and benzos in his system, but it'll be at least a week before the full toxicology report is back."

While she checked out the folder, I added my initials next to her signature on the property list. SA Sorsha Aberdeen.

SASA. That was the acronym on Seeger's video file list. **use for deal with SASA*. Double asterisk. And I specifically remembered that none of the double asterisk file names matched any of the clips used in the stupid mockumentary. Seeger had planned to pass files to her, but never got the chance.

"Miss Crawford? Mind if I take a photo?" Agent Aberdeen lifted her cell phone.

I startled out of my thoughts. "Of me?"

"Why yes. Of your makeup for the Zombie Fest." She smiled, but her gaze was far too intent for my comfort. Beside her, Allen looked as disconcerted as if he'd been asked to drop trou in the middle of Main Street.

The cell phone remained steady before me like a rifle in a firing squad. She wanted a picture, but the natural pre-rot greyness and smudges of black under my eyes weren't exactly photo-worthy. Not with all of the really cool costumes and makeup around town. "Maybe I should go touch it up first?" I said, suddenly desperate to find a mirror.

"No need. It's perfect as is," she said, voice and smile equally steely. "Humor me?"

It wasn't a request. Refusing would draw suspicion. "Sure. It's not much makeup. Just a little something I threw on this morning."

The cell phone camera flashed before I finished speaking. I blinked away spots as it flashed again.

Expression triumphant, she turned the phone around for me to see. Along my left cheek, dead-grey skin hung in tatters with nasty red and black flesh below.

I clamped down on my dismay. "Looks better than I thought," I choked out.

She tucked the phone away. "You have my card."

"I'll walk you out," Allen said. At the door, he looked back and mouthed *Don't fucking move* before exiting with Special Agent Sorsha Aberdeen.

Chapter 26

The instant the door closed, I tossed the clipboard onto the receiving desk and ran for the bathroom. Leaning close to the mirror, I poked at the squishy patch of rot on the side of my grey-as-wet-concrete face. A knot of worry tightened in my chest. I'd downed a whole bottle of brain smoothie not even fifteen minutes ago. I shouldn't be *rotting*.

I dabbed at the spot with a wet paper towel and managed to slough off one of the skin tatters. Hands trembling, I crumpled the paper towel and dropped it into the trash can. I couldn't go out in public with a rotted face, and makeup wouldn't cover this. A big gauze pad could work. The tape might rip my skin, but I'd have to risk it. I tentatively scratched the inside of my arm, relieved and encouraged when the skin stayed intact. There was still a sliver of hope that I wasn't about to fall apart completely. Yet.

I jumped as a fist pounded on the bathroom door. "Angel!"

"Jesus! I'm taking a leak!" Damn it. I flushed the toilet then washed my hands, stalling in the hopes that my parasite would get a fucking clue and pull my face together.

Nope. Face still gross, but hands squeaky clean.

I dried my hands and stepped out of the bathroom. Across the hall, Allen stood in the doorway of the morgue tech office. "Sorry," I said with a totally relaxed and chill smile. "I had a lot of coffee this morning."

Allen slipped his phone into his pocket and didn't return my smile. "Let's talk," he said then turned and moved behind the desk.

I hung by the door. "What's up?"

He snatched a paper lunch bag from a drawer, then dropped it to the desk with a heavy plop. "You tell me."

"You bought me brunch?" My attempt at a laugh came out weak and strained.

His lips thinned. "Are you *trying* to incite an investigation?"

"What do you mean?"

He stabbed a finger at the bag. "Open it."

Wary, I moved to the desk and unrolled the top of the bag. A plastic sandwich baggie held odd lumps—

"Pig brains, Angel?" The words cracked out. "*Pig* brains?"

Ice spread through every muscle in my body. There was no lying my way out of this nightmare. "I guess I'm fired?" My voice sounded tinny and distant.

He slammed the flat of his hand on the desk. "*No* brains in the organ bags is one thing. Pig brains takes it to a different fucking level."

No brains. So he *did* know brains had been missing before. That's why he called me in on Friday. "Look, I'll go. You'll never have to deal with me again." My voice shook, but my thoughts were surprisingly clear. "No more loser Angel in your department."

Allen folded his arms over his chest and leveled a stern look at me. "If you leave now, it will only make your situation worse. I suggest you sit down."

"Sit down and wait so the cops can scoop me up? Sorry, but no." I took a step toward the door then hesitated as it all started to sink in. I was about to walk out of this life forever, leave a job I loved, where I wasn't a loser. It *sucked*.

"Allen, this isn't what it looks like. I . . ." Shit. What could I possibly say? *A girl's got to eat?* "I'm so sorry," I gasped then fled toward the exit.

"Angel! Stop!" Allen shouted after me. "I haven't called the cops."

I slid to a stop with the exit in sight, turned and frowned at Allen where he stood in the office doorway. "Why not? What are you waiting for?"

He exhaled. "I'd like you to answer a question for me. You owe me that much."

I wavered between staying and fleeing. "You won't call the cops?"

"Not unless you give me a reason to."

A bigger reason than replacing human brains with pig brains? Absurd hope flickered that something could be salvaged from this mess. "Ask away."

"In private."

We were alone in the morgue, but maybe he figured there was a chance another employee would pop in. I returned to the tech office but made sure Allen wasn't between me and the door.

He dropped into the chair on the far side of the room. "You're really grey," he stated. "And the rot on your face looks bad."

I tossed off a shrug. "Half the population of Tucker Point is grey or green or rotten. What's your question?"

He leaned back, eyes on me. "I want to know what's been going on with you these past few months. Pig brains. Careless raids on the cooler. Reckless behavior, like jumping into floodwater for that gurney. You were solid before. What changed?"

I blinked stupidly at him. That was his question? Not why was I stealing brains? "I've been on a special medication," I managed to say. "For dyslexia. It messes with my impulse control, but I'm changing meds now."

He blew out a breath. "Thank God. I thought it might be something less, ah, manageable."

What the—? I had no idea what Allen's deal was, but he had yet to fire me or press charges. "How long have you known about the brains?"

"Since the gash on your hand healed without a trace."

My breath caught even as I shoved my hand behind my back out of pure reflex. I'd cut my hand on a scalpel last year, and Allen had stitched it to save me a trip to the emergency room. He'd almost been nice about it, too. "I have this really amazing miracle scar cream," I said. "Works like a charm. What does that have to do with anything?"

"Angel, I *know*." His voice stayed calm, but his eyes were wary. "I started checking the organ bags after that. You're a *goule-gris*."

I didn't know much French, but I understood *grey ghoul*. Blood drained from my head, and I swayed. Allen shot to his feet and shoved a chair under my butt as I sank. A weird numbness set in, as if I was along for the ride in some other person's screwed up life. Allen had *known* for all this time. "I don't understand." I looked up at him, baffled. "Why didn't you say anything?"

"You were doing what you had to do, and no one was getting hurt." He sat on the edge of the desk. "I figured you had good reasons to want your privacy. But when you started behaving erratically, I knew it was only a matter of time before you got caught and by someone other than me. That would hurt the Coroner's Office nearly as much as it would you, and I can't have that."

I felt as if I'd been dropped into a weird dream-world. "How do you know about z—" I swallowed. "—about *goule-gris*?"

"A few years ago I went on a medical aid rotation to the Central African Republic." He grimaced. "We provided emergency services for refugees and victims of armed conflict. There was a local woman, a nurse who I worked closely with. Sorella." His voice softened on her name. "I found out she was *goule-gris* when I accidentally poisoned myself with a wound salve I'd seen her use for a cut on her leg."

A strange calm settled over me. Allen knew what I was, and he wasn't going to have me arrested. "It was toxic to you, but not to her." I cocked my head, intrigued. "Did her wounds heal without the salve?"

He rubbed a hand over his jaw. "Not as well. I don't know how it worked, but as far as I can tell it helped conserve, uh, brains."

I snapped out of my slouch. "What was in it?" I asked. Demanded.

A corner of Allen's mouth twisted. "That's the same question John asked when I told him this story."

"Who the hell is John?" But the answer hit me an instant later. My jaw dropped. "Wait. John *Kang*?"

Allen nodded. "Once you've seen *goule-gris* color, you don't forget it. Less than a year after Africa, John came in to pick up a body, and he had that grey cast. It went from there. He told me—repeatedly—that outing your kind is frowned upon, which is part of why I kept quiet when I found out about you."

My mind spun as I worked to readjust to this bizarre new world. "Did you tell Kang what was in the salve?"

"The ingredients that I knew of, yes. But I have no idea about the proportions or techniques." He tipped his head back in thought. "Okra seed, moringa leaf, stinkblaar." His forehead creased. "Boomslang venom—I won't forget that one anytime soon—myrrh oil. There might've been more, but I'm not certain."

Ideas formed and fell apart only to sprout again. "Did Kang figure anything out with it?"

"No clue. He was a private kind of guy. We didn't talk about the *goule-gris* aspect much after the first few days."

Had Kang shared the word *zombie* with Allen? Too weird. "I know this is going to sound kind of lame, but thanks. For keeping my secret."

Allen didn't quite smile, but his face lost some of its tension. "I kept my eye on you once I realized. But you make it to work on time, do a good job, and haven't fucked up anything that I know of." He shrugged. "As long as you weren't hurting anyone, there was no need for me to butt into your life."

I stared at him. "I thought you hated me."

"There was no love lost for the first few months, that's for sure," he said, then made a sour face. "But you have *no* idea how many times I've been burned by losers who slid into a morgue tech job because of a relative with influence."

I winced. I'd been one of those losers when I started out. "Then why do you still jerk my schedule around all over the place and treat me like crap?"

He surprised me with a bark of laughter. "I treat *everyone* like crap. That's what makes me so lovable. As for your schedule, you never complained about it. I was happy to have an employee who was flexible."

Now that I thought about it, he'd never given me a lick of trouble about arranging my schedule around classes. I'd spent all this time being butthurt because Allen wasn't *nice* to me. "What now?"

Allen sobered and met my eyes. "No more taking all the brains. Leave some every few bags. No more carelessness. Don't do your collecting when people are here. There's a limit to how far I can cover your ass. If you get into a bind, *tell* me, and I'll do what I can without drawing attention. And for God's sake no more pig brains. Anyone with half an eye can tell they're not human."

I nodded meekly. "Does this mean I still have a job?"

"For now." He gave me a mild glare. "But I'll fire you in a heartbeat if you do anything to jeopardize your coworkers or this department."

Relief danced through me. "Got it." I pushed to my feet. "Thanks, Allen. For being decent."

"Don't get used to it."

Chapter 27

"And they use this for zombie wound care in the Central African Republic?"

I grinned at the naked awe and delight in Dr. Nikas's voice. Allen had left to watch the parade with his wife, and I was on cell phone in the morgue tech office, kicked back with my feet on the desk. I'd already given him my update concerning Allen and Special Agent Aberdeen, and had saved the best news—the *goule-gris* salve—for last. "Apparently so," I said. "Those ingredients were just the ones Allen could remember, so it's possible there's a secret ingredient missing."

"We won't know until I experiment," he said. "But even so, the information offers avenues I haven't explored."

"Right. So, this got me thinking. Allen told Kang about this stuff, too. And we've been scratching our heads trying to figure out what was in Kang's system that made him re-grow while the others stayed in stasis." I took a deep breath. "What if Kang spent a couple of years experimenting with those ingredients? Maybe it changed his cells or his parasite, and that's why he has an extra boost for re-growing. Like he's been pickled in zombie steroids."

Dr. Nikas let out a laugh. "Pickled zombie. Angel, not

only are you a ray of light in an often dreary world, but you may well be correct."

With a parting promise to keep me in the loop, he hung up. I had a feeling he was already filling a whiteboard with scribbled notes.

Still grinning, I exited the morgue with a light step and headed to my car. There was still plenty of time for me to make it to the Fest. I'd picked the loose skin off the rotten patch and taped a patch of gauze over it—one that I'd smeared with eyeliner to make it look like it was part of my "costume." For good measure, I taped smudged gauze pads onto my collarbone and forearm to complete the look.

I stopped dead as a muffled scream of rage and frustration reached me from the only other car in the lot. Nick's, parked at the far end of the first row. He sat in the driver's seat, head thrown back and face contorted. I stood rooted to the spot in shock as his long scream trailed off to a guttural howl and finally shuddering silence.

Instinct and worry urged me to rush to him, but I found myself hesitating. Maybe he didn't want help. Maybe he just wanted to be left alone. I had no desire to go through a repeat of the scene at the restaurant, but I also couldn't go on my merry way without checking on him. I approached his car, only to see him violently ripping a sheet of paper into smaller and smaller pieces. At the sight of me, he froze, then quickly slipped on his I-don't-give-a-shit expression and flung the door open.

"Hey, Nick. You cool?" I sauntered up to his door and snuck a casual peek inside the car. Paper bits littered the interior like confetti. On the seat was a torn envelope with LSU School of Medicine in the corner, and beneath it I spied the butt of a gun. What the shit? Sure, his dad owned a gun shop, but I'd never known Nick to carry a gun before.

"Everything's great," Nick said, "if you don't count all the detours for the stupid parade." He grabbed his messenger bag, got out and slammed the door. "I need to finish a report, and it took me twice as long as usual to get here."

I suspected his temper had more to do with the confetti-fied contents of that envelope than traffic. My heart sank. It had to be a rejection of his med school application. Damn. I glanced at the gun. But why did he need *that*? Protection? Murder? Suicide?

No. Not Nick.

I hoped.

I cocked my head at him. "You sure nothing else is bugging you?"

"I'm fine, okay?" He stalked toward the building, but not before I got a good look at his right eye—red and puffy, and promising a nice shiner.

"Nick!" I dogged his steps. "I'm not going away this time. Did your dad do this?"

His shoulders jerked with tension, but he didn't stop. "No! I clocked myself with the lat pulldown bar at the gym earlier."

Right. And I only ate brains on holidays. "Talk to me. Five minutes. If you still want me to go away after that, I will."

He key-swiped his ID and yanked the door open. "What do you want, Angel? I said I'm fine. I have work to do, and the last thing I need is you hanging around."

I ducked in after him. He kept his face turned away so I couldn't see his swollen eye. "Fuck it!" He threw his hands up. "Since your idea of a good time is to screw with me today, go for it. Just don't expect me to help you." He strode off through the morgue toward the front offices.

I followed like a lioness waiting for her prey to wear out so she could pounce. "Did I ever tell you about my mom?"

Nick headed up the stairs. "No. But I'm sure you're about to bombard me with the story."

I took the stairs two at a time right along with him. "She went to jail when I was eleven. For child abuse."

He glanced at me, but didn't give a smart ass remark this time.

"She was mentally ill, but that didn't change or excuse what she did to me. My dad didn't see it, or didn't want to see it. Not until she broke my arm. That's when he finally called the cops."

Nick stepped into his office and plunked his messenger bag onto the desk. "I'm sorry you had a rough time, but I don't get why you feel the need to tell me about it now."

"Because when I was seventeen, I started getting it from my dad."

He flinched as if poised to either bolt or punch me. I'd struck a nerve. "I was acting out and being a little shit," I continued. "And he was an alcoholic who didn't know how the hell to deal with my screwups." I paused, chest tight. "I figured I deserved it."

His face stayed blank, but a multitude of emotions boiled behind the thin facade. He yanked papers from his bag and slammed them onto the desk. "You were a fucked up loser. I bet you deserved every bit of it."

My composure cracked as if he'd taken a sledgehammer to it. "Takes one to know one," I shot back. "You can't even get into med school after all your bragging about pre-med this and pre-med that. Who's the loser now?"

I fled the office before he could respond to my stupid and nasty comeback. I knew damn well that Nick was in lashing-out mode and projecting all of his shit onto me. So why did his words hurt so damn much?

"Angel!"

I kept going toward the stairwell. He didn't want to talk, and neither did I anymore.

"Angel. I'm sorry." Misery filled his voice.

Sighing, I turned to see Nick in the hall outside his office, looking utterly bereft.

"I'm sorry, too," I said, returning to him and the office. "I shouldn't have said that about med school. That was low. I know how much it meant to you and how hard you worked."

Nick collapsed into his chair. "I'm going," he said. "I'm fucking going to fucking med school."

Frowning, I struggled to process that. "Okay, I'm lost. I

thought you got rejected. What were you ripping up in your car?"

"You saw that?" He grimaced and turned beet red. "It was my acceptance. I got it last month."

Baffled, I sank into the other chair. "But that's good, isn't it? Being a doctor is your dream."

"Yeah," he said morosely. "Classes start in August."

"Dude, you make it sound as if you're going to your execution."

He looked away. "I can't help it if I've considered other options."

I mentally backtracked to reassess everything I'd seen and learned about him in the past year and a half. His pompous attitude about academics and being pre-med. His flurry of med school applications and exams and interviews. And his current look of defeat. "You really don't want to be a doctor?"

Slumped shoulders twitched. "It's the smartest thing."

"That's not what I asked." I leaned forward and fixed him with a penetrating look. "Nick, do you *want* to go to med school?"

"I'd be stupid not to after all the work and money that's gone into it." He wadded a piece of paper and hurled it at the trashcan. "I guess I'm stupid."

"You're not stupid, and you know it." A picture began to form of an ugly family dynamic. "It's your dad who wants you to be a doctor." I paused as more pieces clarified. "When I saw you outside Crawfish Joe's, that was when you told him you didn't want to go through with it."

Nick pounded a fist into his thigh. "I *like* being a death investigator here. Right now, all I want to do is work and get back into theater and volunteer with Allen on medical relief missions and keep my friends. I *don't* want to bury myself in stress for the next decade. Even if I did, I'd specialize in forensic pathology. I sure as hell don't want to be a fucking trauma surgeon so Bear's survivalists can have a goddamn medic for the apocalypse!"

I leapt to my feet and slammed my hands on the desk. "Then *do* all that shit you want to do! Get back into theater, and volunteer with Allen on medical relief missions, and for fuck's sake don't be a trauma surgeon unless that's what *you* want. Don't kill yourself for someone else's dream. Fuck that noise!"

"I wish I could just say fuck it." The flicker of fire had left his voice. "But I can't."

"You can't be your own person?"

"I made a deal."

I grabbed his chin and turned his face to get a good view of his bruised eye. "Is this part of the deal? How many times has he hit you?"

He jerked away. "It's not like that. This med school thing blindsided him, that's all. He yells a lot, but he's never hit me before."

"But he made sure you committed yourself to *his* vision of what your life should be." I shoved a hand through my hair, frustrated and aching for Nick. Bear was brawny and a good foot taller than Nick. Not to mention, charismatic and intimidating as hell. I had little doubt Nick grew up walking a line of fear and respect with him. "Look, I get it," I said. "He's your dad. And now he's pissed off because, god forbid, you dared to have a speck of free will."

"You don't understand what—"

"Nick. I swear to God, I've been there, on the receiving end of verbal and physical abuse." I straightened and gathered my thoughts, gentled my voice. "I get that it's easier to stay silent and take it. When you've been beaten down so hard for so long, the last thing you want to do is push back and make it worse."

He shot to his feet and turned away, sending his chair skittering into the wall with a bang.

I moved in and put my hand on his shoulder, felt the stress vibrating through him. "The problem with keeping your mouth shut is that you die by inches," I said softly, willing my words to reach the core of him. "Your own hopes and dreams keep slipping farther away, until one day you realize you never got the chance to live the life *you* wanted."

"Angel." His voice shook as if every pent up emotion wanted to spew out all at once. "I don't know what to do."

"Yeah, you do. But the thought of *doing* it is terrifying." I gave his shoulder a gentle squeeze. "Do you want to live your own life? Or die crushed beneath someone else's dream? You're in control of that, whether you like it or not."

He went still beneath my hand for several seconds before turning to face me. "I want to stay here." He forced a crooked smile. "Someone needs to keep your butt in line."

"Ain't that the truth!" I grinned then poked him in the sternum. "So don't you dare let your dad bully you." I poked him again. "You don't have to take that crap." I waggled my finger to ready for a third poke.

Whisper-faint amusement touched his eyes as he swatted my hand. "Yeah, I don't have to put up with bullies." He let out a long sigh, but looked as if he'd dropped a billion pounds of burden. "I'm such a chickenshit. I couldn't even tell him to keep his stupid tranquilizer gun and shove it up his ass."

Relief washed through me. A *tranq* gun. From his dad. "First off, you're not a chickenshit. Standing up to a parent is the hardest thing ever. Second off, why the heck did he give you a tranquilizer gun? Bears? Cougars? Raging nutria?"

Nick rolled his eyes. "Don't ask. You'll be sorry."

"Aw, c'mon. Spill." I lifted my poking finger in mock threat.

He snorted, shook his head. "Fine. You asked for it. My dad gave it to me so I could defend myself against . . . zombies."

"Zombies?" The word squeaked out.

"Hand to god. Toldya you'd be sorry." A smile lifted his mouth. "It's completely insane. But, just for absurdity's sake, why would anyone think a tranquilizer would work faster on a zombie than a regular gun? Or a baseball bat?"

"A tranq for *zombies*." I managed a laugh and hoped it didn't sound strangled. "Oh, man. That's crazypants. Where'd he come up with a wild idea like that?"

Nick threw his hands in the air. "He must've been talking to some seriously whackdoodle people over the weekend. He's never bought into the woowoo crap before."

Whackdoodle or not, who had given Bear the idea of a tranq gun? Regular tranquilizer drugs didn't do shit to zombies unless it was enough to stop ten elephants, but Saberton had a special formula that took zombies down in seconds. Could it have been one of Andrew's security people? Or Dante Rosario? He'd sure been palsy-walsy with Bear in the gun shop on Friday. I needed to find a way to check the darts in Nick's tranq gun. If they were zombie-grade, that put an ugly spin on everything.

"Well, if Bigfoot attacks, you're set," I said then winced as I caught sight of the clock. "Crap. I'm heading out to the Zombie Fest and need to get going before I get blocked in by the parade."

Nick grinned. "By the way, nice makeup. How'd you get the skin tone so smoo—"

"I really gotta run! We'll chat later. Promise you'll call me if you need anything?"

"Yeah. Sure." He paused and met my eyes. "I'm going to do it. Tomorrow, I'll have it out with Bear."

"I'm behind you all the way. We'll celebrate after Mardi Gras." I gave him a sly look. "I'll even let you help me study for midterms."

Nick smiled, genuine and relaxed, then swept in and hugged me.

I hugged him right back then rested my head on his shoulder as if it was the most natural thing in the world. Thank god the V12 pre-rot didn't come with Eau de Decay. "You're my best friend. You know that, right?"

"I'm not so sure," he said, voice light with humor. "Remember the Nick the Prick doodle you did last month?"

"Which one? I mean, god, there've been so many."

He laughed and released me, then caught my hands in his. "That does it. I'm truly offended."

I grinned and squeezed his hands. The next thing I knew, I had him backed against the desk with my lips firmly planted on his. I hadn't even thought before moving. *Oh god, what the hell did I just do?!*

Nick seemed damn near frozen in surprise—not exactly kissing me back, but not resisting, either. A small and crazy part of me hoped he'd return the kiss, but the rest wanted to run.

Majority rules. I scrambled back and gave a shaky laugh. "That'll teach you to be offended." I knew my statement didn't make any sense, but neither did me kissing him.

His eyes were wide with bewildered shock, but he recovered enough to give me a mischievous smile. "I think I should be offended more often."

A snicker escaped me. I needed to leave before I did something stupid. Stupider. "Gotta go. Call me if you need support with your dad. I got your back."

I didn't wait for a response, and hit the stairwell at a run.

Chapter 28

What the hell, Angel?

Outside, I waited for my pulse to return to a normal rhythm and struggled to make sense of what just happened. The obvious suspect was the V12. With it, the slightest emotion or impulse could turn into action. Annoyance could become rage. A craving might result in me trying to pry someone's skull open. But *what* would prompt me to kiss Nick?

Glancing back at the building, I spied him in the window—for the split second before he jerked back as though he hadn't been watching me. Despite everything, I grinned. I'd have done the exact same thing.

On the street, a car blared twangy country music from open windows as it cruised past. A dog barked in complaint then settled as the ballad about the singer's guitar faded into the distance. Farther away, sirens and the uneven strains of a marching band heralded the start of the parade. Crap. Time to get my ass moving. The Tucker Point PD was great about waiting until the first float was within spitting distance before barricading cross streets, but if I missed the window I'd have to wait over an hour for the parade to pass or backtrack halfway across town.

As I hurried to my car, a man wearing a plastic half-mask and a green satin Krewe of Chiron shirt wandered unsteadily into the parking lot. *Drunk as a skunk*, I decided. Dude must've missed getting on his float in time, and now he was trying to cut across the block to intercept the parade. Too bad the idiot was going the wrong way to catch it.

My this-ain't-right senses tingled, and though the man was still a good twenty feet from me, I angled to give him an even wider berth. Why did he have his mask on when he wasn't on a float?

Alarm bells sounded in my head. *The barking dog.* I shot a quick look toward the street, saw a silver Ford Explorer parked so that the corner of the building shielded it from the view of anyone exiting the morgue. In the back seat, Marla glared at me through the open window.

And it was Dante Rosario behind the mask, a Taser in his hand.

My heart slammed against my ribs. He wanted to capture me for Saberton and would likely succeed unless I came up with a brilliant plan real damn fast. No way could I beat him to my car or the morgue door. If I tried to flee in any other direction, Marla would be out that window and after me in a heartbeat. I was hungry enough that my parasite probably wouldn't be much help against his Taser. At least he didn't have a zombie-tranq gun. I'd have no chance against—

Tranq.

I sprinted toward Nick's car, leaped up onto the hood and over to the passenger side. The tranq gun still rested on the seat, behind a locked door. A quick glance told me I only had seconds before Rosario reached me.

Don't think, just do! With the help of my almost-one-hundred pounds of mass, I smashed my elbow through the window. Pain shot up my arm, fierce and hot, but I pushed

through it and grabbed the gun. Rosario rounded the front
of the car. Glass grated against bone in my arm as I jerked
the gun up and at him.

He skidded to an awkward stop barely five feet away,
hands spread. "Whoa whoa whoa. No need to shoot that
thing."

My finger hooked onto the trigger. "Yeah, well you don't
need that joy buzzer of yours. Drop it and back the fuck
off."

Rosario went still for several seconds, no doubt wondering if the tranqs in my gun were zombie-grade—lethal to
humans. I could survive a Taser jolt, but if he guessed wrong
and I got a shot off, he'd be dead.

To my relief, he apparently came to the same conclusion
and slowly placed the Taser on the ground.

"Kick it away," I ordered. Jaw tight, he grudgingly complied, even as a soft thud reached me from the street. Still
covering him, I shifted position to see the dog out of the
vehicle and loping toward us. "Keep her back, or I drop you
both!"

"Easy, Angel," he said in the same tone he used with
Marla and made a small motion with one hand. The dog
stopped and sat, but her eyes stayed glued on me. "No
harm, no foul. We can both back off."

"I don't think so," I snapped, mind racing. I'd wanted
Tribe security to grab Rosario, and here I literally had the
asshole in my sights. But how could I possibly take him
prisoner—and keep him that way—all by my lonesome?
Especially with Marla poised to have herself a juicy Angel-
snack.

Frustrated and on edge, I punched the tranq gun toward
Rosario, pleased to get a tiny flinch out of him. "How about
you tell me why a Saberton security fuckwad helped Kristi
Charish escape the Dallas lab, and then went on to leak
sensitive company videos."

His split-second jaw drop confirmed that my suspicion
was dead-on. Damn it, I needed answers, and this was a

lousy place for an interrogation. Maybe I could force him into the trunk of my car and . . .

The thought trailed off as a breeze wrapped his brain-scent around me. My stress woke the hunger. *If I tranq the dog first, I can tackle Rosario and crack his skull open on the asphalt, then—*

No. Oh god, I couldn't lose control. I didn't want to kill Rosario, even if he was an asshole. My body count was already way too high. Teeth clenched, I took a step back and tried not to breathe in the tantalizing aroma. "Get out of here," I choked out. "Now!" Didn't want Nick to see me kill and eat a human being.

Rosario must have seen his death in my eyes. He snatched up the Taser and dashed to his vehicle with Marla right beside him. I crushed the urge to chase him down like a psycho cat after a mouse and instead sprinted to my car.

"Angel!" Nick burst from the morgue, phone in hand as Rosario sped off. "The cops are on their way. Are you all right? Who was that?"

"I'm fine. I'm really sorry about your window and the hood. I swear I'll pay for the damages. But I gotta go before the streets close." I scrambled into my car and slammed the door on any further questions. Nick waved his arms and yelled, but I made it out of the lot before he could get close enough to try and stop me.

I headed in the opposite direction Rosario had taken, then tried to figure out my next step. Rosario's kidnap attempt had been sloppy and rushed which made me think he'd received a "Grab Angel ASAP" order. I'd beaten the asshole this time, but he'd be back and better prepared. Son of a pissing hell bitch. This was a mess wrapped in a shit-storm and stuffed into a clusterfuck.

My elbow flared in pain as I took a sharp left turn to avoid parade traffic. Glass shifted beneath the skin when I probed. I scowled. Hungry or not, the parasite would have normally dulled the pain by now. Great. Yet another way I'd fucked myself with the V12.

Before I could grab brains from the cooler, my phone rang. Nick. I put it on speaker. "Hey, Nick." I filled my voice with as much casual cheer as I could squeeze in. "I'm fine, I promise. Sorry I had to run off, but I forgot I had to meet someone, and now I'm running late."

"Who the hell was that? What did he want?"

"Dunno who he was. Some asshole who'd been drinking since morning." I clung to the hope that Nick had raced downstairs the instant he saw me in trouble and therefore only witnessed the initial part of the attack when Rosario was acting drunk. No way did I need the cops involved in this. "Lucky for me, the dude ran like a little bitch when I grabbed your tranq gun," I continued. "And I really am sorry about the broken window. I guess I panicked and went into Angel-Smash mode, but at least it scared the guy off." I tried for a laugh. "If it wasn't for the broken window, the whole thing might be kinda funny."

Nick laughed with me, and I melted in relief. He'd bought it. "Windows can be replaced," he said. "What matters is that you're okay. Do you have a description for the cops?"

I rattled off a description vague enough to fit a quarter of the parade-goers in town since I didn't want the cops involved At All, reassured Nick yet again that I was fine, then finally disconnected.

Hunger grumbled, and I reached for my cooler to grab a brain smoothie.

No cooler. Not on the front seat or the floorboard.

Dread rising, I checked my mirrors for any sign of Rosario, then pulled over and looked for the cooler in the back seat. "No no no no no no," I breathed then ran to the trunk on the slim chance I'd had a brain fart and stuck my cooler in there.

Nope. Just the usual junk. I held back a shriek of rage with effort. The asswipe had broken into my car and swiped my entire stash of brains while I was in the building. Hands shaking with fury, I slammed the trunk and got back in the car. No doubt he was also the prick who'd stolen my gun at the Fest. Maybe his plan wasn't so sloppy after all.

Didn't change the fact that I wanted to kick his brain-stealing ass more than ever.

But first, I needed to find my next meal.

Chapter 29

Dante Rosario wanted to kidnap me, but this wasn't my first let's-get-stalked rodeo. A little over a year ago, Dr. Kristi Charish had ordered William Rook—a mercenary-operative-hitman, a.k.a. Walter McKinney—to bring me in. After several failed attempts, Rook succeeded, but I'd learned a few things from that experience. First, I hated Kristi Charish with the fiery heat of a thousand burning suns. Second, I hated Nicole Saber with the fiery heat of a million burning suns. Third, if I was going to be hunted again, I needed to be ready and well supplied with brains. And fourth, but most importantly, I needed to make sure my dad was safe in case Rosario decided to take a page from Rook's playbook and grab my dad to get to me.

"I'm okay, I promise," I said the instant my dad answered his phone. "But I need you to go hide."

"Jesus, Angel, I just put a damn pizza in the oven and I got *The Godfather* in the Blu-ray."

"Jesus, Dad," I mimicked. "Turn the oven off, and you've already watched that thing a billion times. Get out of the house and go someplace no one would expect."

"Shit. Fine. You ain't lying to me about being okay, are you?"

"I'm not lying. But I need to know you're safe."

I heard the beep as he turned the oven off. "I think I liked it better when you was just a druggie car thief," he grumbled.

I laughed. "I love you. I'll call as soon as I can."

"Love you too, Angelkins, and you damn well better."

That took care of a big chunk of my worry. But my nerves ratcheted back up when I called the lab and it continued to ring and ring. After at least ten rings the line clicked, and a woman's voice answered. "Delancey."

Uggghhhhh. Rachel Delancey. "It's Angel. I have a problem and need to speak to Dr. Nikas." I grimaced then added, "Please."

"Dr. Nikas isn't available," she replied coolly. "Perhaps you can try in a few hours—"

"Dante Rosario just tried to kidnap me behind the morgue," I said in a rush. "Pretty sure Dr. Nikas would like to know that."

"I see. I'll relay the info to Dr. Nikas. But, as acting chief of Security, I'm ordering you to stay clear of the lab as long as there's the slightest chance you're being followed."

My hackles went up at her patronizing tone. "Right. Because it's not as if Saberton already knows *exactly* where the lab is. Oh, wait, you weren't there when they infiltrated and almost got Jacques and Reg and the heads."

Her calm demeanor shattered. "They got in because of *you.*" Pent up anger vibrated through her voice. "Chris Peterson's death was *your* fault. You're a security risk and a liability to the Tribe, and I'm not the only one who feels that way!"

I held back the words that leaped into my mouth. Instead I took a slow, deep breath then pulled onto the shoulder and came to a stop. Not so long ago, I'd have crumpled and accepted that I really was dead weight and a fuckup, whether it was true or not. But in this moment it was as if her venom threw everything into sharp focus, burned away the bullshit and allowed me to step back and clearly see my accomplishments and failures. Sure, I still fucked up here and there, but so did everyone else. I'd done lots of good stuff, too. I knew damn well she wanted me to believe that Marcus agreed with her assessment of me. Maybe he did. But I'd risked my ass to go back into Saberton to rescue him and Kyle. I knew without the slightest whiff of doubt that I'd proven myself to be an asset.

And, in a supernova-bright burst of clarity, I realized it didn't matter who agreed with Rachel. Not Marcus, or Reg, or Jacques, or Pierce, or even the guy who cleaned the toilets. Whoever that was. I knew my own worth, and no one could take that away from me.

When I spoke, my voice remained steady and calm. "I was attacked, and a listening device was placed in my arm without my consent or knowledge. There's considerable evidence to support this, including the testimony of Philip, Brian, Dr. Nikas, and Pierce. You chose to ignore every shred of evidence that clears me of fault and instead decided that, because you don't *like* me, I'm obviously a murdering traitor."

"Don't you dare—"

"You're also a judgmental bitch, so fuck you." I disconnected, satisfied, then texted Dr. Nikas—since I didn't trust Rachel to relay my message. I boiled the kidnapping attempt down to *Rosario tried and failed to grab me at the morgue*, and received an *Oh dear. Do you need to come in for protection?* in response. Fuck Rachel. *Thanks. I'm good for now,* I replied. Sure, I could go hide out and twiddle my thumbs, but then Rosario would be free to do whatever the hell he wanted. I then let Dr. Nikas know that the pre-rot had progressed but seemed stable now, and that I'd confirmed Rosario's involvement in Kristi's escape from Dallas and the leaked videos. After several seconds I received a *Well done* that warmed me to the tips of my toes, followed by *I'll pass it on.*

Duty complete, I continued toward my next goal: the Tribe training ground and the emergency brain stash. As soon as I stocked up and topped off, I intended to turn the tables on Rosario.

Hunger came and went in relentless waves, as if it kept lifting its head to see if food had arrived. By the time I finally made the turn onto Salt Perch Road, the hunger breathed down my neck, prodding me with growing impatience. After two miles of steadily deteriorating road the asphalt finally gave way to a thirty-foot-wide stretch of packed dirt and gravel surrounded by waist-high grass and scattered pines. Farther out, firm land fought a losing battle with stagnant pools and brackish marsh until even that gave way to wide stretches of water between sparse patches of slightly higher ground.

This area had been a nature preserve at one time, with a long boardwalk that threaded through the marsh and nifty signs that identified the plants and wildlife. I had vague memories of coming out here with my parents when I was five or six, shrieking in delight as I ran down the boardwalk, sneakers pounding the wooden planks like a giant drum and sending every resident of the marsh scattering. After Hurricane Katrina destroyed the man-made additions, money for rebuilding was nonexistent, and the land was put up for sale. Pietro Ivanov bought it soon after to use as a training ground, cordoned it off, banned all hunting, and deliberately allowed the wetlands to remain wild, unimproved, and undamaged. Except for the occasional stampede of zombies, of course.

Small noises entwined into an earthy harmony—the shriek of birds and croak of frogs and buzz of insects. A damp and chilly breeze flowed over the grass and set it waving. Fifty yards to my right, a rusted flagpole speared drunkenly up from scraggly bushes on a small circle of dry land. There was no sign of the barbecue pit where the brains were stashed, but Dr. Nikas had said near the flagpole, not beside it. I tugged my jacket on, locked my car out of pure habit, then set off toward the flagpole. The footing ranged from firm and dry to knee-deep muck. I paused long enough to grab a sturdy tree branch for stability and forged onward. There was probably an easier path if I bothered to take the time, but at this point, I didn't care if I got wet. I just wanted to get there as fast as possible.

Not that it made a difference. There wasn't a damn thing at the base of the flagpole but dead grass and a nest of rats. I did a slow turn and scanned the area. No barbecue pit in sight.

Maybe I'd dreamed the part about the barbecue pit? Heart sinking, I clawed through the bushes even though they couldn't possibly hide a shoebox, much less the one I wanted. *No, this can't be happening. How can it not be here?* A sob of panic rose, and I choked it back with effort. This was a problem, but problems had solutions. I just had to work through it. A military-grade hard plastic case full of eight-ounce packets would be too heavy for a swamp animal to drag off, and the only footprints around the flagpole were mine. But now that I was looking more carefully, I also couldn't find any box-shaped depressions in the grass.

Frustrated, I jabbed my stick into the soft dirt. Either someone took the box a while ago, or I'd misheard Dr. Nikas about the location. My phone was in my car, but it wouldn't take long to trek back and send a text. If all else failed and the brains really were supposed to be at this flagpole, maybe Dr. Nikas could direct me to a different emergency stash.

God, I hoped so. At least mosquitos didn't care for zombie blood, so I had that going for me.

The crack of a rifle smacked the air, and bone and blood flew as pain exploded in my right hand. I screamed and dropped the stick, fell back as I clutched my ruined hand. *Rosario.* Goddammit. There was no way he could have followed me here without me seeing him, which meant the asswipe had probably stuck a GPS tracker on my car during one of the break-ins. *And now I'm a sitting duck.*

"C'mon out, Angel. I got you in my sights, and I can drop you before you can get up to run."

I froze. Not Rosario. *Judd*. How the hell had I underestimated the redneck gun nut so thoroughly? And how had he found me out here? No way was he in league with Rosario. Even a Saberton goon had standards. I shivered as I looked down at my mangled hand. To my unending relief the pain was starting to ebb *It's okay, you beautiful parasite. I know you're trying.*

And on the other end of that rifle was an oh-so-savory brain, perfect to give my parasite a boost.

"Get the fuck up, you goddamn zombie freak," Judd shouted, "or I'll put the next one through your head. And you know I'm good enough to do it."

Yeah, I did know. He'd aimed for my hand to get my attention, and was skilled enough to tear me apart, piece by piece. "Why should I make it easy for you to kill me?"

"Makes no difference to me whether you're alive or dead. Either way, you're my ticket outta this whole goddamn mess. Bear's gonna pull the strings I need to get me a new identity once I bring him a real honest-to-god zombie. Now get your ass up before I have to shoot you a few more times to motivate you."

Bear. That fucking son of a bitch. He'd even given Nick a tranq gun for zombies. Fury sharpened my focus to a scalpel's edge. "No, don't shoot me anymore," I said, adding a pained gasp for effect. Judd probably didn't know the parasite dulled pain—when it was working, at least. He might think I was in too much agony to fight back. It was a flimsy advantage, but it was all I had.

Hugging my hand to my chest, I staggered out of the bushes. Judd stood a dozen yards away at a right angle from the watery path I'd slogged to the flagpole. To my annoyance, I saw that the ground between us was damn near bone dry. Great. If I'd taken a minute to look for a dry path, I'd have made it to the flagpole in a quarter of the time and wouldn't be soaked.

Judd kept his rifle aimed at me as I moved toward him. "That's far enough," he said when I'd closed half the distance.

I stopped and kept my face contorted in pretend pain, but a gauze bandage on his right forearm drew my attention. That was my bite under there.

"You fucked everything up, you know-it-all bitch." Anger swept over Judd's face. "You just had to poke your fucking nose where it didn't belong." He steadied the rifle, and my pulse jumped.

"You'll turn zombie a lot faster if you kill me!" I blurted.

"The fuck you talking about?" he demanded, but his tongue darted out to lick dry lips. The seed was already there. I just needed to give it plenty of manure.

"The bite. The zombie virus creates a psychic connection with the one who turned you." I couldn't bring myself to call him my zombie baby. Ugh. I tried to ease forward but the twitch of his rifle stopped me. "Even now, you're probably able to pick up some of my thoughts, such as the number I'm thinking of right now."

His eyes narrowed. "Seventeen?"

"On the nose," I said, adding a sprinkle of awe.

A tremble went through him. "I'm not that stupid, you freak. It's been twenty-four hours, and I'm not sick or turned into a zombie." His throat worked, and a sheen of sweat covered his forehead.

"Exactly. It's not too late to stop the virus and keep you human." I tried to give him a motherly smile. "I can get you the antidote. But, if you kill me, our connection will snap back like a rubber band, and POW, you're as full a zombie as I am right now."

"Shut up!" he screamed, spittle flying. "I'm not a zombie, you fucking monster freak whore bitch!"

Shit. Pushed too far. Fucking motherly smile. "Okay, you're right, Judd. Look, I'll go with you. Take me to Bear. You don't have to kill me."

Judd sighted in on my head. "Don't tell me what—" His

face went slack. The rifle tumbled out of his hands, and a second later he collapsed face down beside it in the dirt.

A tranq dart protruded from his back. A *zombie* tranq. *He's dead*, I thought wildly. *But who—?*

I snapped out of my daze and sprinted toward Judd's body. I didn't have zombie super speed, but I covered the distance in record time. With the sweetest tuck and roll I'd ever managed in my life, I snatched up the rifle, took cover behind a thick slash pine, and fired three quick shots at the stand of trees where I'd seen a flicker of movement.

A choked cry of pain rewarded my efforts. "Goddammit, Angel!" Rosario's voice. "Shit! It isn't what you think."

"Go fuck yourself!" I yelled back. I slammed the butt of the rifle down onto Judd's skull to crack it then once more to smash it open. Moving quickly, I ripped skull pieces away and tossed them aside, then grabbed a double handful of brain and tore it free. Most of it, anyway. The cerebellum and medulla oblongata were still in there along with a mangled chunk of occipital lobe, but digging them out would take time I didn't have. I lifted a handful of brain to my mouth then paused as a horrible thought occurred to me. Judd had been zombie-tranqed. Could I even eat his brain without knocking myself out? My hand trembled as I thought it through. Tranqs were formulated to be injected—not only for speed of delivery, but because ingestion drastically reduced the amount that got absorbed into the blood stream. Since Judd wouldn't have anywhere near a full dose in his brain tissue, I'd be taking in a micro-dose, at most.

Hunger roared in impatience. *Screw it*, I thought and gulped the chunk of brain. I didn't really have a choice anyway. I shoved the rest of the brain into my jacket pocket and zipped it shut, then gave Judd's body a quick search in the hopes of finding the flash drives. His wallet contained four hundred dollars in cash that I pocketed with zero guilt, but his clothing held only keys and a folding knife. No drives. Crap.

Marla let out a flurry of growl-filled barks, quieting only

after a *hush* from Rosario. I didn't need to be fluent in Doggy to know that she'd announced precisely how she planned to tear me apart for hurting her human, despite the fact that Rosario was far from death's door, judging by the muffled curses that drifted my way.

Well, this was a nice little standoff. I had no way to reach my car without risking getting tranqed or mauled. I had Judd's rifle, which was surely the only reason Rosario hadn't sent Marla to flush me out. But if he called for backup I was fucked.

Fine. Time to change the game. I tucked Judd's knife into my pocket then snatched up the rifle and took off running at an angle that kept the trees between me and Rosario. I fully expected to get a German Shepherd between the shoulder blades at any second, but I made it to the water untackled, and a glance behind showed no pursuit.

Yet.

With a vague goal of *get the hell away from here*, I splashed into the water and tried not to think about snakes and alligators and snapping turtles and sea monsters. The setting sun painted the marsh in reflections of gold and orange, and cypress trees cast long shadows over the water. I pressed onward, slogging through waist-deep then chest-deep water, holding the rifle over my head like soldiers in a movie I once saw about the Vietnam war.

Marla's strident bark in the distance was more than enough to spur me deeper into the marsh. It was nearly full dark by the time I stopped hearing her barks and was far enough into the swamp to feel safe from discovery. Exhausted, I crawled onto a small island of relatively dry ground. I heard a slide and splash that was probably a gator, but I was too tired to give a crap. The island was about half the size of my bedroom and crammed full of chest-high marsh grass that I knew damn well was home to all sorts of slithery critters. I wasn't really afraid of snakes, but getting bit by a water moccasin at this point might make my poor parasite throw its hands up in defeat and go sob in the corner. With a stick in hand, I jabbed and poked and whacked the grass as I pushed toward the middle of my little island. Though I didn't see any snakes, I heard plenty of whispers of noise as unseen creatures evacuated the area.

Invasion complete, I stomped a circle of grass flat then plopped my butt down. An almost full moon was starting its climb above a horizon of cypress trees and Spanish moss. I reclined in my nest and watched the curtain of stars shift and shimmer as fluffy clouds drifted across the sky. The various swamp musicians who'd been silenced by my arrival gradually resumed their evening symphony. I was wet and dirty, but the night was mild enough that I wasn't miserable, and I took care of the twinge of hunger with the rest of Judd's brain. Peace stole through me despite the danger that lurked beyond the swamp. Tomorrow, I'd deal with Rosario. And Bear.

For the moment, I was safe. And that was enough.

Chapter 30

I snapped fully awake, primal instincts shrieking so loudly I expected to find a serial killer standing over me with an axe. But no serial killer. No threat of any sort within my trampled circle of grass. It was still full night with at least another hour until dawn, judging by the moon's new position. Heart jittering, I grabbed the rifle, parted the grass, and gave the dark swamp a careful scan. Though I couldn't see anything remotely dangerous, my nerves continued to buzz a low warning. Unsettled, I listened, straining my ears through the silence.

Silence?

No symphony or chorus. Every living creature had gone utterly still, waiting for whatever was out there to pass them by.

A low splash cracked through the air like a cannon. I bit back a yelp, hands spasming on the rifle. An animal going into the water. That's all it was. A goddamn bullfrog.

The moon slipped behind a cloud, plunging everything into a deep gloom. Another splash, and every hair on my body lifted as a weird choking-gurgle followed it. *That was no frog.*

Okay, I was officially freaked out. I peered in the direction of the splashes, breath catching as the water rippled twenty feet away from where I crouched. *Nutria*, I prayed. *Please let it be a nutria.*

As if in slow motion, a dark figure broke the surface, water dripping as it straightened into an unmistakably human shape.

Anger and dismay battled it out in my gut. *Rosario.* Or, more likely, one of his Saberton buddies since gunshot wounds and swamp water didn't play well together. I couldn't catch a fucking break.

Or maybe I *had* caught a break. I didn't know how this guy had found me, but any plans to catch me off guard were toast. I was awake, ready, and armed.

I shifted to one knee and lifted the rifle to my shoulder, but a tremble went through me as I took aim. I was about to kill this guy, and he had no idea it was coming. It didn't matter that I *knew* with horrifying certainty what sort of hell awaited me in Saberton's tender care. I'd killed before, but always face-to-face, in the heat of battle. This was cold-blooded murder.

Damn it. I blinked tears away and took careful aim at the center of my intruder's torso. And now I really am a monster.

Fire leaped from the muzzle as the shot shattered the air. The dark shape fell back with a heavy splash, barely audible beneath the chaos of cries and shrieks as thousands of creatures dashed into hiding. Ears ringing, I lowered the rifle, watched as the water closed over him and went smooth again. "Shit. Shit." I scrubbed at my face with a grimy hand as a stupid ache squeezed my chest. *I had no choice, but hunting me—a zombie—was his choice.* I knew that, and I also knew it didn't change a thing.

I startled at a loud splash and watery gasp, yanked the rifle up again as the man surged upright. I hadn't killed him, but I wasn't sure whether to be pissed or relieved about it. He staggered a step closer, less than ten feet from the edge of my island. Pissed, I decided. That was the better choice.

"Get the fuck back!" I yelled. "I don't care if you're wounded. You're not going to—"

"Annnnnggeellll."

I knew that voice. My blood turned to ice as the impossible figure lurched forward. The moon broke through the clouds to shine down like a spotlight from hell, illuminating the lopsided and ragged half bowl of remaining skull. His mouth gaped open as glistening drops of water fell in lazy slow motion from a stained gauze bandage on his right forearm.

No. This couldn't be Judd. I was having a nightmare. That was the only explanation. A really horrible, terrifying, vivid nightmare. There was no way in hell my bite had made this open-skulled *thing*. Making a zombie was *hard*. It couldn't happen from one bite.

Or could it? Horror crawled through my veins as I remembered Philip turning two Saberton guards with only a bite. But that was only possible because he had a *damaged* parasite. And those two had been messed up, unstable. Not *real* zombies.

So what the hell was this thing?

The Undead Judd sloshed closer, snapping me out of my shock. With every movement, water spilled from the jagged edges of his skull, like a kid carrying a bowl of soup.

He found me, I realized in stunned amazement. Apparently the bullshit I'd fed him hadn't been all bullshit. Whatever kind of zombie he was, he'd glommed onto the weird zombie mama-baby connection and found me, deep in the swamp. It would be amazing and sweet except for the part where he was a godawful walking nightmare who'd been a murdering piece of shit before he died.

I fired twice in quick succession, hissing in frustration as he stayed on his feet.

"Annnnnggelll." His arms extended toward me, hands crooked like claws as he continued to close the distance.

Mouth dry, I fired three more times, cursing when the gun clicked on the fourth try. I was out of ammo, and I'd only managed to blow a fist-sized hole in his chest. Damn it, the dude was missing most of his fucking *brain.* How was this possible?

The answer appeared as moonlight shone down on the pink and grey lumps in his shattered skull. Those lumps included a completely intact cerebellum—a seriously vital region of the brain that handled all sorts of important shit like motor control and coordination. That explained how he could move—sort of. But talk? I'd eaten his cerebrum! Whatever godawful zombie parasite or infection he had inside him was helping him out in ways I couldn't imagine.

Now I had to figure out how to shut him down.

I scrambled to my feet and backed away as he lurched onto the island. "Judd!" I shouted, hoping he still had a few neurons that would listen to reason. "You need to stop!" Oh, who the hell was I kidding. He'd never had any listen-to-reason neurons, even before I ate most of his brain.

Judd's lips pulled back from his teeth as he swung at me in a clumsy blow. I ducked it with ease, then smacked him across the jaw with the butt of the rifle. His head jerked to the side then swiveled back to face me. His eyes skittered in every direction in a creepy, unfocused dance, yet I couldn't shake the feeling he had no trouble seeing everything around him. He made another swing at me, a bit faster this time. Things were getting rewired deep in that brain chunk, and I didn't like it one bit. Especially since I'd obviously left the part that wanted me dead.

I pivoted away then whacked him again with the rifle with the same lack of effect as before. His next swing brushed my shoulder, but when I moved in to whack him again he snapped his arm back with a gut punch that sent me sprawling.

He flopped on top of me, pinning me down as I gasped for breath. I struggled to buck him off, fear climbing as he closed a hand over my throat. He growled like a purr, and a trickle of brain-tinged swamp water poured over the edge of his open skull to spatter onto my face as he shifted to tighten his grip.

Brains in a bowl.

A predator's snarl pulled at my mouth. Time to scrub the dishes.

I ignored the squeeze of his fingers on my throat and reached up with both hands to grab that goddamn cerebellum. I was at a lousy angle and couldn't pull it out, but when I dug my fingers in, it sure as shit got his attention. He spasmed hard and released my throat, which gave me enough wiggle room to jam my knee into his side and shift him off me. He let out a weird howl as I dug my fingers into his brain stem, as if he knew what was coming. In the next instant the howl cut off, and Judd's body collapsed, finally lifeless.

I staggered to my feet with the remainder of Judd's brain clutched in my hand while several inches of spinal cord dangled like a tail. Curious, I took a cautious sniff. It definitely didn't smell like a human brain anymore. No desire to eat it whatsoever. I filed that bit of info away to pass along to Dr. Nikas, then stuffed the brain and its dangly bits into my jacket pocket. Dr. Nikas would definitely want to examine it. And me, for that matter.

After a few minutes to catch my breath, I dragged Judd's body to the center of the island and once again searched him, but this time with the meticulous and thorough care that I used to search bodies in the morgue. It made no sense that he wouldn't have the flash drives on him or in his car, especially considering how he'd believed the whole zombie thing was his ticket to freedom via Bear. Anger flared at the thought of Nick's dad, but I tamped it down. I'd deal with his ass soon enough.

In the year and a half I'd been working in the morgue, I'd stripped and searched hundreds of bodies and found an incredible variety of objects in every possible nook, cranny, fold, crease, hole, or flap that the human body had to offer. My gut told me that drive was on or in Judd's corpse, and by god I was going to find it.

Dawn was happily flinging orange and purple streaks across the eastern sky when I found the penis-shaped flash drive within Judd's tighty-whities and tucked behind his nutsack. I took a moment to revel in weary triumph before shoving it deep into a pocket along with Judd's car keys. One down, one to go.

The original had to be somewhere. I searched again. No drive. He'd either stashed it or given it to someone.

Not someone. *Bear Galatas*.

"Judd, you turd bucket," I muttered then took out his knife and set to work separating his head from his body.

The sun was up, and my mood was shit by the time I finally finished sawing through muscles, tendons, windpipe, and spine. I clambered to my feet and gave the two pieces of Judd the finger. "Shamble now, asshole," I muttered.

Though I wasn't happy about leaving Judd's body behind, there was no way I was dragging that thing with me. Instead, I rolled it into the water and trusted that the swamp's flesh-eating critters would dispose of it, while I silently prayed that St. Edward's parish wouldn't end up with zombie gators.

The head was a different matter. I had *no* desire to carry that nasty thing back through the swamp. But, even more so, I absolutely did *not* want to leave it out here and give some microscopic fragment of brain the time and space it needed to regrow another zombie Judd body. Yeah, it was improbable, but so was the original zombie Judd.

Since the rifle was out of ammo, it didn't matter anymore if it got wet. I slung the strap across my chest, hooked my fingers in the only secure grip on Judd's head—his mouth—and accepted that the feel of his tongue on my hand would haunt my nightmares for a very long time. After half a mile, I broke through a fringe of trees and could finally see radio towers on the horizon as well as a few other distinctive landmarks—a dead oak whose branches formed a twisted thumbs-up, and a bald eagle nest near the very top of a towering pine. I had a fairly good sense of direction, but even so it took me several minutes of confused puzzling before I realized why nothing lined up the way I was used to.

Nice job, Angel, I thought with a roll of my eyes as the answer came to me. In my not-quite-panicked flight of the previous evening, I'd managed to travel two-thirds of a giant circle. If I'd kept going, I'd have ended up right in Rosario's lap. Obviously, I needed to implant a friggin' compass in my hand.

I laughed at the thought. For a zombie, that wasn't a *completely* ridiculous idea. Of course, if I decided to go with that level of body modification, I'd also get the satellite phone option, 'cause that shit would've been damn handy last night.

With daylight to help me make out landmarks, I estimated I had less than a mile to go. Still, it wasn't a walk in the park, and my fading spirits and energy levels perked up at the sight of a flagpole thrusting up from tall grass. But my relief shifted to bewilderment as I neared it. Where was the parking area? I should've been able to at least see the outer edge of it by now. And hadn't the flagpole been surrounded by bushes before?

I stopped in the knee-deep water, Judd's head dangling from my grip as I stared in at the flagpole. It stood almost straight, and not far from its base was the remains of a concrete barbecue.

There are two flagpoles. How the fuck did I not know there were two flagpoles?

I checked the position of the radio towers and other landmarks, then struggled to visualize the whole thing from above. After a few seconds I gave up, splashed to a muddy bank and drew it out with a stick. *Now* it made sense. Not only was this pole near the outer perimeter of where the Tribe did most of its training, but I'd never actually been in this particular section before. Not all that surprising considering I'd only been out to Camp SwampyButt a handful of times to train with the security team. And, since Dr. Nikas had almost certainly never been out here, he hadn't known the need to specify.

I broke into a run and hoped to hell there weren't a dozen more flagpoles with barbecues to find and search. But no, a dull green, hard-plastic case rested far beneath the barbecue, hidden behind a battered sheet of corrugated metal. Hands shaking, I lugged the case out and dialed in the combination. At the click, I swung the lid up then literally cried at the sight of what had to be close to eighty brain packets.

Worry slipped away as I tore two open and sucked the contents down, and when I finished, I counted out ten more. That would be plenty to carry me through the next few days.

Probably. The V12 was using up brains like crazy, and I had a billion things on my to do list. Just to be sure, I went ahead and counted out another dozen.

My gaze fell to where I'd dropped Judd's head in the grass. After a moment of thought, I stuffed both head and brain into the case, locked it, and shoved it back under the barbecue. Leaving them here wasn't the best option, but it was better than my original plan of "stick them in the trunk of my car and hope for the best," especially since I wasn't sure when I'd be able to get to the lab. Plus, I didn't want to risk being the subject of a headline like *Murder Suspect's Head Found During Routine Traffic Stop of Insane Woman*.

Using my jacket, I made a bundle of the brain packets then damn near skipped the rest of the way back. My car was right where I left it, but parked twenty yards beyond it was Judd's borrowed car and my last chance to find the second flash drive. I dumped the brain bundle on my hood then fished his keys from my pocket and went on to search the car from top to bottom.

Nothing even remotely resembling a flash drive. However I did find spark plug wires in the back seat as well as a phone that looked suspiciously like mine.

Shit. I spun toward my car then groaned at the sparkle of broken glass beneath my passenger window. "Asshole," I growled. Judd had wanted to be absolutely sure I couldn't get away from him.

But my years with Randy meant I knew how to reattach the wires. Once I did so, I crossed my fingers and cranked the engine, then let out a whoop when it started without a hitch.

"Suck it, Judd!"

It was several miles before my phone got a signal, at which time a bajillion missed calls, voicemails, and messages poured in—mostly from Nick, with two from Ben Roth, and a couple others from numbers I didn't recognize. Nick's were all of the "Are you okay?" variety, which I couldn't deal with until I dealt with Bear, so I went on to listen to the voicemail from the unknown number.

Angel. A woman's stressed whisper, but deep as if she was trying to sound like a man. Traffic noise and clanging filled the background. *Just letting you know I sent the kid off safe and sound for his camping trip. My partner didn't want him to go, but it all worked out, so don't worry. I'm staying home for now.*

I listened again to make sure I'd heard it right. *That was Andrew's bodyguard, Thea Braddock, calling from a pay phone.* Trouble must have rolled down about Andrew being a zombie, probably because Rosario—or even Andrew's other security guy, Tom Snyder—notified Nicole Saber that Marla indicated on Andrew at the Fest. However it happened, the fallout was serious enough that Andrew felt the need to activate his exit strategy. I played the voicemail a third time to be sure I understood her hidden message. Snyder wanted to take him to Nicole but Thea put a stop to that. Andrew was okay and safe, and Braddock was "home"—with Saberton—which told me she'd pulled the whole thing off in a way that didn't raise suspicion. And if I was a gambling girl, I'd bet that Ms. Eagle Eye Braddock had known Andrew was a zombie long before this shit came down.

Thank all the little pink gods, because now Andrew's safety was one worry off my plate. He was still in a crappy situation, but at least—for the moment—it was stable.

My first call was to my dad to tell him I was okay and that he needed to stay put for a bit longer. To my surprise he didn't argue or whine, and after a quick exchange of "love you"s, I hung up before his mood shifted. After that, I called the lab and got Jacques, then filled him in on Rosario and Bear. But when I told him about the Judd situation, I heard his shocked gasp.

"Dr. Nikas will want you to come in to be checked," he said, agitated.

"I will," I promised. "But if I don't deal with Bear and Rosario, it may not matter. We need that flash drive, and we need to plug the leaks." With that, I told him where I left Judd's head and brain and how many brain packets I took, then made a quick goodbye and hung up before he could get Dr. Nikas, who I *knew* would tell me to come to the lab. I wouldn't be able to put him off anywhere near as easily.

But, right now, it was time to go on a Bear hunt.

Chapter 31

The weather was lovely and perfect, which meant the streets of New Orleans were guaranteed to be packed to bursting with Mardi Gras day revelers. Normally a small parade of pickups and four-wheelers rolled through Tucker Point on Mardi Gras morning, but this year the Zombie Fest was hosting parades and shows and all sorts of cool stuff for a Fat Tuesday special event: *Laissez le bons cerveaux roulent*. Or, in English: Let the good brains roll.

As a result, Tucker Point was a ghost town.

Worked for me. The empty streets simply meant there was no one to get in my way.

The Bear's Den was closed for the holiday, but a check of the alley revealed Bear's truck parked by the back door. *Bingo*.

Four more brain packets had my senses crackling with life, but even the over-tanking didn't change the condition of my face. Still grey with the nasty rot spot on my cheek, and my gauze pads were all somewhere in the swamp. My breath shuddered as I stared at my reflection in the rearview mirror and willed the rot to heal. The Fest ended this evening, which would also be the end of my "zombie makeup" excuse. Then again, I had plenty of sick leave saved up since my parasite kept me healthy. I could do some inpatient time with Dr. Nikas at the lab and get fixed up.

But if I couldn't find the flash drive and eliminate the immediate threat of exposure to me and the Tribe, there might not be a lab to go to.

After parking half a block down the street, I grabbed the tire iron from my car trunk then strode down the alley. My pulse quickened as I neared the back door. I wasn't going up against some random asshole here. Bear's entire existence centered on disaster preparedness and hardcore survival. I didn't have the "preparedness" bit down the same way, but I was the queen bitch of fighting for survival.

A security camera over the door covered about thirty feet of the alley approach. The instant I hit the surveillance perimeter I poured on super zombie speed in case Bear was near the monitor. Leaping mid-stride, I whacked the camera with the tire iron and sent it skittering down the alley, then whirled and jammed the pry bar end between door and frame, and wrenched hard. The door looked damn solid, and for an instant I thought the tire iron would break. Instead, I nearly sprawled on my ass when the unlocked door popped wide open, sending the tire iron flying down the alley and into a dumpster.

Well, that sure made things easier, even though I'd lost my weapon. No way Bear hadn't heard the whacking and jamming and wrenching, but at this point I was committed. I charged into the dark store and slung around a hallway corner. Light spilled from an open doorway near the end of the hall. I sprinted toward it, leaped and pushed off the opposite wall to propel myself into an office the size of my living room.

Gun in hand, Bear was only a couple of yards from the door. The slow spin of the chair behind the desk told me he'd been sitting there working on his laptop when he heard the noise, and I spared an instant to be impressed at the speed of his reaction. Even the sight of a flying Angel coming at him didn't catch him off guard. He fired from the hip and would have hit me if I'd been an inch wider in the gut.

Not that it made a difference, except that I wasn't *quite* as pissed when I plowed into him. He staggered back but stayed on his feet. I slammed a fist into his forearm, wrenched the gun from his spasming hand, then slung it across the room with enough force to send it through the drywall.

Bear knew how to fight. The instant the gun left his hand, he went for a knife on his belt, snapped it open and shoved it toward my gut. But my zombie reflexes were still singing happily. My hand clamped onto his wrist before the blade went in more than an inch.

"You're not playing very nice, Bear," I snarled as I pulled free and sent the blade flying. "I just want to have a little chat, and here you're being an asshole."

Jaw tight, he snapped out a punch. I ducked it, then grabbed the front of his shirt with both hands and slammed him against the wall. "What the fuck were you planning to do with me after Judd brought me in?" I yelled.

I lifted him several inches off the floor. He let out a shocked yelp and grabbed my forearms. "What in god's name are you talking about?"

I dropped him but kept my grip tight in his shirt and my expression fierce. He didn't need to know that I couldn't have held him up another second. The dude was big and *solid,* but my superpower display had been enough to pause his efforts to kill me. For the moment, at least. The look in his eyes was wary respect, not defeat.

"Judd told me the deal," I said, letting a growl bleed into my words. "If he turned me over to *you,* dead or alive, you'd help him get a new identity and escape the cops."

As I spoke, his expression went from incredulous to furious. "He's a goddamn liar and an idiot. A new identity? How the fuck am I supposed to do that?"

"Judd obviously thought you had a way," I said. "And why wouldn't you help a member of your survivalist group?"

"Judd's not a member!" Bear snarled. "He's a hothead who only looks out for himself. That reckless, self-indulgent crap doesn't fly in my community."

"Yeah, you're a real saint." A saint who was also up to some shit. I didn't see a flash drive in the laptop, but I hadn't missed that Bear never once questioned *why* Judd would think I was worth capturing. Sneering, I released him and stepped back. "And you're so level-headed you gave your own son a black eye because he didn't toe your line. Is that how *you* fly?"

Face reddening, he lifted a fist. "You stay the fuck away from my son. I know what you are."

"What is she, Dad?"

I jerked in surprise and turned to see Nick standing in the doorway, eyes wide and hands clenching and unclenching. Bear yanked his fist down to his side, but Nick had already seen his dad threaten me. Given the circumstances, I had zero motivation to explain the situation and let Bear off the hook.

Nick stepped forward, breathing hard. "What is she? A redneck? The wrong breeding stock? Or just 'not good enough' for me? She's my friend, and I have every right to—" He swallowed and flicked a self-conscious glance at me. "—to hang out with anyone I want."

Bear's lips pressed into a razor-thin line. He squared his shoulders to loom over me and Nick, then forcefully smoothed down the wrinkles on his shirt with both hands. Holy shitballs, the man knew how to be intimidating.

"You want to know what she is?" Bear said, voice mild and murderous. "How about you see for yourself." He stepped to the desk and spun the laptop to face the room. I knew what was coming, felt the impending disaster and was helpless to stop it. Not without making it worse.

No flash drive in the laptop because he already copied the files.

Bear hit a key, and the screen filled with a video. Me in Kristi Charish's horrible lab at the abandoned car factory, my hand gripped tight in the hair of the piece of shit who brought me there—Walter McKinney. Faces were purposely blurred out, but anyone who knew me would recognize my bleached hair and scrawny butt. High-definition, color. No sound, thank god. Frozen, I watched video-me repeatedly slam McKinney's head into the bulletproof glass, then rip his skull open and gulp down his brain. On the screen I straightened, hands and mouth covered in gore, and with bloody bullet holes in my T-shirt.

Nick's expression melted into grief and horror that sliced right through my soul. His gaze cut to me for the barest instant—long enough to take in the grey skin and rotten spot on my cheek—before darting away again.

"Your girlfriend is a *zombie*, Nick," Bear said as the video shifted to a new scene: Blurred video-me, looking every bit the monster as I bit and ripped and tore at the flesh of a big blond man. *Philip*.

Nick slammed the laptop shut and backed against the wall, face white.

"Judd gave me a flash drive Saturday night," Bear said. "He told me it would blow my mind, but he says that about all kinds of shit, so I ignored it. Until today, that is, when I heard he was a goddamn murder suspect and started thinking maybe the drive had something to do with that crap." He folded his arms over his powerful chest and leveled a nasty smug smile at me.

The ice holding me immobile shattered. I rounded on Bear. "I'm part of a survivalist group, too, you festering asshole," I shouted, voice cracking. "And all we want to do is *survive*. We're not monsters, but that man whose skull I smashed against the window *was* a monster. He murdered innocent people and kidnapped my dad to get to me. My *dad!*"

Bear's smile slipped, but I was too wound up to stop.

"That fucking worthless prick put me in an animal cage and brought me to that lab"—I stabbed my finger at the laptop—"so that I could be experimented on! I was lucky because I got out, but others like me haven't been. They get chained up and chopped up, over and over without anesthesia, in the name of research. That's my *family* in those horror show videos!"

Bear held his hands before him as if trying to calm a raging beast. "Angel, please settle down. We can—"

"Settle down?!" I grabbed the hem of my T-shirt and yanked it out to show the smears of mud, blood, and swamp slime. "See this? Wanna know why I'm so dirty? It's because your buddy Dante Rosario was hunting me through the swamp so *he* could capture me and put me in a cage and drag me to a lab. I got away this time, but he won't give up."

Bear dropped his arms as I advanced on him. He opened his mouth to speak but I didn't give him the chance.

"Yeah, I got turned a year and a half ago, but I had zero say in it. None!" I stabbed a finger at him. "So, Mr. High and Mighty Bear Who Shits in the Woods, you tell me what the hell *you* would do if one day you woke up as a monster, and people were out to hurt you and your family and friends. Would you just roll over and take it?" I took a heaving breath. "All I want is to work and go to school and have a *life* without hurting anyone and without anyone fucking with me." My throat was raw, and I realized I'd been shouting as I spewed out my rage. I couldn't bear to look at Nick again, but Bear's face was like stone.

The rage drained away, leaving me empty and exhausted. "I've been fighting to survive ever since I got turned," I said, voice hoarse and thin. "But it's never going to stop. There's always going to be someone who wants to hurt or kill us." I moved drunkenly to a chair and sagged into it. "Maybe I need to get the fucking message. Look at me, trying to be a hero. How the hell am I supposed to catch Rosario before he gets me? Who the fuck do I think I am?"

No one spoke. I half-expected Bear to grab a gun and put me out of everyone's misery right then and there, but he didn't move.

"You're Angel Crawford."

I dragged my eyes up to Nick. "Huh?"

"You're Angel Crawford," he repeated, though he couldn't bring himself to look at me. "You're the girl who doesn't back away from a challenge when it matters. I still remember your first day. I detested you on sight, because you didn't seem to give a shit about anyone or anything."

I winced. "You weren't wrong."

Nick snorted. "I knew I was going to waste time training you only to have you quit or be fired in a few weeks, so I figured I'd make you puke and chicken out." He shook his head. "But you didn't. You weren't going to let me win. Then you decided to get your GED, and so you did." I opened my mouth to speak, but he rolled right over me. "Then you started college, because you want to do better. *Be* better. Now this asshole Rosario wants to take all that away from you *and* your . . . people. And you're going to let him?"

My stupid eyes picked that moment to swim with tears. "No."

Nick took a deep breath, nodded and turned to Bear—who could have been carved from granite for all the reaction he showed to my tirade.

"I'm not going to med school in the fall, Dad," Nick said without ceremony, though I noted the slight tremble in his hands. "And I'm *not* going to be a surgeon. Ever. I've already talked to Allen and Dr. Leblanc about staying on as a death investigator for at least two more years. I'll reconsider my options then, but if I decide to go to med school it'll be in forensic pathology, which actually interests me." He took a breath as if drawing in composure for a speech he'd obviously rehearsed a million times. "Also, I'm volunteering in the Central African Republic this summer with a medical relief team. And . . . I'm trying out for *Les Misérables* next week at Tucker Point Little Theater."

Bear remained silent and stony for at least a dozen agonizing seconds before he sighed and rubbed the back of his neck. "Well, shit." He gave me a frown as if I'd suddenly become a referee to keep everything civil. Weird. Not that

I minded the unexpected shift away from the Angel-is-a-zombie crisis. He sighed again and shifted his frown to Nick, though it was a thoughtful frown and not scary. So far. "Just as well. You'd probably wash out of a surgical residency."

"Oh my god, really?" I said in exasperation as Nick flinched. "Could you try again with a little less Asshole?"

"What? Oh." Bear grimaced. "Shit. I didn't mean it like that, Nick. I meant that you have to *want* that kind of thing if you're going to survive the grinder." He exhaled. "Sure, a trauma surgeon would help our community, but it's no damn good if your heart's not in it."

Nick blinked. "Um, right. Exactly."

"It's a big dream, being a surgeon," Bear said. "I wanted it *for* you. I thought you wanted it too and just needed the push."

"Fuck no! Not *my* dream, Dad. You never bothered to listen to what *I* wanted." Nick cut a nearly imperceptible glance my way. "And to think I almost went through with it, because I *did* listen to you and didn't want to disappoint you."

I clapped my hands together. "Good. It's settled. Nick will do what he wants, Bear will become a surgeon, and I'll do something brilliant to turn the tables on Dante Rosario."

Bear snorted. "Two out of three isn't bad. I'm a bit old for med school."

"You'll be just as old if you don't go," I pointed out. "Hell, Nick can even tutor you."

Bear said nothing as he moved to sit behind his desk. He had the strangest look on his face, as if he'd tasted a new food and had no idea whether to love or hate it. Or . . . as if I'd told him that yes, he could go follow his dream. I masked a smile. Had Bear ever consciously known that being a surgeon was where *his* heart lay? No wonder he'd ridden Nick so hard. Not that it excused everything that had happened between father and son. I watched the emotions crawl over Bear's face as it began to hit home what he'd done—to Nick, to himself, and to their relationship. I didn't expect him to run off to med school, since it was obvious he loved his current work, but I couldn't help but take a grim pleasure in his current unsettled state. Not to mention, I highly doubted the med school thing was the only sticking point between the two. But, hey, it was a start.

Bear nodded to himself then leaned back in his chair and regarded me. He knew exactly who helped Nick come to his senses. And he knew I was right about med school, which meant it was possible I was right about other things, too. "Angel, you're a little bitty thing, but you're full of fire and managed to throw me around like a feather."

"A really big heavy feather," I said with a laugh.

One side of his mouth twitched up. "Thing is, you and your people would be one hell of an asset."

My humor vanished like a pricked soap bubble. "I don't want to be anyone's *asset*," I said sharply. "That's the whole reason my kind are being experimented on, so that other people can use us."

Bear lifted his hands in surrender. "Today seems to be my day for saying the wrong thing." At a rude noise from Nick, his mouth twisted. "Okay, *decade*. Let me try again." He took a deep breath. "Angel, you'd make one hell of an ally."

"I have my moments," I said, eyeing him with caution. "Is that an observation or an offer?"

"Offer."

Huh. Ally, until the Tribe yanked up its roots and relocated. Sweet zombie Jesus, Pierce was going to shit himself when he found out how many people knew about us. To hell with the flash drives. All the enemy needed was an Angel Crawford to scatter chaos and secrets like beads from a Mardi Gras float.

"Allies could be cool," I went on, "but I need to think about it and consult with the others."

"Fair enough. How about a truce for now."

"Truce works." For now. Though I didn't fully trust him when it came to his son, I had faith that he wouldn't stab me in the back. "On that note, do you have a gadget or gizmo that can find a GPS tracker on a car?"

"Yes, I can scan for trackers." His brows drew down. "Your car?"

"Yeah. Pretty sure that's how Rosario found me." Judd, too, I suspected, but they didn't need to know about any of that.

"Bring your car into the alley. I'll meet you out there."

Fifteen minutes later, I stared at the *four* GPS trackers lined up on the hood of my car. Ranging from small and sleek to big and clunky, they'd been hidden in various locations throughout my car, tattling its location to whoever monitored the signals.

"You're a popular girl," Bear said, jaw tight.

"I'm the goddamn homecoming queen," I grumbled. How could so many people care this much about where I went? Rosario was one of them, for sure. Judd was probably a second. But I only had wild guesses about who might have placed the other two trackers. The Tribe tracked me, but that was an internal modification to my car that I'd agreed to. Special Agent Aberdeen? Yet another Saberton operative?

Bear scooped up all four trackers and stalked back inside with me right behind and Nick trailing. He dumped the trackers onto a table, then sat behind the desk, expression grim and thoughtful. Nick fidgeted near the door, but I flopped into a chair in front of the desk.

"You knew about zombies *before* Judd gave you those videos," I said, eying Bear. "And I'm betting your source was Rosario."

He muttered a curse. "I'd met him a time or two in the past few years during disaster relief efforts. Always struck me as a straight arrow." He leaned forward and steepled his fingers on the desk, grimaced. "Few weeks ago he comes into the shop, we end up grabbing a beer together. He starts talking about being prepared for the zombie apocalypse—

but not crazy. More like how the concept can be used as a model for disaster preparedness."

"Even the Center for Disease Control has a page about how to survive the zombie apocalypse," Nick offered. "It started out as a joke but ended up being an entertaining way to encourage preparedness for all kinds of hazards."

"Exactly," Bear said. "Rosario never once tried to convince me zombies were real, though he liked to go on about how zombies were all people—humans—before they were changed." His eyebrows pulled down. "I can't explain it, but it was as if he didn't feel he needed to convince me because he *knew*. Like, I don't feel a need to convince you this desk is real." He tapped it for emphasis.

I gave him a doubtful look. "And that didn't make you think he was crazy?"

He spread his hands. "I've been around enough of the whackjobs that I can spot them a mile away, but I never got the tingle with Rosario."

"Because he *isn't* crazy," Nick put in.

Bear gave Nick a slow nod. "Right. That's it exactly." His gaze lingered on his son's bruised eye for a few seconds, then he took a deep breath and continued. "Anyway, a week or so ago Rosario started getting more specific, sharing links to articles that focused on unusual deaths that happened in patterns all around the country. A series of freak accidents in Colorado where heads were smashed. A firepit in the New Mexico desert containing the burned bodies of a dozen homeless people—all with holes in their skulls. And even the serial murders we had here where the victims' heads went missing." He exhaled. "By that time I was pretty sure Rosario knew way more than he was letting on, and started paying closer attention. When he made a 'hypothetical' comment on Friday about how it'd be tough to kill a zombie, but tranquilizing them would likely work a lot better, I figured it couldn't hurt to stick a tranq gun in my kit."

"That's . . . interesting," I said then fell silent to mull over his words. Bear had a wide reach on a bunch of social networks—blogs, videos, podcasts, and who knew what else. Rosario must have realized that Bear would be a seriously valuable resource, a fast and effective way to spread info or rumors or outright lies. But what was the deal with Rosario's "*zombies are people too*" feel-good bullshit? A smoke-screen? It had to be. He'd supplied the horrific videos for the *Zombies Are Among Us!!* film, which was proof enough that part of his goal was to stir up suspicion and fear about zombies.

"The serial killer wasn't a zombie," I finally said, "but his victims were." In my peripheral vision I saw Nick straighten in surprise. "Also," I continued, "you should probably know that animal tranqs don't do shit to zombies. You have to use specially formulated tranqs, which are so powerful they can kill a human in seconds." *And Rosario killed Judd with a zombie tranq to keep him from killing me.* Didn't want Judd to damage the merchandise.

"Good to know," Bear said, but then his mouth twisted into a scowl. "That son of a bitch was going to use me and my people."

"Yeah, that's my guess," I said. "For what it's worth, I don't think he's calling the shots." I gave Bear and Nick a quick and dirty briefing on Dr. Kristi Charish and the oh-so-warm and fuzzy feelings she held for me. When I finished, Bear's expression was grave, and Nick had a haunted look as if he was in a waking nightmare.

Bear opened the laptop and regarded me, long and hard. "You're right. You can't sit back and wait for them to make another play for you."

"Exactly. Can you find out if Rosario is at the Fest today? I'm pretty sure I winged him last night, but dunno how badly."

"I'm checking now," Bear said. "I know he's scheduled for demos at ten and noon." A few clicks later, he turned the laptop to show me the Zombie Fest website and inset live feeds. "FesterCam three shows him on stage now."

The pistol and rifle-shaped hands of the wall clock read ten-twenty. Damn. Not enough time to go home and de-stinkify before the noon show. "I need to buy a change of clothes from you and do a quick cleanup in the bathroom sink."

"Or you could take a shower." Bear hooked his thumb toward a half-open door off the office. "Comes in handy after being out in the field. What are you planning?"

I pushed to my feet. "There's no sense in me waiting for Rosario to make a move. I'm going to get the upper hand and deal with that sonofabitch on *my* terms."

"All on your lonesome?" His mouth pursed in doubt. "That didn't work out so well last night."

"Yeah, well, my people are tied up with the Saberton and Kristi Charish crap," I said. "I don't have much choice."

"But I do." Nick spoke for the first time in ages. "You aren't planning on *killing* him, right?"

"Not unless he tries to kill me first." I grimaced. "That didn't come out right. I mean, all I need to do is catch him, then my people can, um . . ."

Bear picked up for me. "Take care of matters in whatever way is needed."

"Kidnapping," Nick said. He moved to stand by his dad.

I rubbed my forehead. Kidnapping could damn well turn to something uglier. I had a feeling Bear got it, but Nick—

"Look, the less y'all know, the better. I don't want either of you in trouble over my shit."

Nick bristled. "We already did the less-you-know thing, remember? For chrissake, I took in your dad when you were off doing god-knows-what a few months back. You're telling me there was no risk in doing that?" He slammed his hand on the desk before I could respond. "You can't pull this off alone, and I can damn well decide for myself if I want to help."

Shit. A big part of me wanted to walk out and leave him pissed but safe. Yet I knew exactly how infuriating it was to have someone else decide what was best for me without my input. Nick didn't deserve that. "Fine. But let me lay it all out for you before you jump in with both feet."

Serious and sober, Nick doodled patterns on a notepad as he listened to me spell out what kidnapping meant in this case and the possible complications. Not once did he look me in the face. When I finished, he gave a single nod. "All right. I'm going to see you through this."

"I'm in," Bear said. "That prick was going to use me." He pulled a flash drive out of a drawer and set it on the desk in front of me. "And don't worry, I'll wipe the videos off my hard drive."

"Thanks," I said and stuffed the flash drive into my pocket. Bear could have the videos backed up half a dozen ways and I'd never know it. All I could do was trust him. I also had a feeling he was "in" as much to keep an eye on Nick as to protect his own interests, but I wasn't about to argue. I flicked a piece of gunk off my shirt. "Guess it's time for me to shop and shower."

Bear stood. "I'll help you find what you need. That'll save time."

"No," Nick said with a lift of his chin and challenge in his eyes. "*I'll* help her in the store, while you run down the street to BigShopMart and buy her new underwear since that's the one thing you don't carry here."

Bear's ears turned bright pink. "Oh, well, um, you see—"

"Going commando would be an awfully big distraction," I said with a painfully straight face and a shrug of agreement for Nick's position. "And Nick probably has a better idea of my sizes for the stuff here."

Bear exhaled in defeat. "Guess I deserved that," he muttered. "Fine. I'll go buy undies. And once I'm back and you're cleaned up, we'll make a plan and get equipped."

"Sounds good. Oh, and I like the boy brief style with the lace on the bottom."

"Don't push it, Angel."

"It's what I do best, Bear."

"God help us all."

Chapter 32

Bear had all sorts of gizmos, including high-power binoculars strong enough for me to see every pore in Rosario's face from my hiding place behind the Bear's Den booth. I watched as Rosario paced the length of the amphitheater stage with Marla at his side. No limp, no clutching at his side, no lines of agony in his face. Nothing but a barely noticeable hitch in his step. Damn. So much for winging him.

Sighing, I handed the binoculars to Nick. "The only way that gunshot wound will slow him down is if the Band-Aid falls off and he trips over it."

"Best to proceed as if he's at a hundred percent anyway," Nick said. He checked his watch and turned to Bear. "His show ends in five minutes. You ready?"

"I can read a goddamn watch," Bear snapped. "I'm ready. But I'm still not convinced he'll bite on the I-have-something-cool-to-show-you story." He frowned. "I could say there's a kid in a wheelchair who wants to meet him."

"Dear god, no," I said as Nick groaned. "First off, Rosario would bring Marla along, because a kid in a wheelchair would want to see the dog. Second off, I'm already going to hell, and I'd rather not grease the slide."

"Fine," Bear said. "Luck better be on my side."

"Luck? You're so full of shit, we're counting on you bull-shitting him into submission with your bearshit."

A fit of coughing seized Nick. Bear grinned and slapped me on the shoulder. "Oh, I am, and I will!"

Bear left the booth, and Nick and I slipped on my fancy zombie Mardi Gras masks and headed to the VIP tent, sticking to the least crowded walkways and ducking behind booths when possible. Our plan was simple, which I hoped would reduce the chances for things to go wrong. Bear would find Rosario as soon as his show ended, talk him up and feed him a hopefully convincing lie. Rosario's routine after a demo was to crate Marla in his vehicle with the windows open to help her wind down. With Marla out of the picture, Bear would then lead him to the VIP tent where Nick and I would be waiting to spring the trap. Bear would stay outside to be our lookout and backup, then signal us once the parade of four-wheeler all-terrain vehicles had passed and the road was clear enough for us to drive on out.

There were only two possible hitches in our plan, that we knew of. The first was Marla and what to do if Rosario didn't crate her. But after much thought and discussion we agreed to abort the plan in that event. Standard animal tranqs took way too long to take effect, and we had no other way to neutralize Marla that didn't risk injuring or killing her. Most importantly, we didn't want to deal with eighty pounds of pissed German Shepherd.

The second possible hitch was that we had a very specific window of opportunity to grab Rosario. Unfortunately, that was also when the parade started: Fifty or so four-wheeler ATVs, all decorated up to be redneck zombie Mardi Gras floats, blocking the road leading out of the Fest. It sucked, but we were going to have to capture Rosario then sit on him and wait. Patience wasn't one of my better traits, but for this I'd do my best.

A cluster of ATVs rumbled by, complete with plastic beads, brains, and body parts. After they passed, Nick and I continued to the VIP tent and slipped around to where my car was parked at the very back, thanks to a Bear's Den vehicle pass. I glanced at my watch. Almost go-time. I pulled my mask off and turned to Nick.

"Don't say it," he said before I even opened my mouth. "It's settled. I'm staying." He hadn't smiled or met my eyes for longer than a second since that video, and the frowning zombie mask perfectly matched the edge of steel in his voice.

"Okay," I said instead of the really awesome and compelling argument I'd prepped during the trek over. "Thanks."

He gave me a stiff nod then slipped into the tent. I exhaled and followed him.

The fake moon was gone, and ordinary bulbs revealed stacks of chairs and tables, and white tablecloths heaped in a laundry bin. The graveyard had been broken down, and fence pieces, headstones, and other décor lay in neat piles not far from the main entrance. Bear had assured me that no one would be around until the following morning when everything, including the tent, would get carted off. I crossed my fingers that he was right. This was the only spot at the Fest with any degree of privacy.

Neither of us spoke. I took up a position by a pile of fake headstones, while Nick peered through a crack in the tent wall near the entrance, mask pushed up onto his forehead. He was being a stubborn shit about helping me, but he'd agreed to keep the mask on once things got rolling since neither of us wanted him identified. He checked his gun once then slipped it into the holster on his belt and tugged his jacket over it. *That* was the weirdest part so far—watching Nick handle a gun with the ease of breathing, even though it was perfectly logical considering he had Bear as a dad.

Minutes ticked by. The show was over, but it would take time for Rosario to get Marla off the stage and into her crate. More time passed. In the distance, ATVs roared, and music blared. Nick remained silent and still, but I fought the urge to pace. Maybe people wanted Rosario's autograph or photo. Or the parade slowed them down. Or, more likely, Bear was taking his time and playing it cool since Rosario would get suspicious if Bear seemed in a hurry.

Around the fiftieth time I checked my watch, Nick pointed toward the entrance flap, pulled the mask over his face, and crouched behind a stack of bins. He drew his weapon, but I left my Bear-loaned gun in its holster at the small of my back. Our plan hinged on Rosario's desire to kidnap me. He'd likely cut and run if he saw me armed, and even though Bear would be right there to stop him, we didn't need the risk of a tussle.

My pulse quickened as my enhanced hearing picked up approaching footsteps.

Rosario pushed the tent flap aside and stepped in, eyes narrowing at the sight of me. I faked a startle and stumbled back a few steps, while I silently urged him to continue forward. I had faith that Bear would hear if things went to shit and come back us up, but none of us wanted it to come to that.

"What the hell are you doing here?" I demanded, trying to sound just the right amount of panicked. A few more feet and Nick would have the drop on him.

Rosario swept a quick look around the tent then, apparently satisfied we were alone, pulled the Taser from his jacket and advanced on me. "Looks like I'm taking you in—"

"Drop the weapon *now*," Nick ordered as he stepped from behind the bins. Rosario pivoted, but went still at the sight of the gun in Nick's hands. Nick wasn't a big guy, but Rosario obviously had enough experience to see beyond size and note the calm expertise and the rock-steady aim.

Jaw tight, Rosario placed the Taser on the ground. I drew my gun and held it on him as Nick retrieved the Taser and did a quick patdown, then pulled a set of handcuffs from his jacket and secured Rosario's hands behind him.

"He's clear," Nick said tersely then retreated to cover Rosario from a safe distance.

"Don't bother trying to run," I said. "You wouldn't make it two steps. But I'll be nice as long as you cooperate."

"I don't intend to run," Rosario said, drawing himself up. "All I care about is the safety of everyone at this festival." He spoke with calm authority. "Angel, you need to unlock the cuffs and come with me for your own good."

I made a show of cleaning my ear out with a pinky. "Say what?"

"You're destabilizing. Kristi—" He caught himself. "Dr. Charish has evidence that you're suffering long-term effects from Saberton experiments." He lifted his chin toward me. "The grey. The rot. It's obviously progressing. If you destabilize completely you could kill dozens before you're stopped."

Nick darted his gaze my way, but his gun didn't waver.

"Holy shit," I breathed. "You actually *believe* that manipulative psychopath?"

"She's not a psychopath," Rosario replied with heat, then visibly controlled himself. "She only wants to help you."

I let out a bark of laughter. "She only wants to cut me into little pieces!"

"What? No!" He shook his head. "She would never do that."

"Only because I won't let her get close enough." I cocked my head. It sure as hell looked as if the dude was in love with her. I had no doubt whatsoever that Kristi had played him like a cheap fiddle and was still doing so. "After you helped her escape the Dallas lab, she gave you those videos—the ones you then passed on to Grayson Seeger. But what I can't figure out is *why*."

He stiffened. "Dr. Charish and I intend to shine a spotlight on Saberton's cruelty to zombies. The videos were meant to increase public sympathy for zombies—for you—before it hits the news."

"Generate sympathy with that awful *Zombie Are Among Us!!* mockumentary?" I asked, incredulous.

"It wasn't supposed to be like that!" Rosario insisted. "It

was supposed to be an exposé, disguised as entertainment, of cruelty to zombies. An icebreaker to get people thinking about zombies in a different light—before we unmask Saberton. Grayson Seeger and I had a deal. I gave that son of a bitch the footage and paid him to make a short film that showed zombies as victims." Impotent fury washed over his face. "But the studio decided to go bigger, hit harder, and changed it to that hate-promoting garbage. Seeger didn't see fit to inform me."

"And Seeger was a paranoid mess the night of the premiere because he thought you'd take it out of his hide."

Rosario's expression darkened. "He was a cokehead who thought everyone was out to get him. Though if I'd seen the film Friday, his paranoia might have been justified for once." He exhaled. "Enough. Angel, we're running out of time. Unlock the handcuffs. You need to come with me."

I lifted my hand in a *hold on* gesture. The roar of ATVs had been a steady background noise for the last few minutes, but my extra-sharp hearing picked up what sounded like a half-dozen four-wheelers as they peeled away from the parade route and headed through the maze of booths and tents in our direction. I held my breath as the throaty engine noise grew closer and loud enough to rattle the tent wall. The roar abruptly died, only to be replaced by laughter and boisterous conversation. Wonderful. A bunch of rednecks decided to park not fifty feet from the tent entrance. *C'mon, Bear. Run these assholes off.*

Rosario was listening as well. I twitched my gun up. "Don't do it," I warned him, voice low. "If we get discovered, your dirt—industrial espionage, attempted kidnapping of yours truly, and let's not forget the murder of Judd Siler—sees the light of day right along with mine."

His jaw worked, but he gave a tight nod. He knew I was right. To my relief, the voices moved off a few seconds later. *That's a good Bear.* Looked like we still had a bit of a wait before us. Then again, it gave me time to poke a few holes in Rosario's dream-girl vision of Kristi Charish.

I tapped my finger against my chin as I regarded Rosario. "If your dearest love Kristi is so pristine and kind, why didn't she give you the rest of those videos?"

"What are you talking about?" He gave a derisive snort, as if I was grasping at straws. "She selected clips. So what."

I lowered my gun. He wasn't going anywhere. "Why not let you help choose what to pass to Seeger? Did you even stop to wonder why she included clips that portrayed us as monsters when your goal was supposedly the opposite?"

"It was to show the cruelty," he said, but the first hint of doubt shimmered over his face. "It's what was available. She was in a rush. She—"

"But not so much of a rush that she couldn't edit the clips." I lowered my head. "Kristi left out some great stuff, like in the video where I'm mauling the big blond guy. You missed the bit right before it where McKinney shot him twice in the chest then gave me a choice: let him die or try to turn him into a zombie." In my periphery I saw Nick waver. "Or how about the video where I smashed McKinney's head and ate his brain. A minute or so before that, he shot me four times." I held back a smile as tension hummed through Rosario. "You really should watch that one again. Not only can you see the bullet holes in my shirt, but if you look *real* close you can see Kristi Charish behind that glass right before she runs the hell away."

"You're lying," he gritted out.

"You're in denial," I shot back. "She's brilliant, so why would Saberton have her locked down unless they wanted to keep her psychopathic ass under control?"

Rosario summoned a haughty sneer. "She wouldn't willingly participate in their vicious agenda."

"Yet somehow she did all the cruel and nasty shit they wanted. Even came up with new ones of her own. Isn't that weird?"

"They brainwashed her," he said, but his voice wasn't as steady. "That's why I . . . she needed to get away from that place. To recover—"

"How long did it take for her to recover?" I pressed. "A week? Two?"

"It's not like that. She's still recovering! That's why we haven't begun to move forward on the plans to expose Saberton."

"Uh huh, yet she's okay enough to go through videos of tortured zombies and pick out juicy clips for you."

His eyes darted around as if seeking the words to convince me. *As if.* I advanced on him and went in for the kill.

"She told you I was about to go nuclear as a result of Saberton testing and that I had to be kidnapped. For my own good. Funny thing, though. It's been over a year since I was a subject in a Saberton lab. Yet suddenly *now* I'm about to go mega-monster?" I graced him with my best expression of withering scorn. "And let's not forget that she was *brainwashed* all this time and is still amazingly functional. A lesser mortal would be drooling in a padded corner."

"No, you don't understand."

"Oh, I understand perfectly," I said with a humorless laugh. "Here, let me lay it all out for you. Kristi Charish is perfectly *fine*. Better than fine. In fact, she's at the top of her game, especially when it comes to manipulating people to get what she wants." I softened my voice. "Dante, she's playing you for a fool. There's no way in hell she'd publicly expose Saberton, because that would also trot out all of her own dirty little secrets."

He licked his lips, eyes pleading with me. "No, you're wrong. She's not fine. She's fragile. That's why we . . . why she needs me to take care of her."

"Fragile." I gave him a long look. I almost—*almost* felt sorry for the chump. "I guess that word has a different meaning in your neck of the woods. I can't imagine how a person who's been made *fragile* through deliberate brainwashing could mastermind the kind of wheeling and dealing she's been doing with Saberton and my people for the past few days."

Rosario stared at me, mouth working as he groped for a

reply, a comeback. Anything. My last statement had been the one brushstroke that changed the picture—kind of like adding a Hitler mustache—and now he struggled to understand this new image. I had a suspicion there were little details about Kristi that he'd dismissed or excused since they didn't fit into his "poor fragile Kristi" picture. With a little dose of reality feedback, he was starting to realize that those same details fit into this new picture like the smile on that Mona Lisa chick.

The tent flap flew open. *Finally*, I thought with relief. But instead of the bulk of Bear, a petite form burst in.

"Angel!" Justine Chu screeched in delight, a Hurricane drink glass in one hand and a phone in the other. A canary yellow feather boa was draped around her neck along with a dozen pairs of Mardi Gras beads. A tight silver dress barely covered her various naughty bits.

I quickly holstered my gun—without shooting myself in the ass like I had in New York. Nick yanked his gun out of sight while Rosario shifted so that Justine couldn't see the handcuffs. None of us wanted witnesses to this bullshit.

"Hey, Justine!" I said, doing my darndest to sound really thrilled to see her even though worry churned in my gut. Where the fuck was Bear?

Justine tottered forward in high-heeled purple boots, grinning widely and happily oblivious to anything out of the ordinary. "I've been looking all over for you, and here you are!" She flung her arms wide, dousing Nick with rum and fruit juice.

"Why were you looking for me?" I asked. Shit. Did that sound paranoid? Yeah, that totally sounded paranoid.

Fortunately, Justine didn't notice. "Well. About an hour ago I saw a petite little masked blondie and thought maybe that was you 'cause you're tiny and have blonde hair, y'know?" She swayed near Rosario and gave him an unfocused once-over. I tensed, ready to surge to her rescue if he tried anything, but she merely gave him a wink and a chuck on the chin and continued my way. "Then the blonde babe turned and went the other way, and I was like, Oh my god, I know that cute little butt! And now I'm here and you're here, and I have to tell you"—she took a deep breath—"this Mardi Gras shit is *awful!*"

"Huh?" I'd been trying to split my attention between her and Rosario, which obviously wasn't working. "Wait. Why?"

She looked at me very seriously, if not soberly. "Because . . . I am really fucking *drunk.*"

"No. Way."

Justine let out a peal of laughter. "I know, right?"

"Welcome to Louisiana," I said with a cheery grin even as I tried to keep tabs on everything else. Nick had one eye on Rosario and the other on his phone as he sent a text. Trying to get hold of Bear, I was certain, and the tension in his stance told me there'd been no reply.

Rosario. My gut dropped. He was watching Justine with a friendly, approachable smile. His stance was calm and comfortable, as if standing with his hands behind his back was natural and certainly not at all because they were hand-cuffed. He didn't give off the cold-blooded killer vibe, but I *knew* he'd done something to Bear. I needed to wring the truth out of him, but first I had to get Justine out of here.

I took her arm to steer her toward the entrance, but she planted her purple-booted feet and swung a fierce look at the two men.

"This woman *saved me* from Val Kilmer!" she announced. "And because of that she never got a picture with me!"

"Yeah, a picture sounds great," I said. "Maybe outside—"

"Don't be silly!" For a drunk chick, she sure moved fast. Before I could react, she flung an arm around my shoulders, yanked me close, and held up her cell phone. "Selfie time!"

The camera clicked. Rosario tossed the handcuffs to the ground and bolted for the door.

"Fuck!" He'd taken advantage of the Justine distraction to either pick the locks or use a hidden handcuff key. "Justine, I need to fetch my phone from my car so I can get my own picture! Be right back!" I tore out of Justine's grasp and charged after Rosario, hoping to hell it would take her a minute to realize she could simply text me the selfie pic. Or better yet, forget the whole incident in her current inebriated state.

Outside, Rosario pelted along the side of the tent to the parked ATVs and began a frantic search for any with keys left in them. I tried to pour on the speed, but I was operating at pathetic and normal Angel-levels.

Rosario let out a cry of triumph and climbed onto an ATV decorated with reaching zombie arms made of chicken wire, duct tape, and painted papier-mâché.

"You know I won't stop 'til I catch you!" I shouted as he started the engine.

"If you chase after me, you won't find Bear in time," he called over his shoulder then roared off, metallic purple streamers flapping behind him.

I stumbled to a gasping stop then turned as Nick ran up, mask off and his face contorted in worry.

"What did he mean?" Nick demanded. "In time for what? Where's my dad?"

I reached toward him out of instinctive desire to give comfort, then stopped when he recoiled with instinctive need to stay away from the monster.

Swallowing my dismay, I pulled my hand back. "Bear's not dead," I told him. "Rosario's not that cold-blooded." But he was desperate—deep in a pit of lies and trying to climb out before the walls collapsed on him. Desperate enough to put Bear in a life-threatening situation. "Your dad is around here somewhere. Start looking."

"What are you going to do?"

I bared my teeth. "I'm going to chase Rosario down and find out where your dad is even if I have to rip it out of him."

For the first time since discovering the truth about me, Nick met my eyes without recoiling. "Do what you have to."

I wanted so badly to take a precious second and hug him, but I didn't. Instead I took off running. Not after Rosario, but around to the back of the tent and my car. Breathing hard, I threw myself into the driver's seat and downed three packets of brains. But brain-boosted abilities alone wouldn't be enough for this pursuit. I needed the mega-boost of a combat mod.

Warnings clamored through my head as I grabbed the syringe and vial of V12. Dosing myself on top of the grey-rot was downright stupid. But if I held back and Bear died, I'd never be able to live with myself. Not to mention, Rosario would have time to act on his misguided whistle-blowing plans before the Tribe could stop him. I'd done a whole lot of stupid in my life. For once, maybe stupid was the right thing to do.

I drew a dose into the syringe, then drew up more. And more. A full syringe—three doses. I injected myself and drew another cc then hesitated. I'd taken four doses last night and gained zombie overdrive abilities.

But Rosario had a huge head start. Right now I needed to be a motherfucking superhero.

My hands shook as I drew yet another cc into the syringe. Five doses total. I'd worry about the consequences later.

I'm it. I'm the one who can do what needs to be done.

I shoved the needle in and slammed the plunger home, and was out of the car and moving as the first drops hit my system.

Chapter 33

MegaSuperZombiePowers. Holy fucking shit. Fatigue vanished, and every sense flared into ultrafocus. I knew Bear's scent, but there were too many other people-scents around and not enough time to seek his out. Right now it was Rosario's scent that I followed as it floated in twisted, teasing ribbons along the festival paths. The monster within urged me to run the prey down on foot, but I ignored it. Unlike the times when brain-hunger clawed and howled, I was still in full control of my mental faculties, and I had a better idea.

Parked behind a churro booth was an ATV parade float. Colored lights flashed within a basketball-sized plastic brain secured in front of the handlebars, while a man with salt-and-pepper hair strapped a bloody mannequin to the rack behind the seat with bright pink duct tape.

"I need to borrow your four wheeler," I shouted as I ran up. "It's an emergency!"

"What the hell?" Straightening, he brandished the duct tape like a weapon. "You can't just . . ." He trailed off, face paling as he got a good look at me.

I plucked the duct tape from his limp fingers. "Thanks,"

I said, turned and leaped nimbly into the seat then shoved the roll of tape up to my left bicep like a warrior queen's armband. That was me, Zombie Redneck Warrior Queen.

"I'll bring it right back!" I hollered as I sped off. With any luck, he might even believe me.

Rosario's scent trail dissipated as I followed it through the Fest grounds, but I tamped down the urge to race around in a mindless search, and gunned the ATV in the direction of the zombie hunt prep area. I'd whacked Rosario's worldview with a big ol' fact-hammer, and I had a feeling he'd seek terrain where he felt at ease and in control. He'd spent countless hours in the woods with Marla for searches, so for him it would be like having a home court advantage. If I was wrong, I risked losing his trail for good, but it wasn't as if I had any clues besides my gut feeling. Still, I breathed a sigh of relief when I reached the prep area and picked up Rosario's scent.

Now the hunt was on.

His trail floated in the air and clung to the ground, as clear and palpable as tendrils of glowing red. I raced after it, lights flashing in the oversized plastic brain as if the ATV was an undead emergency vehicle. Though I wasn't anywhere near an expert at driving a four-wheeler, the megadose of V12 had cranked my reflexes up to I'm-a-God level, and that made all the difference in the world. Adjusting my weight and balance with precision, I sped onward, ignoring the underbrush that whipped at my legs. I veered around trees and soared over gulleys, handling the machine with ludicrous ease when lesser mortals would have been crushed to death a dozen times over already.

The scent trail thickened, and the taste of him washed over my tongue. Sweat and worry, grief and determination. Worried about Marla. Driven to return to Kristi.

The sound of his ATV reached me next, an unsteady noise that fluctuated between roar and rumble. Rosario's reflexes were merely human, sluggish compared to mine, and that forced him to slow through maneuvers that I took at speed.

I zoomed over a rise and caught a flash of purple streamers through the trees ahead. It didn't seem possible that he could hear my vehicle over the sound of his own engine, but maybe his hind-brain felt the predator on his heels. His head whipped around, eyes widening in shock for an instant before he returned his focus to the woods and his flight.

I accelerated to try and close the gap, but he was making me work for it. He handled the ATV with the ease of a shitload of experience which damn near balanced out the disadvantage of his puny human reflexes.

It felt as if I'd been chasing him for hours, though less than ten minutes had passed since I hit the woods. The clock was ticking down on my superpowers, a looming threat that spurred me on. I'd lost the bloody mannequin a half mile back, but the big brain continued to flash merrily. Rosario skimmed past a tree and sheared off one duct-tape–and–papier-mâché zombie arm. It bounced in my direction, and I had to flatten myself to my seat, chicken wire fingers skimming my head as it flew past.

The distance between us shrank as I pursued with single-minded determination. Nothing else mattered but stopping Rosario, not only to save Bear but also to get Rosario—and his half-baked Save the Zombies plan—safely under the Tribe's control.

The trees thinned and the ground leveled. Rosario poured on the speed, but my ATV was as powerful as his and carrying a lot less weight. Water sparkled in the distance as I gained ground on him. The Colemyke River. Not as big as the Kreeger but still at least a hundred feet across in this section and too deep to ride an ATV through. Elation surged through me. I had him trapped now.

Yet, inexplicably, he continued at full speed toward the river. My elation sputtered then shifted to outright dismay.

No, he wasn't trapped, not one stinking bit. He was going to drive straight in and then swim for it, let the current carry him far away from me. He was probably a good, strong swimmer, too. *Goddammit.* My swimming skills were adequate at best, and all the brains and V12 in the world wouldn't make me fast enough to catch him in the water.

That meant I had to catch him on land, but easier said than done. I inched closer to him, even as the river seemed to rush at us. Rosario and I were still way too far apart, even for a god-like leap from my ATV to his—assuming my V12 supercharge hadn't fizzled. In another thirty seconds we'd both be in the water. He'd win, and Bear and the Tribe and all zombies would lose.

No. We can't lose. If we lose, we die. With a scream of rage and desperation, I ripped the flashing brain from the wires and zipties then chucked it at Rosario with all my might. It sailed toward him, and my anger melted into surprised delight as I watched the beautiful trajectory. I'd been worried that I'd underestimated my enhanced strength and overthrown it, but a long grey object dangled behind the brain, weighing it down just enough.

Wait. That's my arm.

Brain and arm nailed Rosario right between the shoulder blades. He lurched forward, jerking the handlebars into an impossibly sharp turn.

That's . . . my arm.

Brain and arm fell to earth. Rosario and the ATV soared through the air, twisting in a weirdly silent ballet of disaster. I watched in detached awe and horror as Rosario slammed against a tree and crumpled to the ground. An instant later the ATV smashed down inches from him then tumbled away, finally coming to rest on the sandy riverbank.

Sound rushed in, and I snapped out of my daze. Mouth dry, I grabbed the brake with my left—and only—hand and brought the ATV to a wobbly stop. My legs felt weird and shaky as I climbed off, but I chalked that up to the long and crazy ride through the woods. And possibly also the fact that I'd lost my fucking arm, but I didn't have time to worry about that. Rosario groaned, which meant he was still alive. I had to deal with him first.

My left leg gave out when I was a dozen feet away from him, and I covered the rest of the distance in an awkward three-point crawl. I shifted to a cockeyed kneel beside him as he breathed in shallow gasps. Didn't look as if he had a head injury, but from the way he'd hit the tree I suspected his ribs were a mess.

"Where's Bear?" I shouted. Or tried to. My voice had a scraping rasp to it, but he heard me well enough.

"Reefer . . . truck." He gasped. "Blue and white . . . end of row . . . east side."

I grabbed my phone out of my pocket. "If you're lying—"

"Not." Pain tightened his bloodless face as he swallowed. "Wasn't . . . trying to kill Bear."

I'd stopped listening to him. The fingers of my remaining hand had zero dexterity. I set the phone on the ground and dragged my knuckle across the screen to get Nick's number, then gave it a clumsy tap to make the call and another to put it on speaker. As it rang, I shook the roll of duct tape off my bicep and down to my hand.

"Angel?"

"Your dad's in a refrigerator truck," I said, "east side, blue and white, at the end of the row."

"I'm not far from there!"

"Then go warm his ass up." I tried to smile but my face felt as if I'd spent hours in the dentist's chair. "Keep me on the line, okay?" Damn it. The rasp in my voice was getting worse. "Wanna make sure he's there."

"You got it," Nick said in a breathless voice that told me he was running.

Though I seriously doubted Rosario could sit up, much less run away, I'd been through too much to take any chances. With my teeth and one barely working hand, I wound bright pink duct tape around his wrists and forearms. I wanted to wrap his feet and ankles, too, but when I tried to crawl that way I fell to my side in a heap. *What the fuck is happening to me?*

"Angel! He's okay! He was right where you said!"

"Nick." Even through the deepening rasp I heard the panic in my voice. "Something's wrong. Rosario's hurt, too, but I . . . need help." My legs. My left shin and foot were a dozen feet away, back where I'd fallen and had to crawl. And my right . . .

"Shit," Nick breathed. "Do you know where you are?"

Oh god. My right leg lay crooked by Rosario's head. "River." No, that didn't help. The river curved around the property and covered miles and miles. "Marla. Get Marla. Find us. Help me." I coughed out a gobbet of something dark and nasty. "Call . . . call Dr. Ne . . . Nikas."

I heard shouting on Nick's end, and running footsteps. I tried to reach for the phone only to watch my arm pull away from my shoulder like wet paper tearing. No pain. No sensation. Nothing.

"Hur . . . hurry."

"We're getting Marla. Just hang on. Dr. Degas? I don't know who that is."

"Nee Kahs." Had he understood me? I flopped to my back and stared up at the sky, terrified that if I twitched a single muscle I'd disintegrate completely.

White fog closed in. Nick's voice came through the speaker, distant and muddled. Rosario gasped in pain.

Drifting.

Dying.

I'm dying.

No. I can't. I won't. I'm a goddamn zombie, and zombies don't die. Not this zombie.

Silence.

I can't die. My dad. Who'll take care of my dad?

Something bumped my head, and my world tilted.

"Marla . . . off." Rosario.

"Angel!" Nick. Close.

"Oh my fucking god in heaven." Bear.

Nick's face swam above me then whizzed away. Puking. Lots of puking.

"Her phone," Rosario wheezed. "Passcode . . . nine-six-two-four. Dr. Ariston Nikas."

He knew my passcode? Annoyance came and went. "Nick," I tried to say, but nothing came out. Not even a rasp.

Voices blended and dulled.

Thwup thwup thwup thwup thwup. Sound pounded through me. I dragged my thoughts together. Dr. Nikas. He'd brought the helicopter.

Nick knelt by Rosario's head, his hands on each side, stabilizing.

Bear shouted and waved at the chopper.

Dr. Nikas's voice came through the cell phone. *Yes, we see you.*

Movement and hustle. Lots of it.

Jacques and Nick shifted Rosario onto a backboard.

Dr. Nikas knelt beside me. "Angel, hold on. We're here."

This is really bad! Help me!

"We're here."

Bear scraped my rotten arms and legs into a body bag.

Rosario was gone. Only me now. What was left. Nick backed away, face lifeless as Dr. Nikas worked on me.

Nick.

Nick kept backing. Away. From me.

Nick.

Chapter 34

"Angel. Wiggle your fingers."

Silly Dr. Nikas. Far away, muffly, Dr. Nikas. Wiggly. No fingers to wiggly.

"Angel."

Warm. Weightless. Weird. Angel. That's meeee.

"Increase the voltage."

Voltage. 'Lectricity. Tingly. Stingy.

Bright.

"Her eyes are open. Any change in the readings?"

"Fluctuating."

What the hell? Where am I? I can't move. Dr. Nikas?!

"Heart rate increasing. Twenty-six. Thirty-four. Forty."

"Angel. Wiggle your fingers."

I'm trying! I can't feel my hands. Do I have hands? Can't feel anything. Brain is tingling. Everything's blurry like I'm looking through—

Slug snot. I'm in slug snot! Shit!

"Heart rate forty-four."

Jacques, Dr. Nikas, I can't move! What happened? Why am I in the coffin tank?

"Angel." A shape, a hand, wiggling in front of my eyes. "Blink."

I'm trying, I swear. Fuck. I see you. I see you.

"Holding steady at forty-four."

"Take her down again. She's not ready."

Yes, I am! I'm right here. I can hear you. I can see. Don't.

Fish tanks ran the length of my kitchen counters. The call of seagulls and the *crash-hiss* of gentle surf drifted in through the window. Nice and peaceful. I hummed as I moved from tank to tank feeding hungry fish. French fries for the blue ones. Popcorn for the big red ones. Brussel sprouts for the yellow fishies that looked like my dad. Brain chunks for Judd's head floating in a tank all by itself.

I jerked awake, breathing hard. An expanse of beach spread before me, complete with gorgeous sunset, rolling waves, and palm trees. No fish tanks. No Judd.

A dream. Just a stupid, horrible dream. My breathing settled, but confusion rose as I looked around. I was propped in a cushy bed in a windowless room. The screen for an ambiance immersion system took up the entire wall in front of me, and floor-to-ceiling bookshelves filled the others.

It had to be one of Dr. Nikas's rooms, but that made no sense. I wiggled my fingers then tried to lift my hand, but my arm was stiff, wrapped in gauze. A nameless horror crept through me. *I'm supposed to be dead.* Wasn't I? Why couldn't I remember?

I struggled to sit up without success. I heard a knock on the door, then Dr. Nikas stepped into the room. "Angel?"

I sagged in relief. "What happened? I'm . . . alive."

"Indeed you are." A genuine smile lit his face. "Don't try to move. Tomorrow, perhaps." He pulled bandages aside and injected something near my collar bone. I expected a poke or sting, but felt only a brief wave of warmth. "How do you feel?" he asked.

"Like I could sleep for a year."

His eyes crinkled. "Do you know my name?"

"Dr. Nikas? Ariston Nikas." The whisper of relief in his eyes made me suspect there'd been a time when I hadn't known it. Prickly warmth spread up my neck and down through my torso, and hazy memory woke like a fire stirred to life. "Wait. I was in Kang's tank." Dread swept through me. "Was I just a *head*? How long has it been? Did I . . . regrow?"

"The medicine I just gave you will help your memory." He sat on the edge of the bed and took my hand. "It's only Friday. Three days since Mardi Gras."

Mardi Gras. The sickening feel of my arm ripping off shuddered through my mind. "I was in *pieces*. Lots of pieces."

"We recovered your head and most of your torso. The V12 prevented normal regeneration. But you did indeed regrow." He paused. "With assistance."

"Slug snot." I nodded slowly. "I remember warm slug snot. And electricity."

"Modifications to incorporate a variation of the African salve Allen Prejean told you about. Without it, your regrowth would have taken months as opposed to mere days."

The door eased open. Marla padded in, tail wagging, and sat beside Dr. Nikas. The sight of her triggered a flood of memories. "Rosario! What happened to him? Did you get him?"

"He's locked down and sedated. Post surgery from broken ribs." He reached to scratch the dog's ears. "Marla follows me around when she isn't lying beside his bed."

And Dr. Nikas didn't mind one bit, if the mushy smile he gave Marla was any indication. A yawn snuck up on me, and I fought to keep my eyes open. "Rosario was going to whistle-blow on Saberton. Expose us right along with them."

He squeezed my hand. "You stopped him, Angel. Well done."

"Almost didn't." I grimaced. "The plan went tits up when Rosario took out Bear. What tipped him off?"

"Rosario noted your stop at the Bear's Den and the subsequent loss of your GPS tracking signal. When Bear approached him at the festival, he smelled a trap but played along. After he crated Marla, he retrieved the Taser from his vehicle and hid it in his jacket. On the way to the VIP tent, he took Bear down when they passed behind the refrigerated trucks."

"Rosario should have seized the chance to get away clean, but he came after me instead." Anger boiled through me. "Because of Kristi. That manipulative—"

Dr. Nikas cut off my building tirade. "You need sleep." He drew another syringe from his pocket. It didn't have a needle and was filled with what looked like white gravy.

"Isn't that for use with a zombie mod port?"

"You've had one on your wish list, haven't you?" He smiled as he pulled the gauze under my collarbone down again, twisted the syringe and injected the drug. "This is a sedative, but your port's primary use is for auto-dosing V13, your non-addictive, non-damaging V12 replacement."

"That's so cool." My words were already slurring. "But more questions. Nick?"

Dr. Nikas looked pained. "Answers will be clearer after you rest. Sleep, Angel."

Since I was almost there already, I did.

Chapter 35

"I can walk." I made a shooing motion at the wheelchair Jacques had pushed into the room. "I don't need that thing."

Jacques regarded me placidly and didn't budge away from the bed. Only a few minutes earlier, he'd nudged me awake to inform me that Dr. Nikas was about to attempt to wake Kang, and would I like to observe?

Hell yeah, I wanted to observe, and I was grateful to be woken up for the event, but I didn't need to be carted around like an invalid. I'd slept for two straight days, out cold since I first woke and talked to Dr. Nikas on Friday. I felt perfectly fine. More than fine. I was chipper as fuck.

I was wrapped in gauze from ankle to wrist—though not as heavily as the day before—with a bright pink hospital gown over it all. After I grabbed my phone off the nightstand, I set my feet on the floor and carefully straightened. There, that wasn't so bad. Legs were holding me up nicely. Emboldened, I took a careful step. And another. "See, I can walk just *whoa*." My legs folded, and my butt dropped into the wheelchair that Jacques shoved smoothly under me. In fact, his timing was so perfect it was as if he'd been expecting me to need it.

"Thanks," I mumbled and gathered the shreds of my dignity around me. "But I can wheel myself there." I set the phone in my lap, slapped my hands onto the wheel grip things and gave a mighty shove. And another. And one more.

"Okay," I panted after the exertions of moving a whole foot and a half. "I can be a lazy slug."

Jacques smiled and said nothing as he wheeled me to the Head Room.

Kang was back in his tank, floating like a mummy-fish. Jacques parked me out of the way by the far counter, then set to work with Dr. Nikas in a flurry of measurement-taking and probe-connecting. While I waited, I checked my phone for messages. Two voicemails from an out-of-state area code waited for me. Probably a telemarketer. One from Allen as well. But nothing from Nick. My heart sank, leaving behind a giant aching hole. I blinked furiously to keep back tears. What the hell did I expect after rotting to pieces in front of him?

"Oh dear, I nearly forgot." Dr. Nikas lifted a plain white envelope from the counter then crossed the room and held it out for me. "My deepest apologies, Angel. I should have given you this as soon as you came in." At my perplexed look he smiled and added, "It's from your father."

My heart lifted a few inches off the floor as I took it. "It's cool. Thanks." As he returned to his equipment, I tore the envelope open, spirits rising at the sight of my dad's cramped handwriting.

Angelkins you know i love you. You keep doing good like you been doing you hear me?

The tears spilled over, and I didn't try to stop them.

You got you some good people taking care of you here at this place. Ari says your a champ. He's right but i don't need nobody to tell me that. Your my Angelkins.

A lovely warm glow of happiness spread from the center of my chest to the tips of my freshly regrown toes. Dr. Nikas made my dad feel comfortable enough to call him Ari, which meant that my dad made Dr. Nikas feel comfortable enough to invite him to use that name in the first place. Two of my favorite men in the entire world got along. Total happiness.

I been to see you ever day since you got there. Marcus been by too but he looked too tired and sad-like for me to pick a fight with him. Ari says you might wake up tomorrow so thought to leave you this letter in case you get up before i get here. I was fucked up hard with seeing you in that tank and all. Thought they was drowning you. Ari and that french guy finally got it through my thick skull that it was the only way to make you you again. Turns out they was right. I sat by you today and watched you sleep. Sang you those songs you love to hate. I like to think you heard a little bit and it made you smile inside.

"Angel?" Dr. Nikas said in a voice filled with concern. "Is everything all right?"

His worry was justified, considering I was flat out bawling. "Yeah. My dad," I gulped out through sniffles. "He wrote that he sang to me yesterday."

"He did indeed." Dr. Nikas smiled broadly as he tweaked settings. "Loud and long."

"Oh dear god," I said, mortified yet at the same time ridiculously tickled that he'd sung for me and didn't give a shit who heard. "Let me guess: *Pinball Wizard, Paradise by the Dashboard Light,* and *Shut Up and Kiss Me*?"

Humor danced in his eyes. "Those are the ones. His voice is actually quite good. You remember him singing them to you?"

"Only from about a billion times at home." I let out a laugh. "He was probably hoping to annoy me enough that I'd wake up and yell at him to stop."

Dr. Nikas chuckled, and I dove into the last of the letter.

Tomorrow i got to go into Tucker Point for a while then i'll swing by to see you in the afternoon. Wanted to tell you Nick checked in with me to make sure you was doing okay. Way he's feeling right now i don't know if he'll be calling you direct but you need to know he's thinking about you no matter what it seems he'll come around. I love you Angelkins. Dad

My heart squeezed firmly back into place. Smiling, I swiped happy tears away then lifted my phone and took a picture of the letter. I didn't give a rat's ass if it seemed weird. I wanted to be able to look back at that letter anytime I needed a reminder of how fucking lucky I was.

I carefully replaced the letter in the envelope then listened to the voicemail from Allen.

"Angel. Just wanted to let you know that your, um, primary care physician, Dr. Nikas, contacted me about that, er, procedure you're having done, and your sick leave is approved. Hope to see you back on your feet soon."

Yeah, that was one hell of a procedure I'd had done. I looked down at my brand-new body and let out a tragic sigh. Too bad the Angel 2.0 version didn't come with actual boobs.

Since Jacques and Dr. Nikas were still prepping stuff, I went ahead and checked the voicemails from the out-of-state area code.

"Angel, it's Justine Chu."

Okay, that was unexpected.

"I hope you won't be mad or creeped out that I dug up your cell phone number, but I really wanted to call and apologize for my behavior on Mardi Gras. I am SO sorry for behaving like such an ass. I hardly ever drink and so my tolerance is shit, and I know that's still no excuse but I got too caught up in the whole party atmosphere and was having so much fun and then when I saw you, I was just like hey, that girl is really cool and grounded and I need people like her in my life, y'know? Oh Jesus, I'm babbling. Ugh! Okay, anyway, I'm so very sorry I barged into your private meeting, and I hope I didn't say anything stupid and I don't blame you one bit for running after the guy when he got sick of waiting for me to leave." She took a deep breath. *"So . . . I just hope you don't hate me, and I hope your meeting worked out okay and that you're doing okay too."*

Amused—and relieved that she didn't interpret any of the scene in the VIP tent as suspicious—I went on to listen to her next message.

"Justine again, doubling down on the stalker thing. Forgot to say that this is my cell number and you're totally welcome to call or text. I mean, if you want. Shit, I'm going to start babbling again. All right, take care, and sorry again."

Damn, I really liked her. The mega awesome rising star Justine Chu had normal, everyday insecurities like the rest of us. *And* wanted to keep in touch. How cool was that? It called for a little in-the-wheelchair dance, but I stopped when even that wore me out.

Sheesh.

I set the letter and my phone on the counter, only now noticing a softly burbling aquarium covered with black cloth. Curious, I lifted a corner of the cloth then recoiled as I came eyeball to dead eyeball with Judd. Heart pounding, I snatched my hand back and shoved away in my wheelchair. "You can't regrow Judd!"

Jacques glanced over then returned to typing at the workstation.

"We're not," Dr. Nikas said calmly as he wrote in his shorthand on the whiteboard. "I'm merely preserving him until I have time to determine *how* he mindlessly reanimated, and with such speed. It is disturbing, and the matter is on my urgent task list."

Everything about Judd and his creepy head was disturbing. I wheeled a bit farther away from the tank. "Well, I know you'll figure it out," I said with conviction. "You always do. Look at the miracles you pulled off with me and Kang."

Dr. Nikas placed the marker in the tray and turned to face me, expression uncharacteristically bleak. "Angel, your quick recovery was possible because I contacted Allen Prejean, and he in turn arranged direct contact with his *goulegris* connection in Africa. If not for their help, at best you would be in stasis like the people who haven't regrown." He gestured toward the head vats. "Or, more likely, irrevocably dead due to the V12 overdose."

I shook my head. He had no idea how awesome he was. "But *you're* the one who put the pieces together and made it work. You always find the answers, and you will with the Judd mess, too." I gave him an encouraging smile. "And don't forget all the progress you've made on fake brains! You're so close on that one. I bet it won't take you more than—"

"Angel." The force behind the word silenced me. "I am only one man. An enhanced man but limited nonetheless." His voice carried an edge of desperation I'd never heard in him before. "I made more progress in the few months of brainstorming with Kristi than in the three years prior. Together we produced far greater results than either of us could have managed on our own even with all the time in the world. I have only one mind to engage a staggering list of urgent needs. I am doing all I can, but I fear it may be too little, too late."

"But your one mind really kicks ass."

"Not nearly well enough on its own for the challenges we face. Kristi Charish is brilliant, undeniably so." He held up a hand before I could blurt out my own undeniable opinion of her. "I'm not discounting my own ability, but brilliance manifests in different ways, both in cognition and processing. Areas of weakness for me are strengths for her. Through necessity as a solitary researcher, I have a broad base of knowledge and experience founded on the considerable time I've had for study and experimentation. This base is a great advantage, yet information is quickly outdated and new discoveries are made daily, and I am therefore forever two steps behind in my specialties and ten steps behind in other areas. Kristi is focused in her fields of expertise, and we complemented each other well. Two or more minds working in harmony can see possibilities and make connections and draw conclusions that a single mere mortal"—a whisper of a sad smile touched his mouth as he gestured to himself—"or not-quite-mortal, cannot hope to match."

My stomach ached. "Maybe the Tribe will find a way to convince her to come work with you instead of taking a deal with Saberton." I couldn't stand the bitch, but I'd do my best to tolerate her if she could help Dr. Nikas.

Dr. Nikas resumed writing on the whiteboard but with hard strokes that squished the tip of the marker. "Tuesday afternoon she confirmed a deal with Nicole Saber and, escorted by Saberton, left the apartment Rosario had provided. Pierce and the others had no means to intervene. We lost her."

Now I understood why he looked so bleak. "Saberton will set her up in a lab." I rubbed a hand over my mouth. "She'll be back in the game, bigger and badder than ever. That really *sucks*."

"With a small army of staff along with the knowledge she gained while here in this lab." Dr. Nikas sighed. "Not to mention, she'll have access to cutting-edge equipment that we could never hope to acquire. Even if funds were available, the purchases would instantly draw attention to us."

"If we end up having to move the lab for the exodus, that will—"

"There won't be an exodus this time," Pierce said from the doorway.

Jacques froze, slack-jawed. Dr. Nikas simply looked resigned as if it wasn't news to him. Pierce stepped into the room, face tired and drawn but eyes intense.

No exodus? Can't they think of a place where no human will find us?

Comprehension struck me like a hammer between the eyes. "Because it's impossible!" I exclaimed before Pierce could speak. I gave myself a little forehead smack. "Duh. Dunno why I didn't realize it sooner. The last time y'all had an exodus there was no Internet or streaming video or digital records or security cameras everywhere."

"Yes," Pierce said, so stiffly I thought his jaw would

crack. Heh. Guess I just totally stole his thunder. "We've examined the logistics," he continued. "There's no way to successfully disappear *en masse*."

"What then?" I asked, frowning. "Every zombie for himself? Every zombie either goes rogue or fights it out for the available morgue and funeral home jobs?"

"I don't have an answer yet," Pierce said with an edge of annoyance. "However, you bought us time by capturing Dante Rosario and forestalling immediate large-scale exposure."

"What's going to happen to him?"

"To no one's surprise but his, Kristi Charish threw him to the Saberton wolves. She told them the truth—that he intended to expose Saberton—and twisted everything else to make her look like a corporate saint. Nicole Saber knows better than to believe the bullshit, but she recognizes the truth about Rosario and will target him for capture. He's a liability to her as well as to us."

"Man, that's fucked up." I did a slow head shake. "Psychopath Kristi is an asset to everyone. Gets to write her own ticket. But the dude who thought it was wrong to use zombies as lab rats and tried to *do* something about it ended up being between a rock and a hard place as nothing but a 'liability?'"

"Exposing Saberton in the manner he intended would have ruined us."

I bit back an annoyed *No shit, Sherlock*, and instead said, "Yes, his methods sucked, and he was twisted up by Kristi, but his heart was in the right place. I bet he could be a valuable ally given the right handling."

"Angel, every human who knows our secret increases our risk of exposure," Pierce said, as if addressing a child. "Even those with good intentions. Rosario is a perfect example."

"Pierce, that kind of thinking is obsolete." I wasn't *trying* to mimic his patronizing tone. "Zombies have survived by hiding for, what, centuries? But the world is different now."

"And I will adapt our methods to the changing world."

I tossed up my hands in frustration. "You're stuck in a rut! You still think that hiding is the only option."

Pierce snorted. "What's your alternative? Send out a press release that zombies are people, too?"

"Hey, why not? News flash, Pierce. We *are* people, too." I leaned toward him. "Saberton's success depends on us *wanting* to stay hidden. They can do whatever the hell they want because no one knows about us."

His mouth thinned. "The general populace won't be—"

"It doesn't *matter*," I said. "We live in a world full of instant updates and video and selfies and twenty-four-hour news. Exposure is *inevitable*. So why in god's name aren't we planning for it instead of scrambling for the few available hiding places like a bunch of roaches? More to the point, why are we waiting to be outed—in what's sure to be a negative light—rather than spinning it in a way that benefits us?"

Pierce's scowl had grown steadily darker as I ranted, but I mentally crossed fingers that some of his pissedness was at himself for not considering my points. He could be a real asshole, but there was no way he'd have survived this long by being closed-minded. I hoped.

Dr. Nikas spoke up. "With the African compounds, we can greatly decrease dependence on brains within a matter of weeks. It is a starting point for a less negative reception."

Pierce looked like a cornered tiger. "Ari, our history speaks for what happens when we're exposed."

A shadow passed through Dr. Nikas's eyes, but his voice remained firm and calm. "And it is nothing I care to endure again. If there was ever a moment for a new approach, this is it."

"We're victims as long as we see ourselves as victims," I said. "Coming out of hiding isn't going to be pretty, no matter how it comes about. Instead of thinking of Rosario and the other people who know about us as liabilities, maybe we should think about how to live openly in a world full of allies and enemies." I shook my head. "Pierce, we need to build a network of human allies before we get caught with our pants down. You can't protect the Tribe all on your own anymore."

That hit a nerve. Pierce ground his teeth and looked as if he wanted to hit something. "You've started your own little network already."

"Yup. And those allies saved my ass *and* the Tribe's." I lifted one hand and mimed dropping a mic. "Boom."

He fell silent. The anger in his face slowly leached away. "I'll consider your argument," he finally said, "and we will assess Rosario as a potential *ally*."

I decided to take that as a win. Or at least not an outright loss.

Dr. Nikas slid an approving look my way before setting his tablet aside. "Kang is at optimal temperature," he announced.

Dr. Nikas reached into the tank and cut away the gauze that covered Kang's face. I rolled closer for a better view. Kang was grey, but he wasn't sunken and wrinkly like he'd been when Jacques and I wrapped him. Now he looked like he was sleeping. In pink snot.

Pierce watched with pursed lips. "He will wake?"

"With the new formula it is indeed a possibility rather than an outright 'no'." Dr. Nikas stepped back and wiped snot from his hands with a towel. "Jacques, set the first stage voltage."

Beside me, Jacques adjusted the voltage. I peered expectantly into the tank. And continued to peer as absolutely nothing happened.

"EEG unchanged and chaotic," Jacques said. "Heart rate ten. Sixteen. Eighteen." He paused. "Holding steady at eighteen."

Dr. Nikas tweaked settings and peered at the EEG. "Increase to second stage."

Déjà vu. This was all the stuff I'd heard when I was in the tank.

"His eyes are open!" I squealed in a rush of ridiculous excitement and didn't even care that I sounded silly. Hell, if it wasn't for me, Kang wouldn't be here in the lab all re-grown. Maybe from now on he'd listen to me when I told him a serial killer was chopping zombie heads off.

"Heart rate twenty-six. Thirty-two. EEG fluctuating."

"Hey, Kang," I said, loud and clear. "You're doing great."

"Save the cheerleading, Angel," Pierce snapped. "He can't hear you."

"Bullshit." I glared at Pierce. "You've never been in slug snot, so you don't know what the hell you're talking about. When my eyes opened, I heard everything, all this voltage and heart rate stuff, even though I couldn't move." I pushed to my feet, supporting myself on the edge of the tank as I leaned over. "Hey, Kang." I waved. "You're going to be okay, I promise. I've been where you are, so I'm guessing you can hear me fine but can't talk, and I know that shit's scary as hell. You had a bit of an accident, but you're getting healed up. If you don't wake all the way up this time, they'll put you back under to cook a bit more." I grinned. "But don't worry. You'll wake up for real in no time at all."

Kang's eyelids fluttered, and his eyes met mine.

"Heart rate spiking," Jacques said. "Fifty. Fifty-eight. Sixty-two."

Dr. Nikas nodded once. "Take him to zero."

"No!" Pierce pivoted toward Dr. Nikas. "Do *not* return him to stasis."

Dr. Nikas bristled. "Not doing so could cause irreparable damage. We are considerably ahead of sched—"

"Bring him back," Pierce said through gritted teeth. "Do it."

Jacques cut an uncertain glance at Pierce. "Seventy. Seventy-two. Seventy-eight!"

I collapsed into the wheelchair heavily enough to send it rolling back toward Jacques.

Dr. Nikas stepped between the tank and Pierce. "No," he said. "I will *not* do it."

Jacques was the picture of consternation, but I wasn't.

The instant I heard the "No" from Dr. Nikas, I snaked my arm behind Jacques and shut down the voltage. "You said zero, right?" I asked Dr. Nikas with the utmost innocence.

Dr. Nikas looked at me with surprise that shifted quickly to admiration. "Yes, Angel. Zero."

Pierce gave a cry of angry frustration. "Turn it back on!"

"It's over," Dr. Nikas said with considerable force as Jacques scrambled to adjust other settings. "Even if I believed it to be a wise course of action, I can't revive him again today." He moved to the door and opened it. "Now, I have work to attend to that requires my expertise. I'm sure you do as well. I'll call you later." He held the door open and waited.

Pierce swept a dark scowl over the room before stalking out, jaw clenched tight.

"What was *that* all about?" I asked the instant the door closed. "What's important enough to risk Kang's life after all the work you've put in to get him to this point?"

Dr. Nikas sighed. "Through Allen, you captured some of the information Pierce wants. But he has a long history with Kang."

Huh. Interesting. Pierce was downright desperate to get Kang to talk. Ages ago, Kang had told me he was only seven when his parents died in the Korean War. That put him in the general vicinity of seventy-ish. But Pierce was *hundreds* of years old. How long a history could they possibly have? Or maybe it was simply a matter of perspective?

"Well, thanks for letting me be here for Kang's wakeup call," I said then smiled wryly. "Especially since I doubt Pierce will let me come to the next one."

"It is not Pierce's decision to make," Dr. Nikas said crisply, but then his expression warmed. "I am pleased you were here. I had no idea you experienced awareness before full waking. The EEG indicated otherwise. I very much wish to discuss it with you once other urgent matters are dealt with."

He gave my hand a squeeze, then had Jacques wheel me

to a room that could have been a parlor in a grand estate. Rich colors, elegant trim, and bookshelves everywhere. Ranged around the room were several comfy chairs, and near the center was an antique coffee table and a plush couch that begged to be napped upon. No ambiance immersion system screen in here, but in its place the room had the most realistic fake fireplace I'd ever seen.

A plate of brainy finger food rested on the coffee table beside a slim laptop bearing a note in Dr. Nikas's neat print that read "for your use."

I grinned. Who was I to argue? Especially when I was dying to catch up on the events of the outside world.

I checked my email—both personal and work—then sent messages to my professors, telling them I'd been diagnosed with mono and that I'd have to telecommute for a week or so. So far I hadn't missed any classes, thanks to the grand tradition of Louisiana schools' closing for the entire week of Mardi Gras. But I had a feeling I was going to miss my biology lab tomorrow.

Once I finished all of the being-responsible crap, I skimmed the local news to see if the world had decided to end during my slug snot adventure.

The world was still out there, with a familiar face reporting the details: Brennan Masters, the TV reporter I'd loaned a towel to at the Grayson Seeger murder scene so he could clean mud off his shoes. And now he had a follow-up report on that same murder. I clicked on the video from the evening before Mardi Gras and watched Masters announce the then-breaking news. Coy Bates had turned himself in for the murder of Grayson Seeger, and authorities had issued a warrant for the arrest of Judd Siler, whose whereabouts were currently unknown.

To my relief, a quick check through later videos turned up no mention of Randy. This murder was lurid enough that the news would have definitely reported if he'd been arrested on related charges. He'd come out of the crazy mess with a good scare and nothing more serious, which probably wasn't perfect justice but worked well enough for me. Randy had simply been trying to help a friend. Stupidly.

My body informed me that I damn well needed to take advantage of the very nap-worthy couch, and I didn't argue. After a two-hour test drive that earned the couch high marks, I went back online and proceeded to amuse myself with silly pictures of cats.

I was *awwww*ing over a video of a kitten being tickled when my phone beeped with a text message.

From Nick.

Allen said you'll be off work for a week. Derrel and I are covering half your shifts. You owe me. I have your masks. Hope you're feeling better.

I read it three more times, and my smile grew bigger and bigger and bigger. The message was matter-of-fact, with no frills and a tiny sprinkle of Nick the Prick, but that wasn't important. He'd taken a step to communicate directly, which meant he hadn't backed completely away.

"Baby?" My dad stood in the doorway, face twisting with the effort to keep from crying.

"Daddy!" A flood of sheer happiness rushed through me at the sight of him. I set the laptop aside and pushed to my feet, and then he was running to catch me in a fierce hug before I could fall over.

"Oh god, Angelkins." His voice shook, but his arms were firm and strong as he held me close. "You're back. I got you back."

I clung to him as we both sobbed on each other, then eventually he eased me to sit as gently as if I was made of glass. When he settled beside me, I snuggled against his side and released a long contented breath. He curved his arm around me to hold me close, and we sat like that in rich quiet, dad and daughter.

"There's something I need to tell you," I said, breaking the silence at last, but when I looked up at his face I saw expectation instead of question. "You already know, don't you."

"Angelkins, I been knowing for a while somethin' was up, but I never could figger out what the hell kinda drug you could be taking." His voice caught. "Oh, baby. I was trying so hard not to fuck it all up like I done way back before you helped me get sober. Thought I'd screwed the pooch the night of the movie when I got in your face 'bout it."

I gave him a watery smile. "Well, you were right." I leaned into him again, drew warmth as I told him what happened in New York—not the super gory details, but enough to explain about the mods and why Dr. Nikas had to make them. And why I ended up having to use them.

A fire came into his eyes, and he shot to his feet with a speed I didn't think he possessed. "Now you just wait a goddamn minute!" he snapped, glaring fiercely. "Those zombie sons of bitches got you hooked and let you run wild with this shit? Is that what got you into this mess where you done fell apart? Ari sure kept that part real quiet. Who the fuck do they think they are? You tell me who the goddamn chief of this circus is so I can give the prick a piece of my mind. It's goddamn bullshit! They ain't gonna treat a Crawford like—"

"Dad!" I barely got the word out between the tears and laughter. "It's okay, I promise." An image swam into my head of my dad chewing out Pierce, and I dissolved into giggles again. "Oh my god," I gasped. "You didn't let me finish."

He beetled his brows at me, harrumphed, then plopped back onto the couch. "Fine. You finish. But I'm tellin' you, I'm ready to kick some zombie butt."

That brought on another round of laughter, earning me an exasperated toss of his hands in the air. I wiped my eyes and threw my arms around him. "You don't have to go kick any zombie butt," I said. "Except maybe mine." With that, I launched into the rest of it, about my work at the lab, the V12 and the skimming, and getting caught. Told him how Dr. Nikas helped me in every possible way, then I did my best to explain why I took the megadose on Mardi Gras day.

He gave a slow nod as he took it all in. "I seen a lot of weird shit these past few days, and I asked a lot of questions. Like, how the hell you ended up in pieces, and why you couldn't just chomp on a brain and get better." A shudder went through him. "These lab people are pretty tight-lipped and never would give me a straight answer, but I knew it had to be connected somehow. Guess I ain't as dumb as I look."

I let out an exaggerated sigh of relief. "Thank god for that!"

"You little shit." He laughed and gave me a squeeze. I leaned my head on his shoulder.

"I love you, Dad. I'm so sorry I got into this mess."

In reply, he dug an object from his pocket and dropped it into my hand.

My throat tightened as I looked down at the heavy coin. "One year sober."

"Got it last night." He wiped away tears without shame. "I don't ever wanna go back to what I was before, to what we were before."

"We won't," I said with conviction. "You won't, and I won't. We won't let that happen."

"You're goddamn right." He paused, smiled. "Cuz we're Crawfords."

"Dad, the Crawford family tree is full of drunks, criminals, and politicians."

He shrugged. "Then I guess we got no choice but to take up a life of crime."

"Um. About that 'take up' part . . ."

"Jesus, Angel. Next you'll be telling me you wanna run for office, and there's only so much one man can take."

I laughed and hugged him. "Hell no, Dad. I'm not a *monster*."

Diana Rowland

"Rowland's delightful novel jumps genre lines with a little something for everyone—mystery, horror, humor, and even a smattering of romance. Not to be missed—all that's required is a high tolerance for gray matter. For true zombiephiles, of course, that's a no brainer."

—Library Journal

"An intriguing mystery and a hilarious mix of the horrific and mundane...Humor and gore are balanced by surprisingly touching moments as Angel tries to turn her (un)life around."   *—Publishers Weekly*

My Life as a White Trash Zombie
978-0-7564-0675-2

Even White Trash Zombies Get the Blues
978-0-7564-0750-6

White Trash Zombie Apocalypse
978-0-7564-0803-9

How the White Trash Zombie
Got Her Groove Back
978-0-7564-0822-0

White Trash Zombie Gone Wild
978-0-7564-0823-7

To Order Call: 1-800-788-6262
www.dawbooks.com

Diana Rowland

The Kara Gillian Novels

"Rowland's hot streak continues as she gives her fans another big helping of urban fantasy goodness! The plot twists are plentiful and the action is hard-edged. Another great entry in this compelling series." —*RT Book Review*

"Rowland's world of arcane magic and demons is fresh and original [and her] characters are well-developed and distinct.... Dark, fast-paced, and gripping." —*SciFiChick*

Secrets of the Demon   978-0-7564-0652-3

Sins of the Demon   978-0-7564-0705-6

Touch of the Demon   978-0-7564-0775-9

Fury of the Demon   978-0-7564-0830-5

Vengeance of the Demon 978-0-7564-0826-8

To Order Call: 1-800-788-6262
www.dawbooks.com

DAW 176

Laura Resnick

The Esther Diamond Novels

"Esther Diamond is the Stephanie Plum of urban fantasy! Unplug the phone and settle down for a fast and funny read!"   —Mary Jo Putney

DISAPPEARING NIGHTLY
978-0-7564-0766-7

DOPPELGANGSTER
978-0-7564-0595-3

UNSYMPATHETIC MAGIC
978-0-7564-0635-6

VAMPARAZZI
978-0-7564-0687-5

POLTERHEIST
978-0-7564-0733-9

THE MISFORTUNE COOKIE
978-0-7564-0847-3

To Order Call: 1-800-788-6262
www.dawbooks.com